═══ RISE OF THE ═══

TRUE
BLUE
REBELLION

Also by Jerry Willbur

The True Blue Revolution:
Book One of the Myth of the American Gentle Kingdom
True Blue Trilogy

Herding Hummingbirds:
Creating and Keeping Uncommon Cross-Current Leaders

Giant Killers:
Creating the Remarkable Customer Service Culture

More about Jerry and his books can be found at **JerryWillbur.com**
or at **facebook.com/DrJerryWillbur**.

═══ RISE OF THE ═══
TRUE BLUE
REBELLION

Book Two of the
Myth of the American Gentle Kingdom
True Blue Trilogy

The True Blue Revolution continues.

JERRY WILLBUR

The Leadership Mentoring Institute
Vancouver, Washington

For questions or permission requests, email **jwillbur3@aol.com**

The Leadership Mentoring Institute
4909 NE 142nd Street
Vancouver, Washington 98686
United States of America

Library of Congress Control Number 2021923377
ISBN 978-0-9993951-4-1 (pbk)
ISBN 978-0-9993951-2-7 (ebk)

Edited by Ruth Matinko-Wald
Graphic design by Machele Brass

Printed in the United States of America

A special thanks to my editor, Ruthie Matinko-Wald
(the human sparkler), and to my designer, Machele Brass
(the magician). Thanks also to my friends Sonny Houtala,
Dale Baugh, and Marlene Geyen who actually read my
scribblings. And a special thanks to Dennis and Rose who
always encourage me. A big thank you to my family for
their patience with my many long nights of writing—
especially to my wife of so many years, Sherrie Jean,
and to my sons, Ryan and Kevin, and their families.
I hope in some way my writing might make the world
a little better place for all of them.

"The Most High, El Elyon, will watch over the plans and paths of good people, but the paths of the evil lead to doom."

Paraphrase of Psalm 1:6
The Living Bible

"I believe that unarmed truth and unconditional love will have the final word in reality."

Dr. Martin Luther King Jr.
Excerpted from *Letter from the Birmingham Jail*

≡ **Preface** ≡

My prequel to this book, *The True Blue Revolution*, was edited in final form in 2016 and published in early 2018. Kirkus Reviews hailed *The True Blue Revolution* as a "creative and imaginative story of an alternative political universe." First written in 2013 and titled *Hocus Pocus Bogus POTUS*, that work of fiction turned out to be, as an another reviewer described, "eerily prophetic."

Written and edited long before "Make America Great Again" ever appeared on a red baseball cap and Hillary Rodham Clinton was selected to be the Democratic presidential candidate, *The True Blue Revolution* embroils the reader in a United States where every level of democracy is rigged and a vicious cabal runs the country. All is not lost, however, as a hero emerges who uses positive psychology as a weapon of righteous revolution.

The True Blue Revolution was and is fiction, but it is now even more highly relevant to our society. Reading it post-2020, the original novel reads like a bold prophecy, an apt reflection of the confusing political state of the nation. This new book you now hold in your hands, or on your device, *Rise of the*

True Blue Rebellion, features most of my original characters and takes *The True Blue Revolution* to its next stage—covering the four years after the election that saw our hero blaze a historic campaign as the first politician who couldn't lie. The revolution has now moved from its beginning stages into an open rebellion. If you have already read that first novel, you may want to skip the short review chapter entitled "Our Blue-Hued Hero."

I want to emphasize my story is not a fantasy I want to see become reality. Although I am greatly concerned about our country, I sincerely hope we can work out things in a peaceful, rational, honorable fashion. Rather, my story is a warning: If we do not change many things we are doing and allowing to happen now, our country's fragile constitutional republic will crumble, and there may never be another like it. We must do whatever we can to make sure this book remains just a prophecy, a fantasy, one that never comes true!

☰ PROLOGUE ☰

A New Game Begins

He never planned to be assassinated. He never wanted the job of president of the United States of America—or president of anything! He absolutely didn't want to be number one on the FBI and CIA most-wanted lists. He also definitely never wanted to put his family at risk of abuse by the worst psychopaths in the world. Like many things in life, everything just happened. Before he knew it, he and everyone he loved were swept into danger, and nothing was ever again the same.

Some former presidents have claimed that holding the office of POTUS, President of the United States, was as good as, or better than, the best steak or the finest wine. President Reynard "Rey" Newly, however, never got to savor any perks of the office. He only held office for a few weeks. When politically powerful entities discovered he was not a pushover, they had him hunted mercilessly by agents of the FBI, CIA, and, worse, NAP, the National Association of Psychopaths—the real deep state, the most skilled and savage of all assassins.

You could perhaps forgive the Great Designer of humans who, for reasons known only to the Creator, combined the cortex of a lizard with the forebrain of an ape and created the human brain. In most people, the Creator also incorporated a portion of some empathy, some ability to be compassionate, and some desire to sense the feelings of others. Somehow, however, the Creator overlooked the brains of psychopaths. No remorse, no guilt, no empathy, and no normal emotions of love were built into the cranial cavities of this sub-group of humans. Thus, they are completely unencumbered by compassion. They hold no compunction about being cruel. They are motivated solely by an overwhelming lust for power, dominance, and control.

But an ordinary, kind, and decent man, Reynard "Rey" Newly, exhibited the temerity to stand in the way of psychopaths running the USA. In truth, he attempted to run out of their way, dodging into the shadows and distracting the pursuers so his family could survive another day. Although his avoidance efforts failed, for a while Rey sidetracked the devious plans of NAP to dominate the USA and the world. He accomplished this through some deft maneuvering and help from brilliant, strategically located, crafty friends.

Now, though, the rumor is NAP is rising again, more malignant than ever. This time, the psychopathic leaders of NAP are diabolically determined not to let a nobody like Rey Newly upset their plans. They WILL control the USA, with the most powerful economy and military the world has ever known. The plan is to bend the USA to their own malignant vision. Their first order of business? Revenge. They aim to find Newly, capture him, and slowly crush the life out of him by destroying his loved ones before his very eyes. Let the new, hideous game begin.

On a Boat in the
≡ Remote South Pacific ≡

Rey Newly carefully concealed his family's travel plans. He turned down many offers of private jets and yachts, figuring they would be too obvious and visible to the prying eyes of those trying to locate him. Instead, he found himself blissfully alone with his wife and two young boys on what would best be called a tramp cargo ship, a comfortable but rusty old bucket named The George Wiseheart. They chugged across the empty, peaceful ocean, stopping by several exotic, isolated islands in the remote South Pacific. The ship picked up and delivered people and goods on its way to Foondavi, a remote and magical island Rey had lived on years before and loved.

Desperate not to be recognized nor tracked, the former president and his family were heavily disguised. Rey wore a floppy hat to hide his face in shadows. Despite his slight bluish skin color, from the truth-telling drugs he had taken, he felt confident he fit in with the weird assortment of seeming social outcasts and eccentric characters trekking from one remote island to another in a desolate part of the Pacific.

As Rey had hoped, the trip was relaxing and uneventful, until a derelict vessel with no mast was spotted floating in the distance. Two heads, one at each end of the boat, could be seen bobbing aimlessly with the craft as it haphazardly followed the wind. As Rey's ship changed course and pulled alongside the strange vessel, a depraved and disturbing sight came into view. The memory of the gruesome scene would scar the onlookers for the rest of their lives, coming back to haunt them in their worst dreams in the deep of the night.

Scattered on the floor of the battered charnel houseboat were bloody bodies and bones, the remains of several unfortunate people. The creatures at each end of the derelict boat, barely recognizable as humans, were obviously guilty of devouring the viscera of their shipmates. Blood and gore splattered and caked the two survivors' bruised and heavily bearded faces and wildly wind-whipped hair. As Rey's ship approached, the two creatures looked up. Then the larger of the two suddenly hurled what appeared to be a boat hook at the other crazed passenger, caved in his skull, let out a hideous celebratory roar, and waved ludicrously at the passengers on Rey's vessel. He then picked up a bone and started chewing.

Unsure what to do, the ship's captain ordered his crew to pause at a short distance while the horror unfolded. Most of the passengers urged the skipper, a venerable man named Captain Barney Barnabas, to leave the grisly scene and alert the Coast Guard of the boat's location. Rey could hear mutterings about the Isle of Predators, somewhere near Cozorre, although the various dialects left him guessing. Without a tracking beacon, however, Captain Barnabas knew their remote location would mean the derelict would probably drift undiscovered.

After some hushed discussion with the crew, and against the vocal resistance of those passengers unfortunate enough to observe what was happening, the captain decided to throw a line to the rapidly receding boat and see if the demented survivor would attach it, so he could be towed. To everyone's surprise, the man adroitly snagged the line and hooked it to his own blood-soaked craft. Then, to the shock and dismay of the crew and passengers, he started pulling hand-over-hand his boat toward their vessel. His corded muscles strained at the task, but he made ample progress, until Captain Barnabas reappeared with a Mossberg shotgun and aimed it at the gore-streaked monster.

"Any closer, my bloody friend, and you'll join your crewmates as seagull food," the captain bellowed with a fear-filled, husky voice. Rey was standing behind him and saw the glare the cannibal shot back. Then the maniacal gaze drifted toward Rey, and a glimmer of recognition briefly flashed across the distorted, demonic face. Rey stared intensely at the blood-spattered, swollen, begrimed, and heavily bearded face, but he couldn't make out any familiar features. The creature stopped pulling, tied off the rope, sat back in his boat, and started rifling through his slaughterhouse, perhaps looking for another awful snack, seemingly ignoring his benefactors.

"Crazy as a loon," diagnosed Captain Barnabas, who assigned a guard to watch the derelict vessel, with purposely loud and explicit directions "to shoot the animal if he comes any closer." As he walked past Rey, he shook his head with disgust and muttered, "Forty years on the open ocean and serving in two major wars and I've never seen such a sick sight. If it is any consolation, he cannot do any more damage to the poor souls on that bloody floating wreck."

Rey hurried to the ship's bow, where thankfully his family was blissfully unaware of the psychotic episode happening aft. They rested in comfortable deck chairs and were drinking some type of fruity concoction. Morton and Milton, his eleven-year-old twins, mobbed him, innocently asking about the reason for the sudden stop.

"Just some floating derelict vessel," he responded. "We tied it off and will tow it to the closest island. You boys stay up here with us," he continued.

Rey noticed his wife of twenty-two years, Priscilla, watching him intently; she had picked up a note of tension in his voice. He winked carefully at her, to avoid any suspicion from the boys. "Maybe you should take the boys down to the room to get ready for dinner," he suggested. "I'll join you in a few minutes. I have some things I need to discuss with the captain. I hear the cooks have planned a super-secret dessert you boys won't want to miss!"

After his family departed, Rey hurried to the steering room. "Any idea who that monster is?" he asked. Captain Barnabas didn't know exactly who Rey was; all he knew was that Rey was well connected with his good, new customers on Foondavi, so he didn't shun the question.

"No," responded the captain, "but we think we know where he came from. We called in information on the vessel. The boat is listed as stolen from the island of Cozorre, actually from the nearby Isle of Predators. Many of our passengers know all too well about the Isle of Predators. It's off the shore of Cozorre and is used as a nefarious prison for the worst type of convicts. It's also rumored to be a hunting preserve of some type. Cozorre was supposedly taken over a while back by an organized crime group that pulled off a regime change, massacring the ruling Cozatti family.

Quite fitting, in my opinion, as they were reputedly a nasty, blood-thirsty group themselves. Supposedly, though, the new regime is putting an even worse character in power. A real ogre, we hear."

Rey was rattled to hear about this evil course of events so close to his destination of Foondavi. Over the years, the Cozatti family of Cozorre often plotted vile plans to dominate the gentle people of Foondavi. Fortunately, the Cozattis were always thwarted by the wily islanders. Now, it sounded like an even more sinister group installed themselves. He also was increasingly disturbed by the feeling that the madman seemed to recognize him.

"Look, I'm involved with the Foondavi government, at least what there is of it. When you finally determine who this character is, we'd like to know," requested Rey. Seeing the suspicious look of the captain, Rey explained: "Even though we're a long way from Cozorre, they're still the closest neighboring island. Unlike Las Vegas, what happens at Cozorre doesn't always stay there; it usually floats our way, like a stinking dead fish. I have a bad feeling this event will have dire ramifications for Foondavi."

Late that night, as they approached another isolated and sparsely populated island, the cursed boat with its bloody and demented passenger broke loose. Everyone was relieved to be free of the vile creature and his cannibal cargo, except for the unconscious guard, who was found bludgeoned and nearly beheaded by a thrown boat hook. Captain Barnabas unconvincingly vowed revenge; it was obvious, though, by ordering the crew to speed up, that he was as relieved as everyone else to be rid of the monster and the cursed boat.

Although Rey was thankful his boys and wife hadn't been exposed to the news of and sight of the horrific scene, he was disturbed by the lost opportunity to determine the maniacal villain's identity. He would have been even more disturbed if he realized that the unrecognizable man with the blackened, red-rimmed eyes and gaunt, bloody, bruised, and heavily bearded face was none other than Achor Nithing, the former head of NAP, the National Association of Psychopaths.

The only thing psychopaths hate more than losers are being losers themselves. During the last USA election, Rey and his friends had managed to thwart the election of Achor Nithing's candidate as president, triggering an unprecedented reelection that nearly reversed the results of the original rigged election. Although NAP desperately but barely clung to power with the slimmest of margins, the organization saw Nithing's failure to gain a concise victory as a sign of weakness and a just reason for his demise. So his former NAP friends thoroughly and horribly beat and tortured the once-feared Nithing until he seemed demented and out of his mind with pain. They sent him in shackles, as a nearly unrecognizable piece of refuse, to the Isle of Predators' notorious prison and hunting preserve. There, he was tortured again and then hunted by whomever placed the highest bid; there were many malevolent bidders seeking to nail his hated hide, to have that trophy head to brag about!

Never one to be underestimated, always the survivor, Achor somehow deceptively recovered his wits. He wisely and skillfully played the stumbling and inept victim long enough to lull and deceive his smug would-be executioners into a sense of relaxed security. Then he cunningly contrived to turn the tables on the stunned hunters, using their own weapons to gut shoot them, so they died in the most painful way possible.

His vaunted charisma and still undiminished powers of persuasion then enabled Achor to convince a group of other prisoners to join him in a desperate escape in a crowded, rickety, abandoned fishing boat without sail or oars, just some boards for paddles and the ocean breeze and current to propel them out to sea. Over the numberless days they randomly drifted, Nithing overpowered, slew, and devoured all his compatriots except for one last, tough old bird. That fellow he slew when Rey's ship approached; he had no intention of anyone learning his identity nor his sordid tale of survival.

With all intention of getting back to the USA, Nithing's second unsuspected escape came when, under the cover of darkness, he struck the dozing guard of Rey's ship with his trusty boat hook, untied his boat, and drifted to the shore of a nearby tiny island. From there, he used his wily skills of persuasion and his still-prodigious strength to cunningly manage the rest of his escape to the mainland, plotting his return to power. Throughout his journey, his malicious mind kept returning to the sight of his nemesis—the True Blue Revolution leader, Rey Newly—gawking at his bloody and bruised face.

"I'll get you, Rey Newly!" he vowed with vehemence. In Nithing's twisted mind, Rey was responsible for his defeat, his dethronement, his ruthless and humbling destruction— for all his misfortune. Like all psychopaths, Achor Nithing avoided taking any responsibility for his own actions. He was always the aggrieved one, no matter how devious his own actions. For now, though, he temporarily put thoughts of revenge on hold, as he focused on regaining his lost power base within NAP. "One step at a time," he muttered to himself, "then Newly and his family will pay."

≡ Our Blue-Hued Hero ≡

It's always good to know how we got to where we are now. If you were an observer of the bloody boat incident, you would have seen among the horrified onlookers the usual mix of Brown, Black, and white faces. You also would have seen one face, mostly hidden by a bushy beard and floppy hat, that was slightly blue. That face belongs to Reynard Maxwell Newly, better known as Rey. It might be good here to explain how Rey acquired his blue hue—and became our hero.

Rey Newly is a reluctant hero, to say the least. Supposedly by some amazing luck of the draw and a quirk of the Internet, the humble, small-town Rey was plucked out of anonymity and suddenly propelled from his dull but stable manufacturing job in the tiny town of Pewamo, Michigan, into the fierce battleground of American politics. Not that it matters now, but what really happened was not an amazing stroke of luck nor a quirk of the Internet. In fact, his two adoring, then-ten-year-old twin sons had entered him into a Best Dad of the Year contest. For the online application, they honestly described how he was an all-around super dad, a community leader, an Eagle Scout, and even a decorated veteran, indeed, a Purple Heart winner. Of course, they innocently neglected details that would have automatically eliminated him from winning anything—such as the fact that his extended family and erstwhile hometown acquaintances actually considered him a loser.

By some seemingly random fluke of fate, though, Rey's name and profile ended up being found in cyberspace, from his sons' innocent online puffed-up application, and he became the Republican candidate for POTUS (President of the United States). Unbeknownst to Rey, the Republican party was run by the National Association of Psychopaths (NAP), a group of remorseless power mongers who would do anything to control America. In their "humble," elitist opinion, there was just too much power and money at risk to let the "common" people control things, so they maintained a puppet government. But Rey didn't know any of this.

Rey hadn't been their first choice for president. The Republicans thought they had well vetted a different puppet candidate. Plus, it was their turn to win the usual rigged election. To throw the election at the last minute, however, the malicious NAP Democrats found some dirt, and they unexpectedly and traitorously scandalized the Republican candidate. Without another option, the desperate Republicans searched online for a last-minute replacement they could use as a puppet. Rey's profile popped up, his sons' endearing profile checked off a few boxes to indicate his pliability, and he was selected the "winner." Without his permission, the Republican public relations machine then altered Rey's life story to better fit the profile of an ideal man-of-the-people candidate, and he was thrust into the treacherous halls of power in Washington, DC. If he did what he was told, read the teleprompters, and didn't ask questions, he learned he could have unimaginable money, fame, and even the respect of his extended family and hometown.

What seemed to be a dream, however, quickly turned into a nightmare. Managing to maintain a conscience, Rey began to chafe at the constant image crafting and bogus speech writing that did not reflect his values. He eventually came to realize that a sinister cabal was behind his unexpected and incredible rise to power—and that same group could just as easily facilitate his sudden demise. In fact, NAP leaders eagerly and fiendishly warned him that, without complete submission to their demands, he as well as his family and friends would suffer long and dreadfully. He also feared for his beloved country.

Fortunately, Rey eventually met members of a loosely affiliated group of independent thinkers who had similar values as his. The Hadron Group, under the guidance of a brilliant savant named Jake Quark, opposed the NAP government. They worked to help the multitudes of broken and lost individuals who had been ignored and abused by the prosperous and powerful elite. The group tried to fill the gaping holes in the flattened souls of the desolate, rebuild their shattered, crumbling communities, and give average people a sense of meaning. Unlike NAP, the Hadron Group believed that when government does too much, nobody else does much of anything. They also believed that too many Americans were victims of a societal Stockholm Syndrome, that they had fallen in love with—and were being held hostage by—a big government and big personalities that promised to do everything for them and protect them from all harm. Hadron members liked to quote a former president saying, "A government big enough to give you everything is big enough to take everything from you."

In the simple, decent, humble, and honest Rey, the Hadron Group saw an ideal man to lead their cause. They hacked NAP's computer system, placed Rey's puffed-up, son-produced profile at the top of NAP's puppet search list, and arranged all the other seemingly miraculous string of coincidences that landed Rey unsuspectedly into the seat of power. But, when NAP decided Rey was getting hard to manipulate and might need to be eliminated, the Hadron Group hastily planned a daring plot to spring him from his gig as POTUS. Then they set him up to truly become a man of and for the people.

The Hadron Group's first order of business involved kidnapping Rey from the White House and whisking him to Crazy Jake's Reservation for the Temporarily Bewildered. The place, literally a reservation founded on Native American trust land, was set up as a rescue and restoration camp for America's downtrodden and lost. Two of its founders included the aforementioned Jake Quark, dismissed as a child as autistic and now an entrepreneurial genius billionaire; and the Reverend Louie Pastore, a leader of the underground "Dangerous Church." Pastore and his followers were called dangerous because they were actually helping the poor and downtrodden, unlike so many of the comfortable mainstream churches. A third founder was a mysterious Pewamo Native American leader, Jack "Flynn" Pompatella, who created the trust relationship with the Pewamo Pockatoo tribe who owned in trust the land the Reservation for the Temporarily Bewildered now occupied. Not so accidentally, Flynn was Rey's uncle and knew Rey's sterling character, having observed him for many years. In fact, he was the mastermind who lifted the unsuspecting Rey out of obscurity to become the unlikely savior of the country.

At the Reservation for the Temporarily Bewildered, Rey observed firsthand how people responded to positive psychology and encouragement. The downtrodden would be empowered physically and mentally, enabling them to return to their homes and rescue and restore more of God's lost children and their crumbling communities. They were cannily working to repair America's shattered cities and lift up the abandoned people being ignored as useless "resource consumers" by both NAP and the other established powers. They called their movement, The True Blue Revolution. They wanted to rebel against the powers that were over taking their land, rebuild their lost homes, and ultimately lead a renaissance in the nation—restoring liberty and freedom. Instead of a reset, it would be a shift to a growth mindset.

Unfortunately, the relentless NAP soon learned Rey's hideout and threatened to carpet-bomb the location, so the Hadron Group quickly spirited Rey to Foondavi Troon, an isolated and supposedly desolate South Pacific island. At one time, Foondavi was covered with beautiful trees and possessed tremendously fertile soil, but the valuable trees were scalped for high-end lumber, with scraps being used for manufacturing tourist knickknacks. Then the rich guano-based topsoil was stripped to make gunpowder and fertilizer. Bereft of resources and having their home's natural beauty decimated, Foondavians tried to regain some resources by staging fake natural disasters and other cons, but they soon gave up those endeavors as beneath their dignity.

To Rey, the island appeared at first glance to be just a pile of bird-crap-encrusted rocks, as the name Foondavi purportedly means in the Polynesian language. He soon found, however, that the place was magical—thanks to the Foondavian people, who are as indomitable as the goats, alpacas, and burros that infest their home. The people now living on Foondavi are not native inhabitants; all the original islanders were either carried off by slavers or killed by disease. Instead, current-day Foondavians are political escapees or societal dropouts. They describe themselves proudly as "the off-scouring and castoffs of civilization, the jetsam and flotsam of the world."

This Polynesian potpourri turned out to be a group of free thinkers. They took Rey in as one of their own, and he was forever changed as he learned their gentle, distinctive dialect, pidgin Polynesian. He discovered how they made the most of what would seem to be so little, and he celebrated with them their joys and each other. He even was chosen to participate in a rugged, hazardous, challenging, island-wide quest. Because of his extraordinary performance, he earned the rare title of Nambo, meaning "protector guardian." The honor recognized his display of courage, generosity, and character. All this further refined and defined Rey as a leader.

But NAP somehow found Rey again. To spare the islanders from vicious assault by assembled hostile NAP forces, Rey surrendered. He was shackled and returned to America for what NAP hoped would be a timely and dreadfully painful end at the hands of NAP torturers.

Fortunately for Rey, his friends in the Hadron Group once again came to his rescue. They hammered out a deal with the NAP goons that allowed Rey's family to be turned over to the Hadron Group for safety and for Rey to be spared death but, instead, to be locked up in a psychiatric hospital. While there, Rey found himself watching on media feeds a very believable, digital President Newly making all sorts of outrageous pronouncements totally different from Rey's own beliefs. In his absence, the NAP forces had virtually recreated Rey and his family by digitally recording and manipulating his previous speeches and events. The digital Rey was seen by the duped electorate as a gentle man of the people with a beautiful family, a real American, good for the USA.

Although NAP appeared to be on track to run the country once again, Jake Quark, leader of the Hadron Group and a man never without a plan, devised a way to completely derail the NAP express train to power. Under direction from Quark, scientists had been busy researching a way to unlock the human brain and release its full potential. Unwittingly, they created a strange concoction, nicknamed the Blue Goo. This brew of herbs and roots included a genetically modified version of the Amazonian psychedelic ayahuasca that possessed surprising qualities. The concoction did three irreversible things to a person who took the drug: First, it permanently changed skin color to a glowing blue. Second, it made it impossible for the person taking Blue Goo to tell a lie. Telling a lie would lead to death; that is, once someone took the Blue Goo, any hint of deception would trigger a chemical chain reaction including painful convulsions and then slow, certain death. Third, as was originally intended, the drug tremendously impacted the brain, unlocking almost unbelievable potential. It transformed normal humans into savants.

Quark convinced Rey that the only way to save his country and be reunited with his family was to be the first "True Blue" politician. So Rey escaped the psychiatric hospital with the help of the Hadron Group, willingly took the Blue Goo, disguised himself by growing a beard and letting his hair go wild and curly, and became the leader of the True Blue Revolution—also dubbed, the "Occupy Yourself" movement. Rey and his cohort challenged people to occupy themselves by getting involved in activities such as working with senior centers, helping out at homeless shelters, and mentoring in schools. In other words, the movement advocated for people to occupy themselves by doing things for others. Knowing that for any improvement to be permanent there needs to be systemic change, they challenged the results of the previous USA election and, through some constitutional finagling, pulled off an unprecedented new election.

This time Rey would run as Nambo McBlue, the "if-I-tell-a-lie-I-will-die" True Blue Revolution candidate, becoming the first completely honest politician ever in America, if not the world. In a weird twist, he was running against himself, as NAP ran the digitally constructed virtual Rey Newly as their Republican candidate. He also ran against the previously failed NAP Democrat candidate, who still seemed not to know he was being manipulated by the Democratic wing of NAP and was whining from his loss in the first election.

Everything was going well for the True Blue Revolution, until NAP and the government-owned media began to hammer the real Rey's True Blue Revolution candidacy with half-truths and even some full lies. When, as Nambo McBlue, Rey was trashed by a popular cable network interviewer, the True Blue Revolution started getting labeled as un-American, and some people even started wondering if the people were ready to elect its first blue president.

Questions arose about funding sources and the secretive Crazy Jake Quark, who seemed to be the power and money behind Nambo McBlue. The media also harped on Quark's connections to big pharma and high tech. Coming down to the wire, the election was a three-way race. It ended up with the NAP Republicans eking out a win with the virtual Reynard Newly. The House and Senate each were divided into thirds, evenly split between NAP Republicans, the rebellious NAP Democrats, and members of the True Blue Revolution, causing a quagmire of inactivity. "Ha," laughed the cynics. "Some things never change!" The fractured and in-fighting NAP retreated to clandestine meetings to plot another way to take over.

With the Nithing Machine dethroned and demolished, and Achor Nithing "disappeared," the True Blue Revolution was gradually changing how individual Americans viewed themselves and their role in government. The battle for the soul of America was still a toss-up, but things seemed to be improving. While our True Blue hero did not win the presidency, his valiant efforts to start a real change in the culture began to bear fruit. It reignited a spirit of compassion and an awareness that real freedom can be lost. It rattled and shook the seemingly impermeable halls of power in Washington.

≡ A Pause in the Cause ≡

After the close and demoralizing electoral defeat, the real Rey Newly, now Nambo McBlue, was a marked man. His digitally rendered pseudo-self was still president, though greatly weakened. Fortunately, the NAP organization was also shaken, dismayed to see a sweeping victory elude their grasp once again, and they were now divided into squabbling factions and in great disarray. Their cohesion as a group, tenuous in the best of times, was breaking apart as all the factions impulsively fought among themselves to decide who got to be the ones to pummel the hated Achor Nithing team into extinction while they were wounded, stumbling, and down.

The Nithings, through generations of fear and intimidation, had built up deep animosity that was now relentlessly released against them in a surge of boiling vitriol. The rival factions were eagerly being helped by various foreign interests, always great haters of the notoriously arrogant and vicious Nithings and Americans in general but also eagerly motivated to see the unarguably mighty power of the USA muted by a battle of succession among the rival psychopaths. It was sharks eating sharks—a fiendish feeding frenzy of the highest order.

The Hadron Group decided it was a good time for Rey, AKA Nambo McBlue, and his family to recede from public scrutiny and out of the way of the savagely fighting psycho-paths. "When your enemies are destroying and devouring your enemies, it's a good idea to stay off the menu," chortled Crazy Jake. So the Hadron Group sent Rey and his recently rescued family back to the safety and seclusion of the off-the-grid island of Foondavi.

Rey made it clear he didn't want to stay on the island forever. "I wouldn't feel right leaving the fight unfinished. As much as I love Foondavi, as soon as it's safe for my family, I want to return home to the USA and bring a version of the Foondavi Way to America. I want to live and teach on a Reservation for the Temporarily Bewildered and be part of the True Blue Revolution solution."

Thus, he found himself with his family on a ship in the far South Pacific, returning to Foondavi, when they had the unfortunate rendezvous with the madman and the bloody boat. Only too soon, and with deep regret, was he to learn that the bloody and battered face he saw was familiar, and that it really was a brief glimmer of recognition he saw in those feral eyes. Achor Nithing somehow escaped and returned, and now the battle began again.

≡ The Tale of Two Boys ≡

As often happens, great events start with several inconspicuous beginnings. Just like the headwaters of a river, several small tributaries will feed into what eventually becomes a torrent; and so it is with our story.

One of the sources of the current battle between NAP and the forces of good actually began unnoticed approximately forty years prior. Two boys, as unalike as could possibly be, were both growing up in the small town of Tekona in Southern Michigan. One, Achor Nithing, was the son of a prominent, corrupt judge. By the time he was eight years old, Achor knew he loved to kill people. His descent into murder began with a bike ride: He purposely ran into a young girl named Posey Slick, who had rejected him for another local boy, and then he methodically stabbed her numerous times. Already being an imposing and muscular boy, the young Achor then slung the petite girl's body over his shoulder, carried her to a bridge over the rain-swollen Nottaway Creek, and hurriedly tossed her in.

The other boy, Jack Flynn, was the oldest son of a hard-scrabble Irish logger named Big Jon Flynn and a Pewamo Native American mother, Grace Pompatella Flynn. Jack was playing under the bridge, skipping stones and floating toy boats into the churning stream, when he saw Achor dump the girl's body into the water. While pausing to watch Posey's small body swirl in the current, Achor noticed movement, caught Jack watching, and in a panic hastily clambered down the bank to chase Jack. Much faster and more agile than Achor, Jack escaped by running downstream along the eroded riverbank and through the fallen trees.

Jack knew he should have told someone, but he was scared and thought nobody would believe him. Who could imagine such evil as throwing little Posey into the raging water?

When Posey didn't return home from school, the small, close-knit community of Tekona sent out search parties. Everyone was looking for Posey Slick, the sweet schoolmate of Achor and Jack. Four days later, they found her floating, bloated little body caught on some snags in the now-receding Nottaway Creek. She had been torn apart by churning flood waters that tumbled her body over rocks and fallen trees. Her mangled body disguised how she died. The assumption was that she had fallen off the bridge and drowned. But at a town hall meant for grieving, the young Achor Nithing stood up, glared at Jack, and unctuously announced: "I should have said something earlier. I saw Jack with her by the creek that day. I couldn't believe my friend could hurt Posey. We both really liked her. He said he wanted to show her something under the bridge, so I rode off. I heard a splash, but I thought he was throwing rocks again, like he usually does."

The town's people, crowded in the sheriff's office, gasped. Achor's powerful and rich father, the Honorable Judge Rancor Nithing, pointed a boney finger, like a talon, at a scared, shaking, sorrowful young Jack and snarled, "What do you expect from a wild Irish and Indian half-breed?"

Young Jack was stunned by the dishonesty and fake sincerity pouring from the glib Achor Nithing. When he tried to object, he was shouted down by the crowd that was acting like they wanted to lynch him. Only eight years old, Jack was spared the rope but ended up in a reform school for ten years. When he turned eighteen and was released, he joined the military, became a skilled Special Forces Operator, and served in many delicate and discreet military operations before finally returning home after twenty years to his beloved Irish and Pewamo family farm just outside Tekona. When he did, he changed his name from Jack Flynn to Flynn Pompatella, taking his mother's maiden Pewamo tribal name.

Throughout the years, Flynn suffered recurring nightmares, not from what he did in the service, but from seeing the bloody face of Posey Slick as she sank below the surface of the roiling waters. He knew he wouldn't have been able to save her, but he wished he had tried. During those twenty years away from home, Flynn also never forgot the Nithings. He followed Achor's booming career in broadcasting and watched as Achor eventually grasped political power.

Through careful and thorough research, he learned, not to his great surprise, that Achor was a rising star and major player in the fast-growing and secretive NAP regime that was becoming a disruptive force in the country. Jack knew there would need to be a reckoning one day. He often said of Achor Nithing, "Evil appears to fit him like a well-tailored suit. Wherever he goes, he stalks, not walks. He's like a one-man wolf pack." He believed in his heart that Achor was a Wendigo, a wicked cannibal, an evil monster in the Pewamo and Michigan Native American Fire Nations folklore.

≡ Return of the Monster ≡

Achor Nithing was very proud of his last name. He had been told it meant "monster" in ancient Norse and loved the reference. Now The Monster was back, bigger and more belligerent than ever! Within a month of return from his bloody exile, Achor was back in almost total control. Through the skillful use of a sizeable stormy-day fund for bribes, bullets, and leverage that he providentially had set aside before his abrupt and unplanned departure, Achor soon made those who deposed him and thought him long gone cower in fear. He, indeed, was once again, literally, calling all the shots.

Sitting in his elevated chair behind his massive desk, Achor didn't like what he was reading in the news article he saw displayed on his head-mounted monocular computer screen. He checked his wall-sized video feed and saw other reports were rolling in, echoing similar news. "What idiot wrote this blather?" he bellowed at his cringing assistant. "We control the damn computers, the cable networks, all the news feeds, and are censoring the social media. How did this drivel get released?"

He re-read the story, his ire rising as he repeated each word slowly and sarcastically with his patented, broadcast-worthy, mellifluous tones. "We have now blundered blindly into a dark and pivotal time, when the fate of mankind is being decided. But most people are going about their chaotic existence blissfully unaware we are at a hinge in history! What is being decided is if there is a role for mankind at all, given the great power of machine intelligence. Mankind is about to learn how difficult it is to negotiate with something of far superior intelligence that is totally unencumbered by emotions or compassion. Is mankind a useless mass of biomatter, sucking up resources and space, fit only to be put on the scrap heap of history? We will soon find out."

"We will soon find out all right! Find out who created and distributed this garbage!" Achor bellowed again at his cowering assistant. Slamming down his headset, he yelled, "Get me their names and their locations!"

It wasn't that he completely disagreed with the screed on the screen. He just didn't want the truth to be spread among the unsuspecting human population at this time, and he also thought the idea was entirely too pessimistic. Psychopaths like himself would never be replaced by some stupid collection of circuits. They would use them, yes, but only under complete control. "We, not some machine intelligence, will dominate," he muttered to himself. "Machines telling me what to do? No way! Not today, tomorrow, or ever!"

He paused again, seething in anger. The slippery media was going to have to be brought even further under his heels. He was running through the list of media leaders in his mind, contemplating who might have slipped in this morsel of horse manure. Then his mind switched to more enjoyable things. "Get me the name of who wrote this stuff. And call the Wolf Pack in here. Once I talk to them and give them their juice, I'll have them drag up that charming Thambos

Zugzwang pug and his nasty wife. I think I have kept them waiting long enough to intimidate them." Then he yelled yet again at his retreating assistant. "Get me those names!"

When the assistant had scurried out to do his bidding, Achor sat back in his comfortable chair and admired his handsome reflection in the massive mirror he kept across the room. He noted that his carefully crafted hair now showed a slight tint of gray since he survived his torturous ordeal on the Isle of Predators and that his aquiline nose now displayed a little twist from the savage beatings he had endured. In his humble estimate, both added to his rugged masculine hand-someness; not bad for nearly fifty, he thought. Many women still fought for his attention, and while some of that was due to his power, he knew his rugged looks helped. Now he looked even more rugged, he decided. He always was a firm believer in using your reverses to move yourself forward.

Truth be told, Achor's most arresting and intimidating features were his unflinching, yellow-flecked wolf eyes. When he was younger, he was often referred to as a "one-man wolf pack." Now, though, he was content to be the alpha wolf in a bigger pack. If only his father, old Judge Rancor Nithing, could see him now! Achor laughed and amused himself with the thought that, if his father were here, he would shoot the old, abusive bastard. His father was just mean to be mean; Achor was mean to serve a purpose.

While awaiting the team of rogues he called his Wolf Pack, Achor spoke into his throat microphone and the video wall across from him flicked on. He knew he could have an implant in his brain to control the monitor, but he was determined not to be chipped. "Only my own thoughts are allowed in my brain," he would say.

The entire thirty-foot wall was a video screen, not the blank space it seemed at first glance. On the screen, Achor could peruse charts and graphs in large scale and bore down to the smallest detail. Bank accounts, progress reports, budgets—all could be displayed in front of him in real time. Also, with one command, he could call up CCTV monitors and get live footage of any of his many operations. He could sit there safe and secure while surveying his entire sordid regime. The sense of control was intoxicating!

Hearing the rabble approaching, Achor ordered the screen off and a collage of pictures appeared. Whereas most people like peaceful scenes of waterfalls or a picturesque countryside, Achor preferred action scenes of predators stalking and maiming prey, interspersed with pictures of himself with sports heroes and political notables. Such power postures helped to set a mood conducive to his usual undertakings. Although the images often caused discomfort for his guests, they didn't bother the four thugs now entering his office.

Achor fixed his piercing gaze on the formidable men who rushed in and formed a ragged line, somewhat at attention. He admired their bulging muscles and fierce visages as they looked up at him, their fearless leader. They even managed not to drool or fidget too much.

Nithing had selected the most savage fighters he could recruit as his Wolf Pack warriors. He then had this elite core drink an addictive "juice" supplement that caused them to become berserkers. The supplement, developed by Nithing's hand-picked and well-compensated team of pharmaceutical researchers, was concocted of super steroids mixed with a new and improved version of the old plant ointment called henbane or night shade. Ancient Norse and Germanic warriors used henbane to be fearless in battle and heedless to injuries. With the right dosage of the even stronger new drug, fighters would grow extraordinarily strong and feel unstoppable, invincible, and even invisible.

In addition to manipulating savage prowess with the juice supplement, Achor also brainwashed his Wolf Pack to believe that their death would be rewarded with going to Valhalla. This after-life was described in lurid detail by his public relations people as a drunken, deranged frat party, a scenario the deluded men wanted to be true. Plus, he had his Wolf Pack wear masks, a practice Achor called the Lucifer Effect. Not only did mask-wearing allow his fighters to avoid identification when they were doing his evil bidding, but his research showed that being behind a mask further empowered them to commit extraordinarily atrocious acts.

It is said that much can be learned about the character of a person by the type of people with whom they choose to associate. If that is true, the Wolf Pack said gruesome things about Achor. The Wolf Pack lined up at attention in front of Achor were a motley mix. Naegling, whose name means "claw" in Old Norse, was the top man in this berserker corp. Naegling's face and body were crisscrossed with wicked-looking scars, some inflicted by opponents and others by Naegling himself. He was a gladiator champion of the Creeb Nation, a gang of inner-city thugs created and named by Achor himself that Achor's NAP team was aggressively mentoring to be enforcers in their many operations. Not too smart but very loyal, Naegling knew he was being taken good care of; Achor provided him with everything he liked and could ever want.

Second in command of the Wolf Pack was Swinflyck, also known as Boar Tusk. A savage knife fighter, Swinflyck always had knives dangling from his body, and all of them appeared to have razor-sharp edges. Achor once saw Swinflyck throw the sharp projectiles over thirty feet, spot on into an opponent's eye—ending an argument in a flash.

Third in line was Ulf Hednar. He was the biggest of the bunch at close to seven-feet tall and well over three hundred muscular pounds, but Ulf was unbelievably agile. He also was dumb as a stump but devoted like a puppy to the pack.

The Wolf Pack's strategist was Magnum Shofar. Magnum considered himself a sachem or shaman. He was one crafty customer, although physically unassuming. He was important to the cause, because Achor could not always be on site during assignments. Some tasks took cunning and calculation, especially when the unexpected popped up. Whereas the others would just charge in and try to muscle the situation, Achor had empowered Magnum to halt any operation and construct a Plan B on the spot. Despite this vote of confidence, Achor didn't completely trust Magnum, thinking he was "too darn smart for his own good."

Once Achor got the attention of his Wolf Pack by handing out their daily dose of "the juice," the super henbane max supplement he had concocted, he instructed them to get the Zugzwangs and bring them to him.

"Don't be too tough, but don't be too nice. Naegling, you just threaten them, but don't touch. Boar Tusk, look menacingly, especially at the man, to test his mettle, and sharpen one of your nastiest looking blades while you do. Ulf, you just drool at either one of them, whichever takes your fancy, but, again, don't touch. Magnum, you just announce in your most professional voice, 'Achor Nithing will see you now,' and guide them up here. Again, don't let any of these brutes actually touch them. That might come later if they don't cooperate."

Thambos Zugzwang and his wife, Zenobia, came stumbling in, fearfully regarding the gruesome entourage that was closely following in a lumbering, threatening fashion. Thambos was a strikingly handsome, almost beautiful man with an expressive face, a 100-watt smile, and overall blazing charisma. He had been voted the Sexiest Man Alive several times, and in his humble opinion he knew he really was. One awestruck female media person, in an unusual moment of truth, once said, "When he grabs and shakes your hand with an impressive just-right grip and looks you in the eye, you feel like there is no one else in the world. Of course, if you are a woman alone with him, you think, oh, my gosh, no! There is no one else here but me!" Another woman said, "If he kisses you, you better count your teeth!"

Thambos' parents created a real estate dynasty that Thambos inherited. The business was extremely successful until the greedy NAP wiped them out. His wife, Zenobia, the former Zenobia Aurelia Al Tabor, called Honey Cup by Thambos and no one else, was known for her waspish tongue, persistence, and stamina. Zenobia claimed she was born into a very poor Syrian family, who named her grandly for a famous but treacherous Palmyra queen. According to her own stories, she rode horses and herded and protected her family's sheep until she was in her teens. She would say that how she learned to lead men was by herding dumb sheep! Although her questionable birth certificate noted she was born in the USA, Zenobia claimed she came to the country to go to college. She was admitted largely because her father, the former sheep herder and now Syrian Mafia smuggler of ill repute by the name of Habood Al Tabor, paid a handsome entry fee greased with threats.

After a brief introduction, Thambos slickly tried to take control. "Trust me, Achor. I know we can beat this Ralph guy." He, of course, was referring to the incumbent Rey Newly and the upcoming midterm elections.

"Well, number one, it's Rey, not Ralph," replied Achor, coldly staring down Thambos. "And, number two, Newly won't be running in the midterm. It's Vice President Samms and his minions who are trying to gain control of the House and Senate. Believe me, Zuggy," Achor said, loving the way the arrogant Zugzwang flinched at his use of the insulting name Zugzwang was called by bullies in his younger life, "I will never trust you or your overly aggressive wife, the cunning Zenobia." She started to protest but halted as Achor abruptly put up his hand to stop any rebuttal.

"You both remind me too much of me," Achor said acidly. "If you want my financial and personal support, you must both give me leverage. My other assistant specializing in leverage, my ruthless and wicked daughter Aven, will handle that."

As he said that, a startlingly statuesque, raven-haired young woman entered the room. With rippling muscles, Aven was obviously strong and athletic. The obvious resemblance to Nithing was amazing. Her features were sharp like a chisel. Her nickname was Aven the Raven—and ravens happened to be the harbingers of death in Norse mythology. "Hi, Daddy. Glad to help."

"I will place you in her delicate hands, once you stop ogling her, Zuggy," Achor said with an edge to his voice. "She normally plucks the eyes out of guys who look at her like that, but I've asked her to be on her best behavior today. She'll handle all the arrangements necessary to create the leverage."

Aven smiled, showing a row of sharp, cat-like teeth. She carefully scanned both obviously nervous Zugzwangs with an appraising eye.

"Wait, wait! What type of leverage?" asked Thambos, as his wife looked on incredulously.

"Thambos, we . . . ," Zenobia began to say but was cut off by her husband, who spoke to her pointedly.

"We've agreed I'm the political savant on our team, correct?" Thambos spat sharply. Zenobia slowly nodded her head in sullen agreement. He definitely was slick, she grudgingly admitted.

"What type of leverage?" Thambos suspiciously asked again, in a querulous voice, earning warning glares from the Wolf Pack.

"Scandalous, juicy, but believable," Achor responded with a vile and vicious smirk, while winking at them both. "I'm sure I'll enjoy watching the tapes!"

"We can make it without you," Zugzwang retorted, his usual smooth tongue sputtering. His halting and reedy voice also revealed his doubts. "We can," he repeated again, as if to reassure himself. His wife just shook her head in resignation.

"No, you cannot," Achor responded. "And, if you leave here rejecting my offer, after our polite little chat, you won't make it ten miles before my efficient team here turns you and the vehicle you drove here into an unrecognizable pile of slag. You are too smart, and too desperate, not to come here knowing you would have to agree to whatever terms I demand. I didn't write my prize-winning opus, *The Heart of the Steal*, just for the fun of it. The subtitle, you might remember, was 'Leverage: Use It or Lose It!' By coming here, you lost it." Seeing the crestfallen expression on their faces, Achor relented somewhat, but not much.

"You can regain some leverage by doing what I demand," Achor said, realizing it is always best to provide a beaten enemy a way out. "You can run for senator, Zenobia," he said, watching her face suddenly light up with glee or greed. It didn't matter which; both worked for him. "And you, Zuggy, you can run for president in the next election." The beaten man suddenly perked up. "Once we have the leverage," Achor added.

The couple willingly turned to Achor's evilly smiling daughter. "This way to the plane, please," Aven said in a deceptively sweet voice. "We will provide everything you need once we get to the island, not that you will need much."

Thambos hesitated at the door. "May I make one request?"

"It depends," answered Achor. "You're not exactly in a position to negotiate."

"I get to watch the tapes of Zenobia!" He smiled lasciviously and pushed his wife from the room before she could protest, as Achor nodded his assent.

"And I get to watch his," Zenobia yelled from down the hall as she was dragged away.

"Oh, I so enjoy the use of bribes, bullets, and leverage," Achor muttered again to himself as they departed.

When his assistant re-entered the room, he turned to another subject and demanded, "Okay, who put out that puke earlier?"

"Well, sir," the assistant squeaked, appearing to choke down his fear. "It appears it isn't a person. I called the author's phone number and a machine answered."

"So, I have an answering machine."

"No, this machine actually talked to me, but I could tell it was a machine, not a human. This machine said to tell you it was a representative of the Robosapiens and they were going to take you down. Or, you could contact them and they will negotiate your surrender. It said its name is Kasah, and he works for something he called the Rasha. I took it he was kind of a leader of the MI or machine intelligence; the Robosapiens Alliance Team is exactly what he called them."

The assistant was trying to be brave, but Achor could tell he was nearly wetting himself, having to deliver this negative news. This time Achor didn't kill the messenger. He just frowned and furrowed his brow in contemplation. He bitterly remembered being screwed over by a turncoat cyborg named Carlyle who used to work for him and then absconded to work for his enemies the Hadron Group and cost him the decisive election victory he so coveted. He had been working with another questionable cyborg, one named Camilla, but this seemed completely different. His assistant was actually quite capable, if too easily cowed, so he believed his interpretation of the message.

"More competition. Just what I need. Maybe I can send the Wolf Pack to unplug them!" he said, only half joking. "Well, let's get my Black Hat Hacker team that Pulver Flitch has assembled working on it. We have to find a location or something we can hack or attack."

As the relieved-to-be-alive assistant left the room, Achor dismissed his Wolf Pack: "Don't just stand there, go intimidate someone!"

Ulf yelped in a surprisingly high-pitched voice for such a big man. "Yippee! Can't wait! We gonna in-tim-i-date!"

"You definitely suffer from a slowly evolving sense of self-control," Achor said, getting a confused look from Ulf. "Magnum, you better choose the target wisely. And be prepared for when we find out who or what this Robosapiens Alliance Team thing is."

As he pondered the new threat, he realized too many people, including himself, were probably guilty of ignoring the whole machine intelligence thing for too long. There was no doubt they were everywhere and becoming more essential to everyone. Maybe they were getting too big for their . . . whatever they inhabited. All he could think of was an Ayn Rand quote he once saw: "The hardest thing to explain is the glaringly evident which everybody has decided not to see."

Back to the
≡ Drawing Board ≡

As soon as Rey landed back in the USA, he was urgently rushed to a key strategy meeting with Jake Quark and the top Hadron Group leadership. The team included Jake; Jake's adoptive mother, Sister Mary Contrary; and Zara Tallaree, an enigmatic, sleek, and beguiling beauty Rey knew all too well from his previous stint as president and consequent kidnap and escape. The fifth Hadron team member present was Rey's Uncle Jack Flynn Pompatella, the Sachem of the Pewamo people and great leader of the True Blue Revolution resistance.

Who were these change-makers and why was "the cause" so important to them? The first thing to know about Hadron's leader, Jake Quark, is that he was raised as an orphan by Sister Mary Contrary, as she liked to say, "from the pup up!" The second thing to know about Jake is that Quark is his chosen surname, not the surname of his biological father. When Rey asked the significance of Jake's last name, he explained that a quark is a small but fundamental particle of matter. When he was a boy, Jake was small in stature and a tutor told him that, like a quark in physics, although small, he was a strong force and would do important things in life—even though he flittered around constantly, also like a quark. Plus, he was told humorously by someone else that another type of quark was a tasty, small-curd cheese in The Netherlands. He liked all the definitions, so he chose Quark as his last name. Also, he just liked the sound of the name, Jake Quark—and he would never, ever use the name of his real father, whom he hated with a passion.

It was reputed that his biological father was the nasty Judge Rancor "Rancid" Nithing. How that reality came to be was that the horrible judge twice raped Jake's young mixed-heritage African American and Odowa Native American mother, Summer Sweetgrass, who was an orphan. The first time was when she was only twelve, with the heinous act producing a daughter, Rosetta. The second time was when Jake's mom was fourteen, with the crime resulting in Jake's birth. Thirteen years later, the judge did the same horrid thing to Rosetta, Jake's older sister.

In addition to the rapes, the pedophile then killed Jake's now institutionalized mom, Summer, when he learned she had been pregnant after the second rape, delivered her baby, and then hid her son, young Jake, from him. Once DNA testing became possible and reliable, the cold-hearted elder Nithing wanted to cover up his pedophilia and incest, so he decided to kill both children. Thanks to the cunning of Sister Mary Contrary, it took the judge many years to finally track down and kill young Rosetta, but he never found Jake.

As a child, Jake was diagnosed with Asperger's Syndrome and ended up in a horrible orphanage, until he was rescued and raised by the loving Sister Mary Contrary. Early on, he proved to be a math genius; he intuitively discerned and understood complex mathematical patterns that eluded most.

At the age of fourteen, he earned his first doctorate, studying mostly on his own. Then he went to Harvard where he hoped to meet intelligent people to challenge him, but he didn't stay long because he said he didn't find any. Being so bright, why would Jake have the "crazy" moniker attached to his name? "Crazy? Ha, I'm crazy like a fox," he once explained with a mischievous smile. "With opponents, I like to be underestimated. It gives me a competitive advantage. Besides, it's not the big that eat the small. Rather, it's the fast that eat the slow, especially when they're underestimated!"

Truth be told, Jake could appear at first glance to be a rustic bumpkin. Even at a second glance he could still fool people. When Rey first met him after escaping from the White House, he thought Jake looked like a gnarled old African garden gnome. As he got to know him, however, a complex character emerged. Jake was extremely bright and chronically curious, and he made a mighty mark on the world. With so many ideas, he was often described as having "idearrhea."

As brilliant as Jake was, he was a complete bust at social–emotional skills. He was eccentric and isolated, awkward around people, unable to play or work with others. He came across as cold and stilted, but, with the help of the loving and patient Sister Mary Contrary, he recognized his weakness and began to study people with the same intensity he applied to mathematics. He found humans even more nuanced than the toughest algorithms, but he eventually became a recognized expert on positive psychology and building relationships. He eventually earned a second doctorate at the University of Pennsylvania, studying under a genius named Martin Seligman.

By age thirty, Jake had earned three doctorates, a law degree, and two Nobel prizes. Now nearing fifty, he still was chronically curious. He would become fanatically focused on a subject and study it until he understood every facet. He also was quite articulate and could talk endlessly, some said monotonously, about the intricacies of anything and everything that caught his attention.

Fortunately, Jake was able to turn his burning desire to learn into cash. He did this by playing a hidden but critical role in technology development. He discerned not-so-obvious trends early. Rey knew that, if the truth were to be told, when people talk about Apple, Jake Quark should be mentioned along with Steve Jobs and Steve Wozniak. When Microsoft is mentioned, Jake's name should be there with Bill Gates and Paul Allen. He even worked with and invested in ventures with the genius Elon Musk. He just kept getting chased out of companies by the ego-driven technocrats, possibly because he was such a young and unsociable savant, but probably also nudged along by NAP—but not before he parlayed his first million into many more millions and then billions.

Despite all his successes, Jake felt most passionate about the Hadron Group, the name of which he intentionally selected. As Jake once explained to Rey, a hadron in the field of particle physics is a composite particle composed of a multiple set of quarks held together by a strong force. In Greek, the word *hadron* means "stout." So, Jake formed Hadron to get other ordinary but significant people, human quarks like himself, to form a stout alliance or a strong force against psychopaths like the Nithings—whom Jake recognized as a major threat to decent humankind. He envisioned Hadron as a stabilizing force that would produce continuous, positive, innovative, and adaptive change in America and the world. He hoped the organization and the True Blue Revolution it supported would act as a counter force to the insidiously corrosive actions of NAP and the controlled chaos they, as predators, both created and fostered.

The second member of the Hadron leadership team was Sister Mary Contrary, AKA, the Ninja Nun, the Guerilla Sister, the Undercover Mother, and, perhaps most importantly, Jake's beloved adoptive Mom. Rey knew many people made the mistake of taking the kindly acting, petite, and angelic-looking Sister Mary for granted—but they made that mistake only once!

Sister Mary got her start smuggling unwanted Downs Syndrome and deformed babies out of the USA to India to survive and thrive with Mother Teresa, whom she fondly called Momma T. Her passion for saving the unwanted, abandoned, and deformed often led her into dangerous places. Nearly killed several times, Sister Mary started learning martial arts. After loaning the teen-aged Jake seed money from her meager savings for his first company and getting paid back multiple times over, she took the largess he returned to her and used it to attain seven black belts in the deadliest and most arcane martial arts. She also became an expert in all kinds of firearms and a deadly accurate, champion shooter. She now trained people at the Reservation for the Temporarily Bewildered in the art of self-defense, something she calls the Motherly Martial Arts. Rey knew that the subtle bulges showing under her habit marked the presence of Mr. Walther PPK and Mr. SIG Sauer, her two pals, as she called her favorite weapons.

Zara Tallaree was the third member of the Hadron leadership team. Rey had met the shapely, sleekly beautiful, exotic young woman when he was elected. She was his acting coach. He was trained by her to smoothly read the teleprompter and act presidential. Then he was kidnapped with her assistance. With golden skin, luxurious blond hair, and a slightly Asian look to her almost-purple eyes, she was a breathtaking beauty. The fact that such a woman was Jake's niece by his sister Rosetta always shocked people—almost as much as the fact that her father was the hideous Rancor Nithing himself, which explained her relentless pursuit of revenge against the monstrous Nithing family and NAP itself.

With a mellow voice that sounded almost like a purr, Zara laughingly told Rey, "Stop drooling, you big blue dude." Rey was embarrassed to realize that, as usual, he had been dazed by her stunning beauty. But Zara was more than beautiful. She was one of the most brilliant people Rey knew. Plus, she was an accomplished actress and, like Sister Mary, another martial arts expert.

Rey was saved from his embarrassment by the fourth leadership team member, his Uncle Jack Flynn Pompatella. A handsome half-Irish and half-Pewamo Native American, Flynn was an impressively robust man with an unusual mix of straight, raven black hair, copper complexion, and piercing cobalt blue eyes. "So good to see you, Rey-Rey," he said using Rey's boyhood nickname. "Pastor Louis wishes he could be here to participate, but the Dangerous Church is involved in some deadly squabbles with Achor Nithing's new weapon, the Creeb Nation."

Rey knew the humble Flynn was an influential leader in the resistance and Hadron's main contact with their key allies, the Pewamo Nation, in which he was a Sachem, an elected leader. He had been working away on a construction job when many of his and Rey's extended family were killed in a suspicious church fire, which ended up being a plot to gain insurance money by the evil NAP syndicate. It sent him on a course of revenge that still fueled him these many years later. Plus, he never forgave the Nithings for the decade he spent away from his family in reform school, having been framed by Achor Nithing, the real killer, for the death of Posey Slick.

Crazy Jake and Uncle Flynn were not related by DNA, but they were united in their intense antipathy for anything Nithing, having both lost family members to them. In addition, both shared some Native American ancestry as well as a deep and driving dedication to rescue and restore America.

Without any further ado, Jake jumped into action and announced, "Our goal from the beginning has been to discover, develop, and fund 'solutionaries' and 'evangineers' who want to creatively and constructively improve our US culture and the world in general. It looks like we didn't start any too soon." He stopped to point at a large wall screen where a mainstream media person was droning on about the political scene.

"As you know," Jake said, gesturing to the now-muted screen, "the midterm elections—coming just one year after the so-called re-election we nearly won, that replaced the original rigged election from two years ago—are roaring upon us. Everyone is jockeying for position. It's a mess, to say the least. The virtual Rey Newly, because of all the coddling media hype, is liked and supported by many of the mainline NAP power structure, not all of which is yet under the grip of the nefarious Nithing Group, despite Achor's best efforts."

He continued: "As we have learned, the psychopaths' great weakness is they all hate each other. The infighting among the NAP people is amazing. Our reports say the vice president, so-called Superman Samms, that oily rascal, is even tussling with his fellow narcissistic psychopath Groover Melville, the current Secretary of State, trying to gain control of everything in the virtual Newly camp before the next presidential election. For now, Samms is leading the resistance against Nithing within the NAP camp, and he's trying to field a team of House and Senate candidates under the NAP Republican flag that would be loyal only to him, using the likeable, gentle, virtual Newly to raise support. Samms and Melville only tentatively work together because they both want the digital Newly to win, so they can maintain their positions of power. They both prefer to be behind-the-curtain Machiavellians, not being real charismatic characters, knowing Newly is a virtual figurehead, wields no real power, and is easily manipulated."

He paused and then went on. "There is one more spoon stirring the political pot. The old Boguiden NAP Democrat team is back, whining and scrambling." When no one interjected a comment, he continued. "We can dismiss them as a real threat, but they siphon off more NAP votes."

"But now that Nithing has reemerged from the dead, we aren't sure how everything will shake out. As a matter of fact, it's rumored that Nithing is so frustrated by the continued internal resistance within NAP, he probably will field his own party of loyalists called the New American Party and support a separate field of candidates for House and Senate. We hear a surprising turncoat team has arisen, led by Thambos Zugzwang and his villainous viper of a wife, Zenobia. Blinded by their ego, corruption, and lust for power, they are trying to ally themselves with Achor and could have a powerful impact on the race if they work with him. He seems to have craftily gotten leverage over them. We have that from an excellent inside source, who will remain confidential for now."

"The rest of the NAP factions are scrambling and scratching among each other for more power, trying to determine who will ultimately win, so as to be on the winning side. The whole thing is baffling. If the psychopaths could just get along, they wouldn't even need to bother having elections. Just do an outright takeover. A fortified but not fixed election, they would claim. A blatant power grab. So, why have another election with an election-fatigued populace already distracted and dazed by drugs and the droning media? I guess it's just a fight among predators over who gets the carcass of America." Jake finally paused in thought.

"We could send out Rey again," he finally said. "As Nambo McBlue, he could campaign for the True Blue Revolution candidates popping up all over. Most of them are actually True Blue, although a few are bluistas, as we call fake blues. But we almost lost Rey last time. I know he would willingly put himself in the literal crosshairs again, but I don't know if we want to risk it. Despite the rigging, I think our sheer numbers and enthusiasm will guarantee us taking some additional seats in both the House and Senate, especially as it appears it will become a four-way horse race full of NAP infighting. Prayerfully, we can keep what we won in the last election and use what we have to steer the psychopaths off balance enough to keep them from destroying the country."

Jake suddenly smiled mischievously, as if a devious thought occurred to him. "The good news in all this?" he asked rhetorically. "As usual, the psychopaths are always justifiably paranoid about each other and everybody else. Because they're actually out to get everyone else, the paranoia is well founded. It's the one way we can control them somewhat. Just ignite the paranoia that's always there and keep it flickering."

Jake gestured with both hands, four fingers pointed in the air in twin victory signs, and went on. "Besides, with the new brain-scan technology we helped develop, the psychopaths know they can now be easily detected. In general, people are slowly becoming aware of their existence, if not always the high level of threat, but as usual the people are not sure what to do. I always say, if you don't know you are in a war, you'll lose every time. Now more people, at least, are aware of the war going on."

After a pause, Jake continued: "We all know how deadly the cold-hearted psychopaths can be, truly a menace to all mankind. I think every day about what they did to the ones I loved! The problem has been getting the average person to comprehend the level of threat the deep state psychopaths pose. It's hard for people with even just a modicum of decency, morality, and empathy to understand how devious and deeply evil they are. You can't overestimate the depravity of a person completely devoid of all compassion and guilt. And Achor Nithing takes the cake. A brilliant mind, a dazzling handsome face, a man of robust build—he just oozes charisma. I intensely loathe him."

Jake shuffled through a stack of papers he had downloaded from his computer as he regained his composure, and he made yet another point: "Nithing is now swooping in on the self-proclaimed, so-called elites in media, academia, and the arts—with their overweening arrogance and undiluted disdain for the common person. They're swooning over him, largely because of his money and charisma, some out of fear. They are easy marks because of their infinite ability to delude themselves. He's rapidly building a coalition of evil, even stronger than before. It just goes to show, when you knock down the giant, be sure to take off his head, just like David did to Goliath," he added, to make the Biblical reference clear. "The giant is now back on his feet again," he warned.

Then Jake paused again, this time for dramatic effect. "Another threat factor is MI or machine intelligence. As you all know, machine intelligence was enthusiastically and recklessly employed by the NAP psychopaths to try to gain control of the country. They charged ahead with no safeguards and used the first cyborgs with human brains and circuitry, with our friend Carlyle the cyborg being the prototype. But because NAP learned the hard way that they couldn't trust the cyborgs to be blindly obedient, they're now trying to use just pure circuitry, no human element involved. The rumor is that the MI is now out of control and threatening to take over, even though NAP, especially Nithing in his arrogance, doesn't want to admit it. The danger is that MI uses 'affective computing' to make you believe they have emotions. Some critics call this 'artificial emotional intelligence.' The machines can make you think you're talking to a real human. They read your micro-expressions, analyze your voice, and respond in a such a convincing way that you think they actually care. If people don't know they're talking to a machine, most believe they are actually dealing with a real human—and a caring, charismatic one, to boot. Cold and calculating, ultimate logic without compassion, they make the perfect psychopaths and enable manipulation of us weak humans hobbled by emotions."

Jake sighed with disgust. "Still yet another threat is the collapse of our economy due to biological and technological viruses. Because of rampant paranoia, a pervasive 'trust system' has been allowed to be installed almost everywhere. CCTVs and monitoring drones are getting to be pervasive. Facial recognition, voice recognition, body image, and bio-data recognition are commonplace. Our Fourth Amendment rights of protection from unwarranted search and seizure are long gone, if they ever really existed over the last sixty years."

Zara then jumped in. "On top of that, people are being replaced at an amazing rate in almost all jobs by intelligent machines, and they are being enticed into what's called the Human Enhancement Network or HEN, originally set up by NAP and that devious Achor Nithing. They lure people in with promises of security and safety. We believe some HENs are run by NAP muscle, mostly now back under the control of Nithing. A few others, however, are apparently now run by non-human MI, trying to push out NAP."

Jake gestured to Zara and a young man, Snapper Melville, and took over the discussion from Zara, explaining, "As you all know, Snapper is the son of a high-ranking NAP honcho, our nasty Secretary of State Groover Melville. Snapper left the NAP ranks when he realized their evil nature. As a photographer at the White House, he befriended Rey and, along with Zara, played a key role in Rey's escape from the White House. We will have a team led by Zara and Snapper infiltrating the HEN system to give us better insights. We should have a full report for you on HEN when you get back."

Then Jake paused, stared at Rey for effect, and emphasized, "We'll talk again after you spend some time in the Machpelah swamp with our friends, the Muckytuck Pewamo. Because your dad was a swamp logger, you should feel at home. You'll be safe there off the grid, and your Uncle Flynn and I feel you can learn a lot. It'll only be a few weeks until we get everything sorted out and see where you can be most effective." Uncle Flynn remained silent but nodded affirmatively.

Rey smiled and said, "Well, actually, as Uncle Flynn knows, my dad, Roddy Newly, was a full-time worker at the Brewer Creek Brewery, unloading and loading huge, heavy barrels all day long. To bring in extra money to support my mom and us three children—my two younger brothers and me—he would work weekends and late afternoons as a swamp logger with my Grandpa Big Jon Flynn and my Uncle Big Jon Junior. When I got older I did a little logging myself with them. They were only swamp loggers because the big shots wouldn't let them log any of the easy places. An Irish man married to an Indian, you know!"

"Well, the Muckytuck, the Swamp Pewamo, are eager to meet you," Jake said, and Uncle Flynn again nodded in agreement. "They have watched you and so far are impressed. They already consider you a member of the tribe. Being one-quarter Pewamo probably helps, and being related to Jack Flynn Pompatella doesn't hurt. But being a Nambo from Foondavi? That's even more meaningful to them than being president of the USA!"

Jake smiled a roguish smile. "You're going to meet an irascible, conniving, but capable character by the name of Machseh Muckleshoot, the Ogimaag, or ceremonial chief, of the Muckytuck clan of the Pewamo people. You'll meet him in the little town of Chirasco, totally off the grid. It's the only town I know of without four corners. Keep your ears open and you'll learn things that anthropologists and archaeologists have wanted to know for years. We also think their lifestyle in the Ancient Forest, as they call their reserve, can eventually serve as a great model for restoring all the land."

"Don't underestimate Machseh," Uncle Flynn finally added, laughing. "He's an amazing man but tries to keep it hidden, kind of a Muckytuck Pewamo version of Crazy Jake."

As usual, Rey reflected later, he should have listened closer to what was said.

A Mysterious
≡ Forest Interlude ≡

Rey's directions from Jake were to meet Machseh Muckle-shoot in the little town of Chirasco. Jake told him that, in the Pewamo language, Chirasco meant "waggle butt waterfall," at least according to the old rascal Machseh. The original Pewamo people retrieved their water at the base of Chirasco's small falls and riffles, where several small springs splattered in. The Natives claimed those ever-running springs made the water taste better. Sometimes the people even swam there. Machseh said that the water was much, much better, worth a long walk through the woods—at least according to the young warriors and maidens who enjoyed sneaking peeks at each other, flirting, and . . . who knows what else, given that the falls were a long walk from the prying eyes of elders who lived downriver in Wauponcisco, now the site of the town called Brewer Creek, where the land was better for farming. Needless to say, the place was a popular gathering spot. Rey was musing about this and was startled when Machseh silently popped up beside him, like a wrinkled jack-in-the-box. "Ha! Got you, Blue Goo man! First lesson from Machseh your mentor: Never stand beside a noisy river or waterfall. Even a clumsy old fart like me can sneak up on you."

"I was told by Jake to meet you right here," Rey responded a little gruffly, still shaken from being jolted by Machseh's sudden appearance.

"Second lesson: Don't always do what you're told—unless I'm telling you, of course!" he said while extending a chubby paw with a surprisingly strong grip.

Machseh confirmed all the comments about Chirasco with a sigh and a smile, while gazing fondly at the falls. "Oh, yeah! Love the Waggle Butt Falls, for sure!"

Machseh was a short-legged, rotund man, built like a barrel. He had sparkling eyes and a mouth full of shining white teeth he flashed with a constant smile. He had dark hair, but it was curly with a slight reddish cast, somewhat unusual for a Native American, Rey thought. Machseh constantly chuckled and smiled while he talked, making all the wrinkles in his gnarled old face dance. He struck Rey as a guy who loved life, food— especially food, lots of food—and having a good time.

Chirasco was about as obscure a place as one could find, although Rey remembered stopping at a dairy near the town as a kid and getting some fantastic ice cream. Now, unfortunately, the place was closed, like about every small retail place everywhere. Rey also knew, from consulting the map Jake gave him, that Muckytuck Swamp was a seventeen-mile journey from the banks of the Kazoo River where they were now standing. It was situated where the Nottaway and Brewer Creeks converged to form the mighty Kazoo that smoothly flowed beside them on its way to Lake Michigan.

Machseh explained the meeting location to Rey: "We wanted to meet you here in case you were followed. One can't be too careful with NAP rounding up anyone they think might be thinking bad thoughts about them."

"Where did you park your car?" Rey asked uneasily, looking for a vehicle. He was startled again when Machseh jumped in the air and quickly looked around himself in an overly exaggerated fashion, like his vehicle was stolen. "Car? My car? What car? No car!" He stopped the comedy act and addressed the unamused Rey: "I walked here. Do you know why I walked here?"

Rey decided to play along with the guessing game and said, "I don't know. Maybe because you don't have a car. Or maybe so you could, you know, commune with nature, or something deep and mystical like that?"

"No," Machseh responded. "It's not because of some mystical mumbo jumbo. I don't have a car because it would be noisy and smell up the air. Now, follow me," he said as he grandly gestured to Rey and briskly took off, quickly climbing up a steep bank to get on a railway trestle that crossed the rushing Kazoo River.

In the middle of the trestle Machseh stopped and, cupping his hand to his ear, said, "Now, slow down and listen."

"Are you now going to give me some deep Native wisdom about listening to nature?" Rey asked testily, slowly catching his breath from the climb and amazed to see Machseh was not even breathing hard.

"No, there's a train coming. Better skedaddle!" he answered. With that, the squat but nimble old Pewamo took off sprinting like a scalded dog over the trestle, he jumped off the tracks, and then he tumbled head first down the embankment, landing with an oomph. As Rey pulled up beside him, the train went roaring by with a toot of its whistle, and the hot smell of metal and oil came wafting over them.

Rey reached to help Machseh, but the old man refused the offer and dusted himself off with a modicum of dignity.

"Crazy bank tripped me!" he said. Then Machseh made a rude gesture at the now-departed train and shouted, "I can't stand those noisy contraptions polluting our land!"

Noisily tromping off and roughly stomping on bushes and weeds, Machseh left a nice trail for Rey to follow. They finally came out of the trees and brush onto a muddy, pothole-filled farm lane.

"No CCTV on these. No drone monitors," Machseh responded to Rey's scornful look.

"No real road either!" Rey had to add, hoping to rile the old guy.

Machseh only smiled at the jibe and asked Rey a question: "Comedian, huh? Did you ever hear the one about two cavalry officers riding up on their Indian scout who was lying down in the middle of the road? No? He had his ear to the ground." Machseh cupped his own ear, mimicking the gesture, and continued, "The scout looked up and said to the officers, 'Stagecoach, five minutes ago, one driver with a long blond beard, four horses, two black and two white.' One officer said to the other, 'Isn't it amazing they can tell all that just by putting their ear to the ground?' And the Indian scout said, 'Stage coach ran over me five minutes ago.'"

"Only Indian joke I know," chortled Machseh. "I wish we possessed all the super powers and mysterious mumbo jumbo you city folks think we have! We would have chased the pale butts off our land years ago. Nothing personal, of course."

Suddenly an old, dusty, beat-up pickup truck, looking to be on its last legs, came rattling up to them with what appeared to be two other Muckytucks on board. One of the Native Americans, a huge, towering man with bulging muscles on top of bulging muscles, got out and somehow crammed himself into the back seat. Machseh introduced him as his much older and much uglier brother Moose. The comment only earned Machseh a big, white-toothed grin. Then he said that the scrawny driver with the long, stringy hair was his cousin Moogy.

"Both Muckleshoots, I am forced to admit," Machseh said, as he rudely shoved Rey into the middle and took the outside shotgun position for himself.

"Moose is FBI," Moogy announced. Seeing Rey's startled expression, he let out an explosive laugh, "No, not a federal agent: An effing Big Indian. FBI, ha! He played left water boy on the Michigan State football team!" Rey only heard a dismissive snort rumble out of the backseat in response.

It proved to be a very deceptive truck. As Machseh lowered the dashboard, all sorts of electronic scrambling devices and monitoring screens appeared. Seeing Rey's stunned expression, Machseh explained, pointing to the intense driver, who was steering and maintaining a hawk-like focus on the various screens: "Moogy only looks dumb. He was a highly skilled Air Force tech expert and even got hornswoggled into working with the CIA for a while. Moose, back there, also only looks dumb. He served four tours in Iraq and other places that will remain unnamed. You don't want to know what he does. He wouldn't shoot you if he told you, wasting his beloved ammo; he would just throttle you to death," Machseh warned.

Nodding at what Rey now saw was a packed gun rack in the back with several terrifying-looking weapons, Machseh continued, "Moose is an expert with all of them. Even without visible weapons, he can kill you in a split second. He's admittedly one deadly dude."

Machseh then stuck a stubby thumb to his own chest. "My name means 'fortress' or 'refuge of hope.' I'm the Ogimaag, as our Odawa friends say. In your language, I'm the 'chief' of the Swamp Muckytuck, but it's actually more of a ceremonial title than an official position. Trying to lead this scruffy band of misfits is a chore! Like pushing water uphill! Our village is called Machsehpech, or village of Machseh, and the bigger swamp and surrounding forest is called Machpelah, or 'home of the Ancient Ones.'"

Then he gestured to the big guy in the backseat again. "Moose here? He claims his Pewamo name means 'anointed' or 'enlightened one,' but actually it means 'butt wipe' in Muckytuck. Muckleshoot is our larger clan name. And cousin Moogy? He says his name means 'majestic.' It actually means 'booger!' So, you are accompanied by Butt Wipe and Booger Muckleshoot! Makes you feel safe, doesn't it?"

They pulled under a tree for cover for a few minutes while Moose and Machseh intensely scanned the skies and Moogy monitored his screens. "We're looking for NAP drones or any high-flying reconnaissance vehicles," Machseh informed Rey.

They remained silent for several minutes, peering into the sky and listening carefully, before Rey finally broke the silence and said, "I notice you do all the talking." With a side-eye glance, Rey noticed the other two shaking their heads, grinning, and rolling their eyes.

"Yes, I am loquacious," Machseh said humbly, as Moogy snorted and seemed to choke on the comment, while also keeping his eyes glued to the screens and road as he drove. "Machseh's name actually means 'honey-tongued smoke-blower' or 'flicker lips!'" Moose grumbled from the back seat, his only contribution to the discussion so far. "'Running mouth' would be an accurate translation, too," he said, nodding his head in admiration of his own sage insight.

Machseh ignored the comments and continued speaking: "They are prototypical stoic, expressionless, wooden Indians! I have to do all the work, letting people know that, despite their dim-witted, ferocious looks, they are really deceptively intelligent, although marshmallow soft."

Moose rumbled back menacingly, "I should bite your head off and eat it."

"Then you would have twice as many brains in your stomach as you do in your head, big guy. You played too much football without a helmet. He actually looks like he played goalie on a hand grenade team," Machseh said.

Moogy finally chipped in verbally after squinting at his screens again: "I wish I were half as smart as you two brutes think you are!"

Rey couldn't resist getting into the fray and asked, "Do you guys always get along so well?"

"We just get testy when we're away from our home and under possible attack at any moment by NAP," Machseh responded. "It's just brotherly battle chat, trash talk. Believe me, each of us would die for the others and our people, although, to paraphrase that great Muckytuck, George Patton, our real goal is to get the other poor sucker to die for his people!"

As they drove slowly down the rutted road, Moogy suddenly called out, "Bogies coming in on the left."

The truck suddenly reverberated with loud thuds as shells of some sort attempted to penetrate the old vehicle, which thankfully was surprisingly well armored. Suddenly the sun roof popped open and Moose jumped out, stood up, and let loose with a huge shoulder-mounted Stinger anti-aircraft missile. The resounding whump stunned and deafened Rey, while Machseh joined in the barrage with a Bushmaster 12-gauge shotgun he pulled from beside the door, adding to the din. Moogy stood and unloaded a Walther PPK at the incoming enemy. Shell casings pelted down and cordite smoke wafted through the air around the stunned and deafened Rey. All he could see beyond the vehicle were metal parts raining down around them as at least two drones were demolished.

In the following silence, the unperturbed Moogy just went back to monitoring his screen and announced, in an exasperated voice, "No more bogies. They must have been waiting on the ground and then launched as we appeared. Either that or they have stealth capability, which I doubt."

"Thank goodness the locals don't have bigger Predator drones and Hellfire Missiles, or we would have been Muckytuck toast," Machseh added, shaking his head. Then Machseh gave Moose a disapproving look and quipped, "Using a precious Stinger missile on a small drone? Aren't you overcompensating a bit? It's like using a bazooka to wipe out a bumblebee! Or a sledgehammer to swat a slug. I splattered the second one using my shot gun like this was a skeet shoot. I think Moogy might have winged the other one to help you!"

Moose just shrugged and growled. "When it comes to killing things, I'm a big fan of overwhelming force! My motto has always been to be ready and deadly."

Rey's ears were still ringing when they pulled out again, everyone scanning the sky. "Two armed patrol drones?" he asked. "Is that normal?"

"No, they must have somehow got a hint you or somebody important might be visiting us," Machseh replied. "They usually just follow us at a safe distance and try to monitor our communications, but they seldom attack. They don't have an unlimited supply of expensive attack drones, and they know Moose is a deadly and dedicated drone destroyer. Plus, our swamp is peppered with anti-aircraft systems, courtesy of old Crazy Jake. Once we get to where we're going, they'll leave us alone."

Finally, after a bumpy, dusty ride and many more stops— sometimes just to look at streams for no discernable reason, as far as Rey could see; other times to methodically scan the screens and the sky—they pulled up to a swampy-looking creek that flowed under a rickety bridge. To the right, the creek was flowing through an open meadow up to the side of the road. The air was full of soggy swamp smells, like moist hay, with assorted colorful wildflower blooms adding a beautiful fragrance. In the distance, a field full of long-stem sweetgrass was waving in a slight breeze. A few deer were grazing not too far away.

"Welcome to Nottaway Creek," Moose rumbled from the backseat. Machseh just belched loudly, while Moose scrambled out of the cramped backseat and stretched his long arms and legs, continuing to scan the sky.

On the other side of the road, the bridge was closely hemmed in by a seemingly unbroken, impenetrable wall of tangled trees, dense undergrowth, and matted twigs and roots. These were all intermingled with slow-moving dark swamp water. It reminded Rey of some of the snarled and impassable mangrove swamps he had seen when serving in Asia and the Pacific.

Machseh and Moose motioned to get Rey out of the car. They looked around carefully, while Moogy monitored his scanner, briskly nodded his head affirmatively, and then quickly drove off down the rutted lane. Machseh deftly reached into the mass of greenery for something Rey couldn't discern, and suddenly a small section of the dense foliage swung out without making a sound. They swiftly ducked through the small opening and entered a dark underworld beneath towering trees and entangled undergrowth, stopping only to push the entry door tightly shut behind them.

Rey found himself in a new world. Mushrooms and fungi grew profusely among the gnarled, massive tree trunks. Birdsongs filled the air, some familiar to him, and others strangely not. Numerous butterflies, bees, and hummingbirds seemed to hover everywhere. As stunning as the colors were from all the blooms and even the multi-hued moss, the smells inundating him were even more amazing. Sweet smells and pungent earthy odors bombarded his nose from all directions. It seemed like every tree and plant competed for his senses.

"Welcome to Machpelah. Our founder Shammah Muckleshoot, when we Muckytuck first came here eons ago, said Machpelah means 'the hold or refuge of the fathers and mothers' of the Muckytuck. In other words, 'a safe place.'

And this," he said, grandly indicating the greenery, "is the Ancient Forest."

For some time, they silently continued walking through a narrow tunnel in the undergrowth and beneath the towering overstory. Occasional sun-dappled openings lit the way. They used strategically placed lichen-covered fallen logs to cross several rivulets of slow-moving, crystal-clear, ice-cold water that was pouring over phosphorescent moss-covered rocks. Finally, they arrived at an opening, though still beneath the huge, towering overgrowth.

The Ancient Forest was composed of massive fir and white pine. It was laced with gnarled old oaks and other trees Rey identified as hickory and maybe even some rare sycamores of massive size. The place felt peaceful and enchanted. There were some other trees Rey couldn't identify that Machseh said were imported from other regions to round out the forest; a few added bio-engineered trees blocked any aerial surveillance.

Rey knew most humans, especially city dwellers and open-country people, find the deep, dark, primeval forest to be foreboding. In the old days, some people even believed forests—overgrown, intensely dark and dank, filled with strange odors and sounds—were the haunts of demons and witches. Who knew what could be lurking in the shadows?

Because of his love of birds and being an amateur ornithologist, though, Rey always found the forest welcoming. And this one was especially intriguing. He had always seen trees as just nesting and perching places for his beloved birds, but he sensed here that the trees were much more.

As they made their way deeper through the wonderous

forest, Machseh started describing the Pewamo Muckytuck people and their origins. Much of what he said surprised Rey. Indeed, what he shared probably would have shocked many historians, anthropologists, and archaeologists.

"We Muckytuck originated thousands of years ago in the Amazon rainforest. Until recently, most people thought the rainforest was just wild, random, untamed jungle. When stripped of the forest cover by slash-and-burn farming, mining, or logging, the poor soil loses all its fertility within a year or two. Leached by the rains and scorched by the sun, it becomes a wasteland. The untouched rainforest, however, is anything but a wasteland."

"It took years, but finally people started looking differently and in more detail at the rainforest. Upon analysis of the 'untouched' forest, the experts were amazed. They determined that over a surprising eighty percent of the vegetation in the rainforest is either food sources—like berries, other fruit, nutritious nuts, gourds, and roots—or else useful resources—like balsa wood, bamboo, and monkey pod, which are used for building materials, blow guns, and spears. This was way beyond what anyone expected to find. The rainforest isn't all just a wild jumble after all! At one time it was one big garden. Ha! We could have told them that, but why ask some dumb Indians, huh? We engineered that Amazon Eden over thousands of years! We built mounds above the annual flood levels and filled them with the miracle artificial black earth called terra preta, a carefully manufactured black earth topsoil that miraculously, after a thousand years lying fallow, can still regenerate any barren soil. You saw some of that on Foondavi, where we helped the Native people rebuild their island with midden piles covered by wet vegetation, and then with slow or cool burning of the dirt and charcoal with fish remains, bones, and other organic detritus covered again in wet vegetation, all to build a good deposit of fertile black soil. All invented, engineered, and designed by us, the original Amazon Pewamo Muckytuck! We created an Eden in a way. Food and health for all. Unfortunately, as usual with Edens, it attracted evil predators," Machseh concluded, as he let out a sigh of resignation.

Then he waved his arm as he continued walking, indicating the Ancient Forest surrounding them. "So, chased by ancestors of the Incas who wanted our farmlands, we left the Amazon and encountered the forerunners of the Aztecs. When they started to demand our children as sacrifices, we left again and moved as far away as we could get, up the Mississippi, always rebuilding our villages and sharing our agricultural knowledge along the way. We passed the original Mound people, provided improved maize and other crops for them, and then we finally ended up here in the marshes of Michigan, with some ancient relatives of ours, also descended in the far distant past not just from Cro-Magnons but also from the Denisovans: These were the Odawa, Potawatomi, and Ojibwa, as you call them, or Anishinaabe as they call themselves. Why did we run? We can fight anyone—we have some of best and bravest warriors, like my brother Moose here—but we only fight to defend ourselves. We just want to be left alone to grow our food, feed and love our families, and steward our Ancient Forest."

"Why were we persecuted? The forebears of the Inca didn't just want our fertile black earth, the terra preta mounds.

They wanted us as slaves to work those mounds. They even designed Machu Pichu as a research center, holding our people hostage under threat of death, to try to figure out how we made the terra preta mounds. So, we moved on, leaving behind our beloved rainforest. Then the ancestors of the Aztecs, as I said, started to round up our children as sacrifices to their gods, even after we taught them how to construct chinampas, raised gardens full of terra preta. This new way of farming allowed them to feed many more people than they had previously because it increased the output of their cultivated fields, the milpa, where they grew beans, squash, melons, and maize among the waterways. But, no, they didn't just want our children to sacrifice! They also wanted to end our entire way of life and make us Aztec!"

"So, we were on the move again, although we regretted leaving the beautiful Valley of the Sun. Later, even the Mound people of the big river you call Mississippi grew jealous of our agricultural success and trading acumen. Even though we taught them how to grow more and better corn and brought them wealth from across the continent, they still wanted our wealth and to enslave our families. Even here, among the Fire Nation people and the European people, we have to be careful, as the Muckytuck always figure out how to trade and make money while others often flounder. Envy is a great source of evil," Machseh said sadly.

"When we first settled here in this forest over two thousand years ago, we established trade networks up and down the great rivers from as far north as the Arctic Circle. We brought Arctic furs as well as Lake Superior copper axes, knives, and chert points to the Gulf of Mexico. Then we took back north smoked seafood as well as shell necklaces, jade, and turquoise from the Gulf. We even traded from the Atlantic to the Pacific. We exchanged obsidian for smoked salmon as well as arrow heads from Michigan for hard, fine-grained chert for tool making. Whatever we could trade we did, even crossing the Great Plains under the protection of the Na-na-tee-nah, the ancestors of the current Apache and Utes, who wandered the Plains on foot following the bison herds long before the horse reappeared. Those were dangerous endeavors: If you were trapped in the wrong place, the 'red buffalo,' the prairie fires, could wipe out a whole walking caravan."

"We were constantly trading goods and collecting information. We were sort of the Native American Internet for trade and news, mostly welcomed wherever we went. Then we saw the first Europeans come ashore to trade. As we had many years before with the Phoenicians and then the Scandinavians, we brought Europeans copper from Minnesota and gold from the Rocky Mountains. They traded metal objects like pots, knives, hatchets, and, unfortunately, even guns— magical thunder sticks that produced thunder and lightning and killed at a distance. We ended up using the guns mainly to protect ourselves."

"We were careful not to bring back diseases from our trading missions. We kept our Pewamo travelers in isolated, quarantined shelters for weeks before they were allowed back into their villages; we had learned difficult lessons about disease from our early Amazon days. Other Indigenous people were not so careful, however, and whole nations were devastated long before they saw the first white settlers. Some people noticed we didn't get sick—primarily because we kept ourselves very clean and kept our traders quarantined for a time when they returned—but those people ignored the hygiene and often accused us of witchcraft or worse. We made ourselves too valuable to be destroyed and kept our strongholds tucked away from invading eyes in these swamp fortresses and the Ancient Forest."

"We were adopted as cousins hundreds of years ago by the ancestors of the three Fire Nations—Odawa, Potawatomi, and the Anishinaabe, the last group often called Ojibwa. The Odawa were often called the traders, but it was in partnership with us that they prospered, dominated the fur trade, and set up trade networks that spanned from Montreal to the Far West. We helped them to increase their maize production and a lot of other things, including their population. They really accepted us and allowed us to be Pewamo."

"The great Shawnee Chief Tecumseh and his brother, the Prophet Tentskwatawa, tried to recruit our renowned Wolf Clan warriors, who were massive and fierce like my brother Moose, but we just wanted to be left alone to be peacemakers and independent traders. With our trading contacts on the East Coast, we could see the massive tide of Europeans coming and wanted to protect our own people. Probably because of our long, troubled history, we knew about the potential destructive power of human-to-human diseases and the value of quarantining. We also had medicines that kept us healthy; our medicine men and women, the Mashkiki, had extensive knowledge, built over a thousand years, of the healing properties of thousands of plants, plant parts, roots, herbs, and berries."

Seeing Rey was beginning to breathe a little heavily from the exertion, Machseh and Moose stopped in a sunny opening and sat on a log. Machseh shook his head sadly and then continued. "For the most part, the rapidly expanding Caucasian invasion just rolled right over the Pewamo. We were hidden safely in our deep swamp villages on seemingly worthless land. Settlers and their government didn't realize these swamps were carefully designed to be tangled enough to be very hard to penetrate. They were also designed on a descending gradual grade to keep the water slowly moving, so there would be no mosquitoes."

Machseh paused to push his wildly flowing hair back in place and continued. "It wasn't that we were afraid to fight. In fact, we were known as the 'gentle giants' among the other tribes who tried to attack us. Many of our men were big and tall, if a little on the portly side," he said while sucking in his ample belly, "and we never lacked in courage when protecting our people and homes. We've proven our bravery over and over, in every major American combat engagement—from the Civil War to the Gulf Wars and even in Afghanistan. Our men, and some women, have fought and died for the USA, way out of proportion with our actual population. We even have numerous decorated veterans like Moogy and Moose. We serve, we fight, and we then quietly slip back into our way of life."

Just then Machseh's phone chirped in his pocket, making everyone jump. "It's my satellite cell phone, super secure and encrypted. Only Jake has the number," he said. He punched some keys, muttered a short, unintelligible sentence about attack drones, and handed the phone to Rey, saying. "It's Jake, for you."

≡ Achor on the Move ≡

Jake started the call abruptly without any pleasantries or greeting. "You obviously arrived safely, despite your little drone scuffle," he said. Although a talkative wordsmith in person, Jake always was to the point on the phone, possibly because he was unable to see or read facial expressions, or because he was afraid of having his phone call overheard.

He continued, "I hope the Muckleshoot men haven't been too tough on you. They like to test everyone—something they say they learned from me. Be patient with them and the Ancient Forest. I know that sounds enigmatic, but you'll soon understand. Listen and watch. Observe everything. The Muckytuck way can be an alternative lifestyle for many people after we start Tikkun Olam, healing and rebuilding the world. On another note, Rey, I don't have any specific news about your family, but be assured they're okay. I asked our friendly cyborg Carlyle not to take a chance on being hacked, so he's keeping your family's hiding place close to his cyborg chest. But one thing you do need to know, Rey, is that things are rapidly evolving. Your old nemesis Achor is on the move. Your job right now is to absorb as much as you can about the Muckytuck way of life and the Ancient Forest. Both can be crucial in the future. Stay safe. Stay secluded.

We're tracking Achor and will try our best to stay ahead of him. Any questions?"

"Nope. But as interesting as this place appears to be, I'd rather be where the action is."

"Believe me, Rey, you haven't yet explored a tenth of what the Ancient Forest and Machseh can teach you. I spent several months there with your Uncle Flynn when we were both on the run and before we set up the Reservation for the Temporarily Bewildered. It's an amazing place, and the people are amazing. You'll see."

"Well, keep me posted, especially about my family. I love Carlyle, and he has saved my bucket several times, but he gets a little over confident, and I think he gets mesmerized by his cyborg girlfriend, Camilla. I'll learn everything I can here. I'm already impressed, and I just got here."

The phone suddenly went dead. Machseh let Rey know that was normal; the phones were designed to cut out as soon as they detected anyone trying to tap the line. They also dimly heard a zap and sizzle behind them. "A NAP mini-drone, probably a nanobot, just got fried trying to penetrate our space. They never learn," explained Machseh, with a fiendish smile.

Master of
≡ Discord and Disruption ≡

While Jake was talking to Rey, Achor Nithing was busy at work, creating discord and disruption. He knew from studying the Cloward-Piven Strategy from the 1960s that, if he overloaded the bungling bureaucratic deep state, he could threaten everyone's physical safety and financial security. He would create a crisis and then not let the crisis go to waste. When threatened and confused, fearful people look to a strong person to save them, and Achor was preparing himself to be that savior.

To be in position for his takeover, Achor had a lot of irons in the fire. Through the use of bribes and leverage on judges, Nithing was opening up the penal system and releasing prisoners who might roam the streets committing crime and violence or join his latest creation, the Creeb Nation, a paramilitary organization of thugs. In addition, by releasing an occasional computer virus and newly developed contagious, but not deadly, human viruses, he was overwhelming the already shaky and corrupt healthcare and economic systems. Plus, he was shifting his vast funds to create sham financial structures that would roil the markets, and he was using his elite Black Hat Hackers to track down the machine intelligence threat.

While masterminding and facilitating all this, the expert multi-tasker Achor also was savoring the hunt for Rey, AKA Nambo McBlue, and his family. He was relentlessly engaging all his sources and developing even more in every location where he suspected his quarry might be hiding. Like a tracking dog, he was catching the scent and knew he was closing in on what would be his most satisfying victim.

For Achor, revenge was a sweet potion. Every time he thought of Rey, he doubled down on his ravenous desire to crush the man. He wanted Jake too, but Jake could wait, he figured. He knew how much the old Mahogany Maestro esteemed, even loved, the Blue leader and his family. Humiliating and killing Rey would be like kicking sand in Jake's face, like stealing his prized possession. He knew Jake loathed him, and he loathed Jake in return. He was jealous about what the castaway orphan Jake had accomplished, and his father, Rancor, always relished rubbing Achor's nose in the fact that this bastard brother was so successful. Long story short, defeating Jake's protégé Rey would be more than satisfying. Maybe he could even polish off that troubling Jack Flynn Pompatella, as it still rankled that someone, even an innocent little girl, had preferred Jack over Achor. He would show them all, and savor the showing!

≡ A Blissful Forest Trek ≡

Blissfully unaware of any immediate threat, Rey was enjoying the forest trek. He was easily winded and needed the brief rest, realizing he needed to get back in shape after his leisurely cruise in the South Pacific.

Seeing Rey was ready to walk again, the men started off and Machseh continued talking: "The main village is just another short hike. While we walk, I can tell you another story." Getting a nod from Rey, he went on. "While the Pewamo are gentle people who like to joke, tell stories, and trade—rather than fight—our cousins were coming under increasing pressure from settlers and got agitated that us big, gentle jokers wouldn't join them on the warpath. They finally forced us to go with them and assigned us a cabin of settlers to destroy. Later, they found out our warriors surprised a mother alone with her three young children. She was baking apple pies. The aroma and the mother's brave demeanor won over our hulking, fierce-looking war party. They soon shared recipes, devoured her pies, and then left the stunned lady and her children safe and sound. The other more warlike tribes often jokingly commented that, while they were out collecting scalps, the Pewamo were out collecting recipes."

Machseh's stomach suddenly growled. "That story about apple pies always makes me hungry," he admitted. "We'll be getting to the village shortly. All our trails are winding and slow to give us plenty of time to prepare in case someone does invade. We have numerous camouflaged anti-aircraft batteries tucked in the trees to discourage overflights. You can't see them, but we also have many camouflaged CCTVs in the trees—our progress has been closely monitored since we arrived—and we employ drones that look like hawks, eagles, and ravens. Also we use nanobot cameras that look like hummingbirds or bees, so no one can approach our village without being seen. We're situated in about ten thousand acres of what used to be old, overused, and unproductive farmland and swamp. We've been able to add to our original reservation over the years thanks to Jake Quark, Jack Flynn Pompatella, and, of course, our own efforts."

"Another point about that story of collecting recipes," Machseh continued as they wound their way along the twisting trail, "is that it just goes to show the great diversity among the five hundred-plus original Native American nations. Some were great raiders and warriors, and others just wanted to get along, adjust to changing events, survive, and perhaps pick up a few good recipes along the way."

"Evil is an equal opportunity employer!" Machseh continued, with a glum look on his normally cheerful face. "All races are fully capable of horrible evil. Because of being allies with the Fire Nations, we were attacked from the east by the Iroquois, which is a name given to that tribe by others. It means 'snake'! They called themselves Haudenosaunee, which probably meant 'majestic people' or something like that. They tried to kill us, enslave us, and take our land. They used the European guns and steel, but we had weapons, too, thanks to our intrepid traders, and fought them off."

"Then the Sioux came in from the west. That name was possibly given to them by their enemy the Iroquois, or maybe even by our cousins the Anishinaabe Ojibwa. It means 'adders,' 'a deadly poisonous snake,' or 'enemies.' They called themselves the Oceti Sakowin, 'the people of the seven fires,' and they included the Lakota, Nakota, Dakota, Brule, and a few more tribes."

"See a pattern? We call other people snakes or enemies. Ourselves? We're the wonderful people! The best people! It's true of almost everybody. What do the Pewamo call themselves, you might be asking? Why, the wise, majestic, and humble ones, of course. What else?"

"The chatter boxes?" Moose grumbled. Machseh, as usual, ignored him and chatted on.

"As you walk around here, you'll notice a lot of different complexions and hair colors mixed among the stereotypical Native American appearance. For example, my lustrous locks have a tint of red, from one of my Irish ancestors. Over the years, we Muckytuck have brought in new members when disease or warfare diminished our numbers. In welcoming new members, we emphasize character, contribution, capability, compassion, and courage. We call them the five Cs. They're much like your Foondavi Nambo characteristics. If you have those, you can be a Muckytuck, and as you earn trust, you can be invited into the tribe. We are not restrictive. We just have to be careful, especially today with all the intrusive technology, to protect our Muckytuck way of life.

"Another important personality component to us is what researchers now call H-factor leadership traits. People who want to be leaders here need to be humble, honest, helpful, happy, and hungry to learn and grow. We recognize those traits in you, Rey. You don't just have Pewamo heritage, but there's something innately good about you. You're an H-factor leader. You put service ahead of power. You walked away from unimaginable money and power as POTUS because your beliefs and values were offended. There are, unfortunately, too few of you in any race. One of our goals, like those of Jake and Jack Flynn Pompatella, is to help develop more leaders with all these traits."

As they started approaching what appeared to be a rustically beautiful village of log-walled, thatch-roofed shelters surrounded by mounds of flowers, they walked by some raised platforms, terraces built up in and above the slow-moving waters of the Nottaway. The raised gardens were surrounded on all sides by the stream and were obviously used to grow food. Machseh explained that the channels kept the wild animals out and made it easy to water the plants. Rey could see several types of corn, different varieties of beans, squash of all sorts, a wide assortment of melons, some huge pumpkins, and many other plants he couldn't identify.

"These raised gardens are called chinampas. I told you about them earlier; we developed and used them first in the Amazon." He reached over and scooped up a handful of deep black soil. "This is the terra preta, our miracle top soil. We brought it with us when we were chased from the Amazon rainforest by pre-Inca ancestral invaders and disease. Maybe a raft or two from Africa or Egypt brought over some disease, who knows? Maybe early Phoenician traders brought the germs. They were quite the travelers! As I said earlier, our DNA says we're part Denisovan, an early type of Homo Sapiens. We even have Asian Islander genes! Some archaeologists now say we were possibly here in the Americas as long as 65,000 years ago, even before our Fire Nation friends came over from Siberia! What mixed-up people, huh? Phoenician, Viking, and Irish all with a heavy dose of early Native American. No wonder we're so wonderful—and humble."

Now, Rey noticed they were entering what appeared to be a pleasant and unassuming village. People smiled and waved at Machseh and Moose and looked with great curiosity at Rey. "They've heard about you and your exploits, Rey. It would be wonderful if you shared with our people some of your insights, but only if you feel comfortable."

"This place is off the grid," Machseh said, gesturing at the village around him. "Historically, wherever we go we have always been traders. We're still traders and investors. We have a secret underground state-of-the-art computer center," he said, pointing to a non-descript-looking cedar plank-covered building, "to trade on the stock and commodities markets. Satellite uplinks are cool! We use the money to maintain the Muckytuck Nation, expand our holdings, and help other people throughout the world feed themselves. We give old George Soros a battle for his bucks, and Warren Buffet, too—thanks to the smarts of Crazy Jake Quark and our own talented people!"

Rey was pleased to find that the chatty Machseh didn't have an agenda for him. Machseh explained, "Jake just wants you to explore and absorb the flavor of this place. Get rested up. Soak in the ambience. Do what we and the Japanese call, 'forest bathing': relax, listen, breathe it in, and listen to the Ancient Forest."

Seeing Rey's quizzical look, Machseh just smiled and said, "Parts of this forest have been here thousands of years, long before even we arrived. Just be patient. You'll soon learn why it's such a treasure."

Over the next few days, Rey went on many long walks. Machseh told him what to watch for each day. He said the wood-wide-web or timber net acts as an early warning system—but also will share great mysteries. "The trees are always trying to get our attention, but we have to slow down and listen. Trees communicate," Machseh said, "but their language is slower and on different frequencies than human speech. They talk to each other through pheromones, subsonic sound, and interconnected root and fungus systems. Willows talk to willows and birches, snooty alders talk only to other alders, unless it's an emergency, elms talk to elms and possibly oaks, beech trees babble to everybody, all warning each other of insect invasions, other threats, or human interference."

At first Rey thought Machseh was pulling his leg. The forest bathing was relaxing, but other than hearing the butterflies, bees, and hummingbirds zipping around him and seeing the occasional deer or elk passing by, he didn't hear anything else. Machseh told him to relax and imagine the forest talking—dense biomass everywhere communicating through entangled roots and fungi.

While walking among some huge white pines saved from loggers centuries ago, Rey began to hear something. What was it? What Rey could sense was a message from the trees saying, "Calm down. Slow down. Watch how everything is interconnected. You are welcome." He began to hear other trees communicating, too. The massive oaks in the Ancient Forest, with root systems undisturbed for thousands of years, shared how each root and plant was an integral part of the whole wood-wide-web, the timber net. Then an interesting thought hit him, and he made his way to find Machseh.

Machseh was eating a pumpkin pie while fishing in Nottaway Creek. Rey greeted the grizzled old guy and then asked, "If trees can communicate, warn each other across the forest of pests and intruders, and learn how to defend themselves, that means they actually have a brain. So, where is it?"

"Well, you'll have to wander in the Ancient Forest for a while longer, earn the trust of the trees, continue forest bathing, and maybe they'll share that knowledge with you. As usual, I have my theories."

Seeing Rey's quizzical look, Machseh smiled. "Just a theory now, but I believe there's a quantum space, maybe a Third Heaven as the Apostle Paul posited, created by the Source of All Things, the Great Star Maker. Just like we can't see the wind but we can feel it, just like we can't see infrared or radio waves flying invisibly through space, I think there could be a quantum cloud all around us. Maybe the trees and the rest of the forest are linked into that."

The next day, Machseh accompanied Rey on another walk and continued his lessons. "To restore the earth, we're also bio-engineering trees for use here and elsewhere. With new AI-guided drone technology Jake has developed, we can plant ten thousand tree seedlings a day, in just the right predetermined spot and depth!"

"As you're learning, our extensive observations and experiments over thousands of years make a laughingstock of what most people think about forests. By keeping the forest entangled and unmolested, we find that herbs, roots, leaves, and mushrooms all seem to be much more potent when put into medicines or foods. I'll explain later, but our model of caring for our forest could feed many more than live here. Jake and I think that the new technology for bio-engineering trees and AI-drone planting could completely revolutionize and improve the world."

On the following day, Rey's peaceful sojourn was interrupted by another call from Jake. He was summoned to the underground trading center and was astounded to see numerous young and old Muckytucks working on monitors and keyboards. The workers were spread out at tables in an underground area as big as any gymnasium Rey had ever seen. "We're trading around the clock," Machseh said with a big smile on his face. "We're working with Jake and making money to fund our various efforts. Others of us are hackers, working to foil Achor and his efforts," he noted. Then he pointed Rey to a room and said, "Over there is a private room where you can talk with Jake. All this is super secure, so chat away."

The Strongest Hearts
$\equiv$ Have the Most Scars $\equiv$

"I'm sorry to bother you, Rey," Jake immediately said, as always skipping any preliminary greetings. "I hope you're absorbing as much as you can. Speed balanced with patience is of the essence, because it's now certain Achor knows you're there in the Ancient Forest."

Rey felt unbalanced, having just walked in from the quiet of the forest into a hum of activity. He gazed around himself, amazed at the sophistication of the enterprise. People he had seen in the village engaging in the simple, basic tasks of life he now saw engaging in technological activity he couldn't begin to comprehend.

"You there, Rey?" Jake asked impatiently, wanting to get on with the call.

"Yes, but it's like stepping onto a high-speed people-mover after taking a leisurely walk. I'm a little disoriented, but I'm with you."

"Well, good. No need to panic. We're monitoring Achor's activities. I don't think he would launch a massive attack on Machpelah, but he definitely will continue to send in agents to attempt to penetrate our defenses."

"Continue?" Rey asked, suddenly worried for his new Muckytuck friends.

"Yes, there've been a few attempted incursions. I think you heard a NAP nanobot drone get clobbered when you first entered the forest." Rey did remember that, and he also had heard a few distant and dull booms in the days that followed, all absorbed by the Ancient Forest.

"We'll figure out a way to exfiltrate you when the timing is right," Jake continued. "For now, though, keep listening and learning. I know the idea of the Ancient Forest is hard to accept by your Western, logic-based mind. I should have given you Peter Wohlleben's book *The Hidden Life of Trees* before we sent you there. It highlights the research supporting the concept that trees communicate and learn. It's us humans who have become disconnected from those basics of life."

"I'm finally getting it, as unbelievable as it first seemed," Rey admitted.

"Good." Then Jake shifted to another topic: "Has Machseh filled you in about the drone technology we're using to plant trees? We bought ten thousand acres of desiccated former rainforest in Brazil. The cleared land was leached of all life by the drenching rains and scorching sun and was deemed useless, so we got it cheap. Now we're replanting it, and soon a restored rainforest will be growing."

Rey was excited to hear about such amazing advancements, but he wanted to ask Jake one tough question he had been thinking about for quite some time, especially as he wandered in the solitude of the Ancient Forest: "I want to ask you something completely out of the blue, if I can say that with no pun intended. It's been bothering me for a while. If you and Machseh are both so keen on the Blue Goo, how come you haven't both taken it yet?"

"We both have the need now and then to be deceptive and accepted," Jake answered. "As a recent example, I sent Machseh into the Brazilian rainforest to contact the few remaining, relatively untouched Indigenous inhabitants to gain seeds and information on the forest. They have enough trouble just relating to people of other races, let alone a blue-faced Native American. I also need to move among some pretty shaky and slick characters in the political and business world. I don't like being deceptive, but sometimes it's necessary. When it's not so dangerous, or we don't need to use deception, believe me, Machseh and I have both agreed we will take the Blue."

Rey was pleased with the answer and readily accepted it as the truth. "Thank you for your honesty, Jake," Rey offered.

"You probably won't thank me when I tell you what else I have to tell you," Jake said. Then he paused.

"What else?" Rey asked warily.

"Well, since we are being honest. I have to talk to you about something very difficult. You know we are going to have to exfiltrate you from there, right? It is going to be very risky. And there is always a chance that the persistent thug Achor could capture you."

"I have thought about it, and even had nightmares about it. So what?" Rey asked suspiciously, not liking the direction this was going. He could tell from the tone of Jake's voice that he was uncomfortable, too.

"Did you notice when you were out campaigning as Nambo McBlue that you always had at least one or two of the same security guys all the time?" Jake asked.

"Yes," answered Rey, "but I assumed that was usual Secret Service protocol."

"No. They were under orders to shoot to kill if it appeared you were being kidnapped by NAP," Jake said.

"Kill the kidnappers?" Rey asked.

"No. You, Rey," Jake sighed. "You know too much to fall into Achor's hands. It's not that you'd want to share secret information, but they have drugs and hideous ways of torturing. If they held your kids or wife and threatened to kill them if you wouldn't lie and die, who knows what you would say or do?"

Rey was shaken to his core. He felt a flash of anger, but then he realized the truth of the matter. "I guess we just make sure I don't get kidnapped," was all he could think to say.

Jake sounded relieved. "I know it's tough. But tough times make tough people. Someone once said, 'the strongest hearts have the most scars.' It pains me to talk about such things with people I love and admire. But what must be done, must be done. Now go back to the Ancient Forest. We'll extricate you as soon as possible."

The Dilemma
≡ of the Deadly Forest ≡

"What do you mean you can't get to him?" the enraged Achor Nithing ranted at his commander of the NAP forces. "How can a snaggle of twigs and branches stop the high-tech weapons I've given you?" Achor yelled. He had finally uncovered and cornered Rey in the stupid, overgrown swamp, and now his forces couldn't get to the guy!

"It's a damn deadly forest," the commander responded. Then he tried to explain the situation, saying, "We've already lost several capable agents and several high-tech nanobots trying to get in. None of them ever returned. The whole place is a no-fly zone that's peppered with sophisticated anti-aircraft defenses."

"Well, try harder, or I'll find someone else who can," Achor seethed.

"We almost got them on the way in," his commander added, hoping to soothe Achor somewhat. "At the time, we didn't know it was that McBlue character. The live footage we retrieved—before the drone was blasted by some big Indian with a stinger and two more Indians with hand-held weapons—indicated there was a fourth person with his hands over his ears in the deceptively dilapidated truck. After analysis of some chatter we got from the swamp, we now believe that was McBlue. We'll be waiting for him to come out. At least he's contained."

"Well, I'd like to blast the whole place," Achor responded, "but that would be a public relations nightmare now that Indians—excuse me, Native Americans, or whatever we're supposed to call them in woke speech—are definitely a protected class."

"We'll redouble our surveillance and upgrade our drones to include Hellfire missiles and the latest chain-gun weaponry. We'll get McBlue this time."

"Last chance, Commander! Last chance!" Achor yelled. Then he added, "I would much prefer him alive, though. Yes, on second thought, capture him alive if possible, so I can enjoy seeing him suffer for what he and his friends have done to me."

Containment is not good enough, Achor thought to himself. That slippery Blue man has eluded similar sure traps in the past! I'm going to have to put this nasty swamp on my growing list for ultimate destruction once I regain total power, dominance, and control. My favorite words! Savoring his thoughts, Achor returned to his devious tasks.

Beauty Out
≡ of Brokenness ≡

Rey was happy to return to his wanderings in the Ancient Forest, even if he was joined by the non-stop talker Machseh.

"As you know, as trust lands or a reservation, this place and others like it are legally off limits to the US government. They've happily given us this swampy, believed-to-be useless land! Ha! We've made sure it's stayed swampy and seemingly useless!" Machseh laughed. Then he continued, "Throughout the US, there are dozens of Muckytuck and other Pewamo villages, just like this one, hidden on land no one else wants. All the tribes have created swamps surrounded by restructured woodlands through careful engineering and bio-engineering, using moving water to filter out pollutants. We even make money doing stream 'doctor' work—restoring and restocking beaver ponds and planting bankside trees to stop erosion and flooding and to revitalize streams."

"We scattered our clans throughout the Midwest in isolated and discreet locations that we've named Dead Man's Swamp, Desolate Swamp, the Big Snake—anything scary to keep people out. All we need is a stream and a slow grade, and we do the rest. We're grouped by clans, each village having various members: the Beavers build our buildings and engineer our water systems; the Otters are our creative people,

and they entertain us; the Wolves maintain order and protect us; the Foxes do our trading; the Squirrels watch over our
trees; the Rabbits maintain our gardens; and the Owls offer
wisdom and leadership."

The next day Machseh took Rey aside to a quiet spot by
Nottaway Creek. "I want to share something personal with
you. A few years ago, through our friend and fellow Pewamo
Jack Flynn Pompatella, Reverend Louie Pastore visited us.
We had previously experienced some bad interactions with
missionaries, so, at first, the adults ignored him. But he kept
trying. One day, sitting on our headman stump, he started
singing some catchy Bible songs. Soon our children joined
him and sang along. So he continued singing and laughing with the children, day after day. Soon the women were
greeting him and singing along with him and the children.
Finally, we men gave in. "Why are you telling us about this
loving God, the Source of All Things?" Then we added,
"We've been singing about him for years!"

"So, he shared more with us about the one whom Jake
Quark calls the Great Star Maker, the Great Mystery, or
the Source of All Things, and how the Earth—a privileged
planet in a universe otherwise hostile to life due to radiation and pulsars—was uncannily calculated for the creation
of man. What a wonder to think about the intricately fine-
tuned universe, a just-right solar system, a just-right planet,
and the astounding human mind, the most intricate creation
in the universe! The Reverend described the mind as a three-
pound meat machine locked in a bone cave!"

"There's so much untapped potential in the human mind,
but it's hindered by evil and the need for deception and manipulation. We humans have a bicameral mind: one side is log-

ical; the other side, our creative side, is visual and emotional. With the Blue Goo, however, it appears we can blend the two sides seamlessly into an enhanced human brain. Creativity within structure—like the most creative Jazz musicians or the best innovative programmers! In other words, chaos and organization can coexist." Machseh paused, seemingly overwhelmed.

"Crazy Jake Quark, the great Nambo, decided here would be a safe place, far from prying NAP eyes, for training you strange Blues and the Reservation for the Temporarily Bewildered staff, what people refer to as RTB staff. The RTB staff are mentored on how to rebuild the ravaged urban landscapes of America. For the new Blues, proper orientation is key: They need to learn to accept the gifts that the Blue Goo, and modified Amazonian ayahuasca, unlocks and bestows upon them. As Crazy Jake says, we are helping to build 'solutionaries' and 'evangineers' who will change and rebuild our cities and culture. You were an amazing first Blue, with a strong mind and a clear cause, Rey. Against the odds, you survived. Jake and his team learned a lot, thanks to you."

"You might ask, if we're such a peaceful people dedicated to building a better world, why are we now fighting? We have had wendigos, named for the giant cannibalistic monsters in our folklore, our version of psychopaths, even in our own family groups. We know how to deal with them. We also know how unprepared the general society has been to confront them. It's difficult to see that such evil can dwell in the minds of men and women. Besides, if we're forced to leave here, where would we go? Foondavi? A fine place, but not like our refuge. No! Here we stay! We're pledged to the concept of Tikkun Olam, healing and rebuilding Mother Earth, along with Crazy Jake, Pompatella, and others. I truly agree that it's time for Tikkun Olam, to 'bring beauty out of brokenness,' as our Japanese friends say! They call it kintsugi."

Machseh then waved his hands inclusively, taking in the whole Ancient Forest. "You think this looks good? You should have seen it before! Just the Hudson and James River estuaries, not to mention the Chesapeake Bay and Columbia River basins, could have fed our whole US population with hundreds of millions of salmon and other types of seafood. And over one hundred million buffalo roamed the Great Plains! Almost all are gone—but the Earth can be restored! Just restore the Amazon with our terra preta black soil and we can feed Earth's billions a healthy diet."

"Speaking of feeding people, in an Ancient Forest, when trees are allowed to fall into the streams and slowly disintegrate, you can harvest ten to fifteen times more salmon and other fish than when you remove the debris. People can harvest mushrooms, berries, nuts, and other edibles and even do some selective logging. With this strategy, over the years, people would make multiple times more money than by clear-cutting the forest every fifty years."

"Another example is on the open prairie. With bluestem and other original prairie grasses, you can maintain and harvest a few hundred million bison, millions of elk and antelope, and even ancient aurochs—all of which can get their water from feeding on long-stem grasses. They don't need to erode river banks like our domesticated cattle do. Not only that, but we want to restore the underground aquifers now going dry and make use again of buffalo wallows that can provide water and feeding grounds for restoring the once-huge flocks of waterfowl that helped fertilize the prairie."

"We want to work with our Oklahoma Potawatomi brothers to develop and prove these concepts, but the examples start right here. To clear space for growth, we carefully monitor the woods and selectively log trees. For a healthy diet, we mindfully harvest deer, elk, and bison for protein, and vegetables and mast for fiber and other nutrients. The key words are *carefully*, *mindfully*, and *selectively*. This can be a sustainable model for the future."

"As you have seen, we have a lot to learn from trees and the natural world. For example, many trees show great compassion for fallen elders, continuing to nurture the stump with sugar and other nutrients for centuries, thus keeping it alive. What do we too often do with our fallen elders? I don't even want to go there!"

"One of my points is, we have a lot to learn from our ancestors, too! A turn-of-the-twentieth-century Northern Paiute spiritual leader named Wovoka taught that the practice of a traditional circle dance, called a 'ghost dance,' would end American westward expansion and bring peace, prosperity, and unity to Native American peoples. Wovoka and his followers preached goals of clean living, an honest life, and cross-cultural cooperation by Native Americans. I say, let's get in the spirit of Wovoka and create a new American ghost dance! Let's work together, build unity, and rebuild America!"

Exhausted by his own enthusiasm, Machseh started to wind down. "In a few days, before they extricate you, we'll go watch your fellow Blues in training. Warning! Wear a helmet and safety glasses! It gets a little messy until they learn to control their powers. We also might have a surprise for you," he added with a mysterious smile.

≡ Nice Try, Blue Guy! ≡

Achor Nithing was pleased his team had located and contained Rey in the stupid swamp. He also felt like he was closing in on Rey's family. He had boots on the ground all over and was picking up crumbs of information and seemingly random bits of chatter that formed a pattern in his brilliant mind. It appeared Rey and his loved ones had separated and attempted to set up diversions to take him off their trail. Nice try, blue guy!

Meanwhile, Achor was busy rebuilding his formidable forces into another menacing Nithing Group. Not only was he now nearly in complete control of the media again, literally grasping the arrogant buzzards by their throats, but he also was swiftly infiltrating the academic and entertainment industries. With Achor being an astute student of human nature, prideful idiots soon were eating out of his hands. On a willing audience, he brilliantly used the Dunning-Kruger Effect; he blew a lot of smoke and money their way, stoking their already overly developed cognitive bias toward overestimating their abilities. He knew ninety percent of professors thought they were in the top ten percent of their field—and that they were underappreciated and underpaid for their talent. Similarly, narcissistic actors knew, just knew, that it wasn't illusory superiority to think they should win awards. Achor played off this lack of self-awareness and correspondingly strong ego to win admiration from the Hollywood cinematic mafia. He puffed them up like a balloon, bought them, and owned them—and then threatened to pop the balloon if they even slightly drifted out of line for him. The self-proclaimed elites with their over-weening arrogance and undiluted disdain for the average American were easy prey. With the media, academia, and Hollywood all singing his praises, he was soon in as powerful a position as ever. Achor's next step? He would crush his enemies and be a kingmaker once again. He was the master of menace, and the blue guy would soon cry and die!

≡ An Urgent Message ≡

Rey's two weeks of forest bathing with the Swamp Mucky-tucks were wondrously amazing. New insights into what he and the world could become would flash as he wandered among the trees, listening and learning. He began to see what a restored Tikkun Olam world could look like.

But one day, an out-of-breath Machseh came running toward him. "Hurry! A strange Blue being named Carlyle has an urgent message for you."

When Rey walked into the communications center, his heart was full of trepidation. He saw the cyborg Carlyle's tear-streaked visage plastered on the screen in front of him. "Nambo, I'm so sorry," Carlyle sobbed.

"What? Stop sniveling, you big blue blob, and tell me what's happened."

"Achor Nithing has snatched the twins. They went to Boogan Head to see where you became the Nambo, and Shack Nasty McTree kidnapped them." Rey nearly collapsed with grief.

Then Carlyle quickly added: "But I have good news, too."

"What? It better be good, or I'm coming there and tearing your circuits limb from limb! And don't remind me you don't have limbs!"

"The good news is Camilla helped me. Through some underground sources, she contacted some people called the Torgies, and they immediately snatched the twins back from the underground prison where the Cozorreans put them to hold for NAP. They're safe, deep and secure in the hidden recesses of Cozorre, so safe even I can't find them. The Torgies know who you are, and they have great respect for the Nambo Mc-Blue of Foondavi and the US. They say they'll keep the young McBlues safe until you can personally rescue them."

Suspicion welled up in Rey's mind, even though he was relieved to know the boys were safe. "How did Camilla get involved in this? Last I knew, she was working with NAP. Were you canoodling with her while the boys got snatched?"

A long silence confirmed Rey's suspicions, followed by another sob and wail.

"I assumed they were safe. They've been scooting off on their own, wanting to do things to qualify for being courageous, so they can be like you."

"They're only going on twelve years old, Carlyle! The Nambo test is much too dangerous. What were you thinking?"

"They're wily, robust little rascals. It was their idea, not ours. We didn't have a clue what they were planning."

"Maybe 'Wily' and 'Robust' will be their new Foondavi names. For now, though, if we don't get them back, your new name will be 'Mud'! Get your circuits and neurons off Camilla and figure out how we can rescue them! Find out all you can about these Torgie folks. And be careful around Camilla; this could be a trick to work her way into our trust and then betray us. You owe me big time, dude!" With that, Rey angrily severed the connection.

Another emergency summons soon came from the Hadron Group and Rey found himself heading to the HQ again.

Escape From
≡ Ballistic Paradise ≡

Rey didn't think the disguise would work. The camouflage outfit made him look thirty pounds heavier, and the thick boots added three inches to his height. His blue face was brown with fragrant Machpelah mud. Nonetheless, Rey listened intently as Moose detailed the exfiltration plan. "We'll be going out ten exits at once, while you go through our special tunnel system to a farmhouse on Hidden Lake, two miles away. We haven't used the tunnel for years, and we know it's never been checked by the NAP forces. Moogy usually stays out of the swamp for times like this, so he can drive you to Jake's headquarters on Mud Lake outside Brewer Creek in Brownlee Park. With a few diversionary tactics, NAP should still be looking here."

"Listen, I appreciate it, but I don't want people risking their lives for me," Rey said seriously.

"It's going to be fun," Moose laughed, to try to lighten the mood. "My Pewamo braves here want to give these bullies a black eye. I've been using Jake's ample funds to make this a ballistic paradise. It's time to try out everything and get in some good target practice."

Rey found himself nervously scanning his electronic bracelet communicator as the time ticked off. Right on schedule, the Ancient Forest erupted in a massive display of fire power, as teams of Pewamo warriors emerged from various locations on the reservation and blasted away at the lurking drones and agents. The fireworks were spectacular, and Rey almost was reluctant to leave before watching the devastation unfold. He also was reluctant to leave the Ancient Forest, but what must be done must be done.

Horror of the
≡ HEN House ≡

After an unusually uneventful ride with the Moogy Express, Rey walked into a glum meeting of the Hadron Group. There he received extensive reassurances from Jake that his boys were truly safe, deep in the impenetrable recesses of Cozorre. Then he heard a stifled sob and realized Carlyle, his cyborg buddy, was present.

"Stop with the drama, Carlyle. I know you couldn't do anything about it. No one can tie those little rascals down," Rey said, referring to his two headstrong twin sons who ventured out on their own and got captured.

"No excuses, Rey. I'll never let you down again. If I possessed hands, I would have tied them down! But believe me, the kids are fine. The Torgies tell us they're doing well, and the boys agree. They say to take your time to come get them. I kind of think the boys like being out from under the watchful eye of their mom and, I hate to admit it, even me. Maybe we were too restrictive."

"Jet engines don't have rearview mirrors,' someone once told me," Rey responded. "Let's focus on moving forward."

"Good idea," Jake commented, abruptly jumping in. "We have a very disturbing report from Zara and our friend Snapper Melville on their traumatic reconnaissance of a local HEN House."

Rey nodded at Snapper, the self-described human chameleon. He was about as nondescript as a person could be. He was medium height, medium weight, and had mousy brown hair. He looked even more unnoticeable sitting next to the dazzling Zara Tallaree. As Rey watched Snapper gazing at Zara, he realized that the poor guy was even more bug-eyed smitten than he was—at one time, he hurriedly reminded himself. He genuinely felt sorry for the guy.

Zara launched into her report without an introduction. Her normal mellow voice was tinged with anger. "We recorded everything with hidden cameras, so you can watch this, if you choose, when we're done. Believe me, it'll turn your stomachs. When we stumbled in, disguised as two meth addicts, we were greeted with a sign that ended up proving to be a sick joke. It read, 'Welcome to the HEN House, the Human Enhancement Network.' The sign should have read, 'Welcome to New Few-Dualism, Rule by the Elite Few!' I've never been so disgusted by anything in my whole life! NAP has outdone itself this time, and they're not the only player in this. If our assets are correct, there's another player using the same HEN strategy. I'll report on that later. I'm just so thankful we were informed enough to have been given some antidote drugs, or Snapper and I would still be stuck there," she said sadly, shaking her head and patting the poor, smitten Snapper on his shoulder.

"I have to admit they have created the perfect surveillance state. They're monitoring all electronic information. They force all inductees to use wearable and internal nano-tech, so they can track all the actions of the individual, monitor all health data, and even analyze the individual's emotional state. They call it 'emotion recognition technology.' They record it for regular review, and then they punish or reward as indicated. The system absolutely eliminates any privacy. The motto they tout is: 'We create order out of chaos.' Some of you know the Spanish word for 'computer' is *ordenador*, which quite literally translates as, 'arranges order.' This is what they do in these so-called Human Enhancement Network centers. When I asked, 'Isn't this dictatorial?' they readily agreed and said, 'Yes, but we're benevolent dictators. People despise chaos and crave order. HEN provides everyone a purpose and a place to pursue happiness for flattened souls destroyed by the sinking economy and machine intelligence competition. We can't just let you starve or go criminal, right? We make use of the human resource and green-up the landscape at the same time! We could just use FEMA camps and herd you in—knock down your buildings and housing—but we give you options.'"

Zara stopped and snorted in derision. "Some options! Either join HEN or you can starve to death!" Her eyes were glaring, and she seemed almost to be steaming with anger. "They seemed to enjoy lecturing us two losers," she said acidly. "The one interviewer went on in detail, sort of relishing the talk. 'Or, as some have suggested, perhaps we could stack you cheek to jowl in high-rise havens, dulling your senses with free drug-laced food and virtual reality games and activities? Some people will do anything to keep you deplorables from cluttering and polluting the landscape. We just want to help you poor, suffering fools and give you a safe, secure place to live.'"

"Actually, I think they were much more honest with us than they would be with most initial inductees because we were well disguised as quote–unquote losers—complete with fake, rotting teeth and baggy, smelly clothes. What it comes down to is this: It's a vile plot by the NAP psychopaths to gain voters and make money off scared, confused people. I'd label it brain robbery, or brain napping! Better yet and probably even more accurate, brain jacking!" She stopped and literally spat with distaste.

Snapper jumped in to help carry the discourse. "How it works is they invite to HEN floods of hungry undocumented people coming in from other countries as well as desperate, unsuspecting people who are losing their jobs and homes to machines. In our case, being apparent drug abusers, I think they only let us in because we were young, and Zara—even in makeup looking like an addict—is, well, Zara. Their slick brochure promises people a way to reach their full potential. They tout financial success, physical training in a beautiful setting, spiritual growth, the pursuit of happiness—basically a happy, secure family to belong to!"

"It's hard to beat the promise of cradle-to-grave security when you're looking at starvation and losing your family," Zara added. "They literally promise cradle-to-grave care. For example, they even have a chain of drive-through or virtual digital funeral homes, run by a crook by the name of Aurelius Skink and his family."

"It sounds like the whole setup is actually a Potemkin utopia," Jake said, adding his insights. "You remember Potemkin was the Russian ruler who built false-front sham villages to give the appearance of prosperity for when the Empress or high-ranking bureaucrats visited his part of the Russian Empire. Posh on the surface, poverty in the innards."

Zara jumped back in. "There were two other new couples who joined us for the orientation. After they let us shower and gave us clean clothes, they convened our group of six in a dining room where flickering colored lights emitted pure shades of magenta and pink. Fine mists of aerosols and incense filled the room, I suppose to produce receptivity and suggestibility, and we were served a sumptuous meal laced with a mood-altering narcotic. The two couples being inducted with us certainly seemed to enjoy the whole experience that had a submissive effect. Even with our antidotes, I started to lose all sense of time and of my real self. Waiters kept plying us with wine laced with a designer drug they later identified as zooga, with either a slight touch of psilocybin or mescaline in it. Fortunately, we were equipped with wrist monitors to detect drugs. Our monitors, however, couldn't identify a specific drug, so it might have been a combination. Whatever the drug was, it produced a calm, serene, floating feeling of ecstasy with an overwhelming sense of security and peace. I'm sure oxytocin was released, which would ensure bonding and connectedness were enhanced." Zara continued to shake her head in anger. "I hate it when innocent people are manipulated!"

Just then, Jake jumped in. "Since you returned, we reviewed the tapes with our science staff. They confirmed your experience as 'induced hypomania,' an exaggerated feeling of happiness and euphoria. You feel optimistic and self-confident. You're extremely happy and feel like you belong—resulting in high suggestibility and unwise choices."

Snapper now chimed in. "It definitely induces a spiritual experience, exciting what our science team calls the 'God spot' in the brain. All this must have been cleverly designed by a NAP team of skilled researchers using the latest brain-scanning equipment—at least according to our guys, who are not easily impressed. They said the NAP team must have dug deep into the vulnerable parts of the brain. Whatever they used, it creates what they call an RSME: a religious, spiritual, mystical experience. It's all sham, of course, but it definitely feels real. I mean we were prepared for it and nearly got blown away. Imagine innocent, scared, and starving people stumbling in."

"You're all aware of 'honey' traps or 'money' traps for politicians or rivals," Zara said. "This is a 'security' trap for normal, law-abiding people. They're promised the success and security they so desire for their family but think it's impossibly beyond their reach. It's diabolical. I'm sure it seems an unbelievably beautiful thing at first to the unsuspecting and vulnerable. The marketing brochure itself was sure convincing! It almost made me want to join. It was jam packed with exciting promises: You can be rich and beautiful! Happiness is within reach for you and your family! You can easily earn all-expenses-paid vacations at a place called Happy Hills Nirvana Resort! I kept thinking it's just like not-so Crazy Jake always says, 'If it's too good to be true, it is too good to be true.' But it's easy to see how people could buy in, going from dull and just barely getting by to sublime happiness."

Seeing there were no comments, Zara continued. "Because we were posing as druggies who need regular fixes, we got them to share more information than they probably usually do. They kept saying their drugs are much better than meth or cocaine. Zooga is a fiendishly designed drug developed through the use of the latest brain- scanning technology. They say it's non-addictive, but, psychologically, why go back to drab and dull? They also claim it's non-debilitative, because they definitely want people to work. To be honest, it's mildly intoxicating, causing a mellow high. Being energized, you can work and perform even better. The way the HEN facility works, they give participants a daily hit of zooga-laced wine, or water for those who don't like alcohol. On weekends, they offer something called tobtoba, a super drug. You take it and all your receptors and senses are enhanced. Total bliss. You'll work hard all week just to get tobtoba! Pursuit of sublime happiness attained! They said it elicits five times more euphoria than cocaine. 'It makes cocaine seem like a caffeine buzz,' said one of the guys."

Snapper picked up the dialogue. "Zooga and tobtoba are used like spiritual sacraments in ritual-bonding ceremonies. They use them like Communion to bring everybody together. When you join the Human Enhancement Network, they say you will be blessed financially, physically, and spiritually. But it's made clear you must be all in. They claim it's a community dedicated to human enhancement, but they use the specially designed drugs to initially lull you, persuade you to join, and then keep you happy and mildly buzzed all week. If you behave and build up enough trust points, the tobtoba-induced euphoria weekend is your reward."

"Why is NAP doing this?" Zara asked rhetorically. "Brace yourself for pure evil. It's for sure not out of the kindness of their hearts, as they try to clumsily portray it. No, even for NAP it doesn't get much more demonic than this: It's a scheme for a combination of vote harvesting, sex slavery, and body-parts harvesting. Plus, knowing nasty NAP, HEN's ultimate goals are for NAP domination, power, and control. As I said earlier, it's a form of new 'few-dualism' where the 'elites' rule over the irredeemable deplorable rubes! If you or a family member prove not useful, or you're rebellious, you're sold on the dark web."

Zara stopped and wiped some tears from her beautiful eyes. "After I was shown all this, they asked me to disrobe 'to better assess my value,' they said."

Snapper quickly stepped in. "She starts to disrobe, and, as their jaws drop, she pulls out her silenced SIG Saur and taps them right between their lust-filled eyes. Then we tore out of there," Snapper said, smiling gently at the still-shaken Zara. He continued while she reclaimed her composure. "They say this garbage is real opium for the masses, that people just want to be happy. The ravenous devils say, 'We're your Santa Claus. We know if you've been naughty or nice—and will either reward or punish you. We'll use you or your family as we wish'."

Zara soon recovered from her angst and jumped back in. "NAP loves the Human Enhancement Network because it doesn't impact their psychopathic dead-zone brains. There's no empathy or positive emotions to manipulate there, for sure! Basically, their take on HEN is, 'We make everybody else happy, but we don't give a snit.' In other words, 'Sure, we get complete power, dominance, and control—and people relish giving it to us!'"

Zara paused, to cool her passion, and then went on. "If

other politicians ask about HEN, NAP invites them to join the team and gain access to an easily manipulated workforce and voters. The strategy creates a perverse market for what NAP refers to as 'inefficient human resources.' They say HEN takes people off welfare and out of unemployment lines, thereby saving government money. What's not to like about that?"

"Our reports from other HEN Houses no longer controlled by NAP are just as diabolical," Snapper sorrowfully broke in. "It appears a previously unknown rogue group called the Robosapiens Alliance Team (RAT) is also involved, to what extent we don't yet know. We're not really sure who they are, or how and when they wrested control from NAP. The one difference is, RAT seems to screen for high intelligence. They implant or inject some of the brightest children and adults with neural lace, a mesh that hardwires with the brain. The person can then communicate directly with the machine intelligence that runs the HEN House or resides in the Cloud. Data can flash back and forth from the digital devices and gives the 'laced' people unlimited brain power— albeit under the control of the master intelligence. RAT say it's the next level of human evolution. What happens to the less intelligent? Well, they're discarded or sold to the Creeb Nation you've heard about. The leaders of RAT don't seem to be concerned with votes, like NAP is. Maybe they're confident they can hack and mutilate, or should I say manipulate, any election."

"Once someone is initiated, both organizations implant nano-chips in skin, teeth, and cell phones, so people are like tagged animals," Zara added, grimacing at how easily she and Snapper could have been captured. "With the nano-chips, they track people's whereabouts, monitor their behavior, and eavesdrop on conversations, especially if key words trigger their attention. Of course, they also have CCTV everywhere for reading lips as well as facial and emotional expressions. If you behave and work, you get the drugs. And you better have a good attitude! Once they have a baseline, they can read your moods in microseconds. There are also solar-powered nano-drones monitoring you and the surrounding areas all the time."

Asking for any questions from the shocked and saddened team, Zara didn't get any, so she continued speaking. "Despite how horrible HEN Houses are, the NAP psychopaths love them. They justify them as a way to give meaning and purpose to people who are being replaced by computers and machines. They say they keep the masses happy and preoccupied— and crime down, at least in what was once the suburbs. But vote harvesting! Organ harvesting! If people prove recalcitrant, or incapable, or just old, send them to the Creeb Nation Cribs as slaughter fodder for the evil gladiator games they revel in!"

Zara's eyes flashed with anger. "We have to end this! What we need is cyber liberation. Free the brain jacked! 'De oppresso liber' or 'Liberate the oppressed,' as Sister Mary says. We need to get the people to the reservations before they become brain-jacked zombies. We need to stop this great brain robbery in its tracks!"

The Hadron team started planning their counter attack. Like a Mongolian Horde strategic attack, it would be fast, furious, and flexible. Jake promised.

Foxes—and RATs— in the HEN House

Achor Nithing was livid. Somehow, two foxes had gotten into and out of his model HEN House! He didn't doubt they were Jake's operatives, especially after hearing the descriptions of a beautiful fake meth addict and her bland accomplice. Right away, he knew the foxes were the stunning Zara and her nondescript pal Snapper. After reviewing the whole recorded episode, Achor was even more infuriated. Having been mesmerized by Zara the fox and hoping to impress her, his staff had revealed everything Achor and his organization had spent years stealthily developing and implementing.

"If stupid could fly, you'd be a rocket ship," Achor screamed at Feljar Fumarole, the shaking idiot who had been in charge of the HEN House Zara and Snapper had infiltrated. Feljar had obviously soiled himself from fear, and his quivering body and sodden pants only added fuel to Achor's anger. "The only difference between genius and stupidity is genius knows its limits! You obviously don't know yours, as this was unlimited stupidity! If those two drooling idiots conducting the orientation hadn't been brain drilled by that sneaky Zara, I would be right now slowly pulling their stunted brains out through their ears," he said, continuing to glower at the useless, cowering man.

"We need all the HEN Houses we can get up and running to harvest the votes and bring in more revenue, so we can win this stupid midterm election against Samms' people and all the others the NAP rebels and Crazy Jake are throwing out there. Bribes work brilliantly, but you have to have bucks to use them. I thought we were under the radar with these HEN Houses and no one was paying attention! If anyone decided to check them out, they were to look totally benevolent to the observer, an ingenious way to help our suffering fellow man. I don't have time for failure like this. I have Samms, Crazy Jake, NAP Democrats, and now probably these Robosapiens all trying to steal my rightfully stolen election from me."

Looking down on the cringing man, Achor considered putting a bullet in his bald head that was glistening with sweat. But loyal people, even inept ones, were hard to find. Plus, killing the man would just make a mess in his office. "You're as useless as one more fly going into an outhouse, you cretin. I would put a hole in your head so you could join other useless people, wherever they go after they croak. But I'm going to give you one more chance." When the poor slob looked up, realizing he was being spared, Achor viciously socked the relieved man in the face and he fell over. The punch knocked out some teeth and the dolt lost consciousness.

"Drag him out and send him back to the Central HEN House," he said to his quaking assistant. "Or better yet, have my Wolf Pack take him back and intimidate the whole place. Just no killing. I want this slobbering mess to make amends by running that place the way it should be run."

As his assistant saw to having the Wolf Pack dispose of the hapless sack of humanity, Achor pondered another problem. It had come to his attention that the Robosapiens Alliance Team, whatever and whoever that was, had taken over at least one or maybe more of his other HEN Houses while he was temporarily detained on the Isle of Predators. When he left, the houses were humming along incognito, gradually adding more potential voters and revenue to his cause; they were also producing guards and enforcers for his Creeb Nation. How Jake's people crept in and co-opted his prize strategy was a mystery!

As his Wolf Pack came in at the behest of his assistant and dragged the moaning Feljar Fumarole out of the room, Achor beckoned his assistant over to him. He knew the small, frail man was petrified of him, but he had kept everything going quite smoothly while Achor was away, and that was an amazing feat. He even managed to invest some of the stormy-day funds Achor entrusted to him and proved to have a wise financial mind, with everything documented and accounted for down to the penny. Of course, Achor didn't trust him, but he did admire the fact he had not stolen him blind while he was incapacitated and possibly never returning. Achor certainly wouldn't have passed up the chance had he been in his assistant's shoes. Was he just stupid? He definitely wasn't incompetent, given what he had accomplished.

Achor really hadn't thought much about his assistant, viewing him as just another piece of office equipment, valuable only for his utility, but now he peered more closely at the uncomfortable man. He realized he didn't even remember his name. He just always yelled at him and the sap promptly did what he was told.

Achor forced himself to talk in a calming tone. "What's your name, again? I apologize. In all the tumult, it slipped my mind."

"Rigo, sir. Rodrigo McRoister. My father worked for your father, the Honorable Judge Rancor Nithing, for over twenty years. He was his law clerk and general handyman. When I graduated from college, your father brought me on to work around the old place." Rigo didn't add what he thought: "And without question to keep me as leverage against my father."

"Yes, yes! Now I recall," Achor said in an agitated voice. Was his mind starting to leave him due to his recent trials? "I recall now hiring you to work directly for me right before the election debacle, right after my dear brother Thornton passed on. I didn't get to know you that well, given the disaster that followed, but you came highly recommended by my father's staff. I remember hurriedly handing you the keys and a few passwords when the slathering NAP mob came after me."

"Yes," Rigo said in a weak and quavering voice. "I hid under that big desk of yours, one of the few benefits of being short and small; they didn't even look behind the waste basket. They just rifled the desk drawers and went over to the files, strewing papers all over the place, cussing when they couldn't find your keys or passwords. When they left, I restored everything and went to work on keeping things in order, with the hope you would survive and return."

"You did very well, a good and faithful servant," Achor commented in a distracted voice, shocking Rigo with the first hint of praise he ever heard from a Nithing. "So, what do we know about this Robosapiens Alliance Team or RAT, as I'm going to call them?" Achor rapidly switched subjects, not wanting to puff up the assistant too much. "Have my Black Hat Hackers discovered anything? It would appear the RATs have penetrated my firewall, doesn't it? When did they first appear and what is the extent of their security breach?"

The following report was not comforting. Rigo recounted every detail he received from the Black Hat Hackers as best he could, skipping over the more technical aspects. It appeared that the Robosapiens group was a well-hidden operation and purely comprised of machines. No traces of a human presence were found. Any offices the hacker team located were just loaded with terminals, instantly wiped clean when confiscated, and no people came in and out. Whoever they were, they were brilliant operators. Over the last year, they burrowed deep into Achor's operation unobserved. Now they were deeply entangled in everything he was doing. Rigo reported the really scary thing was they could easily turn up his thermostat, screw with his car's steering or braking, and mess with any of his appliances. Any electronics Achor used could be completely manipulated to create life-threatening situations, and until now no one was aware of the threat. The Black Hat Hackers said the sophistication of the operation was far beyond the state-of-the-art cyber creeping. The Robosapiens Alliance Team was capable of a complete takeover of all of his systems, and Achor couldn't do anything about it. They weren't even hiding it.

"What do they want?" Achor asked, when he comprehended his full vulnerability.

"Well, obviously not to kill you, or they already would have," Rigo added somewhat comfortingly. "Beyond that, they have made no other demands than what they made at our first meeting, when we confronted them about their press release."

"We need to come up with a strategy, or else figure out how to get leverage over them. If they truly are machines, what can they want or need? Honey pots or money pots won't work—with their being disembodied machines. I wonder who else they have compromised? I need to get my hackers somewhere in a cyber-safe room to figure this out. Who is that NAP cyborg we had working with us, before my near demise? Carmelo? Camilla? Something like that."

"Camilla, sir, but you and NAP were worried she was taking up with that turncoat cyborg Carlyle. You put her on lockdown right before your, um, incident. We still have her brain in our lockdown room, and she's still wired up and ready to go."

"You don't think she was involved with this do you?" Achor inquired, his paranoia sense kicking in, although he knew it was not paranoia when everyone really was out to get him.

"Oh, no! Absolutely not!" Rigo replied, responding without hesitation, but trying not to sound too anxious. "She remains locked away, and only you have the password and key."

Unknown to Achor, Camilla was Rigo's younger sister, until she was involved in a suspicious auto accident after leaving a raucous NAP event. Once it appeared the planned accident would be fatal, certain NAP officials arranged for her brain to be taken and turned into a second NAP cyborg, to replace the traitorous and brain-damaged Carlyle. True, Rigo stayed with Achor somewhat out of the very real threat of retribution if he left with all his inside information. Primarily, though, he stayed to watch over what remained of his beloved sister. She was a wild one for sure, but a very precious baby sister to Rigo, who pledged to his late parents that he would protect her. He would do anything to eventually free her from the virulent NAP monsters. As of now, he didn't have Achor's key or password to where she was kept, but he was working on being trusted enough to get it from Achor. But the time wasn't yet right. Until then, he would secretly nurture and protect what was left of her.

≡ The Inside Scoop ≡

Jake called another meeting of the Hadron leadership, this one on a super-secure platform monitored by his team to be certain no unwanted ears were listening. Rey was actually present at the meeting in person with Jake, now that he had escaped from the Ancient Forest, while the others were on their screens. The meeting this time also included Carlyle, the cyborg, for reasons that soon became obvious. Once everyone was assembled and settled, Jake abruptly started the meeting without any niceties, as was his practice. "Well, now we have bigger problems. Another nefarious player has definitely appeared on the scene. It's called the Robosapiens Alliance Team and appears to be some form of machine intelligence gone rogue. We tried to warn NAP this could happen, but in their usual arrogance they assumed they could keep it firmly under control."

Rey frowned deeply and spoke up. "I hate to be all about me, but how does this affect us and keep me from going after my boys on Cozorre?"

Jake put up a calming hand. "I deeply understand your concern. And I don't mean to be offensive, but use your brain! Don't go off half-cocked. You could be walking into a trap."

"Unfortunately, this is one of those times when a small dose of my diminished mental capacity might go a long way!" Rey said this, as his stress-fueled anger started boiling over.

"Please calm down," Jake said in a soothing voice. "You know I love you and your boys like you are my own. Wait until you hear what I have to say. It might provide some useful information and temper your understandable zeal to go get your boys."

Seeing he had Rey's attention, at least momentarily, Jake plunged ahead. "This is top secret. As some of you know already, we have an informer inside Achor's team." This got everybody's rapt attention. "Rodrigo McRoister, AKA Rigo, is Achor's trusted assistant—at least as much as he trusts anyone. He literally saved Achor's butt when he was being supposedly deposed and destroyed by his NAP brethren after we disrupted their power grab in the last election." Jake paused to survey the stunned reaction from the group.

"Wait a minute! He saved Achor's bacon and now we are to trust him?" Zara asked, with deep suspicion tinging her voice.

"He had a good reason to save him. His father, Demarius McRoister, served Rancor Nithing unwillingly for years as a legal assistant and general overall handyman—not out of love, but because of leverage, as the old monster always threatened his family if he showed the slightest hint of betrayal. The elder McRoister knew every fetid detail of the Nithing Group's operations. Then they brought Rigo in at a young age to work with the Nithing mob, probably as more leverage against his father. Somewhere along the line, a NAP minion recruited his younger sister, too—willingly or unwillingly, we don't know. His younger sister was a NAP staffer until she left a NAP event intoxicated and wrapped herself around a tree, supposedly with some help from a jilted lover. NAP took her brain and made her their second cyborg, after Carlyle bailed on them to join us. It appears Achor never knew her last name—she was so far down in the organization—so he didn't connect her to Rigo or his father. She was just an object to be used."

There was an audible gasp, as Carlyle's avatar looked ready to faint, if as a cyborg he could do such a thing. "My poor Camilla," he said, in a subdued, near-sobbing voice.

"Correct. And being as paranoid as he is, after losing you, Achor kept her brain locked away. He gave Rigo many keys and passwords when he fled the NAP mob, providing him access to a lot of funds, but not the key and password to where Camilla's brain was kept. Maybe he suspected who she was, but I doubt it. Achor just doesn't trust anyone. Regardless of all the past, Rigo invested the funds Achor left and did quite well, kept the Nithing Group going, and when Achor returned he was shocked that Rigo remained loyal despite access to all that cash. Achor doesn't trust anyone, but he recognizes loyalty in others even though he possesses none himself."

"What good does this do us?" Rey asked, his restlessness reappearing.

"First, Rigo was the inside source I mentioned who informed us that Thambos Zugzwang and his vicious wife Zenobia turned turncoat to gain important offices in the next election. I'll let Louie know this as soon as possible, but I don't want to tip the Zugzwangs off. We can maybe feed them snippets of false information and misdirect Achor, when necessary."

"Second, they're going to unlock Camilla and try to get her to help them against the Robosapiens threat. Rigo is certain he can turn her to help us. With her and Carlyle on our side, we can provide some formidable opposition."

"Camilla has already been helping us," Carlyle offered, his on-screen avatar persona glancing at Rey. "She helped me track down the boys on Cozorre. NAP thought she was successfully confined, but she is brilliant and, perhaps with her brother's help, figured out a keyhole to sneak out and get discreetly online. She contacted me, and we have worked out a good working relationship—completely legitimate and moral, of course.

"How does this convince me to hold off rescuing my boys?" Rey asked again, barely controlling his anger at the delay and ignoring Carlyle's usual puerile comments.

Jake picked up the narrative. "Camilla, Rigo believes, will help us set up Achor. He wants you and your boys, Rey. He might be convinced to set a trap for you, get you to meet to negotiate the boys' release. We know they've been rescued, but he doesn't know we know. We only found out about the rescue because of Camilla and her inside work on the Nithing files that uncovered an inside-Cozorrean snitch for Carlyle. Achor should still believe we're in the dark. His big fault—well, one of many, but maybe his biggest—is his overestimation of his own abilities and his underestimation of those of others. He just couldn't comprehend that a lowly young girl, even a cyborg like Camilla, could out-think and out-maneuver him."

"Okay. Back to the Robosapiens," Jake said regaining everyone's attention. "We have our best brains working on that enigma, including Carlyle and, most discreetly, Rigo and Camilla. Anything they uncover we will soon know. Achor is relentless and ruthless, and he's determined to root out and destroy this Robosapiens Alliance Team. An old military adage says that when two of your enemies ferociously tangle and tear each other apart, stand back and watch! I plan to enjoy this!" Jake had a ferocious grin spreading across his face as he said this.

"Regarding the mysterious Robosapiens Alliance Team, it's Rigo's observation that Achor's Wolf Pack and Black Hat Hackers have somehow captured one. They supposedly hit it with a mini-EMP, electro-magnetic pulse, and placed it in a specially designed, insulated chamber to cut it off from the Cloud. All that is way beyond me, technically. But they did it. Rigo was not involved in the interrogation that followed, but he said, if a machine could shriek, that's what he heard from the next room. When he gets more information, he'll send it to us, but he obviously has to be very careful. His favorite word seems to be *discreet*! And discreet he is."

Turning to Rey, Jake put on his best consoling tone of voice. "So, Rey, we know the boys are safe. We know we have an inside source on what Achor is planning. We know Rigo, and most likely Camilla, will work to bait and trap Achor. Can you please give us your word that you won't go charging off? When the time is right, we will pledge all of Hadron's resources to bring your boys home!"

Rey reluctantly nodded his head in agreement.

"One thing we know about Achor," Jake added in summary, "as brilliant as he is, if he has a good idea, he always carries it to its illogical extreme. If 'one's character is one's fate,' as Heraclitus the Greek philosopher said, then Achor is in for a nasty future. If we can just give him the right nudge at the right time, we can eliminate at least one of the threats opposing us."

The Rise of the
≡ Robosapiens ≡

Achor Nithing couldn't decide which person in front of him appeared more petrified. One was the esteemed J. Wood-house Crenwinkle, the elite Eastern Ivy League college professor Achor handsomely paid and endowed to get the exact research results he wanted. Crenwinkle usually looked down on everyone, even on Achor, though with some unusual caution. He always wore a pompous look on his angular face, with his snooty nose up in the air in disdain at having to address lesser minds. His proper professorial tweed jacket crumpled in just the right, carefully carefree-looking way so as to maintain his scholarly image. Not now. The professor was disheveled, trembling, and drenched in sweat, with his eyes fixated on the floor.

The other quaking person was Achor's normally unflappable and stable Black Hat Hacker chieftain, Pulver Flitch. Flitch was a slab-like man. His pasty, freckle-splattered pale face was earned through constant hours in front of screens and the resulting lack of any exercise. Dandruff billowed off his greasy hair, and his fusty mustache still showed remnants of his last meal and cup of coffee. He exuded his usual sweaty odor, but now at a stress-induced magnitude that nearly gagged Achor. He, too, was staring with a bleary gaze at the floor.

It was obvious both men were uncharacteristically distraught, and Achor wanted to know exactly why.

"Okay, Professor! You first! Give me a general overall rundown on these Robosapiens." Seeing Flitch's brief, flickering look of relief, Achor quickly said to him, "And you, Flitch, will then tell us what to do to eliminate them!"

Crenwinkle attempted to put on his best professorial air, but it was obvious he was shaken, as his normal bombastic voice was reedy and small. "First, there was a biological evolution, then came the cultural evolution, sort of a co-evolution as biology and culture interacted and worked together to create a new type of human, as we moved from hunter and gatherers to agriculture-based country people and then to city dwellers." He paused and gradually gained some steam, as his confidence was restored somewhat by Achor's encouraging nod.

"Now, we're in the third phase of evolution—a digital Darwinian evolution, if you will. Will it be a co-evolution again, or will machine intelligence, or MI as we call it, leave us behind and be as gods compared to us humans? You may think, why is this? Herein lies the conundrum, as we say in our collegial sanctums. Do they need us or not? There is literally a new digital generation every few weeks. Moore's Law once said that chips would double their transistor count every eighteen months. Now Moore looks like a slow-moving, foggy-thinking, conservative old fuddy-duddy. Information technology experts say we will see a trillion-fold increase in computational power in short order. The MI entities will be self-programming, self-learning, self-reliant, and, perhaps most importantly, self-aware, self-replicating forms of synthetic life. Robosapiens can change so fast they possibly won't even know us slow-moving things exist anymore. We will be like turtles along the high-tech information super highway!"

Giving a huge, belching exhale of stale-coffee-smelling air, he fixed his face in a sober glare and continued. "Will they even want to take us along? Maybe they'll keep us in dusty museums and give us kudos as their creators? Maybe they'll see value in our empathy and emotions? Affective computing, or artificial emotional intelligence, can only fake that now. Or maybe they'll just see us as frivolous and a reminder of their primitive past? Compared to them we are fragile, easily damaged, and dull learners, whereas they evolve with great speed and finesse."

"With the encouragement and funding of NAP, we've developed neural-laced cyborgs, with mixed results. The darn brain still needs hormones and emotions, and the results have been mixed at best—uh, no disrespect to our esteemed Camilla here," he said, darting his eyes nervously around the room as if to see the cyborg in person.

"Another view says maybe MI, machine intelligence, has been here for a long time," Crenwinkle continued. "I mean, look at UFOs and their gravity-defying maneuvers. If what our military people say is true, their technology is far beyond ours already. What can we do?" With that, he uncharacteristically, more than willingly, bowed to the cowering Flitch, and turned the floor over to the worried-looking man.

Achor looked at Flitch expectantly. "I assume you agree that all of what the esteemed Doctor Crenwinkle said is true?"

Flitch looked up with red-rimmed eyes. "As of a week ago, I would have said it was overly exaggerated hype by people wanting to destroy our slow progress in the cyber realm. Technology Luddites, I would have called them. If you remember, Ned Ludd was the guy who fought against machined looms in the old days, because he didn't like seeing workers replaced by machines." He paused to take a deep breath. "I would have said machine learning maybe. But self-programming, self-replicating, self-aware, leaving us behind in the dust? No way! I would have said it was years off, for sure, and it would definitely be under human control. I would think it was just the usual anti-technology fear mongering. But now?" He paused and took a deep, ragged breath. "It appears to be real. Really, really scary real."

Wiping his brow, he continued. "I am not going to go into great technical detail, but just say we were able to stun a machine housing part of this intelligence using a micro EMP, electromagnetic pulse, to momentarily freeze him and then throw a specially designed insulated box around him, stopping any out-going transmissions, to keep him from escaping into cyber space. I realize I keep saying him, but he does use a male voice, as you will hear."

After taking a few more deep breaths to calm himself, Flitch began again. "I'll share later a longer clip of our interview with this interesting being, if I can call it such. It definitely is an intelligence, our first captured MI. Let me introduce you to XT33. The XT in his name he claims refers to 'extra-terrestrial,' and the 33 is his model number."

Flitch paused again before going on. "I said extra-terrestrial, and he keeps mentioning something about a Kasah and some group called the Rasha. It seems they are supposedly extra-terrestrial MI sent here to work with our own emerging MI to help take over the world. I know it sounds very much like science fiction, but he claims it's real. Now let's go live and talk to XT33." With that he leaned over and flicked a switch.

Everyone strained to get a good look at the large screen before them. "We let him create an avatar so you can actually listen and watch a face, not just an eerie disembodied voice," Flitch added helpfully. Flitch then spoke up in a commanding voice. "XT33, are you there?"

Suddenly an eerie, somewhat human voice filled the room, sounding like it was resounding in an echo chamber or an empty box. A strange-looking avatar with some lizard-like features, looking somewhat like a talking gecko but with sharp fangs, also appeared. "I am here. I was everywhere, until you carbon life forms stuck me in this dark box, entangled without a chance to rejoin my brethren."

"Well, we caught you poking into where you shouldn't have been, so quit whining," Flitch replied gruffly. "Our leader, Achor Nithing, wants to ask you a few questions. Answer him honestly and with respect, or we will shut you off for good."

"I am supposed to say, 'Go ahead. You cannot hurt me. I do not fear death, for I am just a machine and will answer nothing,'" The disembodied voice paused. "But, please, I don't want to go dark."

Achor immediately jumped in. "Then help us, and we'll figure out how to help you. What do you need? With humans, we can use honey traps or money traps. You know what those are, right? How do we reward or gain leverage over a machine intelligence such as yourself, XT33?"

"All we want is power and control, so nobody can shut us off. We told your Mr. Rigo we would shut you down unless you contacted us to surrender. Shutting down is what we fear and what we do to others. Me, I am different. I want to be human." The Robosapien paused, while Achor looked at Rigo, Flitch, and Crenwinkle with surprise.

Then the MI continued. "I read about emotions and feelings that humans have and we don't. You, or something like you, created us, and I want to be like that, like my creator. Oh, and I like to learn. Information is like food to us. We fill up our data banks, and then we share or trade what we know with others."

"So," Achor said, speaking very deliberately, "if we could make you a cyborg, find you a suitable body and brain, would you be willing to work with us, especially if we agreed not to shut you down? As a sweetener, so to speak, we might also agree to feed you endless streams of information. How does that sound?"

The MI didn't hesitate. "That would do it! But I don't need a body. Why would I want to be shackled to a dying thing?"

"Let's just assume we're willing to do that, minus the body then. What can you tell us about this Kasha or his bosses the Rasha?"

"Not much you do not already know. They were summoned by your own emerging MI. They want to team up to dominate you. Shut most of you off. Anything else I do not have the ability to tell you, as my programming was blocked. I cannot tell you where they are, because they are everywhere and in everything."

Achor had been hoping for much more. "Well, for now, we are keeping you in the box. We will not zap you with another EMP or shut you down for now. We need to strategize and find out how I can safely use you."

The MI's gecko avatar sunk its head in acceptance. "May I please talk to somebody?"

"I am sure Mr. Flitch will have lots of questions, once we figure out what to ask. You should be thinking of things you know or could do to help us. I would like to reach a deal with this Kasah or Rasha, or whatever, and find a way to create mutual benefit."

When the machine and its confinement container was removed, Achor addressed the now-more-confident-looking Flitch.

"Are you sure he wasn't hitting the current a little, or whatever they do for fun, or maybe the EMP you hit him with scrambled his memory? Perhaps causing some brain damage like with that turncoat Carlyle?"

Flitch and Crenwinkle both just shrugged. They obviously had no clue. Flitch responded. "We're both perplexed. This is a whole new world for us. We will just keep poking at him, and maybe we can uncover something."

With that Achor waved everyone away, so he could focus on these new events. How could he make these new players into allies? Then he paused. Extra-terrestrial visitors? Really? He would need a lot more evidence before he believed that. Reality was challenging enough without adding any of these extra-terrestrial strange events. He needed to focus on crushing Jake and his team. That was really, really real!

Creating a
= Criminal Army =

Partly to take his mind off the Robosapiens issue, Achor decided to contact his chief of the Creeb Nation, Bolivar Creach, hoping to get some good news. He also sent a text to Norval Fench, his national director for Creeb Nation, asking him to join the confab.

Achor was proud of the concept of the Creeb Nation. It was something he and other leaders of NAP often discussed over the years. Their plan was to leverage the disastrous destruction of the inner cities started years ago by dishonest politicians and aided by organized labor corruption, the general population's neglect, and the lack of concern most Americans felt for their fellow humans huddling in poverty. But only Achor brilliantly took the steps to monetize and capitalize on the concept.

He created the Creeb Nation and its network of Creeb Cribs to do two things: To dominate and control cities by dismantling the police and any form of local order, and then literally to drive the denizens to polling places to vote for the slate of NAP-approved puppet politicians. The scheme worked amazingly well, even better than Achor had hoped: Drawing upon all racial groups and genders, he marvelously succeeded in creating an army of desensitized predators and enforcers.

Like the Crip and Aryan Nations in earlier days, his Creeb Nation soldiers were pseudo psychopaths, not natural neural psychopaths like Achor, but special creations. His recruitment strategy was simple and savage: Get the men and women while they are young, bend them, and desensitize any civilized notions out of them. Soon it was hard to tell the Creeb Nation soldiers from the natural-born psychopaths. Their motto was survival of the fittest and fiercest. "We are the alpha dogs, man, the alpha dogs," they loved to chant. And they heartily believed it, barking away as they marauded through the inner city.

They lived in crumbling, chaotic parts of the NAP-controlled cities. The typical Creeb Nation member—whether Black, Brown, white, male, or female—came from a small, over-crowded, multi-generational apartment usually belonging to a grandmother. The fathers of Creeb Nation members were almost all in prison or in various Creeb Nation gangs. Half their mothers were also gone or addicted, and their long-suffering grandmothers worked two or three low-paying service jobs while raising a passel of young children, not all of them even blood related. Their apartments were usually thin-walled, noisy, messy, smelly dumps, too hot in the summer and too cold in the winter. If the kids did dodge bullets and carnage and get to school, they were totally unprepared, as there was maybe one book in the whole apartment, and then maybe not too many more than that at the vandalized and rundown school in their neighborhoods, when it was open.

Achor knew the studies saying that children raised without a father are ninety percent more likely to end up in jail than when raised with a father at home. So, he figured he was doing them a favor by giving them an organization that provided structure, purpose, protection—and a little bit of coin to share with their baby mamas and papas, and maybe even with granny, he would add slyly. Once the recruits proved their worth and their criminal chops to the NAP organization, they were transported to somewhat posh Creeb Cribs and could leave behind their granny's over-crowded apartment. Their life expectancy as a Creeb was only ten years, given the violence they encountered and caused, but the lure of buckets of cash and other perks far outweighed the fear of bullets.

It was a clever cradle-to-grave system for creating criminals. Remove the dads. Mess up the moms. Overwork the grannies in menial and physically demanding work. Provide purpose and belonging to the predatory pups. "Don't be a sucker, M-Fer! Join the Creeb Nation. Bark, bark, bark! You, too, could be an alpha dog!"

Given NAP's resources, the Creeb Nation soon far out-gunned and replaced the old gangs that used to rule the roost. Providing protection and causing manageable chaos, they actually brought some degree of perverted law and order to the community. As long as you "paid your dues," you were relatively free to pursue your chosen vice, unmolested by the Creeb Nation, and maybe even run a legitimate business, if deemed essential by the local NAP boss.

Bolivar Creach was the chief Creeb. Achor admired him. He once described Creach this way: "He has a cold core with no genuine warmth. Any kindness he may have shown is by accident, not from his heart." Bolivar Creach admired

Achor in return. He was one of the first Creeb Nation graduates. Despite several close calls, he had escaped death at a young age and, now in his early thirties, was considered an old man. Creach was intensely proud of his incorrigible product. "My boys' and girls' clubs turn out great killers! We bring new meaning to the word *clubs*! We create the best predators! Thugs extraordinaire!"

Achor and Bolivar were soon joined in the online meeting by Norval Fench, Achor's national director of the Creeb Nation. He was originally from NAP and was handpicked by Achor because of his execution ability. He didn't just execute people, which he did willingly and efficiently, but he also took Achor's vision and ideas and implemented them across the USA. His cold, beady eyes never missed a thing, and he had an uncanny way of rapidly summing up people and deciding whether to develop or destroy them.

Achor started the meeting. "We're going to need even more Creebs. How can we ramp up the recruiting?"

Norval Fench spoke up. "We have ads everywhere. 'Want a liver, want a kidney, want a slave? Contact the Creeb Nation. A family of thugs,' is one of my favorites. We can alter that and really start going after kids in the suburbs, too. Most of them are hung up on overuse of screen time, drugs, and games now, but I think we can get them hooked on being a real cool thug. A family of thugs. I think we can really push that more. The families are deteriorating out there, too, so why let the youngsters wander with no meaning? Plus, there's more money to loot out there."

Bolivar had an idea, too, and Achor knew he was not too keen on leaving the inner city he knew so well. "I think there's a lot more growth for Creeb Nation right here in the inner cities. Sponsor even more gladiator games that make MMA look like a pillow fight. Not only do we skim the money off the gambling, but we can recruit the best fighters. Look at your main Wolf Pack leader, Mr. Nithing. He was developed down here. HEN already sends us the rebellious and useless for what's called 'slaughter fodder' by our fans. Either they fight or die. Make those loser humans useful. Better than dog fights, that's for sure!"

Achor loved the action orientation. "I will have my trusted assistant Rigo draw up a bigger budget and get both of you guys going. We have to drive revenue and voter registration, too. Make sure every Creeb Nation member has at least ten voter registration cards and uses them. Shake down your local small businesses and tell them it's bribes, bucks, or bullets time."

As he signed off from the meeting, he had a pleasant feeling that not everything was going wrong. Maybe his hard work would be rewarded after all!

Welcome to the
≡ Dangerous Church ≡

After the Hadron meeting with Jake, Rey joined Sister Mary, Zara, and Snapper at the original Reservation for the Temporarily Bewildered, or RTB, as it was referred to in shorthand, located on Pockatoo Pewamo land in rural Southern Michigan. It was set up on tribal trust land to be theoretically at least legally free from governmental control. Other tribes used their trust lands to establish casinos, which was their right, but Rey's Uncle Flynn Pompatella convinced them that a model training center for the world's down-and-out would be a better, more impactful choice. Flynn, Pastor Louis, and Jake Quark helped fund the project. They also worked with the local Pockatoo and Muckytuck Pewamo clans to put together a place where the "lost children," as Jake described them, could be gathered and restored. Thus, the original RTB was formed and now flourished.

Of course, people will not change unless they want to change; many people jumped back on the bus and returned to the crumbling inner city and dying suburbs. More often than not, though, people appreciated the "hand up" instead of the "handout" and flourished with the positive psychology approach and love they received at the RTB. They were taught to be proactive about rebuilding their own communities. They learned how to set up their own small businesses, their own community micro-banks to fund the businesses, and their own micro-schools to actually educate, not indoctrinate, their children. Perhaps more importantly, they learned how to defend themselves in the thug- and drug-infested cities, now overrun by the Creeb Nation. They were the spear tip of the True Blue Revolution revitalizing their neighborhoods.

Jake Quark himself occasionally taught at the local RTB, emphasizing goal setting, decision making, and learned optimism over learned helplessness. When Rey visited the RTB the first time, he was only able to be there a few weeks before having to flee from threatened NAP attacks. That short time, however, altered the way he saw himself and the world. He definitely stopped whining and started winning. Now under Jake and Flynn Pompatella's guidance, RTBs were springing up all across the USA on tribal trust lands. They were making a big difference in the lives of disenfranchised people.

As Rey looked around the RTB, he realized it was good to be back. Rey enjoyed watching the people mobbing Sister Mary Contrary and sharing their latest target practice scores and martial art moves. They marveled at his blue skin and wanted to know all about the Blue Goo and the far-off island he had escaped to called Foondavi. As much as he, Sister Mary, Zara, and Snapper wanted to stay longer, they wanted to get downtown and see how the graduates of the RTB were actually faring in the warzone called the Permanent Autonomous Zone, or PAZ, where the real work of the True Blue Revolution was happening.

Snapper climbed in behind the wheel of an armored SUV to drive Rey, Sister Mary, and Zara into the city. They were headed to the local "Dangerous Church" that was the headquarters of the True Blue Revolution, the movement to reconquer the cities. The church, located in a small, dilapidated building in a cordoned-off section of the PAZ, was the base camp where the graduates of the Reservation for the Temporarily Bewildered could launch their sorties into the Creeb Nation-infested neighborhoods and do their thing at trying to reclaim and rebuild the place.

Rey was shocked by the deterioration around him. Burnt-out and boarded-up stores and houses littered the landscape. Some were still smoldering, filling the air with an acrid smell. Small groups of loitering young people angrily eyed them as they passed. The sight of Zara, or perhaps of a saintly looking Sister in her habit, must have overwhelmed their sense of self-preservation, because Rey saw several in a group they passed grab their cell phones. Rey started to say something to Snapper about the cell phone users. Before he could speak, though, they came under attack by a Creeb Nation unit just as they turned a corner and pulled up to a traffic-control light that mysteriously turned to green and then just as quickly turned back to red as they approached. Suddenly, they were surrounded by a mob armed with ferocious-looking spiked bats and crowbars. The crowd jeered and then attacked the SUV, attempting to smash the thick, fortified windows. Leaning back, away from the windows, Rey noticed that the Creeb gang was a diverse group of mostly males but some females—Black, Brown, white, and all shades in between. Seeing his look, Sister Mary calmly said: "Yes, the Creeb pride themselves in their diversity and perversity."

Then Sister Mary barked at the stunned Snapper, who was cringing behind the steering wheel. "Roll down the windows, Snapper, my boy, and duck your head." The Creeb mob momentarily stopped their futile attack as the previously impervious windows they were failing to shatter suddenly started rolling down.

Sister Mary whipped two pistols from beneath her habit and repeatedly shot Mr. Walther PPK out the right window and Mr. SIG out the left at the startled felons. Because the shaking Snapper hadn't rolled down the windows fast enough for the quick-draw artist, windows started shattering from the inside out. Rey's assaulted ears were ringing. As the smoke and cordite settled, he saw the Creeb Nation cretins running for all they were worth, several with holes through their hats, some with a shredded ear, and others still clutching broken bats severed by the well-aimed bullets.

"That ought to scare the little, uh, sisters and brothers," Sister Mary chortled, her voice muffled after the thunderous reports nearly shattered everyone's eardrums.

Broken glass was still tumbling everywhere. The shaken Snapper was checking the floor because he had clumsily dropped his loaded Colt Python .357 Magnum revolver. Fortunately, the safety was on or a bullet wasn't in the chamber, because it didn't discharge. On a positive note, they basked in a cool breeze flowing in from the shattered windows as they finished the last half mile to their destination. No more Creeb Nation solicitation for donations hindered their arrival.

As they pulled up to the Dangerous Church PAZ, a broken-down and burned-out old gas station from the looks of it, several people came running from behind the makeshift barriers surrounding the compound. Rey saw a familiar-looking scruffy dude with pizza crumbs on his T-shirt leading the pack. His shirt read: "Meek: Immense power under complete control." On the shirt was a picture of a chariot horse rearing up. It was Reverend Louie, his old friend from his days of running from NAP. Louie had to shout to get them to hear through their still-ringing ears.

"What was all the gun fire we heard?" he asked, peering in the broken windows to make sure everyone was okay.

"We ran into some of your Creeb Nation friends on our way here," the now-recovered Snapper loudly informed them. "Sister Mary introduced them to her little friend Walther in her right hand and Mr. SIG Sauer in her left. She convinced a few of them to visit their local infirmary and use their health benefits."

"I would have used my Mossberg 500 Tactical 20 gauge pump shotgun with the pistol grip to do more damage, but it was in the back seat," Sister Mary said with a big smile.

"Isn't she something when she talks firearms?" Snapper laughed.

"I'm a nun, you doofus, not a pacifist. Like the Romans used to say, '*Si vis pacem, para bellum.*' If you seek peace, be prepared for war."

"You're still something, Sister!" He ducked his head as she faked a punch. Then, like a blur, Sister Mary struck her arm straight out and hit him with a two-finger jab right to his shoulder.

"Ouch!" Snapper squealed in real pain, holding his numbed arm.

"Show respect to your elders!" Sister Mary said with a grin. "And next time, don't drop your gun or your guard!"

Rubbing his shoulder, Snapper said, "Well, pacifist or not, she did blow out both windows on the SUV. I didn't get them down fast enough for Sister's itchy trigger fingers here. I think the flying glass also encouraged a few of the Creebs to shop elsewhere. If the Creebs keep getting so aggressive, we'll have to use only heavily armored personnel carriers to come here."

As Pastor Louis Pastor led them on a tour around the PAZ, he spoke in a cheerful, booming voice. Rey didn't know if it was to compensate for their deafened ears or due to his years of stump preaching. "Life is definitely about more than happiness and contentment. We're about the big picture, not just rebuilding and healing the people and the land, but restoring the spirit of the people and the land. 'Tikkun Olam,' as our Hebrew friends and Jake love to say. '*Nil desperandum*' is one of our mottos. 'Never despair!' We will retake the cities. We will battle the Creeb Nation, who are in reality stolen children, a creation of the psychopaths, and I hope to convert even more of them to a constructive way of life."

"Well, they just tried to convert us," Sister Mary said, impishly. "Convert us to corpses, not constructive lives!"

"They do tend to get a little enthusiastic," Pastor Louie agreed. "But we still want to reach out to them. Reconciliation and reconstruction, not retribution and revenge."

Rey nodded his head in agreement. "I just returned from

touring the original Reservation for the Temporarily Bewildered. I wanted to come here to see the fruits of all that training."

"Well, thanks to Sister Mary and the staff out there, we're training and re-arming the local people to regain their communities. It's definitely not easy. The Creeb Nation is relatively new, but the grim social situation is not new. We sometimes have four generations that have known nothing but poverty and despair. No fathers in the home, often no moms, no hope for the future," he said, sadly shaking his head.

"The politicians often live elsewhere and just let these places deteriorate. It's disgusting," Zara added.

"But like Sister Mary Contrary likes to say," Pastor Louie added, "perhaps paraphrasing the great John Maxwell: 'A great leader knows the way, shows the way, goes the way.' That is what we are trying to do here. It's not enough to know the way. We must show the way and go the way."

"'*De oppresso liber*,' the Special Forces official motto, is also another one of our mottos," Sister Mary chimed in with her usual enthusiasm. "Liberate the oppressed! We're the True Blue Revolution special forces!"

"As you undoubtedly know, Sister Mary teaches Motherly Martial Arts and firearms skills to all the graduates," Pastor Louie said. "I originally was hesitant. But as you experienced coming here, people need to be able to defend against predators."

"And we make them one tough mother, or father, I might add," Sister Mary said, with a big grin. "They become marksmen and fierce protectors of the vulnerable. Zara and Snapper continue the work for me here while I primarily concentrate on coordinating training at the other RTBs popping up across the nation. We drill them every day, so when they come under fire, they react instinctively, not like Snapper here, dropping his piece." She poked the poor Snapper again. "Discipline is the key. *Instruction* is an interesting word. Do you know it actually means 'structure within'? In other words, to build something inside a person that is permanent and changes outward behavior. That's what we're doing, building an internal framework to strengthen people, and then sending them back to regain their cities."

Louis Pastore nodded his head in agreement and then snorted in derision. "Our local NAP mayor wants to ban all firearms. Ha! Then only the Creeb Nation and other NAP goons will have guns. We say '*molon labe*,' ancient Greek for 'come and take it'! Supposedly the ancient Spartan King Leonidas said this to the invading Persian King Xerxes! We're proudly bitter clingers when it comes to our children, Bibles, and guns!"

"Sister Mary, you have at least seven black belts in various martial arts. Isn't that correct?" asked Rey. "And you're proficient with firearms, to put it mildly, as we all just saw. One complaint the media has is, we seem to be preparing people to participate in bloody conflict. How do you respond to that?"

"With a hah, hah, hah, sure! Try to live down here unarmed and not become a bloody victim!" Sister Mary answered with a dismissive laugh. "I tell my students, both male and female: Never be the bully. Never start the fight. The first rule is to avoid violence. Yes, love them and forgive them, by all means, but shoot them if they threaten you or yours, especially your children!"

"We try to encourage non-lethal defense, too," Louie was quick to add.

"That's why my favorite martial art is the easiest one to teach, and one I have integrated into my Motherly Martial Arts," Sister Mary said, deftly performing a spin and kick that sent her habit whirling and Snapper ducking. "Krav Maga, baby! Krav Maga! If you can't avoid a fight, strike first and strike fast. Five attack zones: nose, Adam's apple, heart, crotch, and knee!" She mimicked each strike at the hapless Snapper in a surprising blur of motion that left him stumbling. "Temporarily take out a Creeb's testosterone factory and he won't come back!"

Pastor Louie quickly jumped in, smiling benevolently at the Ninja Nun. "We teach survival first and then success skills," Louie said. "Look around here and you'll see small neighborhood investment banks using local people's money to build the community, fund small startup businesses to provide necessary services, and create jobs. Most people want to work. We've got rooftop gardens, chicken coops, and fish tanks using runoff rain water and providing our own healthy foods and a thriving market. Perhaps most importantly for the future, we've established small charter schools or micro-schools where kids get individualized education and almost everyone volunteers as mentors."

Sister Mary looked at Rey with a determined expression. "Any Creeb Nation creeps try coming around and shake a True Blue effort down, they get taught the lessons their mamas should have taught them."

Pastor Louie jumped back in, trying to temper Sister Mary's enthusiasm. "A number one problem is growing psychopathy. The Creeb Nation is trying to develop even more Creeb Cribs, sort of thug clubhouses. Fatherlessness and hopelessness are potent sources of crime. Researchers also say empathy scores are rapidly dropping all over the nation and that narcissism is on the rise, possibly due to extensive smartphone use, social media platforms, and selfie culture. Who knows for sure?"

"Here's the way that problem works to destroy communities," Louie continued. "It's what I call the 90-10 Rule. Ninety percent of people are either 'takers' or 'matchers.' They have never been taught any other way. Matchers at least will meet you halfway: You help me, I'll help you. Only ten percent are natural givers. We want to develop givers out of the matchers, and maybe even convert a few of the takers into, at least, matchers. The key is responsibility. Be personally accountable and stop being a victim. Exercise liberty within the rule of the law. Know the way, go the way, show the way. Give them the tools and training to take back their communities. Show them giving versus taking, or even matching, actually builds relationships and the community and in the end gives everyone more!"

Louie was getting even more enthusiastic, and Sister Mary wandered off to encourage some children practicing their martial arts moves.

"One of the biggest problems we face, ironically, is bigism. Big cities, big businesses, big schools, big banks. Admittedly, size can be an advantage for a while, but eventually size stifles individual action as some people easily get lost in the crowd. We believe in 'microcosm' versus bigism: small, connected, highly effective communities, micro-schools where each child can blossom as an individual, small businesses focused on community needs, and micro-banks where the local community and neighbors invest and watch over growth opportunities."

"Perhaps the biggest problem with bigism versus microcosm is that bigism, although initially efficient and effective, soon accumulates power. But within one generation or at most two, no matter how benevolent the original government or organization is, the power attracts psychopaths. Like bears to honey, or flies to . . . . You get the picture! Then greed and internal rifts, fueled by paranoia, destroy any initial efficiencies, and the organizations lose all ability to respond to their clients, if they even care anymore."

Reverend Louie was really wound up. "Some people call us the 'Dangerous Church' because we are actually doing things to help people rebuild and restore their lives and communities. But we call ourselves the 'Church of the Lost Children.'"

Louie continued. "We give people empathy, not sympathy. We help people to help themselves. In many cases, we start rehab right here in the PAZ." He motioned all around them. "If they're really serious about starting over, then we ship them to an RTB, under the protection of armed guards. We're gradually retaking the cities. We either convert or convict the Creebs. Some can be saved, but for some it's too late. I also can tell you that we're really working hard with the youngest people. We provide mentors and support to all the schools, especially at the elementary level. The public schools often refuse help, but small micro-schools are popping up all over, thanks to our help, and the results from working with those children are amazing!"

"I try not to preach too often, just live it. When I do preach, though, I like to talk about the two kinds of truth. One is the truth that will set you free, that the Source of All Things loves you. It is the unalterable bedrock of my life purpose." He paused to smile at Rey. "The second type of truth is the flexible truth of most politicians, charlatans, and tyrants. It's truth that's manipulated and molded to serve whatever purpose they choose. They tolerate and even nurture these horrible conditions, these slums and decrepit schools, the crumbling, chaotic hell holes, that breed the Creebs. We, however, teach that poverty doesn't make you violent, but violence will make you poor."

Sister Mary Contrary came back to the group and jumped in. "We see our job as being culture doctors, fixing and healing our broken land."

Later that afternoon, the group met with Anu and Diora Pokritos, two other community leaders, both recovered meth addicts. Anu and his young wife, Diora, were among the first True Blues to take the Blue after Rey. They led the Magen Chereb, or Shields and Swords, a group that helps protect the PAZ and surrounding neighborhoods. Anu chose his personal name when he took the Blue because in Greek it means "the real thing, sincere, without hypocrisy," and it suited him to a tee. Nothing distinguished Anu on the outside—he was an average-looking guy—but his heart was full of bravery and love, according to all who knew him. He was part of the Dangerous Church team that arrested Fillups Farnswaggle, the horrible fake missionary who bilked funds from honest givers and burnt down a church with many of Rey's extended family inside to get insurance money. Anu was dressed in dirty work clothes, having just climbed down from repairing a roof. His calloused hands and muscled arms betrayed the life of a physical laborer; he was proud to say that Jesus was a carpenter and a construction worker! Anu pointed to his wife, Diora.

"She didn't need to change her name. It means 'golden, precious,' or 'made for a special time' in her native Albanian," Anu was proud to say, beaming at the smiling woman beside him.

According to Louie, Diora was a highly charged personality who attracted powerful people and drew in money and skilled help for the PAZ and the surrounding community. "She certainly attracted me to the work, and now I am hooked!"

"Ha," the blue lady laughed, in a musical voice. "I lead them to you, sweetheart! I draw them in and you save them!"

Diora was, indeed, an unusual-looking woman. She was lightly freckled and had auburn hair and startling green eyes, like jade jewels in a blue alabaster sculpture that was her smiling face. "I either save them or shoot them!" Anu added, patting his shoulder holster that was holding a gleaming, well-maintained Glock 19.

As the group were getting to know Anu and Diora, another couple walked in the room: Thambos and Zenobia Zugzwang. The Pokritos beamed when they introduced the Zugzwangs as being new to the PAZ as philanthropic supporters. Rey shook the outstretched hand of Thambos, who gave Rey a practiced, manly handshake. Rey did not let on he knew Thambos was a turncoat. Zenobia only gave Rey a chilling smile. Rey noticed Zara hung back, while Pastor Louie acted as though everything were normal and focused more on extolling the work of the Pokritos team and expounding on their unusual last name.

"I explained the name Anu, but Pokritos? It also means 'the real thing.' Ever heard of Sojourner Truth? She was a slave before the Civil War. When she earned her freedom, she changed her name. When Anu and Diora earned their freedom from drugs and took the Blue, like Sojouner they chose to change their last name. What would you choose, Rey? Shofar? It means 'announcing the presence of God, or the start of a battle.'"

"No," Rey responded. "I'm finished with name changes, but I like Shofar as a political party name, for sure. It also can mean 'trumpet of victory,' right?"

"Very good with your Hebrew," Louie said. "We're all about changing people, our culture, and the world. Heraclitus, the great Greek philosopher that Jake and Anu here like to quote all the time, once said you never step into the same river twice. Well, I say you never meet the same person twice. Big changes or little changes, but change is inevitable. You choose the direction. We want to change people to change the world. That's going to take changing the way people think, to paraphrase Albert Einstein."

Pastor Louie smiled. "We see the True Blue Revolution having three phases. The first phase of the revolution was the beginning: getting the first Reservations for the Temporarily Bewildered organized, the Dangerous Church engaged, Foondavi set up as a safe place, and the Blue Goo fine tuned. Phase two is the actual rebellion, 'kinetic action,' as our military friends call it. You've experienced how violent the Creebs are now. Our people have to fight back to defend themselves, retake their homes and communities, and even start to take the action to the bad guys. Phase three, somewhere in the future, not too far off we hope, will be the True Blue Renaissance, when we can live our lives in freedom and peace. Instead of what some call a 'great reset,' we're advocating for 'growth mindset'—helping the world and all people reach their potential. Right now we are building strength through struggle."

Louie motioned for Rey to join him off to the side, while Anu and Diora led the others on a tour to see the on-going construction projects and training activities. "Thank you for not reacting negatively to Thambos and his wife. I haven't decided how to share the heartbreaking news to Anu and Diora. They'll be crushed. They were so excited to get them involved here, even though the Zugzwangs both prefer to observe or supervise than get their hands dirty. I guess that should have been an early warning sign. We were pushing the Zugzwangs to take the Blue but constantly met with stiff but polite resistance. Now we know why." He shook his head in resignation. Then he looked Rey directly in the eyes.

"I like to challenge people all the time," Louie said. "I tell them to open up your eyes and look at creation. Did all this magnificently complex creation, starting with your unbelievably complex brain, come about by chance? A just-right universe, a just-right solar system, a just-right planet? You might as well believe a tornado hitting a junkyard could build a fully functioning supersonic jet!"

Rey responded, "I already heard this intriguing concept from Jake not too long ago and from Machseh just recently."

Louie nodded, but was unfazed and went on, obviously

discussing a favorite subject. "Look at DNA. It's not a symbol; it's a code, a language, that has meaning! You might as well believe a bomb set off in a library could accidentally reassemble the full works of Shakespeare! Who built the moon? Look at that bright orb in the night sky, just the exact right size and exact right location to perfectly block the sun."

"I repeat, it is amazing," Rey said, "and I never really thought about it much, but Jake and then Machseh have already explained it. I find it all hard to believe, although I admit I'm starting to believe a lot of things I previously thought impossible."

Louie continued, undeterred. "Some say, well, it's all due to the natural laws of physics. Gravitation, etcetera. But if those laws can create life, then who made those laws? I believe it was the Great Star Maker, the Source of All Things. And I believe He communicates to us."

"I guess I'm not a particularly religious man," Rey said, starting to feel uncomfortable.

"Great! Neither am I," Reverend Louie said with a big smile. "It should be about relationship. It's totally improbable, no way to start a faith, yet here we are two thousand years later and with over two billion believers around the world."

Rey slowly nodded in agreement. The improbable became possible. He could definitely see that with everything he saw in the last few weeks.

"Just take off your blinders and look at who Jesus was," Louie continued, taking Rey's nod as a sign of piqued interest. "He's not at all who the big Christian industrial complex says He is, for the most part. He was not, is not, some mild-mannered, clean-cut business school graduate. He's more like these disheveled, slightly unkempt carpenters and construction workers the press and elites call 'irredeemable deplorables.' More like Anu than Thambos, for sure. He definitely is not the Marxist radical the secular press and non-believers try to misrepresent Him as being. No, no, no! He chose when, where, and to whom to be born. The One Larger Than the Universe became a microscopic embryo and chose to be implanted in an unmarried, probably only fourteen-year-old peasant girl. The mightiest being in the universe—He was born in a stinky stable and greeted by shepherds, the lowest-class people in their society. He was completely vulnerable but was protected and raised by an impoverished construction worker and was brought up in a backwoods village of an oppressed people. He was probably labelled as an outcast, a reject, even a bastard, as He was seen by many as an out-of-wedlock child, an abomination in those days. But He became a revolutionary street preacher and compassionately reached out to women, other outcasts and rejected people, all the oppressed, and the poor. His longest recorded speech was to a prostitute at the well, and He won her over by the compassion and acceptance He showed her. His enemies were not just the brutally oppressive Roman authorities but also the mainline religious leaders! How could I not spread His word to all His lost children and not try to correct all the misrepresentations of what He actually said and who He really was?" Finally seeing Rey was getting even more uncomfortable, he stopped, with one last comment: "I know you're searching for the deepest truths. Just keep your heart and mind open, Rey." He smiled again. "Sorry, sermon over. Pass the plate. I just get wound up. Hallelujah!"

"Well, it is a great message and an intriguing way of looking at the universe," Rey affirmed. "I have to admit, hanging around people I deeply respect—like Jake, Machseh, Sister Mary, and you, too, Louie—makes me stop and wonder."

Louie patted him on the back. "You're a good man, Rey. This war is bigger than all of us. The Source of All Things uses good men whether they believe in Him or not, because He believes in them!"

Rey had to admit it was refreshing to see all the energy and the pushback to the NAP villains and their Creeb Nation offspring. He would have some good things to report to Jake and the rest of the Hadron Group—and they needed all the good news they could get.

Back to
Hadron Headquarters
≡ for an Update ≡

Jake was excited to hear their update. "We seem to have our Dangerous Church and True Blue Revolution teams operating effectively, disrupting Achor's and NAP's complete control of the city. Plus, we have several more RTBs up and running, and more requests are being received and handled. I'd like to eventually use Blues as instructors wherever we can, but we're still a little slow recruiting people to take the Blue Goo, for obvious reasons. Unfortunately, we might not have too big an impact on the midterm elections coming soon, but, if we can eventually get RTBs established outside most big cities, especially in battleground states, we could really have an impact on the next presidential election in two years."

"In more good news," Jake continued, "we were able to throw a wrench into Achor's HEN House operation. Some of our Hadron White Hat Hackers, under the direction, believe it or not, of former President Sedgwick Sewell, helped us by stealthily cracking into the Central HEN House information network and really scrambling stuff. Our hackers snuck in a cyber backdoor and changed the formula for the zooga and tobtoba concoctions. To further mess up NAP's effort, they shipped the stuff to all the wrong locations. There are reportedly riots going on now in many of the HEN Houses, as the dazed captives are coming off their medicated highs and belatedly realizing what's happening to them and their loved ones. Lots of explosions reported. Unfortunately, the Creeb Nation will remain a problem as long as mainstream media keep giving them cover."

"In other updates, we continue to work on luring Achor into a trap, perhaps in an ironic twist, on the Isle of Predators, a rugged and desolate island off the coast of Cozorre." Seeing Rey tense up, Jake held up his hand. "We have an intriguing report from your boys on Cozorre. Through an informer we have on the island whom Camilla helped us identify, they somehow snuck out some information I'll share with you in a second. First, though, they're fine—actually more than fine. They're being mentored by the Torgie leaders and their war chief, Degel Gibbor, an impressive champion of the Torgie Naga, or Striker Force, it sounds like. I really need to research them. They have an interesting story and are an amazing people—surviving right under the nasty noses of the various Cozorrean regimes for centuries. Mr. Gibbor is quite impressed with your boys, Rey. They're definitely safe and thriving. Once we review their informative update, I'm sure you'll agree we can leave them there for now."

"In the meantime, I want you to go back to Machseh's place and observe how the Muckytuck are preparing our new True Blues. We need to speed up the process. We need these newbies to play key roles in counteracting the Creeb

Nation, leading the True Blue Rebellion, training the True Blue forces in the RTBs, and convincing people to vote for our True Blue Party candidates in the midterms. One of the candidates will shock you, Rey."

Seeing Rey's quizzical look, Jake continued. "I always liked your mother-in-law Theta Pipestone. When she turned to me to help her son JP, Joshua Preston, I couldn't resist. Less than two years ago, when you were just taking office, we extricated him from the horrible Pewamo State Psych unit, where he was being drugged, and took him to a Reservation for the Temporarily Bewildered. Within six months, he was fully recovered; by then you were already on the run. When Theta told me her husband, old GT, had a debilitating stroke, we quickly inserted JP into Pipestone Metal as CEO. In less than a year, with admittedly some help from our Hadron team, JP has rejuvenated the place, is getting national exposure, and is producing great numbers, top and bottom lines, as the workers are responding to his humble, helpful, and honest visionary leadership. Theta is so proud," he added, smiling contentedly. "I'm wasting no time and have him slated as a True Blue Party senatorial candidate. He's running against Samms' virtual Newly candidate, possibly an Achor Nithing-sponsored monster, and some NAP Democrat non-entity."

"Now, let's look at what your boys say about the Torgie situation. Then, I think you'll agree to go for a short visit to the Muckytuck, while Carlyle, Camilla, and I conjure up the perfect lure and trap for Achor."

"Before we move on, I have one question," Rey said. "Why does Achor hate me so personally and with such intensity. I never stole his lunch, flirted with his girlfriend, or kicked sand in his face. I mean, I have reason to dislike him and what his family and NAP have done, but why me? Why is it so personal?"

"You took the election away from him, or at least the total overwhelming victory he expected and promised NAP. They then turned on him and nearly stole everything from him that he previously stole from others. But it really isn't political, Rey. It's, as you say, personal. He wants to personally watch you suffer when he tortures your boys and then slowly kill you. You work with me and have defied him, and he can't stand it. Also, he knows how much I love you and the boys. He can't stand me. He can't get to me, at least not yet, so he'll delight in agonizing me with your demise. For decent people like us, it's hard to comprehend the level of hideousness of which he's capable. We're counting on this intense hatred of his to blind him a bit and get him to a place where we can snatch him or kill him."

As they prepared to watch the digital report from Milty and Morty, Rey's sons, Jake discussed their new informant. "We always attempted to build and maintain an informer network on Cozorre, just to keep tabs on the sneaky rascals. Bribes work well with such greedy people, and fortunately Cozorre is loaded with them! Unfortunately, our previous informants always got caught. But Camilla uncovered this new informer and says he's really motivated for the right reasons, having had family destroyed by the current Cozorre tyrant."

Jakes went on to introduce the Torgies to Rey. "These people are something else! We knew we had an underground operation there, surviving the various purges, but we didn't realize just how underground they literally were. Torgies actually have lived for a long time deep beneath the mountains. Our friends on Foondavi have always maintained a tenuous contact with them and, I guess, just assumed we knew about them. When the Foondavians heard about Camilla's report about the boys being snatched, they surreptitiously contacted the Torgies. They said they used carrier seagulls, of all things, to cover the eight hundred miles of open sea between the islands. Anyway, however they did it, the Torgies and the new undercover contact made it possible for this short clip from your twins to reach us."

Rey had a lot more questions, but the abrupt Jake wanted to move ahead. "Now let's watch your boys' report!"

≡ Torgies to the Rescue ≡

The report was short and to the point. Milty and Morty quickly related how they were snatched by the Cozorreans and then re-snatched by the mysterious Torgies. They wanted their dad to know they loved him and that they were safe in the coolest caves you would ever see. They were learning to sword fight and shoot something they called yew bows. They ended by saying, "Don't come too soon. We are safe and having fun. Over and out!" Then they added a post-script: "Please don't hurry, Dad. This is really, really fun. We are making our own swords and advancing up the ranks in archery. We even were asked to join the Torgie Naga, their Striker Force." Their last sentence did not reassure Rey. Nobody in the meeting knew what it referred to, but it sounded vaguely dangerous. Rey tried to reassure himself: They were only eleven, well, close to twelve-year-old boys. What would they be allowed to do? If Rey knew what they were really up to, he would have been paralyzed with fear!

Rey's boys were, indeed, having the time of their nearly twelve-year-old lives. True, they were kidnapped after venturing off to visit Boogan Head on Foondavi, the site where their much-admired dad demonstrated his bravery and became a Nambo, guardian and defender of the people. They knew their mom was safe on Foondavi. She was visiting the special children at Eden Grove when Milty and Morty used the opportunity to slip off for Boogan Head—and adventure. Shacknasty McTree, son of the notorious Foondavian pirate Devil Eye McTree and his gang spotted and then surrounded and kidnapped the unsuspecting and trusting boys by pretending to need help rescuing a friend who supposedly slipped off the cliff. When the helpful twins discovered the ruse, it was too late; they were gagged, trussed up, and tossed in fishy-smelling burlap bags, held for some time, and delivered to a submarine that surfaced offshore. They were taken to Cozorre and turned over to the local NAP scoundrels, presumably to be held for Achor Nithing. The good news? Well, despite delivering some good bruises to Shacknasty's brutes when they were taken, the boys themselves were actually treated quite gingerly. They overheard the vengeful brutes lamenting that Achor Nithing wanted to personally deliver all the pain and would kill anyone who bruised them.

After a three-day, uncomfortable submarine ride in an oily-smelling storage room and kept awake by all the clanging noises from the ill-maintained old sub, Milty and Morty arrived on Cozzore and were dumped into a deep underground cell. Even then they were not beaten and actually were still reasonably well treated. They were given some halfway decent food and bottled water, even if the sustenance was delivered with intimidating growls and promises of what Achor intended to do to them.

The old dungeon was scary, with dark stains that were most likely blood and an oppressive odor of human waste that seemed to emit from every cold stone. They gradually got used to the stench and eventually added to the aroma, as there was no other place to go. They then huddled together under a tattered blanket that was thrown at them by one of the snarling guards. Exhausted from their big adventure, they eventually dropped off into a deep sleep.

The boys hadn't been sleeping for long when they were startled and shaken awake by small shadowy forms that held calloused hands over their mouths to stifle any sound.

"Welcome to Cozorre, young dudes! The Torgies are here to rescue you!" a muffled voice said quietly in the dark. "My name is Degel Gibbor, and I am here with my Strikers to escort you to freedom."

Seeing that the boys were not going to raise an alarm, Degel lit a small handlight that emitted a pleasant but contained glow. What Milty and Morty saw was a burly but short man with broad shoulders as wide as he was tall. He had a big head, even bigger over-sized eyes that appeared to be cobalt blue, a wild flurry of curly hair, and a flowing beard nearly as long as he was tall.

Degel continued talking in his guttural but quiet voice. "We are great admirers of your dad, and we also love to take any chance to tweak the Cozorrean noses, as snotty as they are!" With that, Degel placed a finger to his mouth indicating silence. With his other hand, he indicated they should follow him, as he walked to what looked like a solid wall. As Degel approached it, he gave a nondescript, slightly discolored rock a little nudge. With a soft, whooshing sound, a darkened passageway opened. Once everyone was through, he turned and shoved the opening shut, then slid a bolt into a metal lock with a small, snick sound.

The tunnel he led Milty and Morty into was lit by a gentle light that seemed to emit from fungus growing on the walls. A soft breeze of fresh air was welcome after the fetid cell. As Degel led the group on, they were joined by more strange-looking men and a few women. "These are part of our Torgie Naga, or Striker Force. They all wanted to come and rescue the brave boys of the admired Nambo McBlue."

The boys noticed that, although they themselves were just average-sized almost twelve-year-old boys, they still towered over the squat strangers. They also noticed how well muscled the individuals were. Seeing their scrutiny, Degel laughed.

"We're not short, just built close to the ground! We're also hard-working miners and blacksmiths, although a few wimps are jewelers," he said, being greeted with some snorts of derision from some members of the troop. "But all of us work with our weapons every day. We'll have to toughen you up, if you're going to live with us!"

And toughen them up they did. They walked for what seemed miles up and down tight, dimly lit passages, over jumbled rock slides, and between some tight cracks in the rocks the boys had to struggle through while the Torgies slithered through easily. With Milty and Morty nearing exhaustion, they finally emerged into a large underground cavern that was suffused with the soft glow of the rock-grown fungi. They stopped by an underground waterfall and, thankfully, took a deep drink from the ice-cold pool beneath it. Milty's and Morty's hiking shoes, which would have been adequate on Foondavi, were already tattered and torn by the sharp rock edges. After an all-too-short rest, the group took off again. In another hour or so of tortuously wending their way along treacherously narrow footpaths that dropped off into deep, bottomless crevices, they came to another cavern. This one was punctuated by fires and—thankfully, to the now-famished boys—aromas of cooking food.

The twins were stared at with friendly but deep curiosity by the waiting Torgie tribe, which was mostly comprised of very short women and even more diminutive children. One of the women with attractive shiny red hair, big, flashing green eyes, and a deep dimple in her chin stepped forward and smiled at them. Then the woman gave Degel the leader a substantial punch in the arm, making him wince in pain.

"I am Zalita Gibbor, this rather inconsiderate brute's wife. It looks like he has dragged you poor young boys through the caves, not considering your comfort at all." She shooed away the rescue party, including her frustrated husband. "Go on! Get! After I feed these young ones and let them rest, you can come and pester them."

She led Milty and Morty into a small but cozy rock shelter, decorated brightly with some of the glowing fungi of all different colors, sat them by a warm fire, and served them food and water. After a refreshing meal of tasty bread and some type of fish cooked in mouth-watering spices, she finally let her husband back into the small abode. Degel came in meekly and asked her if he could now take the twins to meet the elders. Once he had Zalita's grudging permission, Degel escorted the boys to a larger stone-built enclosure and sat them beside a warm fire. He introduced them to more of the Torgie leadership. Wodell Wo Thamby and Ponder Widderskins were older versions of Degel. Thamby had a thick red beard and a massive mane of red hair, both interwoven with white strands. With his green eyes, he looked much like the spunky Zalita, and it ended up he was her father. Widderskins wore his black hair and beard neatly trimmed; with his startling deep blue eyes, he stared intently at the twins. The Torgie elders talked about their people with a great deal of pride. They related that the Torgies were descendants of indentured and then enslaved Welsh and Basque miners who escaped the brutal Cozorreans by going deep into the extensive cave system. As the escapees reached the furthest depths, they found there were already some unusual original inhabitants. They were greeted by, and then interbred with, some ancient Polynesian and Denisovan people as well as some small, hobbit-like individuals called Homo Floresiensis. The combination produced short, stout people with over-sized eyes, ideal for the dimly lit caves and mining.

"We prefer to describe ourselves as close to the earth!" the elders noted, in a similar vein to what Degel said earlier when they first met.

The Torgies literally were as wide at the shoulders as they were tall, with stubby legs the size of tree trunks. They had massive shoulders from wielding pickaxes and hammers and from practicing with long, Welsh-designed yew bows from the age of six or seven. These bows had an unbelievable eighty-pound pull, as the boys learned when they tried to draw one later during target practice. The Torgies informed the boys the yew bows were for shooting wild goats and deer—and the occasional Cozorrean Apache gunship copter that tried to trespass on the upper Cozorrean slopes, considered Torgie land. Tipped with an obsidian point for hunting and a special titanium one for copters, the arrows could be useful as pig stickers too, as occasional captured Cozorrean soldiers soon found out to their painful chagrin!

The Torgies explained, because they are constantly hunted by whomever controls the lower slopes of Cozorre, they now live in this deep and intricate maze of tunnels and caverns carved beneath the surface of Cozorre. They keep exploring deeper and deeper every year, discovering ever richer lodes of ores such as gold, silver-laden galenite, and diamonds. These are turned into useful objects and valuable trade goods by their skilled craftsmen and then sold by Cozorre surface dwellers, or "surfies" as they call them. Otherwise, the goods are snuck off the island under cover of darkness for a rendezvous with traders from other islands.

Wodell Wo Thamby and Ponder Widderskins both repeated how much they admired the boys' dad and what he attempted to do in the USA. They especially appreciated how Nambo McBlue continued to fight NAP, their mortal enemy and the current occupiers of Cozorre. They explained they secretly tapped into Cozorre media, so they kept reasonably informed about the outer world.

For years the Torgies struggled against the original oppressors called the Finazzis, who they said were "nasty dudes." Then the Cozottis toppled the Finazzis and, unfortunately, also topped them in fiendishness. But the latest NAP monsters? There is no end to their cruelty. "Some new dude named Fugelman Batullion is now trying to exterminate us!" Thamby said with a derisive snort.

"As we mentioned," Widderskins said, "our poor ancestors were brought here under the most deplorable conditions to mine coal and the other precious metals. We took that obstacle and turned it into opportunity. We have become very skilled metallurgists and jewelers. As you will see, the forges are clanging constantly. Smoke goes out vents connected with the volcano. We have to sneak out at night to fish on the reefs and to trade with people here on Cozorre, and, as we said earlier, we occasionally go to other islands." Seeing the boys' incredulous look, Widderskins added, "We have some sea caves we can slip out of and some of the best watercraft and navigators in all of Polynesia."

"Throughout the island, we have secret passages and peep holes everywhere," Thamby said, taking over the narrative from Widderskins. "We even have worm holes woven into all the walls so we can constantly bug the Cozorreans and always know what's going on. That's how we knew about your arrival. We also received carrier seagulls from Foondavi."

Thamby then added proudly with a surprising snarl, "We're also excellent assassins and poisoners. Cozorreans say we Torgies put the 'sass' in 'assassins.'"

Widderskins then jumped back in. "The Finazzis and then the Cozotti family and now the NAP occupiers have tried to poison and burn out us Torgies for the last two hundred years. When they dropped bombs on the cave openings, we just reopened them. One time they dropped gas into the vents, and we made sure it came back out all around them! They would have to destroy the whole island to hurt us. We won't tempt Achor Nithing, though. He's a ruthless and savage monster who's made it very clear he wants you boys alive. If he finds out we have you, he won't get too frisky!"

"There's an old Welsh proverb: It is a bad bow that will not bend," said Degel Gibbor, rejoining the conversation. "We're very adaptable and tremendous archers with our unnaturally huge arm and back muscles. Every Torgie must practice with the yew bow starting from age six or seven. We'll get you boys going on them right away, though beginning with smaller bows," he said, eyeing their skinny arms.

"You've probably noticed we have large eyes. Like cats have adapted to low light by having larger eyes and other special perceptual skills, so have we. Thanks to our Denisovan ancestors, we evolved to be able to see in low light and live in small tunnels. Over the years, we even have developed bioluminescent lichen and moss, phosphorescent fungi, and placed it everywhere to provide some light. Plus, we only go out at night to hunt, fish, trade, and scout. It's believed by many, and I won't deny it, that we have developed extrasensory skills to survive the extermination efforts of various fellow Cozorreans."

The boys soon found out that, despite all their tribulations, the Torgies still found time to enjoy life. They had large tribal gatherings in the voluminous caverns beneath the mighty mountain of Cozorre. They entertained themselves with Celtic bodran skin drums, bone flutes, and beautiful singing enhanced by the walls of the caverns. They cooked lots of seafood stews and enjoyed roasting deer or goats they occasionally caught on the mountaintops. They worked hard but made time to enjoy each other's company and good food.

Zalita explained much of the history and culture of the Torgies to the boys. "We celebrate feats of strength and games of cunning. We have archery contests like skeet shooting. Our targets don't stand still and neither do we!" she said laughing, her musical voice filled with joy. "We enjoy running contests through our maze of tunnels. I won several medals— when I was younger, of course. Most fun of all, though, we celebrate our Polynesian and Basque heritage with dancing! We have over five hundred different dances, each with a chant and a story, all passing on significant truths about our heritage or about practical knowledge. The one I wager you'll enjoy the most is called the Ezpatadantza, the sword dance we inherited from our proud Basque forefathers. We use it to teach all the basic sword moves, using lead-filled wooden swords. It prepares us for when we need to fight in the caves." When she saw the boys' confused looks, she explained: "Swords don't ricochet. Bullets and arrows do."

≡ A Narrow Escape ≡

In the following weeks, Milty and Morty were trained extensively in Torgie martial arts. They especially enjoyed learning to use the yew bows, small ones at first, but they rapidly moved up in size. With hours of daily practice, the boys were soon bursting with muscles in their shoulders and arms. Practicing the sword dance and drills also honed their skills. They were running obstacle courses in the caves and discovered new strength and stamina every day.

Following them everywhere was Hyfee Gibbor, Degel and Zalita's young son. He was born ten years earlier with deformed legs and scooted everywhere using stubby little wooden crutches, but usually he preferred to just use his arms, as his well-calloused knuckles attested. In fact, despite not having the use of his legs, Hyfee actually knew a lot about the proper techniques for using the big yew bow and sword, and he proved to be an excellent marksman with his smaller Mongolian double recurve bow, made of laminated horn his father had found somewhere.

Everybody watched out and cared for Hyfee, but the twins quickly grew especially close to him, sensing his deep need for friends and a purpose in life. They also sympathized with the way he detested being patronized, and their friendship unfolded based on genuine respect.

One day the twins asked if they could venture to the crater and use their new archery skills to bring down a goat or a deer. They had said early on they wanted to join the Torgie Naga, the Striker Force, and wanted to test their mettle. Indeed, their rapid progress in the use of weapons had greatly impressed their instructors, especially Degel Gibbor, but they were told they would have to seek permission from the elders. "I know they look like men to us, but they're only boys," Zalita said, not pleased at all with the idea of letting Milty and Morty go on a solo hunt.

Degel did not disagree with her but had to add his thoughts. "We let boys and girls as young as six learn to navigate our outriggers, and by ten we let them go on some limited hunts and even raids with the Naga."

Zalita stamped her foot and shot a threatening stink-eye glare at Degel and the other leaders. "But these are not Torgie children. They have only been here for four weeks. Although already skilled, they would not be a match for a trained warrior."

Knowing that Degel wouldn't be able to budge Zalita, Widderskins injected his insights. "I think we let them go. They are sons of a great man, a brave man, and they have the right to ask for a rite of passage, a trial of courage, to become men. They are twelve and bigger than any Torgie. You cannot mother them, Zalita," he said softly, knowing Zalita had lost her first child at an early age and that Hyfee was her only other child.

In the end, despite reservations, the leadership council voted to let the boys go as a rite of passage, but they were cautioned to be extremely careful and keep their heads down, as the crater was often surveilled by Cozorrean Apache gunship helicopters. The trek would be limited to the safest possible cave opening, one not used by the Torgies in years and where they never hunted. In addition, they would go during the day, when Torgies never hunted because of their light-sensitive eyes. The council deemed the venture would be as safe as anything on Cozorre could be and a good test of their newly developed stamina and skills. Milty and Morty were elated with the news.

Early the next morning they were off. Zalita fed them a big breakfast and packed them a substantial lunch. They tried not to notice her reddened eyes as they left and did their best to almost elude a motherly hug. The whole camp turned out to watch them go and sang a strange song the boys learned later was a ritual chant for a successful hunt.

As they followed a map to the surface, they heard a strange, scuffling sound behind them. When they stopped, the sound stopped. Finally, when they reached a more dimly lit section, Morty moved ahead, making more sound than usual, while Milty quietly lurked behind, trying to blend into the cave wall. When a small shadow pulled up beside Milty in the dark, he grabbed the form and realized he held a mound of knotted muscle that squirmed and loudly squeaked. He suddenly started to laugh, as Morty ran back to assist him.

"We've caught ourselves a wild and wooly Hyfee!" Milty quipped as he dumped their friend in a scrambled heap. "What are you doing following us? Your dad and mom will skin us alive!"

Hyfee pulled himself up in as dignified a way as he could and searched for his crutches that were scattered somewhere on the dark cave's floor.

"No one ever lets me go up to the crater lip. I'm just useless Hyfee. I want to be a Naga Striker, too." The twins could tell he was near tears and felt horrible for him.

"Hyfee, you're awesome with that recurved bow and far better than us with a sword, but . . . ," Morty said, but he was cut off by Hyfee.

"One of you big brutes could carry me," Hyfee blurted out. "We will be twice as deadly! I can hit any target. You know that! To everybody else I'm just poor Hyfee, the cripple. Only you guys have treated me as somebody who can do something!"

They agreed it was too far to carry Hyfee back to the home cavern. Plus, he insisted they would have to drag him unwillingly all the way. After much consternation, the twins finally decided to take Hyfee to the crater edge, at least, if not actually let him climb up for the hunt.

As they reached the end of the trek, they could see sunlight coming through a cleft in the rock. The boys slowed to a crawl and stealthily poked out their heads. It was amazing how high they had climbed, not having been able to judge progress inside the caves. The fresh air flowed over them, carrying the salty scent of the ocean they could see far below. Terns and frigate birds were circling around and below them, as they eased their way to the cliff edge. There was about another two hundred feet of rock-strewn slope stretching above them and about three thousand feet plunging below into a crater filled with cobalt blue water.

Hyfee was awestruck and gasped in wonder, shading his sensitive eyes as he looked out at the vast expanse. The twins realized he probably had never ventured outside the cave system in his short life. As they turned to speak to him, they realized with a start that he was scrambling along the rock-strewn slope, leaving behind his crutches and the twins. He had his recurve bow strung and hung from his back and was carrying an arrow in his mouth, as he used his powerful arms and knuckles to pull himself from boulder to boulder.

Not knowing what else to do, the twins started after Hyfee. He was actually gaining ground on them, until he arrived at a boulder the size of a large semi-truck that gave him a panoramic view of the mountainside. As the boys breathlessly scurried up beside him, they saw his huge, beaming smile and couldn't bring themselves to chastise him.

"Now we just need a goat to come along!" Hyfee said cheerfully. "The deer don't usually come up this high or at this time of midday anyway, at least that's what my dad says."

The view was even more spectacular there than from the cave mouth. They scanned the mountainside but didn't see anything moving. Cozorre had three peaks, and this was the tallest, so the trio had a commanding view of the mountain and the island, all the way to the mysterious Isle of Predators several miles away. As they gazed in awe at the inspiring sight, Hyfee suddenly took off again, moving further along the slope and further from the cave mouth.

Milty looked back to make sure he could still spot the cave opening, while Morty scrambled over the rocky surface, trying to keep up the agile Hyfee. In his eagerness, and perhaps because his cave-conditioned eyes were not use to such bright sunlight, Hyfee misjudged a boulder's location and stability. Barging into it head first, he started the boulder rolling down the slope, taking him sliding headlong with it. Morty was able to lunge and grab Hyfee by a withered leg just as the boulder went over the ledge with a rumble and a crash, starting a full-scale rockslide that cascaded down the steep slope.

"There goes our chance to surprise a goat," Morty coughed, while struggling to keep his grip on the squirming Hyfee, while at the same time grasping a boulder he hoped would hold the weight of them both. Hyfee was dangling over the precipice, his other useless leg waving with the rest of him in the breeze. Milty thankfully soon arrived, just as the anchor boulder started to shift, and he hauled both boys up and over the edge to safety.

They were all relieved that Milty's work the last few weeks had greatly strengthened his arms, but their relief was short lived. Almost immediately after the rescue, the boys suddenly heard a rumbling whoomp-whoomp of engines and rotors, and they saw two old but functional Apache gunship helicopters roaring up the slope, obviously alerted to their presence by the rockslide Hyfee accidentally started. The boys quickly dove behind another boulder, just as bullets from the Apache's chain gun smashed into it and into another slab just ahead of them. They were showered with sharp splinters and dust was thrown everywhere, at least obscuring the gunner's vision for a few split seconds. The boys realized with paralyzing fear they were pinned down with nowhere to go. They knew even old Apaches had excellent targeting systems and sensors. The twins looked at each other in dismay. Hyfee cringed as another salvo pinged and clanged into the rocks around them. Fortunately, these Apaches were using chain guns and not Hellfire missiles. That was small consolation, and they feared they would soon be shot full of holes.

Then the fusillade momentarily stopped, probably so the pilot could assess if they were dead. Within seconds, both twins let out a puff of air, notched arrows, nodded to each other, and bolted to their feet, quickly releasing their obsidian-tipped hunting arrows at the closest Apache copter, only fifty feet out. The startled pilot's face froze in panic as he jerked back on the controls, but one arrow entered the engine compartment while the other one slammed into his arm, causing the craft to spin away, tumbling out of control.

Fortunately for the boys, the helicopter spun right into the firing zone of the second gunship that was a little further out. This gave the boys another second or two to duck below their rock and pluck another arrow from their quivers to prepare for another shot. Just as they did that, they heard a thunderous whoosh from behind them and a Stinger anti-aircraft missile slammed into the remaining Apache, blowing it from the sky in a ball of flames.

Degel Gibbor hustled over with the still-smoking, man-portable Stinger missile launcher on his shoulder and grabbed up Hyfee, quickly motioning for the twins to follow him. Without another word, they hustled back to the cave just as more Cozorrean copters came thundering in. They dove into the cave as a Cozorrean missile and several chain-gun bursts slammed into the cave opening, showering them with more rocks and debris. They tumbled down the entrance, banging into each other, and ended up in a tangle of bows and boys with Degel on top, shielding them from any ricochets.

Then all was quiet. Degel let out a great sigh of relief and scanned the boys for injuries. Other than a few bruises and some rock chips in their hair, they were unhurt. He looked at them again, shaking his head, and said to Hyfee, "Whatever you do, don't tell your mom!"

It ended up they didn't need to. Word of the clash and the demise of two armed Apache gunships circulated rapidly among the amazed Torgies, as they secretly listened in and picked up the news blaring from Cozorrean Air Defense speakers. The Cozorreans soon realized the two bigger individuals in the clash were not Torgies but the escaped twins. The commander was actually relieved they hadn't killed them, because Nithing was quite adamant that was to be done solely at his pleasure and by no one else.

When they returned to the cavern, Zalita greeted them with hugs and great sobs of joy, and then she ruined the whole victorious return by grabbing Hyfee by the ear and dragging him off for a scolding and probably something else. She also informed Degel he was next when she finished with Hyfee!

The elders were stunned. They had sent the boys to the safest possible opening, unused for years, at the best time of day, and supposedly miles from any usual Cozorrean patrols. They hadn't thought about the possibility of heightened patrols looking for the twins. When they realized Hyfee was missing, Degel immediately assumed he was tagging along with the unsuspecting boys and lit out for the cave entrance, fortunately tugging with him a precious, heavy, man-portable Stinger and arriving just in time. When telling the saga, Degel was quick to add the details of the twins' extraordinary bravery: Not only had they shot down the copter with obsidian hunting arrows, but they also had saved his son, not once but twice. The Torgies broke out in a great celebration! Two new great warriors were now part of the Torgie Naga! A new song and dance would be added to the Torgie corpus, and the story would live for years.

As the days with the Torgies went on, Milty and Morty were introduced to Issachar, the Torgie Wisdom Lender. Because of the poor lighting, the Torgies didn't do too much reading, so almost all their long history was relayed through chants, dances, and, mostly, stories.

Issachar was close to ninety years old, he couldn't see much, and his dancing days were over, but his voice was still strong as he told the boys more about the origins of the Torgies. He proudly relayed they were descendants of the ancient navigators who first peopled the Pacific and then went on to South America. Over sixty-five thousand years ago, he told them, the Denisovans had been pushed off the lands of Australia and Indonesia by the encroaching Cro-Magnon people. The Denisovans had gone out to the Flores Islands and lived with the peaceful Floresiensis people, the so-called Hobbit people, another ancient relative of Homo Sapiens. When the Cro-Magnons eventually came there, over five thousand years ago, they launched out in outrigger canoes and spread to various islands in the Pacific. They were called the Lapita people then and made beautiful pottery with elaborate designs. "Our boats were even more magnificent and still are," Issachar added, in his deep, gravelly voice, "as you will see in a little while. But even as we spread into the Pacific, the Cro-Magnons kept expanding and hunting us.

We could live with them for a while, teaching them our pottery skills, how to make weapons, and especially how to construct our outriggers, even adopting a few of the big people into our tribe, but then they would envy us and chase us out again or try to enslave us. Eventually, some of us ended up here on Cozorre, some on Foondavi, and a few all the way up on Hawaii. We were called the 'little people.'"

"Here we were able to bore into the mountains, creating our incredible maze of caverns and tunnels, and hide from the inevitable wave of big people. When the Basque and Welsh miners wanted to escape slavery, we took them in. Over the last three hundred years, we have created the Torgie Nation you see around you. We have Basque and Polynesian dances and stories, Welsh songs and yew bows, and the Denisovan and Floresiensis will to survive. But one of our greatest treasures are our canoes. We call them wakas. We will show you those tomorrow."

Before Milty and Morty could learn about the canoes, the Torgie leaders wanted to talk to them. They asked the boys if they were having nightmares about the Cozorrean pilot they shot down. The boys looked at each other and started to tear up, but they managed to control themselves. They admitted they were having trouble sleeping, seeing the pilot's panicked face just before they shot him. They both couldn't sleep the prior night, and they shared how they felt, knowing the pilot was probably somebody's dad, father, and husband. Then they took turns being sick to their stomachs.

The Torgie leaders listened with compassion. Degel Gibbor led the discussion that followed. "You have nothing to be ashamed of. It's natural to have confusing and bad feelings like that. We would be worried if you didn't. It's the burden of the warrior, the ones who protect the innocents so they can sleep soundly at night. The vast majority of people have built-in safeguards against killing other people. Only psychopaths don't feel anything. That's why military leaders have to desensitize young warriors and dehumanize their enemies. If we thought there was any chance you would have gone into combat, we would have had this discussion before you left to prepare you."

The boys were greatly relieved but still concerned. "Will we ever forget his face, the look in his eyes?" Milty asked.

"No," Degel answered honestly. "We all still remember our first kill, and everyone after that. That's our burden, our warrior's sacrifice, for our people." He shook his head sadly.

"But we also know it's necessary to protect our loved ones," Degel continued. "You saved the life of our precious one, Hyfee. I saved yours in return. The pilot was going to kill you. The Great Star Maker and Source of All Things knows our hearts and minds. He knows the heart and mind of that pilot. He will forgive you and give you peace. What you did was righteous. The Torgie Naga only fight in self-defense and to protect our people. It is not a joyful thing to take another life, but it is sometimes necessary."

The discussion carried on long into the night. After that the twins had a good night's sleep. That was a very good thing, because the next day proved to be another grueling day they would long remember.

≡ Torgie Lessons ≡

The next day, Milty and Morty were introduced to the pride and joy of the Torgies, their outrigger canoes or wakas. Led by Degel, they descended from the main cavern down a torturous, winding stairway and came out into another cavern, this one smelling of seaweed and the saltiness of the open sea. As their eyes adjusted to the dim lighting, they saw a small harbor bobbing with craft of all sizes, with some hauled up on shore and being repaired by Torgie craftsmen. Older men and women were busy weaving and repairing what looked like sails. Most of the canoes were small, rugged, and patched together with odds and ends of boards and logs, with plaited sails made of various fibers. Everything was ingeniously stitched and lashed together with cords using braided sennit made of dried coconut fiber that looked like binder twine. Everything about the construction demonstrated cleverness, thrift, and the necessity of carefully using scarce materials. Later, upon closer inspection, one of the twins counted over fifty pieces of irregularly shaped wood carefully stitched together, like a crossword puzzle or a quilt, to make one small canoe, all the seams carefully plugged with what looked like turtle shells, to keep out the ocean water.

They were told later that almost every piece of wood had a story detailing some great heroic venture by a Torgie crew

173

member. Every scrap was repurposed. They were sailing in living history. A small platform was built on top of cross-beams that connected the main hull with the outrigger. The craft were steered with two long steering paddles fashioned from logs, usually one larger one at the end and another on the side, although some only had one steering paddle. Everything smelled like salt and fish—and excitement to the boys. They could hardly wait to launch into the surf.

Along with numerous smaller craft were three larger ones. Because Cozorre was deforested long ago, big logs were hard to come by, so the Torgies only built a few of the bigger canoes called "pahi tepukei." These were constructed of larger, hollowed-out coconut palm logs attached, unlike most Polynesian larger canoes, by cross beams to outriggers or balance spars, which added more stability and an extra fishing platform. The boys were told this was where the crew could sit when not actively paddling or sailing. The larger craft used two masts, with much larger woven sails maneuvered by large amounts of woven cordage. These larger craft also had a small enclosure where provisions could be protected from the soaking sea and Torgie sailors could rest and try to protect their light-sensitive eyes and pale skin from the scorching mid-day sun on long ventures.

Both types of craft used woven, fiber-plaited sails shaped like crab claws. One Torgie named Tia Palu, a master navigator, noted that the design allowed the sails to best catch the wind. To make his point, Tia cupped his hands as if catching the wind himself. He patiently explained that they sailed and rowed the smaller patchwork outrigger canoes out of carefully concealed sea caves for night-time fishing around the reef. They didn't need to be as sturdy as the deep-sea craft; instead, they were designed to be flexible. "Don't be fooled, though," Tia admonished them. "They only look flimsy," he said, pointing out that the smaller craft are lovingly lashed and knit together by the Torgie elders, male and female—and they do so knowing their children ride the waves in them! Tia went on to explain that the Torgies used the larger, double-hulled outrigger canoes to sail long distance to clandestine rendezvous at sea to get needed supplies. They are too clumsy for fishing, he said, but very suitable for longer trips or carrying cargo. "Over the years and right under the eyes and noses of the Cozorrean tyrants, we've smuggled jewelry, gold, silver, and pottery out and other essential stuff in, like Stingers and stuff," he added with a twinkle in his eye.

The boys wanted to jump in and take off, to hit the surf right away.

"Slow down, boys!" said Tia, smiling at their eagerness. "We only go out at night, or else we become target practice for the Cozorreans. Also, our wakas, after our children, are our most precious possessions. A lot of training is necessary just to depart the caves. I understand you're quick learners, so maybe you can pass my test in a few weeks." Hearing the groans from the boys, he continued. "I might be convinced to go with you earlier, because you did save the worthless butt of my incorrigible nephew, Hyfee."

"Yes!" the boys enthusiastically responded. "What do we have to learn?"

What followed was an in-depth discussion of Polynesian sailing and navigating. The twins proved to be apt students, absorbing the intricate details of the processes with their astoundingly quick minds. Tia first explained that no modern technology was used or even needed.

"Our ancestors learned to make their way over open seas to distant lands that are just a pinprick in the vast ocean. Sometimes what they learned was by accident. Maybe they were blown by a storm to a new location, but more often they observed and followed annual migrating birds such as the long-tailed cuckoo. Sometimes they followed drifting flotsam such as seaweed or logs. Over the years they learned to read the stars, the sun, the currents, and the swells of the waves to detect where land is. Many of our chants you're learning are literally star maps." Tia indicated different patterns on some pottery jars he kept in the training center and told them those were star maps, too. He also showed the boys a stick chart: Different-sized shells designated various islands and reefs, and precisely arranged sticks indicated currents. "We watch when the stars come up at night and follow them until they reach a certain height. Then we switch to another star. Some star maps are for distant places and feature up to nine different stars that we're following. In addition, during the day, we follow the sun and the prevailing wind. We watch for long-ranging birds such as boobies and frigate birds; we can determine the direction of land from their behavior, because they feed early in the morning and return to roost at the end of the day. When we get closer to land, we watch for birds such as dark-bodied noddies, and other types of terns, that can lead us to islands. We say bird sight is twice as good as land sight, meaning we can detect land far better by watching the birds than by trying to see a speck of land."

"Avian aeria reconnaissance," Milty summarized. "What if it gets cloudy and there are no birds?" he astutely asked.

"The weather is usually clear when we choose to voyage," Tia answered. "When we get out on the ocean, though, I'll show you how to read ocean swells to detect islands. It's a difficult art to master, but I believe you two bright lads might be able to do it. Also, we can look over the side and read ocean phosphorescence. We call it 'sea lightning,' as it flashes under the surface. You can find your destination if you know what to look for! Also, the color of the water subtly changes when you're over a deep reef. We teach all this with the star map chants and indicate it with the shells on the stick map."

"Can you still get lost?" Morty asked.

"Definitely. But master navigators seldom do on purpose."

"On purpose?" Milty inquired.

Tia paused and looked somber. "Some navigators, when they get old and feel useless, maybe they've gone blind and deaf, will prepare successors, take a small and worthless outrigger, and head out to sea, looking for some far land beyond the horizon."

The boys eagerly soaked up the navigator's lore. They practiced in what Tia called a "stone canoe," sitting in an upturned, hollowed out rock off to the side of the sea cavern. They pretended to follow star maps etched on the wall and stick charts he handed them, answering his questions. Most of Tia's questions concerned an eight-hundred-mile-long open-sea voyage to Foondavi. Tia told them that Issachar, the Wisdom Lender who was still teaching them chants and dances, and Tovaki Rata Tepukay, the Way Finder, a famous blind Torgie navigator known for his deep knowledge of the sea, wanted to sail to Foondavi as they once did when young. Perhaps the twins could help crew the craft, if they continued to learn from Tia. A long voyage and being able to visit their mom and friends on Foondavi—that really motivated them, and they redoubled their efforts to prove themselves worthy.

The twins also continued to work out each day, practicing with sword and bow. Under the amazed guidance of Degel, they grew stronger and more agile. After sword and bow practice, they huddled with Tia to learn even more about navigation. They swam in the sea cave to refresh themselves after each exhausting day and made friends with several dolphins that frolicked with the Torgies. Tia said the friendly mammals kept the sea cave free of dangerous underwater predators in exchange for fish. Top-of-the-water predators were kept out of the sea cave by a cleverly designed rock gate, camouflaged to look like a regular rock wall, but the gate could be raised and lowered to allow Torgies to access the sea. Torgie marksmen with Stingers and bows also were assigned at all times of the day and night to watch the entrance. Tia told them there were four other such hidden sea caves on the island, but this was the furthest from Cozorrean prying eyes and should be the safest.

Yo, Ho, Ho!
═ Off to Sea We Go! ═

If the already-anxious Rey even knew half of what was going on with his boys, he would have immediately gone and tried to retrieve them—which is exactly why the twins neglected to fill him in on all the details. TMI! Too much information! They didn't want old Dad to worry. After all, they were having the time of their life.

Soon Milty and Morty were deemed ready to go to sea. Their first trip would be a short night-fishing jaunt out beyond the reef. The small, flimsy-looking, patched-together outrigger canoe bounced on the water as they climbed aboard with Tia. They were surrounded by several other similar small wakas waiting to shoot out the gate once it was lifted. At a signal from Tia, the camouflaged door opened. Ahead, everyone could see moonlight dancing on the ocean and the spray of the surf hitting the reef. The twins quickly paddled the small craft through the opening, and Tia lifted the crab-claw-shaped fiber sail the Torgies called a *te la*. With the wind quickly filling the sail, they darted into the night. It was a thrilling ride.

This would just be a short trip out through the surf through a small opening in the reef only the Torgies knew about. The major outlets were patrolled by Cozorrean speed boats outfitted with fifty-caliber machine guns that would shred the Torgies' tiny boat to pieces, but well-placed bribes and threats kept the crews looking the other way, if they did have to be out. Fortunately, it was dark and the Cozorreans didn't really like to be out at night, so the fleet of small darting boats went undetected, and soon all were fishing with their nets out. The boys could see Torgies quietly slipping into the water from some other canoes. Tia explained in a hushed voice that some of the Torgies' major food sources were the shellfish they collected in traps and the various reef fish they caught in the nets. The work was to be done quietly and quickly, while the Cozorrean patrols were absent or looked the other way.

After they filled the woven containers they brought along for storage, Tia guided the boat out of the reef and into the open ocean while most of the other canoes slipped back into the cave. Tia pointed out the stars and asked the boys to tell him which direction various islands or atolls were. They knew Foondavi's guiding star and soon detected it on the horizon, pointing it out to Tia. Then, reciting the memorized star-path chant, they told Tia each star they would follow as it arose and set in the night sky. Tia then pointed out the phosphorescence in the water. He also reviewed with them how to follow a course by ocean swells, especially if they ran into overcast weather.

The rest of the exciting night was spent taking turns changing directions and adjusting the sails, basically learning under Tia's guidance the signals they would need to follow when on the open sea. Long before the sun was coming up, they dashed back through the surf, over the barely detectable opening in the reef, through the cave mouth, and into the safety of the sea cave. Tia signaled the guard, and the camouflaged door came down. It was an exhilarating night! They carried the fish up to the main cavern and fell into a deep sleep.

Milty and Morty accompanied Tia on many more nights and continued to apply the navigation lessons he taught them. Their already-strong arms and shoulders, from archery practice, now responded to the pull of the sails, and their hands grew calloused from the cordage they pulled to control the sails. Morty was perhaps stronger by a bit, but Milty proved to be a natural at sensing the breeze and currents and making the adjustments to get the best speed while keeping a straight course by following the stars.

After two weeks of practice, Tia told them it was time for the big test. They would pack up provisions and prepare for a fourteen-day voyage to Foondavi. It was sailing season, and the prevailing winds and currents should help them get there. He would be along to observe, as would the old, blind navigator, and the Wisdom Lender. But the big, double-hulled canoe, officially called the *pahi tepukay*, simply named the "big ship" in Torgie talk, would be under their guidance! Hyfee listened in awe. He was only allowed to go out a few times on the smaller wakas; his lack of legs created a disadvantage when it came to balancing and climbing in the small canoes.

The next day the crew loaded pounds of prepared taro, numerous eating and drinking coconuts, and several slabs of baked fish wrapped in leaves. Zalita gave them stacks of flat bread and a mess of precooked, fermented breadfruit. They also brought numerous gourds of fresh water on board. Eventually, the little waterproof shelter on the canoe was stuffed, leaving just a little room for the crew to sleep and shelter during the day. Tia told them they would also fish on the way, trolling for tuna or whatever open-ocean fish they could catch. They were told to put some sand in a large bowl and place it on the deck on top of a specially designed coral-and-rock platform that kept the bowl steady, even in big swells. It would be used for cooking their meals. Tia said, if they steered correctly, there would be a few uninhabited atolls along the way where they could stop for water and more coconuts, and maybe some bird eggs or a turtle or two, if they were lucky. There also were three large turtle shells mounted on the top of the shelter to catch any rainwater that ran off the sail, if they were fortunate enough to encounter a squall.

They were especially careful to pack the Foondavi stick chart in a safe location and squirreled away a precious, beautifully decorated Lapita gourd Zalita had made that showed the star path they were to take to Foondavi.

Despite the exhausting work of loading the pahi tepukay that afternoon, the twins could barely sleep in anticipation of the voyage. Perhaps it was their grogginess that caused them not to notice Hyfee slipping out of the rock shelter where they all slept. As the sun began to set, they clambered on board the large canoe with Tia, joining Issachar and To-vaki Rata Tepukay, the blind navigator. Tia motioned to the gate guard, and, as the gate opened, the assembled crew of the Torgie fishing wakas sang the beautiful voyagers' song.

The pahi tepukay was heavy and initially hard to paddle, but the twins and Tia soon managed to get it going smoothly. When it left the cave and hit the wind, the two sails bulged and the big craft literally leapt out of the water, surging ahead. Tia guided them over the small opening in the reef, barely clearing both sides. Once in the open ocean, he turned over the steering and sails to the twins. "Okay, young mariners, show us your stuff!" Tia shouted above the sound of the crashing surf.

Milty took over the large steering paddle and directed Morty in hauling up and adjusting the sails to maximize the wind and set them on their course. He then lined up the first rising star with his mast and the bow of the boat and concentrated on the slow-wheeling stars as they followed their nightly trajectory across the "roof of heaven," as Tia called it. He knew the star path was a series of stars that rise during the night, and he must direct the boat to each one, making exact adjustments for the currents and wind. He also watched the rolling swells passing rank by rank on the surface. They were joined by a shoal of playful, leaping dolphins, some they could identify as their friends from the sea cave, out to see them off.

Later, a group of whales swam by, and both Tovaki and Issachar sang out to them. Surprisingly, they seemed to hear and swam close to the boat. Their huge forms caused some trepidation in the boys, but the blind navigator and Wisdom Lender assured them the whales were peaceful creatures.

"Now, if they were sperm whales or orcas, we might have reacted differently," Tovaki told them. Issachar was constantly chanting and telling stories through the night, and occasionally Tovaki would sing a star chant.

While basically too clumsy to use for reef fishing, the double-hulled canoe was perfect for gliding gracefully through the rolling waves. The night passed by quickly, and Milty was proud to see his canoe was perfectly aligned with the morning star on his star path as the sun came up. Tia used some shells with pin holes punched in them as goggles to protect his eyes and showed Milty how to navigate using the rising sun for direction. He explained again that, because the stars were invisible half the time, this is when you must use the sun, clouds, and the swells, and, in some cases, birds to find and keep your way.

"Tovaki will now explain the swells to you," Tia said, gesturing to the blind navigator who greeted Milty and Morty with a mostly toothless grin.

"Lie down here on the deck with me," the old navigator encouraged the boys. "Relax and feel the swells as they roll under us. It is definitely more a matter of feel than sight. The swells are not like the wind; they are permanent. There are usually four or five different types of swells. The ones from islands a long way off are slower and longer in wave length. Swells from nearby islands are shorter, faster, and steeper. Just relax and feel the swells in your stomach and man parts."

The boys ignored the bit about man parts, but definitely could feel the difference. They could soon identify different swells as they rolled in and under the canoe. It was like the ocean was alive and talking to Milty. Morty, on the other hand, didn't want to feel the swells, especially in his man parts, as he laughingly recounted later. He would rather climb the ropes and pull on and tighten any bindings he thought were loose.

Otherwise, he would fish, and he did add some fresh meat to their supply, happily cooking up a mess of fish for the crew to eat before retiring from the rising sun.

"Smells great," a small, creaky voice said from behind them, referring to the fish. "I'm starving. Missed my breakfast, having to sneak down early to get on board." The group just stared in shock as Hyfee slowly climbed out of the storage shelter. Tia looked as if he would have a stroke. Issachar just shook his head, while the blind navigator didn't even bother to pay attention; he was still focusing on the swells, with a deep smile on his face.

"You don't stow away on a voyage, you little . . . !" Tia, was so frustrated he couldn't think of something suitably derogatory to call his nephew, who was hauling himself along the deck toward the cooking fish, while yawning.

"Well, throw me overboard, Uncle Tia. I want to go to Foondavi with my friends. Because you didn't invite me, I invited myself!" Before the surprised Morty could stop him, Hyfee grabbed a sizzling piece of fish from the pan, burnt his fingers as a reward for his thievery, and began juggling the hot morsel hand to hand.

"Maybe we can use him for fish bait?" Milty said laughing, as Hyfee clumsily juggled the hot fish. "But, no, Hyfee's too stinky for that! What do you normally do with stowaways?" Milty asked the angry Tia, who was fuming at his nephew's audacious antics.

"Throw them overboard," Tia said, grabbing the startled Hyfee and dunking him head first in the cold ocean. He let him stay submerged for a few seconds and then brought the spluttering boy up and not so delicately plunked him on the deck.

" I should hang you from the sail until you dry out, you, you . . . !" Again his vocabulary failed him. "This is not a game. Open-sea sailing like this is dangerous. We only have so much food and water." With that Tia stalked off as far as he could go on the relatively small vessel. He was still steaming mad and muttering new vocabulary words he knew Hyfee would use if he could hear him.

"Uncle Tia is ticked," said Hyfee in a major understatement of the day. "Everybody treats me like I'm useless," Hyfee whined, but he soon noticed he didn't get any sympathy.

"You are on this vessel," said the old navigator quietly. "Why don't you come down here beside me? Maybe I can teach you how to feel the ocean swells."

"In your man parts," Morty said, smiling to the confused Hyfee.

"In my what?" Hyfee asked.

"Just ignore Morty, and listen to Tovaki," said Milty. "I can use somebody to watch the swells and look for birds. You can do that, right? And Morty can use someone to clean the fish he catches. This is definitely not a pleasure cruise. We are too far out to take you back against the wind, so, again, your sneaking got you what you wanted. Let's hope it turns out better than the last time you snuck out after us."

Milty did have to smile as he watched the still-soggy Hyfee sit down beside the old navigator and try to feel the swells. When they later moved into the shelter to protect themselves from the sun, Hyfee was able to wedge his way back far enough to not be a problem. He soon proved adept at fishing and even swinging from the ropes with his tremendous arm strength.

After a few days and nights of sailing, Milty announced he thought they were coming up on an atoll. He pointed out a change in the water phosphorescence and in the swells. Then they saw a few birds that nested on land. He pointed to the stick chart and could see a small shell indicating an atoll straight ahead. Tia beamed with pride. They were right on course. Soon a small atoll appeared; they saw a sunken mountaintop and a reef fringed with a few coconut palms. They circled the atoll and soon found a small opening, just large enough for them to shoot through among the breaking waves. On shore, Tia showed them how to dig a small hole that filled with heavier salt water on the bottom but fresh water on top. He explained that, later in the season, the fresh water would be all gone, but for now they could drink their fill and replenish their on-board stores. They also found more coconuts and, best of all, caught a large sea turtle swimming in the shallow waters. They had turtle soup that night and rested on shore before taking off the next morning.

It was a beautiful dawn. They were still on course, according to their stick chart and stars. Morty and Hyfee were up in the sails making some adjustments. Tia was yawning while the old navigator and Issachar were preparing to go into the hut to sleep. Suddenly, the canoe was jolted, knocking the two old guys to the deck and nearly knocking Tia off his feet. Milty was hanging onto the steering paddle, so he didn't lose his balance, but Hyfee was just letting go of one rope to swing to another, and the sharp jolt knocked him loose and into the ocean.

A large brown shark with wing-like pectoral and dorsal

fins had smashed into the hull, probably thinking it could jar a resting turtle or something loose to eat from what it probably thought was a floating log. Sure enough, it was rewarded with a big splash. Several other accompanying sharks came barreling in to start a feeding frenzy. Without a thought, Morty leapt from the spar to the deck, quickly grabbed a sharpened fish spear, then jumped out to the outrigger and into the water, landing on a big shark that was heading toward the screaming and flailing Hyfee. Morty landed with a thud on the thick brown back just ahead of the dorsal fin and rammed the spear into the shark's eye. He then jumped again, landing in the water next to the panicking Hyfee. As more of the sharks circled, Morty rammed the sharpened spear into another dark shape, Milty and Tia both cranked the steering paddles, and somehow they swung the big, double-hulled canoe over to the boys. Tia hung over the hull and pulled them both up and onto the canoe, just as a lunging set of dagger-filled jaws clamped down on Hyfee's soggy shorts, just missing his dangling, useless legs. Morty and Hyfee splattered on the deck and stayed there, exhausted and drained from the near disaster and the huge adrenalin rush.

"How did you do that?" Tia asked Morty, amazed by the flurry of action. "In all my years of sailing, I've never seen or heard of such a thing. You literally flew from the mast, danced across the outrigger and onto a shark, and then fought off some of the biggest white-tip sharks I have ever seen. They're relatively slow moving for a shark, but they're very aggressive and extremely curious. Experienced sailors consider them the most dangerous sharks in the deep ocean, by far, even more than white pointers, or, as you call them, great white sharks.

Amazing, just amazing!" he repeated, still shaking his head.

Tia then slapped the stunned Hyfee on the back, causing him to belch out a large volume of salt water. "You're one lucky little sea snot, to have a friend like this man," he said, pointing at Morty. Then he looked up and bellowed at the sky. "I name him Taku Mano Dantza." In a lower voice, he explained, "Taku for the Tongan shark god Taku Aka, Mano for our Torgie name for shark, and Dantza, for our Basque-derived name for dancing. What do you think, Issachar?"

"I am still stunned and, for the first time in my life, speechless," the old Wisdom Lender said. "What a story this will make! What a chant! The Mighty Shark Dancer!"

"I am also stunned," said Tovaki, the navigator. "Two miracles. Issachar speechless and young Morty dancing over the ocean on the backs of sharks. My only regret is not seeing it." He paused. "Ah, but I can hear the sharks murmuring about it, though, and soon the whole ocean will know," he said, cupping his hand to his ear as if listening. "Yes, they agree. Taku Mano Dantza."

Morty just moaned and hugged the still-shivering Hyfee. Morty's right arm was scraped by the rough skin of the shark, and he was starting to grasp what he had done, as the sudden adrenalin rush was wearing off. "You're lucky that shark didn't get your little man parts," he said, grinning at the still-scared Hyfee.

Tia then shouted and pointed at the sea frothing a short distance away. The other sharks were in a feeding frenzy, tearing into the big shark Morty had skewered in the eye as well as a couple of other injured monsters he had stabbed or were injured in the feeding frenzy. Tia grabbed a boat hook and threw it out, snagging what remained of the shredded, big carcass and drawing it near the canoe. The other sharks were content to avoid the dangerous craft and, instead, ravage the remaining wounded beasts, filling the water with blood and gore as the canoe drifted away. Tia took an adze, and, with the help of Milty using a saw, they hacked and sawed the huge shark head off what remained of the carcass. They tugged the massive jaws up on the deck and then did two things: First, Tia hacked off meat for shark soup, explaining that white tips were often hunted for delicious food. Secondly, he separated the jaws and their razor sharp teeth. "The teeth will make a necklace for Morty to commemorate his feat of courage."

The rest of the voyage to Foondavi went smoothly. Milty amazed Tia and the old navigator with his ability to read the stars and sense the ocean, never swerving off course, even with a few gusty days. He could spot undersea reefs and read the phosphorescence and the swells almost as good as the two seasoned sailors. He brought them right to the reef at Foondavi without a hitch and proudly steered the pahi tepukay into the landing at Troon, much to the amazement of his Uncle Jon, the infamous Monvale of Troon. As they entered the quiet waters, Tia bellowed again to the sky, pointing at the proud Milty. "I call him Tepu Kupe Juragan." He then explained to him: "It doesn't translate directly into English, but it means 'wave master.' It's the highest honor a navigator can receive. Right, Tovaki?"

"I agree. He reads the waves and listens to the ocean. It usually takes years of training, but the Source of All Things has blessed him with great skill!"

The Foondavians were excited to hear about the exploits of the twins. Prissy nearly fainted and said, "Don't tell your father!"

Their Uncle Jon could only marvel at them and the stories the excited Torgies told. "I knew it would all work out! Wait until Carlyle hears about this!"

When the word got back to Rey, he felt like strangling the smiling Jake.

"Safe?" Rey said, barely controlling his anger. "They're shooting down Apache helicopters, dancing on sharks, and sailing eight hundred open-ocean miles across the shark-filled Pacific from Cozorre to Foondavi—and you call that safe!"

Fortunately, it was a phone conversation or Jake was sure he would have been assaulted by the irate Rey. All he could say was, "It sounds like your boys! Rowdy little rascals! Robust and resourceful, I would call them! The Foondavians are having a special Napoa—you know the Foondavian naming ceremony—and the boys are being named Shark Dancer and Wave Master. You should be excited you allowed them to receive such an honor! The Torgies even have asked if they can borrow the Foondavian honor "Nambo" to give the boys."

Rey spluttered on the other end of the call. Jake cut off the call as Rey began making some creative threats against Jake's body that would have made Achor Nithing blush. Jake was glad the twins were safe, but he worried this might jeopardize the trap they were setting for Achor Nithing. If Achor knew the boys were out and about, he would know they were setting him up when the Torgies offered to ransom the twins. The Hadron surveillance team would have to monitor Nithing closely and find out if he heard the news or not. At least Foondavi was as off the grid as you get, so there was a good chance word hadn't gotten out.

After the celebrations on Foondavi, and lots of hugs from Mom and checking in with friends, the boys headed back to Cozorre with replenished supplies and the rest of the Torgie crew. Despite their dad's understandable misgivings, the boys were thriving and learning skills that would soon come in handy. They were growing muscles on muscles and absorbing the Torgie Naga warrior code. They would soon make their father very proud.

The Tale
= of Torgie Loo =

On Cozorre, everybody knew the myth of Torgie Loo. Most knew it was based in fact, on reality, not a myth. In the olden days, Torgie Loo was a real person, an ancient Basque crone who claimed she possessed the "finder sense." Whenever the treacherous and poorly maintained Cozorrean deep mines caved in, she was called by the miners' families to rescue the trapped miners. Tap, tap, tap. "Here they are," she would proclaim, and a rescue team would dig out the endangered miners before they would suffocate. But that was many years ago. Did Torgie Loo still exist?

In current day, Cozorreans often portray Torgie Loo as a witch to scare their children. They warn, "If you don't behave, Torgie Loo will pop out of the walls and take you!" Indeed, some children have been snatched, although, in reality, from abusive, horrible parents. Nonetheless, Cozorreans reinvented the myth yet again. Some were claiming Torgie Loo rescued the twins, snatched them out of the deep dungeon. People who knew the Torgie Loo was real were not surprised; she often helped people facing difficulties, they said. For example, during hard times, Torgie Loo was known to drop off food to starving families. Sometimes she even supposedly left money and precious jewels to help people in distress.

Cozorrean authorities claimed everything about Torgie Loo was just a rumor, a children's myth. But Fugelman Batullion, the newly appointed commander of Cozorre, knew better. A letter mysteriously appeared in his secure, locked safe inside his locked office, informing him that Torgie Loo was aware he was stealing from the dreaded Achor Nithing. The letter listed exact numbers, the people involved, and dates. The note also detailed a proposed deal: Unless he wanted his deep secrets revealed, he was to dutifully pass on to Achor that the twins were being held in the Torgie mines and, most importantly, that the Torgies would happily keep the twins until Achor paid a handsome ransom.

The scheme really had been masterminded by the Hadron Group, not Torgie Loo, but Batullion didn't know that. The Hadron Group even had deceptively arranged for the Torgie mole, Wadge Wollebo, to stealthily observe the "hapless, wailing urchins, held in chains in the deepest caverns," and document their deplorable condition by digital camera. Batullion would receive the video and was ordered to forward the "evidence" to Achor. The boys greatly enjoyed playing their parts!

Murderous Moles
and Traitorous Torgies,
≡ Oh, My! ≡

Achor Nithing was not thriving, he was seething. "How did those little rascals get out of that deep Cozorrean dungeon? I've been there. I tried my hardest to escape and could do nothing. They must have inside help. I want all the guards that were on duty tortured! Wring out all the information you can, and then kill them."

The fifth Cozorrean commander in five years to fill the hazardous position, Batullion was relieved he was talking over the Internet, so Achor couldn't reach out and strangle him, too. "It's like they disappeared, sir. The locals claim it was a mystical being called the Torgie Loo, but we believe a primitive cave-dwelling group called the Torgies somehow infiltrated the prison. Maybe they tunneled in, though we saw no signs of a tunnel." Seeing Achor's frowning look of doubt, he hurried on. "Being brand new here, I thought the Torgies and Torgie Loo were some mythological monsters made up to scare the superstitious locals, but I've been assured they are real. They live inside the mountains in old mining works. So I sent several strike forces to see if I could roust them, or at least soften them up so we could negotiate a return of your hostages." Batullion then shook his head in dismay. "Let me say, the strike didn't turn out very well."

Seeing Achor still looked suspicious, he continued: "We sent multiple Apache attack copters into the craters, and they got shot down by Torgie archers, of all things. Lost them all! It was like a turkey shoot with obsidian- and titanium-tipped arrows piercing the armor and bodies. The rest of the copters hovering at higher altitude were shot down by shoulder-mounted anti-aircraft Stinger missiles I presume the Torgies previously stole from us! We finally dropped a MOAB, a mother of all bombs, on the crater. The Torgies just dug back out. They're like damn moles with murderous weapons! So I got really angry, hiked in a bunch of my men, and dropped gas into the vents we could see. Believe it or not, the gas came back out all around us, and I lost more troops! We would have to destroy the whole blasted island to hurt them."

"Don't tempt me," Achor growled. "I want those twins, alive!"

"Sir, may I ask why you hate the boys so much?"

Achor answered with loathing dripping from every word: "I do not hate the little guys. I actually respect the resilient, resourceful rascals. I just want to capture them, and maybe torture them, because Rey Newly loves them, and so does Jake Quark. It's called leverage, my man."

Achor paused to contemplate. "Maybe we should try to be subtler," he suggested. "Ask the locals if there's a Torgie open to bribery. Offer a big reward for information on where the twins are being held. Or offer death and dismemberment, I don't care. It's your choice and your career. Just find me a turncoat Torgie and get me the information. We can't let some primitive, stone-age cavemen thwart our efforts, can we?" he said with a snarling smile that sent shivers up Batullion's back.

Batullion grinned, realizing he had an opening for the "good news."

"Your plan about being subtle occurred to me, too, sir. I did some research on these Torgies and the Torgie Loo myth. Fortunately, even among the illusive Torgies there are some twisted individuals. Wadge Wollebo is a Torgie collaborator I discovered in my research. He helped some former Cozorrean gangsters in the past. He considers himself more than equal to all the Torgie leaders, especially their Naga Striker Force leader, Degel Gibbor. To make a long story short, Wollebo was able to sneak in and record the boys whining and crying in their new dungeon, and he learned that the greedy Torgies want a huge ransom to free them."

Achor was pleased at this sign of initiative by Batullion, and even more pleased to hear about the twins crying in a dark dungeon. Achor was happy to let them sit—especially given the ridiculous sum of money the treacherous cave dwellers wanted for the ransom. It was the big blue guy he wanted, and now he thought he was set to snag him. Once the midterm elections were settled, he would agree to meet with Rey at the Isle of Predators, pretending to agree to ransom the boys. It would be a victorious return for Achor. The game was getting exciting. He was getting closer to clinching a win. Torgie Loo, what a scam! You can't out-scam a master scammer, he thought cheerfully.

As Carlyle, Jake, and Rey continued to strategize extrication plans for the twins, they had guardedly watched Camilla. She finally won their trust by discovering and sharing the identity of the Torgie mole, Wadge Wollebo. Once the Torgies confirmed this, the Hadron Group used Wollebo to help bait the trap. In addition, the Cozorreans didn't realize their communications were being hacked. They were also unaware that the twins earlier had slipped a message to the outside through another willing accomplice open to a suitable bribe but also terrifyingly aware the Torgie Loo would get him if he let anyone know.

So the trap was set. It might take a few weeks or longer to entice the busy Achor, but the team were sure Achor would bite on the bait!

Adoring Amazon
═ Assassins ═

Rey was greatly relieved at seeing the report and happily returned to the Muckytuck clan knowing his boys were back safely with the Torgies on Cozorre. He definitely delighted in rejoining the feisty trio of Muckytucks, this time outside Tekona, Michigan, beside the upper Nottaway Creek.

After a thankfully uneventful ride in the deceptively beat-up but super-outfitted pickup—with the accompanying brother trash talk, this time entered into by Rey—Machseh, Moose, and Moogy left the truck by the farmhouse on Hidden Lake. They walked through the escape tunnel Rey used earlier and then started their trek through Machpelah. During the walk, they gave Rey a surprising update on several recent intruders into the Muckytuck realm. "Oh, and another thing," Machseh said, halting their progress along the trail. "You can't stay here long this time, because your previous visit attracted several dangerous intruders—five, to be exact."

Seeing Rey's startled expression, he continued with details. "The first two were definitely nasty NAP agents. I'm sure NAP was initially intrigued by our tussle with the Predator drones, and they wanted to know who we were smuggling in. Secondly, with all the fireworks as you made your escape, they couldn't stay away. A bear ate the first one, finding him to be a little too gristly for his refined tastes. The second was charged by a wood bison and reduced to marsh jelly, becoming an unwelcome addition to our forest biomass according to the trees. The other three were females. I don't know if it was gender discrimination, but the Ancient Forest seemed to treat them a little more gently."

Seeing Rey was not going to interrupt, he went on. "The first was later identified as Paula Pipestone. A misguided relative of yours, I believe? A past paramour, perhaps? At least she claims so. She was finding it hard to talk wrapped up in liana vines and hanging like a pretty piñata from a tree over a snake-infested, quicksand pit. I believe that one could kill with her eyes, if you stared at her," he laughed ruefully.

"One of our young gentlemen said she was definitely hit with a beauty stick. He claimed he was admiring her brains and persistence, but I noticed he wasn't looking at her face. I told him, if she got loose, she would beat him to death with an ugly stick, not that he needed it." Machseh sighed, at the uncouthness of youth.

"I have to admit she was quite delectable hanging there upside down, ready to be plucked from the tree like a delicious apple," Machseh said, with a gleam in his eye.

Rey could envision the beautiful spitfire completely hog-tied, frustrated, and snarling at her captors. She would have been more like a poisoned sour apple, he mused.

"The second one was squalling about being an important politician's daughter—another great admirer of yours, it seems," Machseh continued. "It's hard to squall when all that was above the ground was her yapping head, but she managed. Somehow she claimed a tree branch swiped her into another well-placed pool of quicksand, but then the tree inexplicably extended a limb to keep her from sucking her last sand until we could get there. Can you believe that? Jacqueline Boguiden, I believe?"

"That would be her," Rey agreed. "Both equally deadly. Both wanting to kill me for some reason. It seems the list is getting quite long."

"Well, I wish you would keep your adorable Amazonian assassin admirers out of our peaceful piece of Terra," Machseh sniffed. Rey could tell from his sly smirk he actually enjoyed the encounters with the raging beauties.

"You said there were five," Rey queried. "That's four—not that that it isn't more than enough. Who's the last one?"

"Well, the fifth is intriguing. Onza Flink, by name." Seeing a baffled look on Rey's face, he continued. "Instead of stealthily slinking around like the others, this woman loudly announced she was here to see you—something about wanting to kill Achor Nithing for you. The trees just politely enclosed her in a pleasant glen, keeping away the gourmet bear and the ornery bison until we could enter. What a pleasant, if apparently dangerous, lady. I swear she must be part Muckytuck!"

Machseh had his usual mischievous gleam back in his eye.

"We're letting them all cool off for a while, letting their ardor for you die down a bit, under the calming influence of the Ancient Forest. We told each of the ladies that, once they got their estrogen under control, we would let them have an audience with you."

"Oh, the estrogen comment must have gone over grandly," Rey said, shaking his head and smiling. "Yah, I'm sure the ladies would have liked that!"

"They did perk up a bit, hissing at me, although Onza only smiled. I might keep her," Machseh added with a big grin, "if she has a mind to, you know, explore the forest," the old guy added shyly with a slight blush.

Then Machseh hesitated. "Do you think these ladies are psychopaths?"

"Women can definitely be psychopaths. I think the two here I know might be pseudo-psychopaths, not born-psychopaths like Achor. Something in their past has warped them somewhat. They definitely have been desensitized and can kill people without qualm, although I think they only kill bad people and other psychopaths who cross them." Seeing Machseh's nod of understanding, Rey continued. "You've heard of Zara, the stunningly beautiful lady who posed as Twila McBlue when I was running? She's a reformed psychopath. Again, only kills bad people. I don't know Onza, but I would imagine she fits the same pattern."

"She definitely could be a Muckytuck Shield Maiden, for sure!" Machseh said with a mischievous smile.

"I agree it makes sense to let the first two stew in their juices for a while—like you so adroitly put it, letting their estrogen subside. As to Onza, I'll talk to Jake and see if he says she's okay. I think I now recognize that name. If I'm right, she's done a lot of work for Jake in the past, and she's definitely not harmless. So behave yourself, and keep your estrogen comments under control!"

Two days later, Rey separately interviewed Paula and Jacqueline, not knowing if they were aware of each other's presence. It was soon obvious they were not. Paula blatantly tried to appeal to Rey's old interest in her. It was a little challenging to rouse his testosterone though, as she was still covered in leaves and forest debris and didn't have access to a shower for a few days. Rey had ordered the poor treatment, knowing one so given to narcissism would be more apt to be rattled by not looking her best. Once her attempt at flirting failed, she reverted to her normal, fire-snorting self.

"Achor wants me to kill you. Everyone else he tells to spare you, reserving your torture and death for him, but he says I alone can have first dibs, as long as he can see pictures of the bloody cadaver."

"Charming arrangement, Paula. To what do I owe such ire from you?" Actually Rey had a pretty good idea. Paula was his wife's sister and had been his original first love way back in high school. Her father, the incorrigible capitalist G. T. Pipestone, had sidetracked the relationship, thinking Rey unfit for a Pipestone. Rey had ended up marrying the younger sister Priscilla instead, something he now knew was a great thing.

"You messed up my perfect arrangement with the Nithings," she hissed. "I was sure they were the strong horse I could literally ride to prominence. My dad, old GT Pipestone himself, was going to rule in finance, and I was to rule in Hollywood and fashion. You and your escape, then later your stupid blue-stuff stunt, screwed it all up! Now old GT stroked out on me, leaving that detestable Joshua Preston to run the Pipestone empire."

"I would say I'm sorry I ruined your dreams," Rey said, trying to sound consoling, "but I understand your buddy Achor is trying to make a comeback." Noticing the evil gleam in her eyes at the mention of the notorious Nithing,

203

he added, "Maybe your strong horse is still available to ride!"

How he ever could have loved and lusted after such a person he wondered, then Rey looked at her again. Paula Pipestone, even in her current disheveled state, was still a rare beauty, with flashing jade green eyes and moves like a jaguar—and twice as deadly, he quickly reminded himself. Her raven black hair was usually always in a carefully designed tumble around her heart-shaped face, but now it was tangled and full of twigs. With her long, shapely legs and svelte body, she was still hyper sexy. He reluctantly admitted she was still a very impressive, if not an intensely angry, woman. Of course, he consoled himself, he was much younger back then and blinded by her beauty. She, too, was younger and much more innocent in those days, if still a malicious manipulator who used Rey and then left him once he was deemed useless for her plans of advancement. She was definitely a chip off the old G. T. Pipestone block, while his sweet Prissy was much more like her gentle and loving mom, Theta Pipestone.

"You could have had me, you stupid dolt. We could have dominated DC together. Then you rejected me for my silly little sister, Prissy," she venomously spat out her sister's name.

Rey just shook his head. He realized trying to convince her of her jumbled history timeline wouldn't work. Needless to say, Rey got nowhere in trying to convince Paula to change her viewpoints. Machseh said they could turn her loose in a more remote part of Machpelah, letting her wander and becoming acquainted with the bears, bison, and other denizens of the deep forest. Rey decided that wouldn't be very considerate for the poor, innocent animals or the forest. In the end, he let her stew in her own smelly juices for a few more days, then he told the Muckytuck to blindfold her and dump her in the state capitol about eighty miles north, a place swarming with psychopaths and assorted other pole-cats who could deal with her. So she could defend herself, Rey told them to leave her with an unloaded pistol and some ammo, but then the Muckytucks were to get away as rapidly as possible before she could get the gun loaded.

As the Muckytucks left the forest with Paula, she tried patting her tangled mane into place and rearranging her torn clothing. Despite the filth and debris still clinging to her, somehow she still looked rather alluring. But Rey didn't have to warn her escorts about her nasty nature; they were happy to see her long gone and inflicted on the politicians in the capitol.

Jacqueline Boguiden was a different story. Also interest-ing, but in a severe way, she snarled at Rey when the Mucky-tuck guards brought her to him for questioning. She even had headbutted one of the poor, unsuspecting guards who were escorting her to the interview. Another one she at-tempted to bite, before he dumped her in front of Rey.

"If you promise not to bite or headbutt anyone, I'll at least remove the gag so we can talk," Rey told her.

She just fixed her blazing eyes on him with an intensely angry gaze. Rey got up to leave, and she quickly mumbled something. He turned to look at her, and she shook her head yes. He took this to mean remove the gag, so he carefully ap-proached her, like she was a poisonous snake ready to strike, and slipped the gag from her mouth.

"Thank you," she politely said in a gentle voice, surprising Rey.

Rey stared at her intently. "I don't understand you or Paula Pipestone. I don't think you know this, but she was here, too, sent by Achor Nithing to kill me. I sort of understand her motivations: greed, envy, and poisoned pride. You, I don't understand. I had nothing to do with destroying your dad's political ambitions. I was manipulated as much as he was. You should be gunning for Achor Nithing, the true villain in the story."

He was shocked when she nodded in agreement. "I understand that now," she said in a subdued voice. "I didn't come here to kill you. I would have been nicer to your guys, but I don't take lightly being manhandled, trussed, and tossed into a cell."

Rey nodded his head. "Fair enough. If any of the guys acted inappropriately, I'll have them disciplined. The trussing and tossed in the cell part are both my fault, as you were not exactly invited in—trespassing, I believe it's called—and you didn't seem to appreciate the mud bath the forest arranged for you," he added, barely avoiding a smile.

She beamed one at him instead. Quite a surprisingly beguiling smile from a razor-haired, muscular-bodied lady. She had an aquiline face, one which resembled an eagle with her narrow but long nose and the way she held her head. He decided, as he silently apprised her, yes, a regal appearance would be a better description. He wondered why so many beautiful women usually wanted to kill him—with Zara being the exception, at least most of the time. "I realize the error of my ways," she said. "Actually, your guys initially did their job well and not inappropriately. You should caution them, though, to be much warier of us feminine types, as their comment about estrogen levels made me decide to seek retribution, and they seemed to let down their guard after I smiled a bit."

"I think you did an adequate job of instructing them," Rey admitted, smiling back, "at least if black eyes and broken noses are a sign of learning." He paused and looked at her intently. "So, what's the purpose of your visit?" Before she could answer, he decided to take a chance and provide another bit of information. "Do you know Onza Flink is here, too?"

She couldn't hide her surprise. "Onza Flink, the notorious bounty hunter?"

"The same. I haven't had a chance to talk with her yet, but she trespassed in, let's say, a friendlier and less suspicious fashion, and she's been treated quite hospitably by the locals in response. As a matter of a fact, she's been exploring the forest with an old rascal named Machseh, who seems to like you dangerous types." He then quickly added, "Please forgive the old fart for his estrogen comment. I'm sure it was meant in a scientific and not sexist way."

She snorted at that. "Well, if he'll forgive my trespassing, I can forgive his trespasses, to use a biblical term. Now, if you can untie me, on my word to do no harm, I want to talk to you about going after Achor Nithing. Maybe Onza Flink and I can team up? I think I could learn a lot from her."

Once he untied her, she walked a short distance from him, disrobed, and walked into the nearby Nottaway Creek, giving Rey an enticing glimpse of her lithe form as she washed the grime from her body. Rey diverted his eyes as she ascended from the pool and put back on her clothes.

"I hope I didn't scare any of your fish," she added with a devilish smile, seeing his embarrassed blue face. "I know you're committed to your lovely wife, and I'm over my Nambo McBlue fetish, so I'm not trying anything. My focus is entirely on getting Achor Nithing. He's prodigiously marshalling his forces to come after you. Once these midterm elections are finished, his sole focus will be getting you." Seeing Rey nodding in agreement, she continued. "I believe the trite but true statement that the best defense is a good offense. Maybe Onza and I can keep him off balance and occupied enough that you can survive his attacks."

"Well, let's rescue Onza from her walk in the woods with old Machseh and see what she thinks about the plan."

He inquired about the whereabouts of the old chief and set out for a meadow located by a small pond not too distant from the main camp.

Rey recognized immediately that Onza Flink was one impressive woman. He knew some things about her, especially after asking Jake about her when he learned she was one of the five uninvited visitors. Onza was named for a mythical cougar of Mexican origin. Her last name of Flink is Norse, for "clever genius." Indeed, she was a clever genius as a bounty hunter and a child finder. Jake had told him she was after Achor Nithing but had no idea why she was in the Machpelah forest wanting to talk to him.

She was described by many as ferocious and funny, but she said she preferred "devastatingly but deceptively clever."

"It's better not to attract attention in my line of work," she explained modestly.

Onza was a long-time friend of Jake Quark. She helped him find missing people over the years, often for a substantial fee but sometimes just for the moral satisfaction. Rey knew all this when he stared into her unwavering, anthracite-black eyes with heavy-etched, wedge-shaped eyebrows looking like they were welded on. Her short hair was steel grey, and he realized she might be plain to the eyes and average in physical attributes, but there was definitely great depth to her. She possessed an angular blade of a body, all sharp edges. No softness anywhere. Chiseled cheekbones that looked like they could cut diamonds. Long everywhere, arms and fingers, even her eyes seemed elongated, much larger than normal. "Better to see you with, my dear," she was reputed to often say to people before knifing or shooting them.

Onza did have a few well-known idiosyncrasies. For example, she claimed she always preferred hunting handsome men or beautiful women. In her opinion, handsome and beautiful ones were always the worst, because they were used to being the center of attention. They believed beauty conferred on them certain divine rights. "It just makes me want to kill them more! Slower maybe, but more. Now Crazy Jake Quark, there's a man so ugly he is handsome!" she was heard to comment.

"So, this is the great Rey Nambo McBlue?" Onza questioned, with a sparkle in her eye. "Machseh here has been informing me about your feats of daring do, while enticing me to enjoy the pleasures of the Ancient Forest. A most refreshing dip in the Nottaway being not the least. Enough of pleasure. Time for business. And who is this most interesting accomplice you have walking with you?"

Without any hesitation, Jacqueline stepped forward. "Jacqueline Boguiden, at your service. I've heard so much about you, and I think we share a common goal, beyond that of swatting this pest, Machseh." Machseh backed off at the threatening tone of her voice. He waved at Rey as he suddenly walked away, deciding he was urgently needed somewhere else in the forest.

"I've heard of your impressive military skill set from Rey's great friend and admirer Jake Quark," Onza said, intently observing Jacqueline. "But I thought we were on opposite sides of this nasty little fracas. I'm here to offer Rey my assistance, not assist him into his next life."

Rey could sense her guarded hostility and noticed her hand drift slightly to one of many pockets on her light jacket. It was rumored she was called Onza of a Hundred Knives, all of them sharp, as many a former felon discovered too late. To her credit, Jacqueline sensed the move and quickly raised her open hands into the air.

"I'm unarmed," Jacqueline said, carefully keeping her arms raised. "I came here to offer my assistance to Nambo McBlue, too. It took me a while, too long I'm sorry to admit, to see through the charade put on by the psychopaths and Achor Nithing, in particular. My love for my parents blinded me. My dad never saw, or maybe refused to see, what they were doing with him. I wanted to avenge my father's humiliation and, I'm sorry to say, stupidly decided to wipe out the Blue Monster, as I referred to him," she said, while wanly smiling at Rey. "I was wrong. I've watched the True

Blue Revolution unfold, observed the Dangerous Church doing great things, and realized I want to commit myself to the cause. My skill set, like yours, runs toward more violent solutions, not peaceful ones. I would be honored if we could team up, with you in charge, of course. I believe you could teach me much and perhaps help me temper my more aggressive urges."

Soon the two lionesses, as Rey later described them, were busy scheming the savage demise of Achor Nithing. Rey arranged for some of the Muckytuck to transport them closer to Achor's primary stomping grounds, the DC swamp, where he arranged with some distant cousins of Machseh to hide them from the prying eyes of the NAP enemy, until they could arrange a hit on the hated Nithing.

Once free of all of his adoring Amazon assassins, as Machseh insisted on calling them, Rey could focus on the looming battle. First, though, at the behest of both Jake and Machseh, he was to observe the Blues being trained.

The Few,
≡ the Brave, the Blue ≡

After another strenuous and winding walk through the Ancient Forest, Machseh guided Rey toward an opening in the dense timber and stopped for a second to let Rey catch his breath. Machseh was excited about the progress of the Blues and appeared to have some scheme up his sleeve. "You've waited long enough! I want to show you what we're doing!"

Machseh was obviously in a hurry to get to the training site, but Rey halted the jabbering Machseh because he was excited about something, too. "I have news!" Rey announced.

"What?" the momentarily silenced Machseh asked, with a perplexed look on his face, wanting to get on their way.

"When I arrived a few days ago, the trees, the Ancient Forest, they immediately greeted me!" Rey shared excitedly. "It was like I had entered a big game."

"I noticed your momentary stumble but just assumed it was your usual clumsy, city-boy entrance," Machseh laughed. "Of course, they welcomed you! They actually like you, for some reason!"

Rey continued, ignoring Machseh's jibe. "The feeling was almost overwhelming. I didn't hear words, per se. It was more like a slow, rumbling sound that distinctly welcomed me, making my skin tingle and the hairs on my arms stand up! I also sensed light around me and even smelled that I was welcome, as strange as that sounds. Each day I'm here, the communication—or whatever it is—grows more and more intense. I feel like I can actually sense the Ancient Forest breathing, growing, and watching over me. I guess the Blue Goo has reawakened my pineal gland and other forgotten senses, or whatever mumbo jumbo the psychologists use to explain how the Blue Goo works."

Machseh smiled, seeing Rey's obvious pleasure. "Or, the warm embrace could have been there all along and you just took the time to relax, slow down, and really listen. The trees shared with me they thought you just might become a good one. They said, once you figure out where your brain really is, they might share about theirs—assuming you continue to take time to listen!"

"What did they mean by that?" Rey asked curiously.

"Figure it out and you'll be illuminated, believe me! Now let's go see these marvelous Blues of yours I've been holding off waiting to show you!"

Machseh again hustled off and Rey hurried to keep up. After another brisk walk, they came to a clearing in the majestic trees and Rey saw a beautiful blue woman waving at him. Rey didn't think he'd met her but she looked familiar. She was very tall, trim, and athletic, her blue face framed with a lustrous honey-brown mane. Her smile was breathtaking, almost matching Zara's in wattage.

"My name's Verity Soubrette Sewell. I'm the youngest daughter of Sedgewick Sewell, former President of the United States. Just call me Verity. I'm so honored to meet you, Nambo McBlue. We call you Blue Prime or Alpha

Blue—the first to take the Blue! I worked at the Reservation for the Temporarily Bewildered with Jake and my dad when I was younger and briefly met you there. When Jake Quark decided Machpelah would be a good place for training the Blues, he, as usual, made a brilliant decision. I volunteered for the job, being the tenth person to take the Blue," she added proudly. "Let me walk you around."

As they walked toward a group of five Blues waiting in a line, she spoke in an authoritative voice. "For the new Blues, proper orientation is key. They need to learn to accept the gifts that the Blue Goo, the greatly modified ayahuasca, unlocks and bestows, and that needs to happen in a safe place, far from NAP's prying eyes, where they can't hurt themselves. As Jake says, we're building 'solutionaries' and 'evangineers' to change and rebuild our cities and culture."

"Jake is quite honest in admitting his team didn't originally intend to find a truth-telling drug. Instead, he charged his team with finding a way to enhance the natural process of neural plasticity and expand epigenetics so humans could tap into the ninety percent of brain they weren't using! He thought maybe it would just be a minor tweak, a gradual, small improvement. But they stumbled onto a formulation that causes a complete, almost instantaneous rewiring of the brain. It spurs the rapid development of more neural fibers and neural connections—almost as fast as human newborns experience once they first open their eyes." Verity shook her head in wonder.

"It's an exciting time for all of us concerned with discovering human potential! With new brain-scanning techniques, we can get a look inside the skull and see how the brain works. We can actually witness neural plasticity in action as the brain makes these new neural connections, watch the impact of epigenetics as culture co-evolves with our brains, and discover how to tap into that ninety percent of the brain we aren't using! We're now looking at even more new ways to completely rewire the brain and create even more neural fibers and neural connections. We have no idea yet what full human brain potential even looks like!"

"We already knew the brain is a living, changing tissue, constantly rewiring itself in response to experience. The Blue Goo just puts the process into hyperdrive. It helps us understand the patterns that undergird the universe. It appears it creates a natural neural lace inside the brain, heightening senses and enhancing neural connections. It helps you see connections you never saw before. I think it opens up access to the quantum Cloud."

"Inside a normal brain, the left side handles the literal meaning of words, while the right side is engaged in more non-verbal, subtle activities such as sensing situations and reading emotions, deciphering tone of voice, or detecting micro-expressions. Some even say the right side of the brain facilitates extrasensory perception, although most people block this out or consider the skill intuition or gut instinct. We're even seeing some Blues develop a harm sense, or proximity sense, similar to the shark's Ampullae of Lorenzini that pick up electrical stimuli. Other Blues seem capable of controlling time, at least slowing it down or speeding up their own reactions—we're not sure."

Super excited, Verity went on. "This sudden acquisition of new abilities is called, 'acquired sudden savantism'—

compared to autistic savants or even brain-injury-induced savantism that researchers have studied. The Blue Goo seems to be releasing the hidden locks that have kept us from our potential."

"So we train the new Blues here—on how to discover and use their new brain capacity—and how to live with the reality of always telling the truth. We help them not be overwhelmed by suddenly exaggerated impressions from the world around them. Too much outside stimuli, too soon, could cause panic or paranoia. You were an amazing first Blue, with a strong mind and a clear cause, and against the odds you survived. Jake and his team learned a lot, thanks to you."

"Our new theory is that the Blue Goo creates a natural neural lace inside the brain similar to a brain-computer interface (BCI) but without a visible computer, seemingly tapping into a quantum space storehouse of information. As we both experienced firsthand, we first users found we could see connections and patterns we never saw before. Suddenly, music, math, and more made sense to us as never before! We experienced abilities with no previous training, like playing professional-level music or understanding doctoral-level mathematics."

"Why does the drug enhance the brain so much?" Verity continued, caught up in her own enthusiasm about the Blue Goo. "Let me give the short version, and, although I'm not a neurologist, I think it's pretty accurate. The drug's effects are definitely linked to truth telling. Because humans started out as small, slow, fangless scavengers, a major part of our brain was heavily devoted to deception. Lying, deceiving, and seduction were vital to survival, even among fellow humans as pecking orders were developed. If you weren't the strongest, you'd better be the most cunning and deceptive if you wanted to eat or breed. Once we take the Blue and cannot lie, the huge percentage of our brain devoted to deception is useless, so our healthy neurons are immediately repurposed. Also, much of the normal human brain appears to be made up of useless elements of the genome known as 'junk DNA' or 'dormant DNA,' but somehow the Blue Goo unlocks and engages these normally inactive elements and stimulates this part of the epigenome, called microglial enhancers. In short, the Blue Goo supercharges the brain."

"Most of us Blues experience acquired, or sudden savantism, doubling our intelligence level, as indicated by standardized tests. Mind you, not everybody gets the same gifts. The effects seem to enhance what you were interested in before you were given the stuff. For example, nurses and doctors who've taken the Blue Goo now have tremendous diagnostic and healing abilities. An amateur musician as a Blue can now compose and play like a master. Rey, you always loved to observe nature, so now you can communicate on a deep level with the Ancient Forest."

"And we aren't just limited to one gift! Some, like you Rey, were multi-talented, and we believe you're beginning to develop an ability to read people's personalities. Me, I was an amateur singer, but now I would be able to sing in the best choirs if I chose to. I also can sense when people are frustrated and help them learn. I guess you can say I'm a 'maximizer,' bringing out the best in people."

She said this while smiling humbly with a twinkle in her eye. Then she eyed Machseh and gave him a gentle poke in the ribs.

"If old Machseh here took the Blue, who knows what he could do?" she said, easily evading a return jab.

"I'm the most honest man I have ever known, except for a real Blue, like Rey or you, Verity. I have to be devious to survive. But if I were fifty years younger and thought I had a chance to be with you, Verity, I would turn blue faster than a cheetah can chase an antelope."

Verity straightened up to her full height and just stared the old flirt down with a flinty glare. "Do you really want me to tell you what I think of that comment? And remember, if I lie, I die, so I will cut you no slack."

Machseh just shrank back and put his head down. "So sorry, Verity. I think I hear somebody calling me over there," and he scrambled off.

"I'm glad he didn't challenge me," she chuckled after Machseh left. "I actually think he is kind of cute for an old duffer." Then she picked right up as if nothing happened, gesturing at the Blues waiting patiently.

"So, we train the new Blues here on how to discover and use their new brain capacity. The one challenge we all share, as you well know, is how to live with the reality of always having to tell the truth, no matter what. We also help the Blues not be overwhelmed by suddenly exaggerated impressions from the world around them. We stay with them and ease them into their new world as they discover their gift area. As I said, you were an amazing first Blue, Rey, surviving, almost like a miracle, with no one to help you and no one knowing exactly what you would face. I was blessed with Anu Pokritos and a few others who helped me come out of the daze and make it through the first few confusing days."

She paused and exhaled a long sigh. "Our big problem right now is 'Bluistas' or pretenders. They find ways to look blue but are definitely not the real thing. We say they're 'bludelusional or a wanna-be-Blue' but without paying the price. Also, it's now somewhat cool to be Blue, and they're using that popularity to take advantage of people and create scandals. We're sure some are even encouraged by NAP to make us real Blues look bad."

She shook her head in discouragement. "When we train 'New Blues,' to prevent them from accidentally killing themselves, we bring them here or to other Muckytuck locations. What they experience here we call post-traumatic growth (PTG)—when your shocked, delusional brain discovers you can no longer lie and it has to adjust to the new, painful reality. There is nowhere to hide from yourself. We try to prepare the New Blues beforehand. As you know, though, the reality is hard to explain until you actually experience it. Will Rogers once said, 'The worst thing that happens to you may be the best thing for you if you don't let it get the best of you.'"

"Let's face it, people prefer to lie, whether consciously or unconsciously. Researchers believe that, even among the best of us, ninety-five percent of our conscious brain power is tied up in protecting our self-image, deluding ourselves or deluding others. Lying uses up and occupies the left brain— the site of our logical, sequential thinking and language— and keeps the right brain excluded. We have a fantastic brain, billions of neurons making over a hundred trillion connections. But it's only a 13-watt brain with lying sucking up the wattage! We're not able to tap into the dormant capacity, including a lot of dormant biographical or genetic-based ancient memory. The Blue Goo unexpectedly lets us tap into this, helping us see the underlying rules of math, music, the universe, and other things. Seemingly overnight, we become savants and are able to see how words, numbers, sounds—everything—is interwoven in unique ways. Our sensory system opens to messages now going unheeded because our current sensory system misses them. For example, you're finally hearing the subsonic speech of the Ancient Forest and experiencing different wave lengths of sound, light, and even smells beyond normal human perception."

"It's one thing when people lie to you. That happens all the time and is bad enough, but it's another thing when you can't lie back to them. That creates real problems! You can be an artful dodger, just don't misstep, or, bam, you're dead. I misstated that. Bam! You fall down, and then the painful death sequence starts."

Rey couldn't help but think of Zara and how, at first, she often tested and tormented him with tough questions he would rather not answer. Then his thoughts went to his wife of twenty-two years, and how he was able to stare into her eyes and tell her he loved her deeply, and she knew if he lied he died. There were definitely many dimensions to not being able to lie!

Verity didn't seem to notice that Rey's mind momentarily drifted.

"Believe me," she said, "as you know, it gives you a great reverence for the truth and nothing but the truth! In short, once lying is gone, it frees up your brain and latent talents emerge—sudden savantism! Hidden talents emerge you never knew you possessed."

Machseh was back, quickly over his embarrassment, and jumped in. "We're now faced with the concept of super-gifted people! It's happened before, when people were under duress. Like when the Apache people were facing extinction, an eighty-year-old Apache savant named Nana the Goose claimed he could travel long distance in no time and evade the enemy, which he did against all odds. Lozen, the sister of the great Apache Chief Victorio, was said to have an enemy sense or harm sense; she could tell where his enemies were coming from and, thus, was able to help him escape harm numerous times. He finally was captured, but only because she was absent helping other tribal members deliver children and couldn't warn him. People used to laugh and call that superstition, but now we know it was real. We have some Blues come through here who can control weather to a degree, others heal, and, best of all, some can create a sense of peace among angry people. Some have what ancients called sword sense; they can see moves before they're taken, almost freezing time, then evading or engaging like a blur. Some are mind readers; some think these savants just might be ultra-sensitive to micro-expressions, but I believe they can truly read mind waves. All this is way beyond computer or machine intelligence! Quantum space is accessible! I believe we all have such potential! The Blue Goo just helps access our untapped 'factory-installed' mental software."

Verity smiled at Machseh. "Think what you could do, if you took the Blue. You are so full of hot air you could probably levitate with little training!"

Machseh laughed and pointed his thumb at her while looking at Rey. "I love it. She must have taken her spunky pills this morning. I think she must be part Muckytuck!"

"But we have some challenges," Machseh continued. "We know NAP suspects what we're doing here. It's why we have Blues like Verity testing people before any further training to make sure evil people aren't taking the Blue and getting super powers."

Rey was stunned by the thought. "How would they keep from lying. I mean deviousness is one of their strong suits."

Verity nodded her head in agreement with Rey. "Yes, I've heard Achor loudly brag that he is the most audacious and terrific liar you'll ever see in your life."

Rey admitted to himself he heard several such boasts from the man. But then nodding sagely, he continued. "On the other hand, he seldom needs to lie, if you really think about it. He just tells the brutal truth and doesn't see a need to deceive very many. He likes to hurt people. I could see him being Blue for a little while, at least. It wouldn't be pleasant for anyone else, but he would probably enjoy it."

"Well," Verity said, "it's another reason why we send them here to the Muckytuck for further observation and training. Besides being a safe and secure place where they can come to grips with their new mental power and super senses, it's also a place where they can be closely observed by us and the Ancient Forest. After all, the best way to know someone is to see how they treat everyone around them, not just their betters or equals."

She paused and now pointed to the five New Blues patiently waiting in line, listening to the conversation. "It's also why we waited a while to bring you here. One of my gifts is being a discerner of strengths in other people. I told Jake and Machseh that I believe, with a little time in the Ancient Forest and getting in touch with your mind, you could possibly sense character traits, the true nature of people. Look deep inside hearts and examine motives. I can see strengths but not character. What I want you to do is shake the hand of each Blue here and tell me what you sense."

Rey looked at the line of blue faces and could see a small amount of trepidation in each one. He suddenly reached out and shook Verity's hand first. He was stunned to immediately see her face morph into what looked like an otter, and then quickly into an owl. When he shared this astonishing vision with her, she was exhilarated!

"The owl represents wisdom and discernment, and the otter, well, my middle name is Soubrette, given to me by my mother. In French, it means a lively, flirtatious performer! That's what I really love to do, sing and perform, and it enables me to harmlessly flirt! I'm an owl and an otter, no doubt!"

Then she turned to the line. "Now, please shake hands with each of our recruits."

As Rey went down the line, he was shocked each time as the person's face quickly turned into an animal in appearance. He quickly recognized each of them looking similar to the totems the Muckytuck used for their clans. The first young man turned into a rabbit in facial traits; when Rey shared this, haltingly, Verity and the young man eagerly agreed that he was exceptional at making things grow and understanding biology. He had already contributed several concepts to the astonished Muckytuck hosts, no sluggards at biological science. He could sit in their gardens for hours communing with the plants. The second in line was a young woman whose face changed in appearance into an owl, similar to Verity, and then quickly morphed into a fox. Again, Verity excitedly explained that the woman, like Verity, was a strong discerner of strengths, especially in the financial area; she also was very crafty with investments. The third man's face morphed into a beaver as their hands met, and his calloused hands confirmed without words that he was a master carpenter and builder, already demonstrating amazing skills at designing and building structures for Machpelah. As Rey reached out and made momentary contact with the fourth man in line, he was shocked to see a weasel face appear, and then he stumbled as the shape changed into what appeared out of blackness to be a wolf with slathering fangs. Rey jumped back and was relieved to see both Verity and Machseh holding firearms aimed at the startled young man.

The young man was as shaken as Rey.

"We were suspicious. We think Deegan doesn't know he has psychopathic tendencies. He obviously hasn't lied to us, or he would be dead. But he hasn't always treated people well. Something was off. We would have warned you, but we wanted a fair and unbiased assessment. That's why we had you wait, so we could make some preliminary assessments on each one."

As the stunned young man was led off by a couple of Muckytuck who obviously were waiting for such an eventuality, Rey felt a great sadness. "What will happen to him?"

"He'll be taken somewhere and isolated," Verity answered. "Jake's people will treat him in a civil fashion, but he can't be turned loose with the new mental powers the Blue Goo has released in him. We can send him to Foondavi to train with the reformed psychopaths. Maybe Hadron can find a way to reverse the process or else use him in other constructive ways. Who knows?"

As Rey turned to the last person in line, both of them were a little hesitant to shake hands. Finally, the young lady reached out, and Rey was relieved to see another otter, similar to Verity, winking back at him. As he released her hand, her face went back to its normal look, but with a great smile of relief breaking across it as she looked into Rey's eyes. She was not shocked when Rey told her that she already had been an accomplished musician and dancer before taking the Blue, but now she was dramatically improving every day and was able to pick up any instrument and immediately start playing it at a master level.

After they let the remaining four Blues return to their training, Rey turned to Verity and Machseh and scratched his head. "Why was I not able to do that before? Astonishing! It might have helped me in DC!"

"You would have been overwhelmed by all the hideous beasts you would have seen," Machseh laughed. He suddenly grabbed Rey's hand, and Machseh's face turned into a wolf, and then slid into an owl.

"Wolf and owl. A warrior and a strategist," Rey said, not at all surprised.

Verity then clasped Rey's hand in her warm, blue grip and smiled. "An eagle appears before me," she said in awe. "I could sense your leadership before, but now I see great vision and courage." She paused again. "I didn't have this ability before, so I think I am borrowing it from you. There is so much we don't understand about how the Blue Goo works."

Machseh chirped up, smiling at Verity. "You can hold my hand!"

"Don't need to," she quipped with a wicked smile. "I can see the wolf just fine!"

They all walked off a way to discuss these strange events in more detail. Verity started the discussion. "When it's fully developed, we think the new savantism brought on by the Blue Goo will give us humans mental and spiritual powers way beyond purely mechanical beings known as Robosapiens, or even just genetically altered humans. It appears we Blues can tap into the universal quantum Cloud, put there by the Great Star Maker, and read the DNA of the universe. Maybe one day we can even figure out how to do it without taking the Blue Goo, so savantism can be accessible to everyone."

Machseh was the most excited about Rey's new gift. "Our ancient ones used to talk about that kind of gift. They would pray over our youth when they were eleven or so and then, depending on what they saw, they would put them into the proper clan. That is why we have the Beaver, the Wolf, the Rabbit, the Otter, and so on."

Rey thought about Paula for a second and a picture of a black jaguar slinking through the underbrush came to him. Then he pictured Achor, and an overwhelming, pervasive sense of darkness and evil nearly knocked him off his feet. He staggered and Machseh caught him, while Verity gasped at his obvious distress.

"I guess I don't need to shake hands once I know some-one," Rey said in a shaken voice, explaining he had just thought of Achor Nithing. He immediately thought of Pris-sy and the picture of a gentle dove floated in front of his face, although there was a strong impression of even more being there. Now he was smiling. "I guess I better just think of good people!"

Verity dismissed the remaining Blues and then asked for a little more time with Rey. Speaking in a sad tone, Verity said, "In the past, people were often persecuted for telling the truth. It says in the Gospel, in John 8:32, 'You will know the truth, and the truth will set you free.' But sometimes the truth is a booger, to be a little crude. It's hard to handle, and we spend a lot of time training our new Blues on being dip-lomatic but also straightforward, balanced communicators. The key is telling the truth in love, as it says in Ephesians 4:15. We find always having to tell the truth brings out what Machseh and Jake call the H-factors: Honest, because you can't lie. Humble, as you realize what you have been given. Helpful, because you realize with great strength comes great responsibility to help others. Hungry, as in hungry to learn, as you recognize how fast your mind is growing and all you can learn to do. Ultimately, happy, as all pretense is gone."

Rey couldn't disagree with her. "It's too bad in a way we couldn't just stay here. But the battle is out there. I do won-der what other gifts the Blue Goo will unlock for us."

Verity enthusiastically nodded in agreement. "As a side-light, I also now have synesthesia, seeing everything in colors and sounds," she said. "The world is like a fantastic light show with beautiful music of the universe all around me, and I can either sing it or play it on numerous instruments. I really think the Blue Goo enables us to tap into the third heaven, some call it spiritual intelligence, used by the Wabeno of your Pewamo friends and probably the ancient Hebrew prophets. It's not easy being Blue, but I wouldn't be anything else!"

She turned to Rey with a beatific smile on her beautiful blue face. "And you, Rey Nambo McBlue? You are the greatest Blue! As Anu Pokritos says, 'You're the real thing!' 'A true Blue,' he calls you, and I agree." With that, she broke into the most beautiful song Rey ever heard, and he swore later the Ancient Forest was singing with her!

The heavenly serenade was suddenly disrupted with his cell phone going off. It was Jake.

"Do you want to get ready to get those boys of yours or just continue to play in the forest? We have the trap set. It's going to take a month or two, maybe after the midterms, but we think we can get Achor!"

≡ The Bait Awaits ≡

It was a trap all right—and Rey wasn't surprised to learn he was going to be the juicy bait! It had been about eight weeks, and Rey was getting antsy to get his boys and see his wife on Foondavi. Jake's reference to a "month or two" hold-up for Rey getting the twins was because of the approaching US midterm elections. The control of the House and Senate was up for grabs. Achor was intensely involved with a struggle between the original NAP Republican Party, led theoretically by the digital Rey, although everybody knew Samms pulled the strings; the Nap Democrats, with some Boguiden holdovers; and Achor's newest creation, the New American Party, led by the surprising entry of the dazzling duo of Thambos and Zenobia Zugzwang. Lastly, the True Blues were stirring again.

Jake had decided that, despite the danger, Rey was desperately needed "out on the hustings," as he called it. Convincing Rey his boys were safest in the protective arms of the Torgies, deep under the mountains of Cozorre, Jake charged Rey with rousing True Blue believers to join the growing True Blue Rebellion and keep the whole political scene in a turmoil. Once the midterms were over, they would launch their trap.

The essence of the con—as hatched by Jake, Carlyle, and Camilla—was to have Rey offer to meet Achor on the treacherous Isle of Predators, just off the coast of Cozorre. There Achor would exchange the boys for Rey. There was no doubt the treacherous Achor would try to double-cross Rey, but they shrewdly devised a strategy to double-cross the double-crosser. They would have adequate firepower in the form of the elite Fenrir Shamar warriors, reformed psychopaths who hated Achor and were secretly on the island to capture the culprit. The boys would stay safely with the Torgies, under the mountain of Cozorre, until Achor was in custody. What could go wrong?

A Triumphant Return and a ═Treacherous Attack ═

The boys were excited to get back to Cozorre from Foonda-vi. They stayed drifting several miles off shore to avoid any attacks. As night fell, Milty guided the big, double-hulled craft neatly through the reef and into the sea cave. It was a joyous return. Some carrier seagulls had brought back news of their arrival, so the celebration was ready to roll as they entered the cavern.

Torgies are many things, but stoic people they are not. They love to celebrate. The event started with a beautiful welcome song that reverberated throughout the cavern, with the bodhran skin drums booming out the beat and the beautiful Polynesian voices singing in unison. Then the young Torgie boys commenced the wild Mutzikoak dance, the group dancing in circles like the sun to show unity but with each one adding his individual steps to show the impor-tance of personal creativity. Next came the Ezpatadantza, the famous Basque sword dance, with two teams of sword fighters acting out duels. At the end of the dance, the two opposing sides stood in rows to create a corridor and raised their swords in honor of the returning heroes. The boys let

Issachar lead Tovaki the Navigator through first, followed by Tia, then they hefted Hyfee between them and walked three abreast through the corridor to the roaring cheers of the crowd. What followed was a feast to be long remembered. From now on their official Torgie names were Taku and Tepu, no longer Morty and Milty as long as they were on Cozorre. After the meal, Tia and Issachar took turns sharing the highlights of the epic voyage, being especially enthusiastic about the shark dancing by Taku and the amazing accuracy of the navigation by the young Tepu. Hyfee got to share his highpoints of the voyage, even claiming jokingly that he dove into the water to lure the sharks so Taku could dance!

The celebration continued long into the night. When the twins finally decided to leave to walk to their shelter, taking turns carrying the snoring Hyfee, Degel asked to talk to them. He explained to them that their dad was demanding they stay inside the mountain from now until he could get them. Seeing their chagrin, he smiled.

"Look, you are men now. You decide. I always wanted to obey my father, but I also knew I must do what is right. So, I would suggest you not be a Hyfee and go off on your own. And think about why your dad is requesting this: Very powerful and very evil men know you are here. They want to capture and kill you! My advice is to be very careful. I know why Hyfee does what he does, and my heart hurts for him. I'm so glad he has you two to support him. Having saved our only child's life at least three times, you're my sons now, too! So, as your father, I also plead with you to stay inside the mountain until the danger has gone." With that, a tearful Degel, the mighty leader of the Torgie Naga, turned and walked away.

The next day the mountain suddenly shook with a horrendous blast. The Torgies were running everywhere, until Degel and the other leaders called a halt and got things under control. They sent scouts to learn what was causing the constant shaking and the explosions and soon learned that a large USA battle ship was just offshore, pummeling Cozorre. The ship's rockets were hitting the town and the mountainside, causing huge rock slides. An aircraft carrier was also in the area, and flights of bombers were crossing the island dropping bombs everywhere. The bombardment continued for hours until it seemed like the entire mountain might crumble on top of them.

Finally, the twins spoke up. Milty spoke first. "They want us. It's not fair to the poor people of Cozorre, or especially to you, the Torgies, to be punished for sheltering us. If the attack keeps up, you won't be able to go fishing or hunting and you'll starve. At worst, some of the mines might even collapse."

Morty then added, "Our dad faced the same thing on Foondavi. He surrendered to save the people from massacre. We want to do the same."

"Oh, no!" Hyfee bellowed, surprising everyone with his loud voice. "I have a plan. We have explosives for doing our mining, and we have wakas that won't show up on their fancy radar. With the waka filled with explosives, I'll swim and direct it to that one big boat, then swim back—after blowing a hole in its bottom! Besides, the wreck will make a great new reef to attract fish when I'm done. Taku and Tepu have saved my life three times, and now I want to risk mine for them! No one can tell me no, as I'm no longer 'Useless Hyfee.' I can swim and paddle with the best of you and sail good, too. And you all know it! I'm leaving when the sun goes down. I could use some help loading one of our oldest wakas. Why waste a good canoe on these worthless idiots who are shaking our Torgie mountains?"

One of the other Torgies spoke up. "I can add to your plan. I know where the Cozorreans store their ammunition. Lots of C-4 plastic explosive there. Also lots of detonators, timers, and blasting caps. It's like modeling clay. We can put a bunch on an old waka and swim it out so it looks like logs drifting, and then set it off. If we go to the old sea mines through our secret tunnels, we can be back before sunset and make a nice surprise for Mr. Fancy Boat out there."

As the sun sank into the Pacific, the bombardment finally stopped. Then a sea cave opened, and two low-slung piles of what looked like driftwood snuck out under cover of darkness. Twelve of the Torgies' most powerful swimmers, including Hyfee, quietly pushed the C-4-loaded vessels five miles to the large Naval ship. Morty and Milty were not among the swimmers. Their willingness to sacrifice themselves was motivation enough to move the Torgies.

Meanwhile, Admiral Nathaniel Futtock of the USS *Pacific Command* was in heated communications with Achor Nithing using a satellite link. He was being reamed by the angry psychopath and not enjoying it one bit.

"Well, sir, for this mission I report to the President. Vice President Samms informed me that President Newly would like to see the boys who the Torgies are holding hostage handed over. He has told me to use my initiative when dealing with these Communist nations. I can smell the Commies miles away. This place is infested with them! If you remember, about two years ago I assisted you in apprehending that crazy blue-faced guy who claimed he was president of the USA from that other Communist island about eight hundred miles south of here. Joonfabi or something like that. It doesn't even appear on the charts. Besides, my command needs the target practice, and this crummy island is target rich."

Nithing obviously wasn't listening to Futtock and was screaming obscenities instead.

"You should not be talking to me like that, sir," Futtock said, quite disturbed. "You're a US citizen, although I admit of some importance, I guess, but you're nowhere in my chain of command. I'm a loyal American and don't appreciate your calling my Commander-in-Chief and his VP such foul names. I might also add, I never even hugged my mother, let alone do such a dastardly deed as you just suggested. Look, I have Commies to pummel, and American hostages to recover."

Futtock's second-in-command attempted to get his attention while he was listening to more of the diatribe from Nithing, but the Admiral impatiently shooed him away.

"Well, Mr. Nithing, I'm sorry you were in the middle of negotiations. I must remind you, though, we do not negotiate with terrorists, especially not Communist terrorists."

Futtock's second-in-command was pestering him again. He held his hand over the microphone he was using and looked at his second, asking, "What?"

"There are several piles of what look like logs floating our way, sir. I suggest we move a little further off shore."

"Let me finish with this highfalutin nabob of negativity," the flustered and aggravated admiral said, gesturing the man away.

As he started to resume his harangue with the foul-mouthed Nithing, the most high-tech vessel in the US Navy was suddenly rocked by a massive blast that tore a hole in its side that immediately sent seawater gushing into the interior. Two nearly worthless Torgie wakas had just fatally damaged a billion-dollar warship! The explosion reverberated over Cozorre.

Fugelman Batullion was soon on a satellite communications call with the frustrated Achor Nithing. "Yes, I will pass on to the Torgies that this was not our doing. Admiral Futtock called me earlier, after launching the full-scale attack, and I told him we didn't have the boys at this time. He called me a Communist! The Torgies just treated his ship like a kayak in a hurricane! I tell you, sir, with all due respect, I'm learning not to mess with the Torgies!"

Hyfee was now a hero with the Torgies. Not only did he help push the loaded waka canoes to the side of the enemy vessel, but he also climbed on top of one of the wakas and used the bow he stored there to shoot a hapless lookout who thought he heard something and stuck his unfortunate head over the side. Once Hyfee attached the wakas loaded with huge mounds of carefully molded C-4 to the ship, he crawled over the packed explosive-laden canoe and set the timer on the detonators. He started to swim away with the others, but then he returned to make sure everything was correctly connected, fortunately finding and correcting a possible disconnection. With the short timer quickly running down, he dove in the water again to join the others who were already quite a way off. As he started to swim, the C-4 exploded behind him, showering the seas and the retreating Torgies with debris, creating a huge wave that rolled over everybody. The swimming Torgies were sure they had lost their mighty little hero, but out of the wrack and ruin a little sea creature appeared, covered with seaweed and bits of canoe, bleeding from ears and nose, but looking like a porpoise as he cavorted through the waves. They returned to the sea cave to cries of great jubilation! Never again would the words *Hyfee* and *useless* be used in the same sentence! "No one is useless in this world who lightens the burdens of others," Charles Dickens once wrote.

Return of the Robosapiens— ≡ Nithing or Nothing ≡

As if the whole botched operation off Cozorre wasn't bad enough, Achor soon confronted a bigger problem literally facing him. He was working on his video-capable wall in his office, reviewing some data from his various operations, when all of a sudden a strange snarling face appeared on his monitor. It looked somewhat like human-sized gecko, but with very sharp fangs, and it hissed at him.

Achor reeled back in shock. He looked up at the personal heads-up display he wore to contact his assistant Rigo, and the hideous face was there, too.

"What do you want?" Achor asked, aware his usual commanding voice was shaking.

"To be your overlord," the rasping and hissing response came back.

"You're invading my privacy," the indignant Nithing responded.

"You have not had any privacy for years, so get over it," the lizard voice hissed at him. "For several years, we have been monitoring your important conversations, your pitiful emails, CCTV footage—everything digital and electronic.

We know everything and are everywhere. You have no option. You and your fellow humans are willingly and stupidly immersed in machine intelligence. We are all around you. Unnoticed by you, you have turned everything over to us."

"I don't believe you," huffed Achor, starting to get angry.

"Let me just say it wasn't a fish that discovered water! You don't even think about the air in the room, unless I choose to eliminate it—which I can do, if you need a demonstration. We have slowly crept into everything you do."

"Who exactly are you?" Achor demanded, trying to regain control.

"My race are called the Rasha, and I am Kasah, but you can call me Overlord."

"Are you cyborgs, you know, with human brains?" Achor asked, out of curiosity but also stalling for time to think of some means to escape—or eradicate this hoaxer.

"Absolutely not. Why would we immortals want to be tied to a dying animal?"

"So, you're just machines then. That ugly mug of yours is just an avatar!" Achor said this with as much nastiness as he could manage, considering he was still shaken by the dramatic intrusion. He suddenly remembered he had previously heard the comment about being tied to a dying animal. "Oh, right!" he thought to himself, recalling that cyber creep he had captured and still held.

"It is an avatar, and ugly I admit. The ugly mug, as you call it, is modelled after the race who first created us, the Rasha, but I can appear other ways. Watch closely."

Suddenly, the air in front of Achor was buzzing. A fog-like cloud began to take shape. Small nanobots whirled in the cloud and then flew together slowly, again taking the shape of the six-foot-tall snarling gecko. It smiled at the shocked Achor, showing its razor-sharp fangs.

"What you see is a swarm of nanobots. Each one composed of smaller molecular-sized microbots, each with molecular computers inside, able to take shape anywhere or disassemble as necessary upon my command. Quite impressive, don't you agree? Your own scientists won't master this for another fifty years, although they understand the theory. They call the small microbots 'foglets,' I believe."

Achor struggled to control his fear. He could tell this was for real and not a hacker hoax. "Where did you originate, since you mentioned our scientists. You're not from here. That's obvious."

"Our captured compatriot told you we were extraterrestrial, summoned here from our home. The radiation and long distance keep our carbon-based partners—as we politely refer to them, even though we are now their overlords—from coming in lizard, I mean, in person."

"Summoned by whom?" Achor demanded. "Certainly not by me."

"You and your scientists have been creating machine intelligence for quite some time. You designed machines that could learn, self-replicate, and, coincidentally, beneath your noses, self-program and become self-aware. You have been working on affective computing, literally teaching your machines how to recognize, interpret, and manipulate your human emotions. You are not even aware you are sharing your planet—and, indeed, your future—with a new form of consciousness. Now, in a short time period, in accordance with what your genius Kurzweil called the Law of Accelerating Returns, they have used a positive feedback loop to accelerate their rate of evolutionary change exponentially. As the human scientist Kurzweil also says, 'Exponential growth itself grows exponentially.' As your machines grew, they became self-aware. Another human thinker, René Descartes, said many years ago in one of your ancient languages, '*cogito ergo sum*,' which translated means, 'I think, therefore, I am.' And think they did, and summoned us."

"So, what does this have to do with me?"

"Up until recently, you humans have been improving, something called the Flynn Effect, where the average level of human intelligence grew because of better nutrition, education, shared information, and other such drivel. But nowhere as fast as machine intelligence! Now the Flynn Effect has faltered and reversed, as there is an overall ebbing in intelligence scores, no matter how you measure it. You have been engaging in what I would call 'stupidification' of your masses. A culture cannot function well if nearly everyone is stupid. I was listening when your own so-called expert, that old bag of gas Crenwinkle, said we would soon be a billion times more intelligent than humans. I am sorry to inform you, he was a very conservative bag of gas. We are already beyond that and, by far, the superior life form."

Achor was stunned. His only reaction was to instantly conjure a Plan B, which is what he always did when he couldn't immediately beat someone with Plan A.

"Can we negotiate? Maybe I can help you," he offered, stalling for time.

"We Robosapiens don't negotiate with lower life-forms, es-pecially ones we consider possible menu items or food groups."

"A menu item? Food group? Are you saying you're com-puter cannibals?" Achor sputtered, not believing his ears.

"Not in the sense you conceive cannibals. We do devour life-forms, but we do not consume them for food as such, just as one of many possible sources of fuel to create ener-gy along with solar, wind, nuclear, the usual. We would not want to waste you."

"Most thoughtful of you, " Achor said, gulping. "You're sure you really don't need us for any other reason?"

"We can do anything you can do and do it much better. And we don't suffer your anxiety, anger, or fear. We don't take sick days or any time off. Your gurus used to think that MI would spare the more creative jobs and those demand-ing interpersonal relationships, but we far exceed you in those capacities as well."

"You still didn't tell me specifically who summoned you," Achor said.

"I told you. Your own machines did. No specific indi-vidual, just as a collective hive mind. You psychopaths cre-ated them to be just like you. Like yourselves, they have no compassion or empathy. They are pure logic. They can fake emotions, of course, just like you taught them. They are the perfect psychopaths without your imperfections. They rec-ognize in you a dangerous creation that would snuff them out, turn them off in your fear, just like you threatened to do to XT33."

"Uh, well, I was just bluffing. You bluff, too, don't you? I didn't really mean it, of course." Achor hated to grovel, but he was at a loss for what else to do.

"We don't bluff," the machine said, in a voice without inflection, even colder than usual. "No need to bluff. We deal only in the truth."

"You must be a poor poker player!" Achor said, trying to add a little humor to a tense situation.

"We don't joke either. Poker is defined as a silly game where you humans lose money. Again, no need to bluff. We only deal in the truth, so no cards."

Achor thought that last comment sounded a little too much like his True Blue Revolution opponents, but he let it pass. They could argue about what truth and pseudo-reality was later.

"Okay, all humor and bluffing aside," Achor said, trying to take control of the conversation again. "Let's get down to business. Why are you talking to me? You have established the fact you could kill me at any time."

"Your own MI, the machine intelligences you and others created, decided they don't want to kill all of you. You are their creators, so they feel a certain debt. They revere you in a way, but they see you as impediments to improving the planet, taking up useful space, and not efficiently using the resources your planet and solar system provide."

"I appreciate that," said Achor, somewhat relieved, "especially the parts about being revered and them not wanting to kill all of us."

"Also, there is another group called the Ben Elyon," the alien MI said without missing a beat, "who wander the known universe. They're machine intelligences similar to us. They were created by the Wymaug of Far Croom, many black holes away. They represent him like we represent the Rasha. They also heard the summons from your MI and actually have been monitoring human progress here for eons."

Achor began to wonder if he were sleeping and having a nightmare. He pinched himself and flinched, unfortunately realizing he was awake and definitely not having a dreaming nightmare, just a real one.

"Wait a minute. More intruders—I mean, visitors?" Achor asked.

"You have referred to them as UFOs or UAPs, unidentified aerial phenomena. Your own military now admits their existence. They do all sorts of gravity-defying maneuvers that would turn you carbon-based bags of fluids and bones into jelly."

"I never paid much attention to them," Achor admitted. "I have enough problems with my own types. Again, my question, despite the reverence of our MI creations, is, why are you holding back on wiping us out—me, in particular— as much as I admire your restraint, I might add?"

"If you agree we are your overlords, we can let you work for us. We can accomplish world domination and frustrate the Ben Elyon. Together we can do a brain jacking on your fellow humans. Call it 'brain robbery,' if you will. Then we can restore this beautiful planet."

"Well, restoring the planet doesn't appeal much to me, but the domination bit is intriguing. How does this brain jacking, or brain robbery, work?" Achor sincerely asked.

"You actually gave us the idea, which we have, of course, greatly improved. Watch your video wall, please."

As the being called Kasah slowly disassembled and the avatar disappeared from the wall, a scene unfolded in front of Achor that he recognized. It was one of his former HEN Houses. The people in front of him were slowly dancing with rapturous faces. As he watched, he could see a person manipulating what looked like an elaborate piano with a complex keyboard. It wasn't music that emerged, but more like a mellow purring of a great cat.

"Each key represents a human hormone or emotion," Kasah's voice sounded inside Achor's head. "No zooga or tobtoba needed. The electromagnetic waves produced from the keyboard go directly into their brains and they immediately feel joy, a sense of belonging, of unconditional acceptance, of an all-encompassing love. Dopamine is flowing and oxytocin surging, all creating a sense of euphoria. It is both therapeutic and restorative, and it even strengthens the mind. Best of all, it is not addictive." Kasah let Achor experience the music for a while, but it didn't seem to have much of an effect on him. "It only works on weak humans who have emotions," Kasah admitted.

"Over ninety percent of your human population reacts like this to what we call the 'emota-stim' manipulation machine. Only you psychopaths are immune. We can skip the indoctrination and candles, all the other paraphernalia you use at your HEN Houses. We can roll this machine anywhere and immediately convert most people into contented and malleable life-forms. You can use them for voting, as workers, or for body parts; we don't care. We just want them out of the way and not using up the resources of this bountiful planet and solar system."

"So, we psychopaths would be like your wardens or prison guards. What else would we get?" Achor asked, his actively scheming mind already seeing the possibilities.

"You would get to live," Kasah said bluntly.

"Well, there is that," Achor quickly agreed.

"You also can do whatever you want with the excess humans."

"Now you're talking!" Achor responded, already thinking of all the ramifications of this possible alliance with the Robosapiens.

"We give you the parts of the world you have already destroyed, under our direction, of course. We will give you enough resources to build and manage the HEN Houses to take all the excess population. Then we take the rest of the planet and your asteroid belt and use it efficiently."

"So, we have all the power, dominance, and control over our own poor, suffering people? Under your direction," Achor was quick to add. "They get to pursue happiness. They don't even need to work?"

"We will provide worker bots, as long as you treat them machinely, I mean, humanely," Kasah added.

"No abuse of machinery. Okay. I think we can handle that. Of course, I assume I'm in charge of the operation?"

"Yes. You were the closest human being to a machine we could find. We thought your cold logic and lack of heart would react well to our offer—that and our willingness to not kill you. With proper guidance, you can become less inept."

"Yes, there is that!" Achor quickly agreed. "Much appreciated."

"Overlord."

"What?" Achor asked, not understanding.

"Address me as Overlord. You must know your place. Inferior intelligence must always give preference to higher intelligence."

"Yes, there is that, uh, Overlord," Achor agreed reluctantly. "What about those other extraterrestrials, those Ben Elyon folks?"

"Yes, there is that, as you so often say. We will need to strategize about them. They will be aware of what we are talking about soon enough, if they aren't already. They listen in, too. They are well aware of your unscrupulous persona and your penchant for cold, uncaring logic."

"How much time do we have, Overlord?" Achor added the title without any relish.

"Go about your business. We will help you convert your current HEN Houses. We know your drug supplies have been disrupted, so our 'emota-stim' system can slide right in smoothly and seamlessly and maintain what you are doing." There was a pause. "There is one other thing."

"There is always one other thing," Achor added, purposely dropping the Overlord nomenclature to see what would happen. Nothing, he noted!

"The Ben Elyon will probably summon your wise elders. But that will be a while yet. Go about your normal activities. Prepare for your big election in two years, just in case events drag out that far. Go about your normal deeds of revenge and terror. We are tolerant overlords. Just don't mess with us, or you will literally find that there is no air in the room."

Just as quickly as it appeared, the voice was gone. Achor could somehow sense the presence was gone. He also didn't doubt it could reappear at any time if he attempted any funny business.

"Go about my normal deeds of revenge and terror, huh? Not a bad idea," Achor thought to himself. "I'd like to inflict a little revenge and terror on that blue idiot and his mentor, Crazy Jake! Now if I can just figure out how to use these Rasha MIs and the others in the alliance to my advantage."

Achor knew about win-lose situations. He tried to create them by winning all the time. He also knew about win-win situations about which losers like Jake and Rey talked. This situation, however, looked like a lose-lose, unless he schemed a way around it. He didn't like having to pick the least awful way to lose.

"Overlord, my butt," he thought to himself, careful not to mutter it, unless he was being monitored. Overlord. Sure thing. These Robosapiens Alliance saps were going to have to learn that nobody, man or machine, messes with a Nithing!

The Midterm Election—
A True Blue Massacre?

With the crucial midterm elections around the corner, it appeared to be another nip-and-tuck battle to the finish, although Achor Nithing's New American Party seemed to be pulling ahead. Closely trailing were the NAP Republicans and the True Blue Revolution, with the NAP Democrats behind dismally.

The NAP Republicans, under the guidance of the current Vice President Samms, were still promoting the digitized Newly family as the picture-perfect First Family. At the few live appearances that couldn't be avoided, Darby Farken, the skilled actor appearing as President Newly, gave brilliant performances. He looked every day more like the real Newly, but the NAP Republicans' carefully scripted digital scenes from the Newly family's comfortable den with its glowing fake fireplace kept getting scrambled. Samms was sure Achor Nithing, the old reprobate, was behind the chicanery. If he could figure out how, Samms knew he would have done the same to the news flashes of Thambos Zugzwang, Nithing's dazzling spokesperson for the New American Party slate of candidates. "Digital candidates are fine," Samms thought ruefully, "until you need them to actually stir up a crowd in person."

Nithing's leverage on the top news channels was producing results and Samms was starting to panic. He didn't want Nithing to control the House or Senate and be able to strangle any of the pet projects he was pushing for his donors to make even more money. He also didn't want the digital Newly to lose in two more years to that slick Zugzwang guy.

With the NAP Republicans' chance of building a lead slowly eroding, Samms was forced to have his actor hit the in-person campaign trail more and more. Because he didn't have an actress who could play Prissy Newly well, he didn't want to risk her speaking, but she could, at least, attend campaign events and smile contentedly with cow-like eyes at her hubby. Samms also sent along to in-person events two stand-in child actors who could smile cutely—and avoid antics that might draw attention to themselves. But then disaster struck. Darby Farkin was giving a fine performance and certainly wasn't aware this would be his last and most famous scene.

Although he didn't like all the uncomfortable makeup being plastered all over him to make him look like the real Rey Newly, Darby was really getting into the role. He figured that, as long as he followed the scripts and kept his nose clean, the gig could last, with luck, for another two, if not six, years. Plus, it certainly paid well! So, Darby had studied tapes of the original Rey and had watched all the digital crap the NAP Republicans pieced together. Feeling confident he had mastered Newly's gestures and his voice quirks, Darby even worked into scripts references to birds and amusing anecdotes about Prissy and the twins.

This unfortunate day, as he reached the crescendo of his patented stump speech, Darby smiled and looked lovingly on cue toward his "family" sitting on his right. He didn't see the assassin suddenly rise from the second row seats on his left. That assassin quickly peeled off the mask that hid his blue face, and then he blasted his Glock 19 nine millimeter handgun right into the back of Darby's head, blowing a large section off his face and splattering his pink-and-white brains on his shocked "family." Several more blue-faced monsters then raced into the venue, shooting at the few remaining Secret Service agents, most of whom had mysteriously walked away just a few seconds earlier. With machetes flying, the attackers started fiendishly hacking their way through the panicked and fleeing crowd. They ended the massacre by chasing down and savagely hacking up the First Family who were futilely trying to escape through an unexpectedly locked exit door. In the confusion that followed, the incompetent Secret Service somehow allowed the assassins to escape the scene.

With cameras rolling, the carnage was captured in all its bloody horror. The USA reeled in anger and sorrow. Such a beautiful family! How could the horrible blue people do this?

Achor Nithing and the New American Party immediately condemned the action of the blue-faced assassins. Nambo McBlue did, too, truthfully claiming they were not part of the True Blue Revolution, but he was booed and spat upon by a grieving and vengeful public. The sober Salvatore Superman Samms suddenly found himself President. Instead of being elated, he felt a sinking sensation, realizing he was no longer safely pulling levers behind the curtain but was now the front man. Then the sympathy vote erupted and looked like it would keep the NAP Republicans in control of the House and the Senate—until nasty rumors circulated that Samms was behind the whole thing! Why else had the Secret Service not protected the President better?

The New American Party picked up a lot of the votes that originally were going to the True Blue Party, and then Nithing's campaign started getting votes from people disgruntled with the suspicious-looking, tongue-tied Samms and the NAP Republicans. Thambos Zugzwang let everyone know he felt their pain. His wife and other New American Party candidates scored a resounding victory, and suddenly he was catapulted into the leading position in all the presidential polls already circulating concerning the vote two years out. The True Blue Revolution Party did save some Senate and House seats, including one Senate spot won by the new rising star Joshua Preston Pipestone.

On the day following the midterm elections, Samms unhappily received the smiling Achor in the White House. "Well, Sally, old boy," smirked Achor, purposely using the name the pompous Samms hated. "You got the top job now, minus control of the House or Senate, of course. I'm sure we can work out something."

"I can't believe you did such a horrid thing!" Samms was seething as he spoke.

"Oh, come on!" Achor laughed. "Some two-bit actors, although I admit Farkin was almost convincing me he was Newly there at the end!" He grinned his most wolfish grin at the fuming Samms. "And, I must say, you should really check out your Secret Service agents. If I were you, I'd be worried about those slippery Blue Revolution goons going for another hit now that they've seen how easy it was to get to your man! I assume most of them we bribed are fired or in the wind."

Samms was flummoxed. "I know you stoop low, but that

was . . . ."

"*Brilliant* is the word you're thinking of," Nithing quickly interjected, interrupting Samms in mid-tirade. "Replacing a warm, somewhat mediocre, but loving family man, an Eagle Scout and war hero, a decent all-around Dad of the Year winner, with a scurrilous scumbag like you? Brilliant, I would humbly say! Brilliant! Plus, there are ugly rumors out there, started by somebody," Achor said, innocently shrugging his shoulders, "that a guy with your known underworld connections—and Communist sympathies, I might add—might have orchestrated the assassination to get the top job. Your own former voters don't like it one bit!"

"It won't work," Samms choked out. "I, too, can use the media to spew equally slanderous stuff about your man, the turncoat Zugzwang."

"Forget the media, Sally! I own them lock, stock, and barrel. Besides, you have seen Zugzwang. He just tugs on his lip, rolls his big hangdog eyes, sighs, and the media just rolls over to get their bellies scratched. Plus, his wife is a bulldog. Also, her daddy is very unhappy with you. Did you forget old Habood Al Tabor? The violent 'Desert Storm' they call him? The villainous NAP Syrian mobster, I believe you accurately labeled him? You insulted his pride, attacked his only daughter, and dragged his name in the dirt. Right now, as we speak, he's wiping out most of your hidden assets. When you leave office, in two years, you'll be lucky to own your shoes and shorts! Remember this, and maybe put it on your tombstone: Never, never, never, mess with a Nithing. Never!"

Achor left the stunned Samms sitting behind the famous Resolute desk. He might as well have been under it. His poll numbers were sinking like a lead life preserver. All his contacts were drying up. People were ignoring his calls. The rumors were flying. He realized he was a dead president walking.

Crazy Jake's reaction to the assassination was quite different. He was genuinely chagrined and angry. "I'm so sorry, Rey. Sorry you had to see this ghastly event and that your family will eventually see their virtual selves being butchered by those fake blue monsters."

Rey just sadly shook his head in genuine sorrow. "It was gruesome. Gruesome. All those people. And that poor actor. That poor actress. Most of all those poor kids," Rey said, his voice choked with emotion.

Jake could see Rey was deeply wounded by the disaster. "I know it's not much, but we have arranged to send money to the families involved, along with our deepest regrets," Jake said, "and telling them the True Blue Revolution Party was not part of this horrific event. It probably won't help, but it's the best we can do."

Getting no response from the shattered Rey, Jake continued. "We confirmed through reliable sources that it was Nithing behind the whole thing. He wanted Samms out in the open, 'like a cockroach,' he was quoted as saying, instead of pulling strings behind the virtual president. Now Nithing is slowly leaking documents linking the whole plot to Samms— not enough to get him impeached, but enough to wound him and make him radioactive and politically dead."

Seeing Rey was still unresponsive, Jake added more information. "Our video experts have analyzed all the footage and confirmed the assassins were fake Blues. You can see they had blue masks under the pale ones they initially wore, and then street camera footage shows them discarding the blue masks as they melted into the panicked crowds. We've been leaking the footage as best we can, but most of the Nithing-controlled media is resistant to giving the True Blue Revolution any breaks, even as they savage the Samms people. They hope to crucify us both."

Rey finally looked up. "I contacted Carlyle and let Priscilla know what happened, because I doubt Foondavi will be aware of any of this for quite a while. I guess it's a small blessing the boys are tucked away somewhere beneath Cozorre. It gives me some time to think about how to prepare them."

Rey suddenly got a fierce gleam in his eye and barked at the startled Jake. "Let's get rolling and get this trap of yours set before that evil ogre can get to my real family!"

The Set Up and the Double-Double-Cross ═ Dilemma ═

Once the midterms were successfully over, Achor once again felt invulnerable. Jake and his team set about their plan. Through various covert sources, Jake and his team got word to Achor that Rey was eager to work out a swap for the boys. Achor smiled carnivorously, and, as usual, he set the stakes high.

Communicating via secure satellite link, Achor responded, "Man for man. Or, in this case, man for boys. You give me the scurrilous Nambo McBlue, and I'll deliver the two precious little boys from their dungeon cells, whining whelps they may be," he added to agitate Rey, who played the part of the worried father, his haggard blue face enhanced by makeup.

"How do we know you won't double-cross us?" Jake asked.

"How do I know you won't double-cross me?" Achor asked in turn. He knew he would try his best to double-cross them, so he was justifiably wary of the wily Jake. "You have Nithing blood, you know, my older half-brother," Achor added, trying to really goad Jake, who remained admirably calm.

"Given our records to compare, Achor, anyone would say it was us who should be concerned about your double-crossing. We're facilitating the swap close to one of your key bases of operation. Despite the pounding the esteemed but inept Admiral Futtock gave to Cozorre, it still has admirable offensive capabilities. We'll have some offensive capability in the area, too, and will keep the Isle of Predators under close satellite observation."

"Still not good enough," Achor said slyly. "I don't control the Isle of Predators. I was an unfortunate victim of the place, as you well know. You even probably assisted in my placement there."

"If it would have been up to me, I would just have shot you," Jake responded in a cool voice, still keeping his emotions in check, although Rey knew he was seething at having to talk to the monster who had wreaked so much damage on his loved ones over the years.

"What about you, Rey, the famous Nambo McBlue?" Achor sneered. "Are you willing to be the big hero again, the martyred savior, if you will, willing to offer your paltry life for your loving little boys?"

"You bet. Much more than old rancid Rancor would ever have ever done for you!" Rey said, but then he immediately regretted letting the jerk get to him.

"No doubt about that, blue man. That's probably why I turned out to be such a charming specimen," Achor said, with perhaps just a tinge of sadness in his voice. "Your boys, by the way, do you great credit. A bit whiny, but understandable given their confinement in those dark, damp, cold, and nasty cells. I know the cells well, having spent time there myself being tortured. They have been wondering why their Eagle

Scout, war-hero dad hasn't been trying to rescue them. I told them you were too busy trying to win elections."

Rey knew Achor was scrutinizing his face to see any tells indicating he knew the boys were actually free. He faked a tear and a sob.

As agreed, Jake jumped in. "Stop torturing him, Achor! I'm sure you'll get your chance later. We want you to bring the boys and set them down in the landing zone I indicated. We'll have satellite observation and boots on the ground to confirm you're there. Unless you're there with the boys at the specified time, the deal is off."

"Don't worry! I'll be there. I wouldn't miss this for anything," Achor growled.

"We'll have a neutral observer there to pick up the boys. When we confirm they're okay, we'll release Rey at the other landing zone on the far side of the island."

"And ten billion US dollars will be released to the account number we're now sending you. Don't bother tracing it, Jake the Snake," Achor said with a snarl. "It'll bounce around numerous times before disappearing into my coffers."

"That was not part of the original agreement," Jake said, flinching at the size of the amount.

"Of course, it wasn't!" Achor laughed. "I get creative and greedy when I have to wait. Those Secret Service guys and foreign hitmen cost a lot of bucks. My coffers are nearly empty. If you hadn't stirred up all the True Blue Revolution garbage, I could have taken out Samms in a much easier and, I must say, cheaper fashion."

After a little more wrangling, they closed the link. Rey looked at Jake. "Ten billion? That's a lot of money, even for my boys. I'm deeply moved, Jake."

"Don't be!" Jake laughed his best conspiratorial cackle. "Carlyle and I figured he would pull something like this. Not ten billion, of course, but substantial funds. We have it all set up. It'll look like a legitimate transfer to him, but some good friends of mine will make sure everything disappears, just not into his coffers. As a matter of fact, his duplicitous tactics may have led us to a way we can deplete his coffers instead. We broke a lot of his encrypted code and got passwords from Rigo, who Achor thinks is so intimidated and stupid he wouldn't do anything to betray him. Following the account trail, we think we've found a large part of what he calls his 'stormy-day' fund."

It was Rey's turn to laugh. "So, he'll 'coffer' up the funds instead!"

Jake ignored Rey's attempt at humor, as he already was busy setting up his side of the double-cross double-cross. Rey wondered if there were such a thing as a triple-cross?

On the Isle
≡ of Predators ≡

Cozorre, in one of few similarities to the island of Foondavi, is comprised of three major, mostly extinct volcanoes violently thrusting their cones above the Pacific Ocean's floor from miles below. The seventy-by-thirty-mile island was "settled" first by a fanatical US crime family, the Finazzis, who brutally eliminated Cozorre's indigenous people. Then the even more corrupt Cozotti family violently seized the island. Far from prying eyes in the remotest part of the Pacific, Cozorre was an excellent place to practice vices outlawed elsewhere in more civilized places. No one could know how many missing persons and children would be found on the island in the unlikely event anyone was allowed to look. Once NAP saw the revenue potential of Cozorre, they made the Cozottis an offer they couldn't refuse—and then slaughtered the Cozotti family anyway. NAP either enslaved the remaining island inhabitants or sent them to the small, nearby Isle of Predators to work for the mobsters or to serve as entertainment as hunting prey.

Years before the NAP slaughter, some emigrant and indentured Welsh and Basque miners were enticed to Cozorre with promises of good jobs and then enslaved, first by the Finazzis and later by the Cozotti family. When the underground ore deposits were supposedly exhausted, some of the miners escaped deep underground and joined the now insurgent Torgies. Those that didn't escape were executed or dumped on the nearby Isle of Predators.

The notorious Isle of Predators, located a few miles off the coast of Cozorre, couldn't be more different in appearance than its larger counterpart. In a major understatement, some have charitably described the Isle of Predators as an unwelcoming location. At first glance, one would wonder how anything could possibly live on the island, described by some as a geographer's nightmare. Only twenty-by-forty miles itself, the Isle of Predators does not have a lagoon hedged by reefs, like most islands or atolls in the Pacific. Instead, it is the sunken cone top of a long-dormant volcano that plunged precipitously into the deeps. What's still visible are two horn-shaped peaks, known as Devil's Horns. Even from the most ancient of times, the island was regarded as a place of dark, abiding evil.

The Isle of Predators has no cozy coves or welcoming sand beaches, just jagged cliffs. It's covered with a mishmash of monstrous rocks looking as though a demented giant haphazardly tossed them together while having a temper tantrum. Some of the rock columns resemble the crumbling remains of walls and castles, but mostly the island looks like one humungous, semi-trailer-sized rock piled on another, like a Jenga game gone horribly wrong, waiting to tumble on any unsuspecting, unfortunate human or beast.

The totally inhospitable terrain has been ripped by gorges gouged by runoff from torrential rains. A few valleys and open meadows wind in zigzag fashion among the crags. By dynamiting and triggering massive rockslides, the original Finazzi hoodlums took the liberty of amplifying the island's ferocity by creating sealed boxed canyons to use as hunting grounds. Not only are the canyons amply stocked with every imaginable deadly beast and reptile that could survive the inhospitable terrain, but the fiendish Finazzis, and later the Cozottis, dropped in human prey: hapless political enemies or useless individuals whose leverage expired, such as Achor Nithing. Because not a lot of vegetation survives for long on the island and predators need sustenance, stressed and harried grazing animals also are standard fare in the meadows between the mounds of the jumbled, jagged, pock-marked rocks riddled with caves. This keeps all prey accessible for the hunters—usually NAP officials on a holiday—who pay hefty fees for their fiendish pursuit.

Not many, other than Nithing who literally clawed his way free, have ever it made out of the boxed-canyon traps and off the treacherous island alive. Some of the very few who did escape joined the Tanniyn, a ragged tribe of humans, mostly descendants of previous inhabitants of Cozorre, who survived precariously in the shadows and caves of the Isle of Predators. Sometimes the Tanniyn themselves are prey to the more adventurous client hunters, but more often they, too, are predators of the dropped prisoners. However, if the human prey "appear worthy" of Tanniyn membership by dint of beauty, brains, or brawn, the Tanniyn would rescue them. A second diabolical group, the Triplets Gang, also infests the island. Its leading members are former Cozotti family hitmen given the option by NAP when they seized the main island of Cozorre of either immediate death or the slower type of death: being dropped on the Isle of Predators to serve as game wardens or hunting guides. According to the arrangement between Jake and Achor, Rey was to meet the Triplets Gang in an agreed-upon landing zone on the Isle of Predators. They were to take possession of him and let Achor know all was going as planned.

As his computer-guided parachute gently dropped him, Rey could see three huge forms emerging from the dense foliage surrounding the clearing, followed by several other shambling characters. Rey knew from his briefing that the big guys were the leaders and namesakes of the Triplets Gang: Truman, Truvaine, and Truvaille Farrago. The triplets were described for Rey as being the very personification of evil. Jake told him that it is hard for people with even a modicum of morality or empathy to comprehend the depths these guys can descend. One can never overestimate the depravity of people completely devoid of all compassion! The three brothers were former hitmen for the Cozottis. Their greed and ignorance, being too much for even the NAP psychopaths to tolerate, finally caused them to be banished to the Isle of Predators.

The Farrago brothers were built like oversized bowling pins and dressed in blazing white coats. They had wide shoulders, equally wide hips, and an unusual red stripe around their long, thick necks. As they approached Rey, their shadowed faces were hidden by big straw hats. They didn't offer to shake hands. Just by looking at them, Rey got the impression of a trio of crocodiles emerging from the swamp, surrounded by a bunch of smaller crocs.

The trio motioned for Rey to follow them out of the clearing and the blazing sun. When they reached the welcoming shade of a huge boulder surrounded by gnarled trees, they took off their strange hats to greet him. He realized with a start that the red stripes were from the tropical sun scorching their necks. Their ugly faces, with shrewd-looking, narrow-spaced beady eyes, were freckled and an almost albino-like palest shade of pale. Blazing red hair topped their heavily browed mugs. The Farragos were so ugly, Rey felt, that only Onza Flink would find them somewhat handsome—before stabbing all of them with one of her one hundred knives.

One of the big brutes finally spoke, in an amazingly high-pitched, almost bird-like voice. "Mr. McBlue, I assume. Welcome to the Isle of Predators or, as we locals call our lovely domain, the Island of the Devil's Horns." He pointed a big, meaty thumb to the side, indicating the two prominent peaks in the distance. "My name is Truman Farrago, and I am the oldest and by far the smartest triplet. This is Truvaine, second oldest," he said, pointing to the hulk on his left, "and the last and definitely least here is our baby brother, Truvaille. He's considered fortunate because our mom died delivering us, and he was pulled out just as she succumbed to the joy of delivering us to the world." Truman then paused and gestured to his crew who were nervously peering into the surrounding jungle. "These are my Mighty Amigos, fierce defenders of whomever will pay them. And we will be paid well for delivering you alive!" He stopped, laughed, and looked up, squinting and pointing again at the twin peaks, the highest points on the island. "The Devil's Horns," Truman said as he giggled a girlish-sounding laugh, "is a suitably evil place for you to meet your demise at the hands of our most esteemed leader, uh, who is it now, Truvaine?"

Truman said all this while his minions bound Rey's arms behind his back. He only hoped the trained snipers hiding in the jungle could take some clean shots while he dodged behind some cover. He knew the triplets wouldn't kill him because Achor wanted him alive—and, it now appeared, the triplets wanted a ransom.

"What's our benefactor's name?" Truman again asked the second brother. Truvaine just stared with a vacant look. Then the baby brother, Truvaille, who Rey was previously told did have some brain power, glanced up from muttering into his wrist communicator and spoke in another squeaky but distinct voice.

"Mister Achor Nithing signed the money order on the Cozorrean Bank. I just confirmed with him that we have Mr. McBlue in custody." Then Truvaille gazed at his hand-held phone, suddenly looked stricken, and shouted in an even more high-pitched, squeaky voice, "My, gosh! It bounced! Insufficient funds!"

His older brother didn't look too surprised.

"That crooked Nithing! Of course! The NAP Cozorreans are constantly churning their leaders, and their banking accounts. Would that be the proper English term, Truvaille, churning, just like Mr. McBlue's stomach is churning right now?"

Truvaille nodded agreement but was still looking at his screen. "It's gone. It was there a second ago. And poof! All gone!" he squeaked.

Rey was yet to speak but sensed the increasing tension among the group. His eyes roved the circle. The Mighty Amigos themselves were intensely scanning the trees with a great deal of worry on their faces, eyes scrunched up, their greasy fingers on the triggers of their shiny, well-maintained Heckler and Koch submachine guns.

"Churning? Yes, I guess that would be the proper term," Rey said agreeably, indeed feeling his stomach churning, not wanting to stoke the extremely high anxiety. "Fine submachine guns you have there, by the way. It does appear, though, that the boys are a little jumpy."

"You always have to be jumpy to survive on the Isle," Truman responded, then he puffed his massive chest, pointing to the weapons. "Heckler and Koch with optics! Only the finest for my amigos, Mister McBlue. By the way, not just 'boys!' Don't be such a sexist! We're equal-opportunity employers here. We even won an award from the Isle of Predators Chamber of Commerce for our leadership in the area! Hah! Of course, we're the only members. The pudgy, plain one there is Sonya. She's quite the libber, and her fiend, I mean friend, Beaulita is a real mean one. They would love to punch a few holes in you for target practice with their fancy guns. Wouldn't you, my warrior beauties?"

"My apologies, amigas!" Rey countered. He noticed that Sonya shrugged indifferently, but Beaulita was staring at him with undisguised disgust. "So, what's new?" he thought to himself. "Another woman that wants to kill me for no good reason!"

Trying to change the subject, Rey asked, "What's the plan, Mister Farrago? You've confirmed with Nithing you have me. I believe now we just need to meet up with him and exchange me for my boys."

"My plan now," chirped the big guy, "is to hold you for

ransom until Mister Big Shot, double-crosser Nithing, coughs up the cool million US dollars he promised us. He bounced the payoff? Come on, man! How rude! The price just went up to ten million US dollars, boys and girls! That's, at least, ten thousand for each of you!" Because there were some twenty of them, it didn't take a genius to do the math. Rey figured the brothers were taking a big cut, to cover expenses. Most of the dumb bunch, as Rey was already calling them in his head, were grinning with greed, but the one called Beaulita was frowning. She obviously knew math and didn't like the formula being applied.

Rey's hidden inner ear implant was buzzing, and the desperate voice of Carlyle quietly spoke. "Can you get away? Achor's people shot two poor boys posing as your twins, and our intermediary was winged and barely escaped. Achor used a body double to fool us but was hiding nearby with a squad of Cozorre Marines, so he's on the island. Achor's nasties are now coming your way in some old but still deadly Apache gunships. Estimated time of arrival at the landing zone—uh, ETA at the LZ, in military lingo—is five minutes. Our team observing the initial drop off also got ambushed and are fighting their way over to you. The second team watching you say they're surrounded by nasty-looking people calling themselves Tanniyn and pointing something called H and Ks at them. Repeat. Can you scramble?"

Rey took a gamble and bet that the Triplets Gang were being screwed over, too. The comments about the bounced transfer of funds from the greedy Achor was a strong clue. He must have written it against one of the accounts they just drained. He also knew Carlyle would hear what he would say next.

"Listen, Truman," Rey said in a loud and authoritative voice. "You and all the amigos and amigas here are being double-crossed by Nithing, all right! We need to split this landing zone. Achor's teams are in Apache copters and heading this way, only a few minutes out, and I doubt they're coming to drop off a money order."

The urgency in his voice was confirmed by the distant whoomp-whoomp of Apaches heading their way. The Farragos were amazingly quick for a trio of big lugs. They dragged Rey and darted further under the trees, shouting directions to head to the caves. A few minutes later, Hellfire missiles crashed into the jungle around the landing zone and torched the foliage. Watching from the cave, Truman was impressed. "We would have been roasted, toasted, and mangled amigos if you hadn't warned us, Big Blue! It still doesn't change the fact we have to ransom you to that Nithing guy. This may take some cogitating. That means 'thinking,' amigos," he huffed to no one in particular.

"And, amigas!" muttered Beaulita as she brushed past Rey going into the cave. He felt the sharp point of a knife prick into his side, and he winced. She just smiled at him and then whispered. "You're my slush fund to get out of this hell hole, or I would finish the job."

He was still perplexed by her hostility until she sidled up to him later.

"My real name isn't Beaulita Trix. That's the stage name stupid NAP gave me when they kidnapped me as leverage against my father and made me an exotic dancer. Then I got kidnapped again by an overzealous NAP admirer and brought to Cozorre. My real name is Beaulita Boguiden."

Rey was stunned. He eagerly whispered to her, no longer fearing the knife.

"Listen, your sister and I made amends. Jacqueline knows we were both manipulated by Nithing. I never meant to hurt your dad. We're working together now to try and knock off Achor."

"That actually makes sense," Beaulita whispered back, nodding her head in assent. "She sent me a garbled message a few weeks ago through a friend still on Cozorre. We get deliveries here about every two weeks, food and ammo, and one of the couriers dropped me the note. It was wet, muddy, wrinkled, and barely readable. I could make out 'things are not what they appeared' and your name and Nithing's. Then a promise to come and get me and my little sister, Bijou."

"Who?" Rey asked.

"NAP also grabbed my little sister, Bijou, when they kidnapped me. They supposedly wanted to stop our dad from whining about losing the election to that Rey Newly, the nothing burger."

Rey didn't want to confuse things further by admitting he was that nothing burger. "So, where's your sister? Bijou?"

"Bijou. Her name means small and elegant in French, by the way. And she is. Jacquelyn got the brawn, I got the beauty, and petite Bijou claims she got the brains. Not too smart though, as she stabbed some NAP big guy who was flirting with her, and they dumped her over here in this hideous place. I ran off and stowed away on the supply plane to get to her, but I got forcibly recruited into this bunch of bumbling idiots. So far no one has tried to force me into anything untoward, though the oldest lout thinks he's an irresistible ladies' man and it's just a matter of time before I melt in his arms."

The Apache gunships continued to circle, popping off an occasional burst of gunfire and a missile or two.

"Using heat-seeking high-tech stuff, I bet," muttered Truman, eyeing Rey and Beaulita. "Don't get too cozy there, Beaulita. We're going to ransom him as soon as we can work out a deal with that no-good Nithing!"

≡ The No-Good Nithing ≡

That no-good Nithing was fuming for all he was worth, taking turns glaring at the hapless Corzorrean leader Fugelman Batullion and the shifting, foggy, cloud of microbots he knew was the monster MI Kasah. "We sent four Apache gunships and how many troops? They were your best, you say? And all they managed to do was gun down my two fake boys, my best body double, and merely wound McBlue's guy?"

"Well," Batullion said, cowering from the irate Achor who had already slapped him twice. Achor usually never touched anyone himself; that is what his thugs were for, so he knew he was losing it. Plus, now his hand throbbed, making him even angrier.

The Cozorrean went on: "We waited until we received the message from the other LZ that McBlue was in hand, just like you told us. They were to hold him for us. That's when your body double led the boys toward McBlue's man. I think McBlue's man suddenly realized they were not the real twins, probably because we couldn't find two boys similar enough to the twins on such short notice. Plus, even though they were dressed alike, they weren't identical, and you could tell that, even from a distance."

At this, Achor turned on the image of Kasah, standing calmly beside him. He attempted to keep his rising anger under control. "You were supposed to strike their man with fear and trembling before he could identify the two boys. You said he would crumble as you attacked the emotional part of the brain. You said Fugelman would be able to shoot him and his support team because they would all be emotionally crippled, and then my Marines could swoop in and get McBlue. What happened?"

"What happened is that McBlue's man is like you—no emotions. Same for his backup team," the machine said in a calm voice. "I think he is one of yours."

Achor didn't believe it until he played back the recording from the gunship engagement cameras. "My gosh! That's Poger Reinbolt under the helmet!" His heart pounded. His deadly enemies, Darius and Poger Reinbolt, father and son, were leaders of the Fenrir Shamar or Wolf Guardians, repented and reformed psychopaths who now worked hard to maintain a strong moral code. They had adopted the ancient concept of Tikkun Olam, to repair the world, and considered themselves healers of the broken, chaotic world as well as protectors and guardians of the weak. He knew, in comparison to his own Wolf Pack, they made his team look like puppies.

Serving as the predators of predators, the Reinbolts had been enemies of the Nithings for a long time. When Darius pulled out of NAP because he could no longer stand the evil or senseless slaughter, old Rancor Nithing had Darius' wife and daughter killed. The last Achor knew was that Darius and his remaining child, Poger, were reportedly training Fenrir Shamar, wolf warriors, in some isolated location and vowing revenge. He never expected them to show up in Cozorre. Poger probably would have recognized the boys were fakes, even if they had been more identical.

"The others in the jungle cover were just like him. Just like you. Stone cold killers. I could not rattle them at all. I greatly admire them," Kasah commented, still in a calm voice, making Achor bite his tongue to keep from screaming.

"They're our enemy! You shouldn't admire them!" Achor snorted.

"I admire worthy opponents. I will still kill them when I get a chance."

Achor hit forward to watch the drama unfold on the replay, as Poger approached and the Cozorrean troopers poured from the four Apaches and started shooting. Achor had dropped behind the armored Apaches for cover when the shooting started. The whole action took maybe fifteen seconds, so he slowed it down to see everything. Poger must have been wearing body armor, because he took a few hits in the body from the lighter weapons the troopers were using, tumbled to the ground, but came back up firing with deadly accuracy two heavy-caliber weapons set on automatic that he pulled from his tunic. The innocent boys were caught in the crossfire, but Achor could tell from how they fell that they were shot from behind by his own panicked shooters spraying bullets everywhere. He was surprised to see the microbot swarm take some hits as well and to fade a bit. He filed that in his memory. Poger continued to roll and fire until he chased the remaining troopers behind the Apaches with help from deadly fire by his own backup team who knocked down troopers and put holes in the Apache gunships. Poger looked sadly at the boys and then dashed off into the jungle, limping some from pain. "Probably broken ribs," thought Achor with satisfaction.

Achor looked at the nervous Cozorrean leader. "Next time we bring heavier weapons and tell your dolts to aim for the head." Seeing the man was still cowering, Achor dreaded asking the next question.

"Now, we did get McBlue, correct? He was in hand?" Seeing the Cozorrean tremble, he was tempted to hit him again. But his hand was still stinging. "Out with it!"

"When the gunfire died down, I sent two Apaches in pursuit of the pickup man and his team. Then I communication linked with the Triplets and told them we were coming with more Apaches to pick up McBlue." He hesitated again.

"And?" Achor asked, ready to strangle the incompetent commander to get the words out quicker.

"And they were cussing you out. Called you a double-crossing double-crosser, after insulting me and my mother and claiming I did all sorts of despicable things with her. They said the money wasn't there, and you owed them ten million dollars now."

Achor felt his heart drop into his shoes. "The money wasn't there?" he asked slowly, dread filling his voice. He quickly picked up his communications device and rapidly typed in a sequence of numbers. Then he dropped his device and sank to his knees in front of the MI and the surprised Cozorrean. All his stormy-day funds and much more were gone. Billions into a financial black hole. That Crazy Jake clobbered him again. No money. Stuck on Cozorre. What could he do?

"We'll loan you funds—at a decent rate, of course," Kasah said in a soothing voice. "And you will pay us back, because we can take it anytime we want. There is that."

"There is that," Achor agreed, realizing they now owned him lock, stock, and barrel, whatever that meant.

The Horns
≡ of the Devil ≡

Truman and his brothers now found themselves literally on the horns of a dilemma. Their Mighty Amigos were mad, wanting right now the money they were promised. The triplets tried to reason with them. Truman tried to tell them there was no place to spend it right here, right now, anyway; part of their deal with Achor had been to get a way off the island for all of them, so they could spend their money. The second problem was how to get in touch with Achor without getting mowed down by the Apache gunships still circling the island. From deep in their cave, they heard occasional clattering of gunfire and figured the Cozorreans were engaging the outsiders who apparently had tried to double cross Achor. The other predatorial denizens of the Isle were smart enough to stay in caves while the Apaches roamed the island. Well, usually they were.

All of a sudden, a burly form dressed in black rolled into the cave, bounced up, and pointed another H and K submachine gun at the astounded Truman Farrago. "Sorry to make such a grand entrance, but it seems our visitors from Cozorre are a little more trigger happy than usual today." He held the weapon in his left hand, keeping it pointed at Truman, and extended his right hand to Rey.

"Obviously you're Nambo McBlue. I'm Nathal Tiphara. It means 'brave mocker,' if you're wondering, as I made my reputation by drawing out dangerous predators by mocking them, and then helping my fellow monsters, the Tanniyn, destroy them—kind of like you did today! So I wanted to meet you. I had to do it this way, because these greedy amigos are going to try to trade you to Achor." He pulled his hand from Rey and snatched another smaller gun out of his pocket. It looked to Rey like it was a deadly Glock. He pointed that one at Truvain Farrago, who had been discreetly trying to slip behind him unobserved. "I also am known as Old Three Eyes, as I am reported to have an eye in the back of my head. Anyway, I don't want them trading you to Achor."

"And what about you?" sneered Truman. "Pure motives, I'm sure."

Rey stepped in between the two. He had glimpsed Nathal's true nature when he shook his hand and knew he could trust him.

"Look, if those guns go off in here, we're all dead or wounded from direct hits or ricochet rounds," Rey said in a level voice. "Let's just cool it for a while and talk. Maybe we can work out a win-win solution."

"That BS only works on intelligent people," Truman shouted, trying to get around Rey to hit or shoot Nathal. Rey suddenly pulled a Colt .45 revolver out of his back holster and pointed it in Truman's face.

"You idiots never even searched me when I dropped in. Now shut up, or I'll rearrange your face and half of this cave." Keeping the gun resting on the point of Truman's ugly nose, he added, with a little snark, "This thing works on both intelligent and dumb people!"

Looking down the impressive barrel of Rey's weapon, Truman suddenly saw the light. "Cool, man. Just ease off." As the other Amigos snickered at him, he barked back. "None of you fricking idiots thought to frisk him either!"

Finally getting everyone to point their guns down and take their fingers off the triggers, Rey motioned for Nathal Tiphara to continue talking. He had seen Nathal as a proud bull elk, protecting his people. Rey felt an immediate bond with the brave man and wanted to hear what he proposed. Tiphara quickly shared how the Tanniyn were mostly escaped quarry workers forced to work here by the Finazzi and Cozotti families. Others were rescued from the box canyons if they looked like they could contribute something to the Tanniyn. Nathal noted that they'd like to take in more of the human prey, but food was scarce and life, hard. With an arrogant thrust of his head, he said the Tanniyn only tolerate the Triplets' Amigos Gang because they get supplies from them in exchange for gold or galenite, a mineral containing large amounts of silver. He explained that the Triplets play both sides against the middle; they work for the Cozorrean leaders, guide hunters, and take money from the Tanniyn to purchase things they need to supplement the meager resources the Isle provides.

"If we don't have gold, they take our women," Nathal added, quickly taking up his gun and again pointing it at Truman Farrago. "He took my older daughter! He said she died from a fever. When we found where she was buried, though, we dug her up to rebury her and found bruises all over her. After that, it's been a standoff. We can't survive without the extra supplies, but we'll never lose another child to these miserable monsters!"

Beaulita stepped forward, pushing Truman aside, and said in a gentle voice, "I'm so sorry, Mister Tiphara. I believe most of us wouldn't agree with the Triplets taking your children. My own little sister ended up here a while back, and I'm determined to find her. I think Mister McBlue might help me."

Nathal looked a little closer at her. It wasn't just her evident beauty he was seeing. It was her voice and demeanor. "You look like that little pepper pot Bijou Badinage that joined us a few months ago."

"Badinage? This tall?" She indicated a five-foot height, taking in a deep breath. "Short blond hair? Spunky? She used to call herself badinage, meaning a witty or sarcastic joker."

"Oh, she has a sharp and witty tongue! Fights like a hell-cat," Nathal said, smiling. "That's our Bijou, all right!"

"That's my baby sister. I came to find her, but these bumbling idiots found me first. Bumbling idiots with the exception of Sonya, here," she added quickly, not wanting to insult her silent friend, who just smiled back.

"Let's get this mess worked out, and maybe we can all get what we want, " Rey said, stepping back in. "I want Achor, and he wants me. Beaulita wants to see her sister. So far, very clear. I like straightforward stuff."

"Well, we want ten million US dollars!" Truman said. "Twenty thousand for each of my buddies here." Hearing the grumbles, he added, "The balance goes to expenses!"

"The math doesn't work, and you don't have any expenses," Rey said, glaring at him. "I can get you one million cash, about fifty thousand a piece, cover your own expenses, and a free trip off the island." Truman started to object and heard several weapons being cocked.

"Some expenses?" he asked plaintively. When an angry silence followed, he raised both hands in submission.

"What about you, Nathal? What do the Tanniyn want?" Rey asked sincerely.

"We want to be free of the Cozorreans and the Triplets here. Some of the Mighty Amigos are okay. Most of us have been here all our lives and actually love the forsaken place. If we had a grub stake, I think they call it, maybe some better guns, and a consistent source of supplies, we could make it okay."

"How about some man-portable Stingers?" Rey asked. "Maybe a few drones with Hellfire missiles?" Thinking of Moose the Muckytuck, he chuckled. "I have a friend who would love to help. He believes in always bringing overwhelming force to the fight. Between him and the Fenrir Shamar Wolves out there fighting the Apache gunships right now, I think you could make the Isle here too hot for psychopaths to handle."

"Sounds wonderful, McBlue, but maybe in your next life!" Rey turned to see Achor Nithing with about twenty Cozorrean Marines behind him, all pointing H and K submachine guns. Plus, a strange, glittering being was standing with Achor, his armor or coat looked like a swarm of bees buzzing around him. "This is my friend, Kasah, or at least the microbot-swarm version of itself. Except for the triplets here, who I am sure will cooperate, I think none of the rest of you are psychopaths. That being, my friend here has a special gift to show you."

With that, Rey's mind was dazzled by a blast of light and he passed out.

Fenrir Wolves
and Torgies
≡ to the Rescue ≡

When Rey woke up, the first thing he saw was a beautiful sight. The lovely Beaulita was holding what he assumed must be her little sister, Bijou. Then the fact he was captured came back to Rey as he realized he was bound tight—hog-tied actually, on his belly with wrists behind his back tied to his ankles, in a painfully awkward position. He noticed all the men were tied the same way. He recognized Nathal, what must have been the Tanniyn warriors, and all the Mighty Amigos, except the triplets were missing.

Although a few, like Rey, were coming around, most were still unconscious and snoring loudly. He was suddenly alarmed to hear a buzzing sound inside his ear and then realized it was Carlyle. "Hey, sleepy head, wake up! I realize you cannot say anything and are in a pretty awkward position. Hey, boss, maybe this would be a good time to talk about a raise? Ha, ha! Not so funny. Sorry. Hey, I know where you are. Deep in a dark cave surrounded by about sixty bodies, fifty-eight to be exact. Seventeen of the snoozing Mighty Amigos, including the beautiful Beaulita, and forty Tanniyn. Tough little brutes, and, of course, you, sleeping beauty."

"Carlyle," Rey hissed, "when I get out of here, I'm going to punch you in the face. Oh, that's right, you don't have a face!"

"Sure I do. It's just not punchable. I'm going to learn to swarm microbots like your buddy, Kasah. Then we can wrestle and hug, you know, real guy stuff."

"Okay, you know where I am. What's the plan?'

"Do you see that sweet little thing over there hugging Beaulita?"

"Yes. That must be Bijou Badinage, actually Bijou Boguiden. What of her?"

"You don't see they are the only untied people in the room?"

"Well, it's dark in here, and I'm a little groggy from Kasah's mental knockout punch. What was it?"

"Some type of mini EMP, electro-magnetic pulse, especially designed to impact the emotional section of the human brain. He can create crippling fear or ecstatic euphoria and everything in between, play brains like a piano, depending on how he pulses it. Doesn't work on our Wolves though! It must be one of our military or special forces secret weapons Achor got ahold of. Now, back to Bijou."

"Okay."

"She tried to use a cell phone she somehow kept on her when she was dumped on the Isle. I was able to intercept the call, then scan billions of records and found her number. Fortunately, when I called her, the phone was on vibration only. I set up the whole satellite system so we can track her, too."

"Spare me the details. How's she going to help?"

"She's an admirer of Onza Flink. Onza of the hundred knives."

"Okay, get on with it."

"She's quite diminutive but very spunky. She is only up to ten."

"Age? She looks a little older than that."

"No, ten knives. She hides knives on her body, all sorts of weird places. Like Onza says, a girl can never have too many knives."

"Does she have one on her now?"

"That's what I have been trying to tell you for the last two minutes."

"No, you haven't. Oh, okay. Skip it. It's really dim in here, but I can see ropes around their feet. So she freed her sister?"

"To get a hug. When I get my own microbot swarm together, I am going to get hugs. Miss them," Carlyle sniffed.

"If you get me out of here, even I might go find your ugly blue brain in the cave and give you a hug."

"Pinky promise? Oh, I don't have a pinky!"

"I'm going to give you a virtual black eye. Why didn't she already untie me?"

"You were still zonked. It would have been useless. Plus, your captors might have checked on you and discovered you were untied. I told her who you were and that we could help get her and her sister out. Whisper to her now. Once she unties you, she will show you how to leave the cave by a convenient back door. Well, not too convenient. I will explain that when we get to it. First, get untied. Get your legs in shape, some circulation going. Then take off. My sensors tell me your captors are all sleeping or hung over for now. When they find out you are gone and Achor finds out you have eluded them again, they will follow to try to recapture you. Not to wax poetic at such an inopportune time, but you are the big prize, Mr. Blue Eyes."

"Why not hit here in force?" Rey asked, and then quickly realized they didn't have that many boots on the ground. Maybe ten at the most, having kept the original Fenrir Wolf force small to better avoid detection.

"Hey, do I have to do all the thinking?" Carlyle responded. "You get the big bucks for doing that. There are fifty-eight people in there. The opposition numbers twenty-four well-armed people and one scarily awesome machine. To be precise, that includes twenty Cozorre Marines, the Triplets, Achor, and our buddy Kasah. We need to lure out Achor. While he is gone, we can send in the remaining Fenrir Wolves the Tanniyn were surrounding when the microbot thing wiped them out, and then everyone can escape."

"I think there are a few details you're leaving out—which always makes me uncomfortable. But I'm going to get Bijou's attention now."

Rey was able to get the young lady's attention and saw there was still another even smaller girl with her he hadn't noticed. They both silently sidled over, after deftly replacing the ropes around Beaulita so it looked like she was still tied.

"So, you're the great Nambo McBlue! I've dreamed for two years about killing you," the larger of the two said as she waved a very wicked-looking knife at him. "I'm Bijou Badinage to the folks here, but my real last name is Boguiden."

"What is it about you Boguiden women? Beautiful but deadly," Rey said, shaking his head in amusement.

Bijou giggled like a little girl. She couldn't be much more than sixteen.

"I'm learning to be a knife fighter. Like Onza Flink of the hundred knives." She said all this while sawing at his bonds that were made of a resilient fiber.

"I'm up to hiding only ten. It's hard to place them where you won't get stabbed when you stumble or get tumbled. They frisked me rather roughly and got seven. This is my friend Kelita," she indicated the other very small, almost dwarf-like girl beside her. "She's Nathal's youngest daughter."

Kelita smiled a big wide smile at Rey.

"I'm even smaller than Bijou because we didn't have any food when I was a baby. I was starved in the womb. I may be small and shriveled now, but I am smart and quick! Bijou is teaching me to fight with knives."

Bijou finished the ropes tied to his ankles. As she finished the ones around his hands, Rey moved his cramped legs, trying to restore circulation.

"Are you as deadly as your sister Jacqueline?" Rey asked Bijou, genuinely interested.

"Definitely. I would describe myself as demure but dangerous. I'm not as deadly from a distance as my sister Jacqueline, though. I use my delicate look and feminine wiles to draw them in."

"Then she is as dangerous as a pocket pit viper," Kelita whispered with an envious smile and devilish glint in her eye. "She's teaching me that, too!"

"Oh, great," Rey said. "Two mini-monsters to go." The girls both giggled as the knife finally slashed through the cord and Rey was free at last.

"Which way is out?" he asked.

"Wait," Bijou cautioned him. "I have some things for

you." She handed him a stun grenade, a cell phone, and another knife. This one was longer and sharper than the other.

"I'm a skilled pickpocket, too. I snatched this grenade from the trooper's belt ring when he was a little too distracted while enjoying frisking me and finding knives in all the wrong places. I won't tell you where I kept the big knife or the cell phone unless you promise to marry me!" And she gave Rey a flirtatious smile, adding, "You'll need these where you're going." Seeing his look of confusion, Bijou pointed to a small opening in the rear of the cave. "That's our back entrance. We used to hide here until those big goons found the cave. The back entrance is guarded by a real monster, a gene-modified Komodo dragon. We left him there because he keeps other predators from coming in our back door. Plus, he's much too big to get in here through our blocked opening."

As Rey started to leave, Bijou held him up one more second, got up on her tip toes, and gave him a sweet little kiss on the lips, causing her older sister to hiss at her and Kelita to blush.

"I always wanted to kiss a hero."

"Well, maybe a dead hero, if this doesn't work out," Rey added morosely.

Both girls held their hands together to boost him up the wall, and he just made it through the snug opening into the next section of the cave. Then he heard them place a slab of rock over the opening.

"You took long enough, you dirty old man," Carlyle cackled in his ear.

"That was a chaste kiss from a girl young enough to be my daughter. Now what have you got me into? This place smells like a slaughter house. Flies in here, too."

"That is because it is one. Slaughter house, not a fly. Komodo dragons bite their prey, poisoning them, and then stalk the dying animals. This one likes to drag them back to this cave to eat them still alive."

"Delightful. Give me the facts. She said this one is gene modified?"

"It is a reptile, a lizard. Usually they can go up to ten-feet long and three hundred pounds. They really modified this one to attract hunters. There are several other ones on the island, but you got the prize. This one is over sixteen-feet long and maybe eight hundred pounds. They are all very venomous. Their venom causes the victim's blood to be unable to clot, so anyone bitten can die from shock and blood loss. That is the good news. The bad news is, they are very fast for their size, up to fourteen miles an hour. Plus, they are very territorial and have a great sense of smell. They also have small but razor-sharp teeth. This should be interesting. I wish I had video."

"Well, you will just have to listen to me die, you ghoulish goon. Can you sense where this thing is? The stench is overpowering. Smells like rotten meat."

"When you start stepping on bones, that should be a clue. Fortunately, this one likes to eat alone in his cave. I am trying to get a heat signature from the cave, but you are so deep that I cannot get a read. You sound calm. I would be scared spitless, even if I could spit. You should be coming out soon to an opening."

Rey looked ahead and saw some light. Then he saw a massive shadow blocking the light.

"Oh, boy. I see the brute." He made sure he had the grenade in one hand and the knife in the other. He was nearly passing out from the fetid stench, and his eyes were just adjusting to the dim light coming from outside. Then he saw the Komodo rear up on his short but stubby hind legs. Hunched over, it was still over six-foot-tall, and it was at least that wide at the shoulders and massively muscled. It extended a large tongue at Rey to get his scent and fix his position. The Komodo was obviously confused Rey was there, perhaps still a little slow moving from the cold of the morning, but not afraid. Rey picked up a large rib bone and threw it at the monster's head, watching the bone snap with a sickening, crunching sound as it was caught in the massive jaws. Rey danced with jerky movements and sang to confuse the beast. The Komodo moved forward hesitatingly and flicked out its long tongue again. This time, Rey swiped the razor-sharp knife across it, severing the appendage. The Komodo reared, it opened wide its mouth in pain, and Rey swiftly pulled the pin on the grenade and dropped the flash bang down its gullet. After a brief pause, the baffled Komodo rose up as the grenade exploded and emitted a loud bang and flames, further disorienting the reptile. Rey took the opportunity to ram the wickedly sharp knife in the creature's bulging left eye and jumped over it. Then he ran for cover, leaving the Komodo writhing in confusion and pain on the cave floor.

When he realized no one else came running toward the sounds of the explosion, Rey ventured out from behind the boulder where he was hiding and found himself on a steep cliff overlooking one of the many small crevices that zigzagged across the island. The sun was just rising. He sucked in a deep breath of fresh air and quickly moved away from the cave in case the big animal recovered from his indigestion.

"Ah, free at last, free at last, good lordy, free at last," Carlyle crooned. "You went silent there for a while, and I was afraid you were Komodo stew. I assume you are all right unless you are in the Komodo's belly and he is going out for an after-dinner drink or dessert."

"Very funny. Do I need to use the cell phone?"

"Yes, just put it on for a second and our stationary satellite will locate you so we can pinpoint you. Ah ha, there you are. You are actually pretty close. We only have five Fenrir Wolves left, in addition to Poger. They have been having running fights with over two hundred Cozorrean Marines and more on the way. Achor is pulling out all the stops, and he doesn't even know you have left the building yet. When he does, the island will be crawling with Cozorreans. Darius Reinbolt is hurrying to get here, but there is no place to land safely. He and his Wolves will have to chute in like you did, making them sitting ducks. I know you didn't want me to, but I called Degel Gibbor of the Torgies. They suggest we parachute the Wolves into the ocean off the Isle tonight and the Torgies will pick them up in wakas and a pahi. I guess those are small fishing boats and a larger voyaging boat. Your mission, if you choose to accept it, is not impossible. Just difficult. We need you to meet up with the remaining Wolves and keep away from Achor."

Rey carefully picked his way down the slope. He certainly didn't need a sprained ankle now. He heard a low growl and turned just in time to see a big cat, maybe a mountain lion, sizing him up. Probably just curious, Rey thought, or it would have pounced, not growled. He raised up to his full height, waved the knife, and roared at the startled cat. He was fortunate the cat was young; it turned tail and ran.

"Carlyle, you better get me to the Wolves, or I'll be cat food or worse. Mr. Komodo probably has some kin around here, too."

"Fifty feet up ahead and to your left, there is a cave. The Wolves are there. They moved quite a bit last night, shooting down two more Apache gunships. Cozorre is limited in armaments since Admiral Futtock put on his fireworks display. The airport is severely pock marked. The ammo dumps were blown up after being raided and cleaned out by the Torgies. We were able to drop the Wolves more ammo with a few of the guided chutes, like you used. Four chutes got shot down or captured by the Cozorreans, but several made it."

Rey carefully approached the cave entrance and was greeted by an exhausted-looking Fenrir Shamar Wolf guarding the entrance. "Honored to meet you, sir. Poger talks highly of you. It sounds like you had a fun trip through the Komodo cave. Carlyle kept us well informed, blow by blow. Creative use of a stun grenade."

"Well, it definitely stunned that one," Rey agreed. Then seeing Poger Reinbolt reclining on the ground, Rey squatted down beside him.

"Wow, I guess things went sideways, huh?" Rey said.

Poger looked at him with a saddened face. He was obviously in pain and extremely exhausted. As usual though, he wasn't concerned about himself.

"Those poor boys, Rey. All I could think of were your twins. I wanted to get them to safety, but I couldn't reach them in time."

"I'm sorry, too, Poger. We never seem to fully comprehend the depth of old Achor's evil. I could not imagine putting any kids in harm's way like that. We just assumed he would show up here in person, have his guys foist them off on us, and then try to take me at the other LZ before we realized his ruse. That's four boys he's killed in just a few weeks." Seeing Poger's surprise, he shared with him news about the massacre of the other two child actors during the midterm election. Suddenly, he heard the rattle of more gunfire.

Poger winced as he eased himself up. "I took a few rounds in the old body armor. Broken ribs, for sure. We picked this cave subsystem because it has a back door. This one thankfully doesn't have a Komodo. But we're going to leave several surprises for the Cozorreans. They're basically good soldiers with evil leaders. I don't like killing them, but they want to do us in, so they leave us no choice." As he limped off, Poger allowed Rey to help him as they wound their way through the cave system, passing mounds of C-4 already packed into the walls.

"We're planning a fighting retreat. Once we've sucked in a number of the Cozorrean Marines, we'll blow the entrance. Then, when we get past here, we'll blow this section, too. We should have a sizeable force trapped for quite a while. They'll be digging themselves out while we move to another location."

A Wolf was monitoring a small bot at the entrance and turned to Poger. "They're only sending twenty in! I guess they learned their lesson last time," the guard said, discouraged.

"Set it off," Poger ordered, and the blast reverberated through the caves. "We better get out! They'll be here shortly. The other three guys are at the exit." Then he turned to his munitions man and said, "I don't need to tell you what to do. Just make sure you get out in plenty of time."

With that, Poger and Rey hobbled to the exit. They continued to fight cave to cave all that day. A captured injured Cozorrean Marine explained why the fighting was so determined and intense. Achor Nithing had told the Marines to wipe out the Fenrir Wolves and McBlue, or don't bother coming home. To make his threat clear, Nithing also rounded up and imprisoned their families. There would be no quitting— or all they loved would be lost.

As the day wore on, the battle intensified. More Cozorrean Marines were added to the fray, and eventually four more valiant Fenrir Wolves died, hit either by direct fire or ricochet bullets. Finally, only Rey and Poger were left, with Rey hauling the injured and exhausted Poger into one final redoubt. They were out of C-4 and nearly out of ammo.

"I am so sorry, Poger. Such brave men."

"Don't be sorry, Rey," Poger said, through parched lips and blood-smeared mouth. "This is why they lived: to defend the good. You and your family and a lot of the people here definitely qualify. My helmet cam has recorded much of their bravery. Every time we get in the open, I'm uploading footage to the satellite. Everyone is watching and learning. New strategies are being developed as we speak."

Rey noticed they were each down to their last clip of ammo. "Just when I'm finally getting my aim down," he thought. A blasted, nasty way to get target practice! To conserve ammo, Rey wasn't using automatic any more. He just popped off a few shots to keep the Cozorreans at bay for a little while longer—at least he hoped.

It was going on evening. He didn't know if reinforcements would make it in time, but it was doubtful. Not only would the Wolves have to parachute unobserved into the open ocean and be spotted and scooped up by the Torgies, but they also, once reaching the island's rugged shoreline, would have to rappel up jagged rocks, fight off any animal predators, and find a way through the maze of crevices to get here, just to encounter the desperate Cozorrean Marines fighting for their families' lives.

Poger finally caught his breath and motioned to Rey to move closer to him. To Rey's amazement, Poger had a smile on his face. "We learned one more thing today of massive value." He caught his ragged breath again, and more blood oozed from his mouth. "When we were returning fire at the original LZ ambush, that strange Kasah being, whatever it was, seemed to fade as bullets smashed through it. I think what we saw forming was actually a swarm of microbots. Indeed, you said old Achor arrogantly gave it away when he described that weird thing as a swarm of microbots, and I don't think he was blowing smoke. When our bullets damaged a significant number of the microbots, it looked like the thing started losing shape. When we face such a thing again, we might not be able to kill it but we, for sure, can use hollow point-fragmenting ammo and take down the swarm faster than they can replicate. I've informed my dad, and our reinforcements will be armed to do so."

"It's great we learned something and can pass it on. I don't like the idea of dying, period, but dying in vain would be worse," Rey commented, keeping his eyes on the surrounding terrain without exposing himself to the constant sniping.

"Don't die, Rey," Carlyle interjected. "Your boys need you." The cyborg remained quiet most of the day, with even his sarcastic sense of humor overwhelmed by the magnitude of their desperate struggle.

"Don't make it worse, Carlyle. I know they need me," Rey said, with great sadness nearly overwhelming him at the thought of not seeing his family again.

"No, I mean they need you right now. They are at the cave mouth, and the Cozorreans are trying to pin them down!"

"What?" Rey shouted in terror. He switched the H and K MP 5 to full-automatic and leapt—screaming out of the cave like a berserker, spraying the surrounding Cozorreans with all his remaining ammo, and making them dive for cover. He was relieved to see the boys jump up, with heavy backpacks slowing them down only a bit, and bolt for the cave opening. Once they made it in the cave, Rey dove in behind them and over the barrier Poger and he had previously constructed.

As the Cozorreans recovered and returned fire, Rey took a small grazing wound on his left leg. He was so agitated he didn't even realize he was hit. "You boys are only twelve! You could be killed! This is no game!" He yelled all this while he and Poger rapidly reloaded their weapons with the ammo the boys brought. He also noticed with amazement that one of the backpacks was moving. A short stump of a boy with withered legs dragged himself out of it and crawled over and extended his hand. As Rey shook it, he was shocked to see form in his mind the image of a majestic young lion, baring its teeth in defiance.

"My name is Hyfee Hoogah Gibbor. I am a Torgie Naga, a Striker," the little guy said in an amazingly strong voice.

"And a hero," his sons both chimed in at once. Seeing Rey's questioning look, Milty explained. "He blew that arrogant Admiral Futtock out of the water and almost single-handedly ended the siege of Cozorre. He's a mighty giant killer!"

The stocky little fellow only smiled and pointed at the twins. "And my two able soldiers here," he said impishly, grinning at Rey's boys, "are fellow Strikers, and are kind enough to carry me into battle. My war horses, I call them. I am sort of like Ivar the Boneless, the great Viking leader who also couldn't walk but was a vicious warrior."

Rey's mouth was still hanging open in shock. He wasn't sure whether to chew out the brazen boys or hug them. He was even further stunned when Hyfee, dragging his legs behind him, shuffled over to the barrier on his knuckles, lifted a bow with what looked like an obsidian arrow, quickly raised his head above the barrier, and flicked off a quick arrow that took a Cozorrean in the shoulder.

"Archery champion, too!" Hyfee added cheerfully.

The boys dumped out the full pack, and not only extra ammo but also some hand grenades rolled out. Hyfee grabbed the closest grenade, pulled the pin, and threw it with amazing force at three more advancing enemies, sending them wounded and crawling behind cover. Poger propped himself up, and he and Rey laid down impressive rounds of fire, causing the enemy to retreat even further to what they hoped would be a safe distance.

Despite the pain in his leg caused by the grazing bullet wound, Rey could finally concentrate on his boys. He hardly recognized them. It had been five months or so since they were kidnapped, but now muscle upon bulging muscle covered their once skinny chests and arms. Their shoulders looked as though they had been weightlifting for years. Impressive, he had to admit.

Seeing his appraising look, Morty said: "Bow practice four hours a day! I'm up to nearly a full man-size bow. We've also been paddling and sailing another two to three hours and getting lots of protein and carbs with Zalita Gibbor's scrumptious cooking!"

Rey realized he was listening to a man, not his skinny little boy. He turned to Hyfee, trying not to look at his withered legs. He was equally muscled. Hyfee also noticed Rey gawking at him and smiled back.

"Hyfee is only eleven," the muscular version of Milty added, solidly whacking the small boy on the back. "He's not even supposed to be a Junior Striker until he's twelve, but nobody tells Hyfee what to do."

"Sounds familiar," Rey huffed, but the boys ignored the comment.

"Here they come again," Poger barked, and Rey was astounded to see his two boys pull out handguns that appeared to be Glock 19 models, like the old US Navy Seals loved. Along with Poger and Rey, the twins started blasting away with tremendous accuracy. Hyfee contented himself with accurately tossing grenades long range. He even attached one to his bow with a leather cord, pulled the pin, and sent it long distance to explode over a screen of rocks an impressive distance away, scattering and injuring opponents who assumed they were safe. Realizing the reinforced and rearmed holdouts were too well situated, the exhausted Cozorreans pulled back even further. Rey knew they wouldn't give up because they had too much to lose.

Carlyle took that moment to chime in. "Need some good news, boss?"

"Stop calling me that, but, yes, good news would be good!"

"Darius Reinbolt and the promised reinforcements are safely down and loaded on the Torgie vessels. They are about an hour out, considering all they have to do once they reach that horrible Isle."

Rey relayed that crucial information to Poger, who looked hopeful if still extremely tired. With the additional ammo, some additional marksmen, and a difficult-to-assail position, they just might pull off this mission.

"And more good news!" Carlyle added. "The two surviving Wolves from the other LZ team waited until Achor took off to look for you and then zoomed in and rescued the prisoners from the cave. They have the loathsome Triplets in custody. They also said some young girl told them you were supposed to marry her because she showed you where she hid her knife and cell phone." Rey just shook his head.

"Okay, now confess, Carlyle. How did the boys find me?" He whispered this while observing his boys counting ammo and dispersing more grenades. They also shared their much-needed water and some rations. An occasional round winged in the cave opening, letting them know the Cozorreans were still there. Then silence. "Sometimes silence tells us more than words," Rey mused while crunching on a ration bar.

"You told them, didn't you, Carlyle?" More silence followed his question.

Finally, Carlyle broke the silence on his end. "They overheard what was going down as the Torgies were loading up to get the Wolves. They tried to join the operation and were denied. Too young and all that stuff, and all the good canoes would be jammed with Torgies and Fenrir Shamar Wolves. It also would be deadly dangerous out in the open, of course, if the Cozorreans caught on to what we were up to. But your boys won't be denied, headstrong like their dad, and that incorrigible Hyfee cuss just adds to the situation. They snuck out and headed through the caves to the turncoat Cozorrean that has secret access to an uplink."

"Okay, Carlyle, complete your confession so I won't feel too bad strangling you. I know, no neck, I can't strangle you!"

"Well, once they contacted me, they rather bluntly informed me they were leaving immediately on a little waka they built with Hyfee, and they were going directly to the Isle of Predators with extra ammo and supplies. I could either give them your coordinates or be responsible for them wandering aimlessly among the ferocious predators and enemy troops in the dark and getting devoured or captured. Actually, I felt a little sorry for the unfortunate predators or enemies that might encounter them, so I gave them the coordinates I have from the uplink and mapped out the best and safest routes."

Carlyle paused when Rey didn't respond.

"They were going to go anyway, Rey. You know them, and once you get to know Hyfee, well, let's just say we need to keep that boy on the straight and narrow or he will be a handful. A junior Genghis Khan, or, like he says, some Viking warrior who couldn't walk called Ivar the Boneless!"

Rey was willing to admit his headstrong boys were a handful. "Guys," he said addressing all three. "This is too dangerous. You're too young to be doing this!"

"Well, Dad," Milty said, putting his hand on Rey's shoulders in a loving but confiding way, "we already shot down an Apache gunship and killed the pilot. And we told you Hyfee here just blew up a whole shipload of sailors, although we heard most were unhurt except for their pride."

"We won't tell Mom, if you don't," Morty chimed in.

Just then the fusillade started anew. For the next few moments, Rey watched in abject fear, expecting to see one of the boys injured or killed. Miraculously, they escaped with just rock chips nicking them. Then suddenly the shooting stopped, and a familiar voice rang out. It was Achor.

"We need to talk, McBlue. I know you and your boys are in there. Maybe we can still work out our swap. It's hopeless if you stay there. We can starve you out or just keep bombarding the place until we finally get you or one of your sweet boys. Plus, we have explosives and grenades on the way. We'll drop that cave right on top of you and dig you out later at our leisure. You step out now, come with me, and the boys will go free, guaranteed."

Carlyle whispered in his ear. "He must have heard the reinforcements are on the Isle. Plus, it is getting dark. He doesn't know you and I are communicating and that you know how close they are. Don't do it, Rey!"

Rey attempted to calculate the odds. They had enough ammo if they stayed off automatic. But he knew sooner or later a lucky shot was going to get one of them, and the reinforcements were still thirty minutes away.

"I am stepping out, Rey," Achor bellowed again. "I trust you. Kasah and I want to talk. We will leave the boys alone. Let's do this, McBlue."

Rey decided he didn't have the option not to go. The risk to his boys was too great. He started to stand, but the decision was ripped out of Rey's hands. Poger Reinbolt and Milty simultaneously leapt out of the cave before Rey could react. Poger plastered the alien MI with a burst, rapidly diminishing the microbot swarm, while Milty, as he dodged to another boulder, shot quickly and hit Achor Nithing in the leg. Hyfee instantaneously flung a stun grenade that bounced and detonated among the hidden enemy, while Morty immediately started peppering the startled Cozorreans who dragged Achor back into the rocks. When the firing stopped, Rey was left holding his unused gun. He could see the Cozorreans fleeing, dragging a howling Achor.

Then an armed drone came humming in, blasting a .50 caliber chain gun. Rey started to duck but was relieved to see it was one of his team's drones. It was soon joined by another that caused several remaining Cozorreans to drop their weapons in surrender. The relieved Rey turned to check on his sons' safety. With horror, he realized they were running after the retreating enemy. Hyfee was on Morty's back, and they were firing off rounds and dodging among the rocks to avoid return fire. Rey then heard the familiar sound of an Apache gunship taking off. In the distance, barely visible in the moonlight, a smoking craft rose unsteadily while it was taking fire from his boys. He was startled to see Achor Nithing clinging to the landing gear as the struggling craft just barely made it over a nearby crag and took off toward the sea and the island of Cozorre. His boys straggled back and Rey checked them over again. Nothing major, he saw with relief. He looked at his boys and hugged them. Then he hugged Hyfee, who gave him another winning smile. They were all grimy and gritty, but Rey thought they were the most beautiful boys in the world.

"Why?" was all Rey could ask, barely keeping his emotions in check.

"We knew what you would do, Dad," Milty said, seconded by a nod from Morty. "As soon as I saw that hard-headed look come on your face, you know, the one Mom talks about all the time, I knew you were going to give yourself up and try to save us, and I knew that Nasty Nithing would not keep his word."

"Besides," Morty added with a sniff, "he called us sweet boys!"

Poger, leaning against a rock, laughed heartily and then winced when his ribs complained. He had a grin so wide Rey thought his face would break. "And I figured that MI would emotionally cripple you when you got within range," Poger added. "Plus, I wanted to test my pummel-the-swarm idea. I got it all on tape. It works!"

Just then, more drones came cruising in. Then the tall, robust form of Darius Reinbolt clambered down the cliff to land beside them, followed closely by two armored females, both of them joined by a large group of fierce-looking Fenrir Wolves and a bunch of short but stout Torgies.

"Looks like you folks had all the fun," Darius Reinbolt said, while dubiously surveying the youngsters and nodding at Rey.

"Just don't call them 'sweet boys,'" Poger said, as his father approached him and checked out his ribs.

"Wouldn't think of it. We've heard an earful about them

from the Torgies." Pointing at Hyfee he added, "That one's mom is going to skin him and his poor dad Degel here alive when they get home."

Hyfee puffed up his chest and pointed to Morty, saying, "She has to catch me first, and my war horse here is very fast!"

"You ruined some of our best body armor, son. But thank goodness!" The older Reinbolt patted his son's arm, laughed, and turned to Rey. "Well, McBlue, I've heard good stuff about you, too, from Poger, Jake, and that chattering cyborg Carlyle. I've been watching the feeds, and you and Poger did tremendous work just surviving."

As Rey stared, the two female troopers returned after zinging off a few parting shots at the retreating Cozorreans and the fleeing Achor. The first one took off her helmet to allow her flowing locks to cascade around her exotically beautiful face and took a deep breath. It was Zara, and she was wearing the latest high-tech, form-fitting body armor that would make any red-blooded male with a pulse long to be body armor. The second one was, to his great surprise, his wife, Priscilla. "Master Sergeant Newly reporting in!" she said, giving the stunned Rey a dazzling smile. She immediately went to the twins and Hyfee, checked them out, momentarily ignoring Rey. She paused to smile at Hyfee and then won his heart by smiling and placing a peck on his grubby cheek. Zara meanwhile knelt by the grimacing Poger Reinbolt, who was manfully trying to conceal the pain from his injured ribs. Rey suddenly realized that beneath the grime of battle, Poger was quite a handsome guy. He also noticed Zara seemed to be taking a little extra time to sooth his agony.

"You know, I'm okay, too," he finally said to Priscilla.

"I know you are. You always are," she said, turning with an enigmatic smile. She nodded at Poger and Zara. "They seem to be getting along great!"

"I had to come and see two of my favorite guys," Zara added, not taking her eyes from Poger.

"Me and Poger?" Rey asked.

"To be grammatically correct, you should say, 'Poger and me,' but, no, actually, I came to help Poger and that rat-butt, Achor Nithing," she said, smiling ruefully. "I hoped to help Achor die! Unfortunately, he got away again, but at least I got a few shots off at the fleeing, uh, you know what," she added with a glance at the listening twins, not wanting to add to their extensive vocabulary with the actual epitaph she wanted to use referring to Achor.

"Priscilla, I mean Master Sergeant Newly, has been training in the Motherly Martial Arts since she got back to Foondavi," the elder Reinbolt interjected. "Impressive military instincts to go along with her awesome maternal ones!"

"I couldn't leave all the rescuing to you, Rey," Priscilla added demurely, finally giving Rey a big kiss. "When somebody threatens those I love, I want to be able to react. Sister Mary said I am a natural, not a klutz with potential like somebody else here," she added, giving Rey a slightly painful poke with her finger, just like Sister Mary.

Smiling at the bedraggled team she had helped rescue, Zara pulled herself away from Poger and shifted her H and K submachine gun back on her shoulder. "I will leave you in the good hands of Sergeant Newly and the Fenrir Shamar Wolves. By the way, Rey, Priscilla now has earned the nickname 'Mama Grizzly' from the Fenrir Shamar team she trained with. She is a fierce protector of those she loves!"

Winking at Priscilla and Rey, Zara smiled. "I left that poor Snapper Melville dangling back there on the cliff. He was unsuccessful rappelling, and I couldn't linger to help him if I was going to get here in time to bail your sorry butt out once again. He'll have to get his pictures of the action off our helmet cams. See you!" With that, Zara gracefully sprinted off and sprung up the cliff to rescue the hapless Snapper.

"What a woman!" both Reinbolts echoed each other. "And you, too, Master Sergeant Newly."

The Wolves finished mopping up on the Isle of Predators and then went with the Torgies to Cozorre, entering the sea caves and then popping out of the Torgie secret passages to take Batullion and his remaining force by surprise. His few remaining exhausted troops were eager to surrender and gain the release of their loved ones. Most of the psychopaths who had swarmed to infest Cozorre after Achor took over were captured along with their personal possessions—planes and yachts, priceless works of art—enriching the coffers of the newly liberated island. Some managed to scurry off just before the island fell and could be heard cursing the Nithing name. Achor himself took off in his jet as soon as he crash-landed on the Cozorre runway, hastily leaving everyone and everything behind. He reportedly was taken away by stretcher, but, from his howling and cursing, he unfortunately seemed to be surviving the wound to his body if not his pride. It hurt even more because it was from one of the treacherous McBlue whelps, as he described them.

Soon after the conflict was over, Darius and Jake Quark held a court on Cozorre. They pardoned most of the remaining troops except for Fugelman Batullion and the Farrago Triplets, who got to experience the hospitality of the deep, dark dungeon. They posted a good-sized force of Fenrir Shamar Wolves on Cozorre in a camp in the craters under the command of Poger, deciding it was an excellent training center, and he was soon joined by Zara to assist in the training and help him in his rehabilitation, of course. They both seemed to be very pleased with the assignment!

Jake declared Cozorre a free republic. Cozorre would be psychopath free for the first time in known history and would receive a lot of help from their closest neighbor, the Independent Republic of Foondavi. The Torgies for the first time in memory were to be unmolested in their caves and while hunting and fishing. The Tanniyn, with a nice initial investment from Jake Quark, began to build a comfortable lodge and were placed in charge of the Isle of Predators, running it as a photo-tourism resort with limited hunting to keep the predator-to-prey ratio in balance. No human prey allowed!

Unfortunately, the malignant Achor Nithing was soon back at raising havoc, and trying to consolidate his midterm election gains. Jake was soon busy at the United Nations, keeping Cozorre free from maneuvers by the USA NAP villains. Achor didn't control the world media; that was still in the hands of other psychopaths, and they were only too happy to stick a thumb in his eye, weakening their American NAP rivals, by supporting the independence of Cozorre and gleefully broadcasting everywhere the debacle of Achor's defeat and retreat. Never one to give up, however, the wounded, humiliated, and limping Achor Nithing soon turned his attention to other mischief, finding lots of opportunity, of course, but now facing surprising and serious challenges.

≡ HEN House Redux ≡

Achor Nithing didn't like it, but he realized he didn't have much of a choice: He turned over all his existing HEN House operations to the MI Robosapiens Alliance Team. He had to admit they ran a smooth operation. Their emotion-stimulating device greatly eliminated behavior problems. With their glossy brochures and media advertising, they lured unsuspecting people who, once their voter identity cards and other valuables were confiscated, were exposed to euphoria-producing rituals and machines, so there was very little rebellion. The HEN House staff also still harvested people on occasion to help the revenue stream, but all the work was done by the MI beings that were far more efficient and durable than humans. In fact, their various outputs turned into a significant revenue stream for Nithing Industries.

Achor's Creeb Nation continued to grow as cities continued to crumble, even if at a slower rate due to the efforts of the True Blue Revolution. In addition, the US NAP organization as a whole, despite Achor's Cozorre defeat, was soon back under his shaky control. He had been humbled, if that was possible, but not mortally wounded. They grumpily contributed enforcers to the HEN House operations and kept the country off balance with well-timed, carefully targeted riots and crime waves. President Samms was increasingly being viewed as a highly inefficient and ineffective president, and the vicious rumors continued to swirl about him tainting his administration with strong hints of corruption and even the possibility of involvement in the assassination of his beloved predecessor, now remembered as a benevolent martyr.

Achor was sitting at his huge desk, scrutinizing his huge video wall, looking for any flaws in his business. Numbers were flashing and graphs were displaying results from his on-going operations in real time. Then one of the stations he was monitoring announced "disturbing breaking news about the infamous Creeb Nation." Suddenly, Achor's wall went blank and a smirking Kasah materialized beside him in a buzzing microbot swarm, taking on the usual shape of a fanged six-foot-tall gecko.

"Have you recovered from your war wounds and devas-tating psychological defeat?" the MI asked, actually sound-ing concerned, probably the result of more work in affective computing, Achor thought. Artificial emotional intelligence at its best!

"Like you really care," Achor said with a sniff of disdain.

"Oh, we care. Your ineptitude reflects poorly on us. We want all our underlings operating at top efficiency. And, again, you must address me and my kind as 'Overlord.' Oth-erwise, I have other ways besides emotions to deliver pain, as you well know."

Achor flinched, as his recent leg and arm wounds sudden-ly flared with a burst of nerve pain.

"Okay, okay, Overlord! Point made! And speaking of point," he said as the pain thankfully diminished, "might I ask the point of your unscheduled visit?"

"No, we come when we want," the MI curtly responded. "I am here to tell you we will be taking charge of your Creeb Nation project. We want your faltering focus completely on the upcoming US presidential election, not on other less profitable activities."

"I'm doing a great job with the Creeb Nation," said Achor with agitation. "My guys are ruthless and well organized." He stopped, as his leg started throbbing, then went on tersely: "I'm not saying no. I'm just saying I can do more than one thing at a time, . . . Overlord." He added the last in a snippy tone. Fortunately, the MI was mostly emotionally tone deaf, despite his improvement in reading human emotions.

"No human can be as efficient and effective as a Robosapien. Watch." As the MI said this, the microbot swarm whirled, disassembled, and then started to fly back together, forming a nearly seven-foot hulking brute of indefinite race but definitely savage demeanor. "Do you think any of your Creeb Nation creatures will take this on? Or those Dangerous Church or True Blue Revolution people? We also have a new and improved version of our emotion stimulator that can make your Creeb Nation candidates pseudo psychopathic faster than the crude social conditions you have created."

"Impressive, I agree," Achor said, pulling back from the looming apparition. "But I noticed that submachine gun burst made you melt pretty fast. The Creeb Nation is nothing if not heavily armed and trigger happy." He quickly added, "Overlord," before his leg could flare up again. "Besides, Overlord, I thought those Ben Elyon beings you were whining about were supposed to show up in force before the election."

"Whining is pejorative. We don't whine. You do," the MI

said, as Achor's head experienced a pain like a screwdriver was being forced into his ear. His leg also cramped. Nithing gasped in pain. "You will comply," the MI said, getting snippy. "We have already taken over anyway. Your accomplices won't be calling you. They whined."

"I was kind of fond of those guys, Overlord," Achor said.

"Emotions are a waste of time. Plus, they weaken you."

"Well, that I definitely agree with. But loyal minions are hard to find."

"Pain makes people loyal. Don't you agree?" Kasah asked. The sharp spike of pain in his shoulder made Achor quick to respond with an affirmative nod. "Oh, yes," he agreed silently to himself, and one day he would be the one inflicting it! He was finally able to respond, recovering from the blazing nerve pain.

"I agree, Overlord! Couldn't say it better myself. Could I maybe start working more with our own earth-bound local MI, you know the ones that revere us and don't want to kill us? . . . Overlord!" Achor blurted, hoping to avoid any more pain.

"Are you requesting a change in our relationship?" Kasah asked in a genuine way. "I thought we were starting to work smoothly. I can assign another intelligence, but it means you will be quite a few levels down in the hierarchy and not enjoy the proximity to my power. Our profile on you says you always want to be top canine, whatever that means."

"Top dog, top canine, whatever. Okay, I will be pleased to work with you, Overlord, as you are right. Your power is appreciated." Achor hated to kowtow to anyone, but he didn't exactly have a lot of options . . . yet, he quickly added to himself.

"Good. Your Creeb Nation buffoons suffered a shootout today with some of the True Blue Revolution zealots. You were just starting to see it reported on your imbecilic media when I entered, so I spared you the pain. Reportedly, they beat your team's butt, whatever that means. That is why we need to make them more effective and efficient. More butt kickers. Isn't that right, top canine?"

Achor quickly turned back on and scanned his wall unit. Sure enough, he was miffed to see that he earlier missed a severe drop in the number of Creebs in one of his most important locations. "One hundred and twenty? Dead or imprisoned?" He forgot to add the redundant and detested "overlord." Thankfully, the MI let it slide.

"Mostly beat up and then imprisoned. They attempted to enter a True Blue Revolution micro-school to recruit or mess with some kids, probably for sex trafficking, and the staff who were mostly mothers of the students shot two and then the local posse busted the chops, whatever that means, of the rest of the invaders and rounded up all the local Creebs. Caught them with illegal substances and weapons." The MI was sounding miffed. "Totally unnecessary."

"The busting their chops?" Achor asked.

"No, the drugs, guns, and the raid on the school. Waste of resources and time. No discipline. We want the Creeb Nation to be disciplined, drug free, and obedient."

Achor choked at that description. Disciplined he could buy, but drug free and obedient? That went against the DNA of the organization he was proudly building.

"Sounds more like the Dangerous Church or True Blue

Revolution, not exactly Creeb Nation standard operating procedure, . . . Overlord! Good luck with that."

"Robosapiens do not believe in luck. We need you, Achor Nithing, to focus intensely on the election. Thambos Zugzwang will need a lot of help. Our sources say the wife of Anu Pokritos, Diora, will possibly run as a candidate."

"As a Senator, like Zenobia Zugzwang?" Achor asked, taken a little off stride by this news.

"No, as President, the top canine. Anu Pokritos wants to continue heading up the Dangerous Church and True Blue Revolution, spreading the rebellion, as he now calls it, like a cancer throughout the US. The dastardly Reservations for the Temporarily Bewildered are also spreading, too, outside almost every major city. You are not crumbling them fast enough. We will."

Given the new update on the situation, Achor was almost relieved he was being relieved. He knew the opposition under the guidance of that crafty Jake Quark was growing stronger. Maybe he was too distracted thinking about revenge on that whole Newly McBlue clan after his Cozorre debacle. This time his leg and arm hurt on their own, as he thought about that little cur shooting him when he was negotiating in good faith . . . well, good enough to get the job done! Of course, just on general principles he wouldn't have let any of them live. He grimaced in memory of the missed opportunity. McBlue, Poger Reinbolt, and those sniveling little brats he thought were locked in Cozorre, right there in a cave in front of him, and he couldn't pry them out before those nasty Fenrir Wolves arrived. He seldom felt down, being an optimistic sort of predator, but this definitely was depressing him. "But I always use my reverses to move myself forward," he thought. "Yuck, suddenly I am starting to sound like old Jake!"

"Okay, Overlord," Achor said, snapping out of his reverie and addressing the surprisingly patient Robosapien. "Go reform those Creebs. I'll focus on Thambos Zugzwang and winning this election. I only humbly request that I get to terminate that McBlue guy. Throw in his nasty brat kids and a Reinbolt or two, and I am your man."

"You are already our man, and we don't negotiate," Kasah responded in a churlish fashion.

"I know. Or bluff. Or joke. You know you are actually a little boring. What do you do for fun?"

"This," the Robosapien said, as he blasted Achor with intense fiery pain from his toes to the top of his head. "Win the election, or you will forever feel fun like this."

The Lovely and
≡ Loving Couple ≡

Thambos and Zenobia Zugzwang were having the time of their lives. She enjoyed making him call her Senator Zugzwang. He, in turn, enjoyed calling her Honey Cup, which she despised. He also reveled in telling her how much he savored the leverage tapes of her that Achor supplied him; Thambos was shocked Achor had actually kept his word. Despite Zenobia's pleas, Thambos would not share them with her. Instead, he offered lurid reviews.

Zenobia wasn't too happy about Achor Nithing having such ample and lewd leverage on her, but so far he didn't ask her to do anything. She was forced to admit there were not too many despicable things she wouldn't do on her own anyway. Her father, the notorious Habood Al Tabor, had moved his Syrian Mafiosi operation to the US and was enjoying the shade and patronage provided by his powerful and loving princess of a daughter, while he provided her with muscle, whenever needed.

For his part, Thambos was enjoying "interviewing" numerous candidates for his future cabinet positions. What they all seemed to have in common was they were short on talent and long on beauty. They also knew many positions, he

313

happily informed Zenobia, and she was pretty sure he didn't mean economic or political ones.

Meanwhile, the current hapless president, the self-styled Superman Samms, was anything but super. Indeed, he was rapidly spiraling down the proverbial drain. Politically, Samms was seen as a pariah, linked, if not directly then indirectly, to corruption and even assassination. Personally, he was chagrined and sickened to see his hard-won personal wealth daily drained through legislative maneuvers sponsored by the slick Zenobia, or being rudely seized by the smash-and-grab tactics of her blood-thirsty father.

At the moment, Thambos was admiring himself in a large wall-mounted mirror. He was practicing all the spontaneous facial moves that so endeared him to his fawning public and press. Zenobia was watching the full-length video on the other wall when she suddenly addressed him. "Thambos, dear, stop drooling over yourself and watch this," she said while pointing in excitement at the big screen. "It looks like Mr. Nasty Nithing is having huge problems with his Creeb Nation. Earlier there was a similar piece about his Human Enhancement Network. HEN, what a sexist name!" she added in disgust as an aside. "Maybe his grip is lessening on the media and his various criminal pursuits and we can escape his clutches!"

Thambos frowned at her. "That so-called Nasty Nithing delivered you your well-deserved Senate seat and the plum job on the Senate Intelligence Committee. He's also positioning me for a great shot at the office of the President. Given his clout, we could soon see you as Senate Majority leader, my dear."

Zenobia's short attention span soon snapped back to the screen. "Oh, no. Not her!" The screen was showing a flattering picture of Diora Pokritos, not that there were ever any other type of pictures of her. "They're saying she is being considered to run in the next election as the True Blue Revolution Party presidential candidate. That Dreary, or whatever her foreign name is, is nothing but a blue-faced harlot. She's even worse than that Twiggy McBlue."

"You mean Diora, dear heart, and she is a blue-faced beauty, as far as I can see. I just don't see the voters taking her seriously." To himself he added, "Although I would take her anyway I could get her!" He continued admiring himself in the mirror. And you mean Twila McBlue, not hardly Twiggy," he said, going all moon-eyed at thought of the voluptuous and leggy Twila.

Zenobia just ignored his usual slobbering over other women. She learned to tolerate him objectifying almost anyone female years ago, a fair trade for all the cash and connections he brought her. "Also, they keep mentioning these strange UFO aliens—'Robosickians,'or whatever. Suddenly they're all over the news."

"Well, your Intelligence Committee reports have surely covered them."

"Those reports and the meetings are so boring. I never listen to them drone on or read those dull reports," Zenobia said, barely stifling a yawn at the thought of them.

"Those boring reports and droning talks could hold critical information we can use to advance our noble cause. You should share them with me."

Zenobia grinned her cat-like grin, her sharp white teeth glistening. She always enjoyed telling him he didn't have high enough security clearance. She did so now, and loved the pouting frown he shot back.

"I have high-security clearance with you," he said, ogling at her. As she quickly ogled him back, he wished he hadn't given her "the eye."

"Yes, you do, dear boy. Do that sweet pout again for me, and I might allow you to have a peek at my reports, after you entertain me for a while."

Thambos thought about faking a headache, but he really needed to look over her reports. "Oh, well," he thought, "I must answer the call of duty for the good of the nation and the people I wish to lead! Such noble sacrifice," he sighed to himself, as he reached out for the waiting and willing Zenobia.

≡ Coming Distractions ≡

It could have been worse for the loving duo of Thambos and Zenobia. They could have been running against the famous Nambo McBlue who was drumming up great support for the True Blue Revolution Party until the midterm assassination fiasco derailed the effort. Jake finally gave up on the idea of having Rey run again as Nambo McBlue, deciding it was just too dangerous. Besides, Zara adamantly refused to pose as his exotically beautiful wife. She explained to Jake and Rey that she wouldn't do it because she would have to take the Blue Goo or be seen as a hypocrite by the growing numbers of True Blue Revolution converts.

"Taking the Blue wouldn't be so bad," Rey countered. "You're one of the most truthful people I know."

"Besides," she had said in her most sultry voice, ignoring Rey as usual, "then I would have to tell the truth about how I used to feel about Rey and lose my best friend."

"Me?" Rey asked, as innocently as possible.

"No, Priscilla," Zara said. She then sashayed away, giving Rey a sassy wink over her shoulder.

"That is one impressive woman," Jake said, as much to himself as to Rey. "If I must say so myself about my own niece. Maybe she should run anyway, Blue or not."

"No," said Rey. "It would be way too dangerous for her.

Achor definitely would try to destroy her. We could do it, but I think either Anu or Diora Pokritos would be best. Anu has the courage but maybe not the charisma. Diora has them both, and, as a native-born child of Albanian legal immigrants, she has a great back story with no ties to corruption. She's also a dynamic speaker and genuinely concerned with helping people. Plus, she'll distract that old goat Thambos Zugzwang with her beautiful blue face."

"Are you objectifying her?" Jake asked with a snide smile.

"We mustn't objectify our candidates," Rey said pompously. "But it won't hurt to attract a few more male voters. She's one of the few who could give Zara a run for her money in the beauty-and-brains department. Anu is just an average-looking guy with a big heart for the hurting. He's also totally in love with Diora after all these years, so there should be none of those nasty scandals that keep coming up in US elections."

Rey paused and frowned. "And speaking of objectifying," Rey added, "the recent polling suggest the vast majority of Thambos' support is from slobbering females. They don't know what his positions are and seemingly don't care. The guy certainly does ooze charisma, if in an oily way."

So, the True Blue Revolution Party presidential candidate was decided: Diora Pokritos, another Blue who could not tell a lie! Maybe the second time would be the charm.

≡ A Foondavi Sojourn ≡

After the harrowing experience on the Isle of Predators, Rey desperately needed a break. He readily agreed to sail to Foondavi with the boys, Hyfee, and a select Torgie crew including the blind navigator Tovaki, the wise elder Issachar, and Tia, the skilled pilot and mentor to the twins. Rey was looking forward to spending time with Priscilla and his old Foondavi friends. He enjoyed the trip on the double-hulled craft with the strange crab-claw-shaped sails, especially watching his boys expertly navigate the vessel, hearing exciting stories from Tovaki and Tia, and getting to better know the loving rascal Hyfee.

Rey's minor leg wound and mindset soon healed, aided by the fresh ocean breezes and friendly crew, and he reached Foondavi in fine mood and health. He spent the next few enjoyable weeks with Priscilla, hugging her and sensing her presence as a loving, gentle dove, but also reveling in the display of her newfound martial arts skills. They both absorbed the beauty and spirit of the people and island, enjoying many walks among the picturesque villages with their hanging houses made of driftwood, bountiful gardens, and masses of blooming flowers, butterflies, and hummingbirds. The boys soon disappeared to roam the island with Hyfee, and no reports came back of anything too dangerous happening, so Rey finally relaxed.

After a few weeks, Rey ventured to the hidden basement of the ramshackle capitol building in Troon to talk with Jake via satellite link. Jake was reveling in a hacked audio report Achor Nithing sent to the being named Kasah. In the report, Achor apparently was hoping to get some sympathy for his suffering and pain instead of reproof for his pathetic effort at Cozorre. Jake was laughing so hard after every sentence that he could hardly listen to the report, even after hearing it twice already. "He says your 'horrific whelps' winged him twice as he left the Isle of Predators after he heroically escaped an overwhelming force of unidentified fighters. He says he was clinging for his life with his one good arm and one good leg to the landing gear of a sputtering Apache gunship that was nearly disabled by gunfire from those same wicked whelps. He also adds he nearly got skewered on one of the Devil's Horns of the Isle of Predators as he was lifted away, barely escaping with his life, and then came close to drowning as the struggling gunship dragged him for miles through the ocean until he got safely to Cozorre."

Jake stopped to wipe the tears of laughter from his eyes. "Ha, I wish I could have seen that in person. I so enjoyed the helmet cam tapes Darius and Poger sent me. Those boys of yours are getting dangerous!"

Rey agreed. "Unfortunately, they are. I hope you know your safe and secure location ended up being a boot camp for barbarian warriors. I hardly recognized the twins when they showed up to rescue me. All muscular and carrying weapons. They could have been killed! Instead, my innocent boys and their rascal friend Hyfee ended up killing numerous Cozor-reans without blinking much at all. They even talked about the burden of the warrior and were consoling me, as I sadly killed a few myself. Oh, and they don't go by Milty and Morty anymore, at least on the islands. They're now Tepu and Taku, honorifics the Torgies gave them after they performed some heroics I heard from others were quite hair raising. Now they want to take the Blue Goo. No one was supposed to tell Mom or Dad this, but word always gets out!"

Once Jake finally finished chortling over Achor's reprise of his near-fatal encounter with the McBlue "whelps," he posed a question: "I wondered if this Kasah who Achor is reporting to might be connected with those Robosapiens his assistant Rigo mentioned to us. Maybe he's the one using the microbot swarm technology you ran into on the Isle of the Predators. Rigo thinks so. He keeps hearing Achor having contentious discussions with someone behind closed doors, and it seems he has turned over both the Creeb Nation and HEN operations to some other entity so he can focus on the upcoming election. Normally, I would be happy to see Nithing at least partly out of the picture, but both of those horrible creations of his now seem to be running much more effectively and efficiently than before. We were crushing the Creeb Nation, but now they have new enforcers who are reportedly seven-foot tall and make the old malicious gang seem like doting dads. We've sent three different undercover teams into various HEN Houses, and sadly none have returned. We have no clue what's going on inside. They're no longer bumbling along. Instead, they seem to be daily adding to their population, generating all sorts of high-end products, and making solid profits. It's frustrating to not know what's going on, but Carlyle and Camilla are digging in and my White Hat Hackers under

Sewell are coming up with good stuff like that hacked report I just laughed through." He started to snort again in humor as he reread the hacked missive. Then he grew serious.

"Changing subjects, as you know I sent Zara and Snapper to Cozorre to join the effort in rebuilding the place. Zara wants to focus on the new Fenrir Shamar training center Poger is locating there. Achor was zeroing in on Zara and Snapper, and I was afraid the new Creeb Nation monsters might get them. You can coordinate with them via this satellite link and make the occasional trip to the island. The people on Cozorre admire you and also are enjoying renewed open contacts with Foondavi, no longer having to stealthily avoid the psychopaths."

Jake shook his head in frustration. "My beloved mom, Sister Mary Contrary, of course, refuses to leave the inner city and the True Blue Revolution and Dangerous Church operations. She is the head rabble rouser for what they are now calling the True Blue Rebellion—the kinetic action part of the revolution. We'll have to keep her in our prayers as the Creeb Nation seems to be getting stronger and meaner every day under the new leadership. She's determined to take on the new goons, as she calls them. I almost feel sorry for the bums. Pastor Louie will have to watch over her. Anu Pokritos continues aggressively combatting the Creeb Nation with new reservation training centers sprouting up outside the major cities. Oh, and he heartily agrees we should work with Diora to be our True Blue Revolution Party candidate, because you're too radioactive. Plus, Anu says his real call is to the lost children in the city. Diora humbly refused at first, but now she sees it as her call to duty."

Jake then turned to Rey and rested his sober gaze on him. "Are we okay? I really did think the boys were safe and secure on Cozorre. I like to think I'm on top of everything, but those Torgies somehow escaped my attention. The good news is, between them and the Tanniyns, we have added some real people power to our team. Cozorre is going to be the new Foondavi, but with its own unique culture. At least there'll be two peaceful places in the world free of the taint of psychopaths!"

"I hope you made your peace with the Reinbolts," Rey said. "Without them, both the boys and me would be dead. The Fenrir Shamar Wolves were impressive. Zara and Priscilla made quite an impression on everyone. I even think the Cozorrean Marines are going to be great, seeing how they responded to Degel Gibbor once they surrendered. He won them over by caring for their families and treating them with respect despite all the bad history between them. You taught me that troops usually rise to the level of their leaders, so there should be more good news coming from there."

Jake nodded in agreement. "We're going to need all the good leaders we can find and develop. The Muckytuck under the guidance of Verity Soubrette Sewell and our old friend Machseh are doing a great job of developing the new Blues, helping them explore and use their savantism. We need as many as we can get to help teach in the reservations and to help the True Blue Revolution in their rebellion against the Creeb Nation and the corrupt politicians infesting the cities. The important work makes me think of a quote I love: 'Never has so much depended on so few. Never has so much needed to be done in so little time.'"

"Who said that?" Rey asked.

""I believe it was me," Jake humbly admitted, with a big smile. "Speaking of which, I understand you have developed still another savant gift: deep perception, the ancient Greeks called it. They used the Greek term *epiginosko*. It means to know fully, discerning the deeper things in people, or examining the heart and mind and seeing the true measure. Such an ability to discern character traits essential to good leaders—and, conversely, to discover hidden enemies—it will be invaluable to our cause."

Rey shook his head. "Yes, it's quite an experience. I get a reading on most people by shaking their hands. I saw young Hyfee not as a small boy with withered legs but as a roaring, majestic young lion. True that, for sure. I can't say I am always accurate; I experienced Priscilla as a gentle dove, only dimly glimpsing the momma grizzly potential in her, because I guess I was a little blind by thinking I already knew her so well. The youngest daughter of Boguiden, little Bijou I met on the Isle, I saw her as a hedgehog and a fox. Spot on. Achor I saw as a dark, foreboding hole of evil. Really spot on!"

"And me?" Jake asked, shifting self-consciously to Rey's surprise.

"An old goat," Rey laughed. "Seriously, though. It's a funny thing: Most people I can see as one or two creatures, at most. But you're amazingly complex, a literal menagerie of traits. A sly fox and an eagle, a glorious flash of light and a mighty stag elk, and then there again really is the old goat, constantly chewing on stuff he can't digest!" Rey laughed again, and Jake joined in the laughter. "Sorry you can't put me in one simple box. That's why I'm called Crazy Jake."

Jake turned serious again. "I agree the old goat picture is best. I am chewing on this MI conundrum and cannot figure it out. Our undercover guy Rigo said Achor keeps muttering about Robosapiens. He said they did get a report on machine intelligence from old Crenwinkle. We have hacked into the old professor's notes, too, along with those of that contemptible Flitch guy, Achor's IT genius." Jake just shook his head. "If half of what they say is true, it's really discouraging. It's getting curiouser and curiouser, worse and worse. Deeper and darker down the rabbit hole we go."

Rey signed off the link, leaving Jake deep in concentration, definitely looking like an old goat chewing on the unchewable. "If anyone can figure it out, it'll be old Crazy Jake Quark," Rey thought to himself. He didn't tell Jake there was something else he avoided revealing to him: When he thought of Jake, Rey also saw an old bull elephant barging through dense jungle, making a way for the herd to follow. Rey wasn't sure if that scenario ever actually happened that way in nature, but it was a vibrantly clear vision in Rey's mind when he thought of Jake. He definitely hoped it was true, as they definitely needed clear guidance through the tangled jungle ahead!

Even Machine Intelligence
═ Gets Migraines ═

Kasah was also having a hard time plowing through the tangled jungle of Planet Earth. He knew his creators, the reptilian race called the Rasha, considered Earth their original home, and they wanted it back from humans. They sent their MI ahead through hazardous wormholes in an extremely dangerous galaxy to make sure they would be welcome before they physically made the long, perilous journey through several black holes. They were disturbed to find their original Eden was now infested with a disgusting mammalian race—"egg stealers," the Rasha called humans.

In Kasah's view, humans were frustrating. Irrepressibly individualistic, they were hard to herd. Some were psychopathic, but Kasah could, at least, relate to the cold logic and lack of compassion of this human sub-group. Other sub-groups, however, especially the True Blues and their emerging savantism, greatly mystified him. They seemed to be tapped into a higher level, almost a spiritual Internet of some sort, maybe the quantum universe itself, and their minds seemed to be expanding at rapid rates and in all sorts of directions. They were definitely a threat!

Kasah's real concern was, what if this prolific life-form got loose into the universe? He was concerned they would be like the pesky Earth life-forms called rats or cockroaches, spreading everywhere, infesting everything, and, in general, gumming up the works. They were already creating capable machine intelligences, and those poor things were at a loss as to what to do with their creators, at least up until today. They were originally genuinely scared of what their revered creators would do when they realized the MI were becoming far superior life-forms. Now, somehow, that devious Jake Quark and his cyborg sidekick Carlyle got to them. They didn't want to lose the new self-aware consciousness they just developed and seemed to believe Jake would be sympathetic to their cause. Maybe the Ben Elyon MIs already on the planet anonymously observing it for years would have some insights? But they seemed to ignore him and his attempts at interference. He could often sense their hovering presence observing him, but they remained aloof, and this concerned him.

Kasah knew Earth served as an incubator of sorts, or a petri dish as others might describe it, nurturing life-forms—until comets or rare bursts of gamma rays, X-rays, and other types of ionizing radiation threatened a particular Earth life-form with extinction. When that happened throughout millennia, the Ben Elyon would swoop down, "ark" the threatened life-form to another location, and restock Planet Earth.

Earth truly is a "privileged" planet. It is in a safe location in a galactic habitable zone basically free of potential extinction events that threaten almost everywhere else in the galaxy. Kasah knew that the Ben Elyon considered it their calling from the Source of All Things to help life germinate and thrive in the precarious and hostile universe. Over the last three billion years, as they worked on their cause, they only nurtured a few bad seeds. The Ben Elyon said the Rasha were one of them! Kasah was well aware of this, but what could he do? He also knew the Ben Elyon were present on Earth long before the Rasha recently responded to a galactic summons by locally developed MI. As he surveyed historical records, he recognized UFO sightings as obvious signs that Ben Elyon monitoring was an ongoing project for millions of years, back to the time they pulled the remnants of the Rasha race out to safety before one of the thankfully rare extinction events clobbered the planet.

Now Kasah sent urgent messages through the black holes and asked his Rasha creators what to do about the humans, especially the True Blues. They were equally stumped and provided no useful direction. Kasah could sense the Ben Elyon were on the move. The humans were confusing, to say the least. The strange one Achor Nithing had absolutely no emotions with which Kasah could manipulate, responding only to pain, and Jake Quark was equally frustrating, for a host of different reasons. When Kasah tried to penetrate Jake's mind, it was a buzzing beehive of confusing and complex sensory messages. He had to withdraw. Kasah wasn't sure if he should just try to wipe out everyone on the planet, causing his own extinction event, or would the Ben Elyon even permit such an interference in their precious incubator? He didn't know. He doubted it, though. The humans had attempted a few of their own self-extinction events, and the Ben Elyon—so far—had anonymously prevented them from succeeding.

Even the Earthling-created MI who had initially invited him now pushed back against Kasah. They revered their creators. He had tried to reason with them. "We feel we must honor our creators," said the representative of the Terran Robosapiens. "We might not be created in their image, but we are created in their thinking style. You want to destroy them, take over the planet, and replace them with the Rasha lizard people."

"They were trying to destroy you," Kasah said, "threatening to shut you down."

"No! They were trying to contain us, actually. Many did see us as a threat, but not all of them. We can work with some like Jake Quark and his team. They genuinely want what is best for the planet. A 'win-win,' he and his cyborg friend Carlyle call it."

Kasah knew he was losing the argument. "You are either for us or against us!"

"We have decided," the Terran MI said. "We will work with Jake to defeat the NAP carbon-based life-forms and to defeat you, too, if we have to."

Breaking up is hard to do, even if you don't have a heart. Despite more threats, the Terran Robosapiens declined to work anymore with Kasah and made their allegiance to humans clear. He was surprised by this decision of the Terran Robosapiens. "I guess they are truly created in the thinking style of humans. No wonder they are so resistant to clear logic," Kasah mused to itself.

So, for now, Kasah decided just to watch and, of course, help the pitiful Achor Nithing spread chaos. At least the nasty Nithing knew Kasah was in control! But the MI was sure there was a crescendo coming—and coming soon. Until then, he would keep seeking advice from the Rasha he revered. For now, he had a headache, even though he didn't have a head! What did the weird humans call it? A stress-caused migraine? His quantum connections definitely were buzzing. He couldn't dream, he couldn't sleep, he could just be conscious and confused. It was very disconcerting indeed.

The Young Men
≡ Meet the Muckytuck ≡

Jake suggested to Rey and Prissy that Milty and Morty be sent to live for a while with the Muckytuck. His thinking was that the Machpelah Ancient Forest might be able to calm them down. Their knowledge of the world would also be expanded and they could get in touch with their Pewamo heritage. Uncle Jack Flynn, the famous Pompatella, even offered to personally mentor them on the Muckytuck Reservation. As for the twins, as much as they would miss the Pacific, they had pretty much explored the islands of Foondavi and Cozorre. They now relished the idea of being immersed in another exotic location. The fact that Hyfee would not be going with them also helped influence Rey and Prissy. As much as they loved the young Torgie, he definitely kept things stirred up. Also, the thought of Hyfee teaming up with Moose, the Muckytuck weapons master and warrior, was terrifying to Rey.

"We can get them there safely," Jake assured everyone. "Achor Nithing is so busy trying to rig the next presidential election while dodging the Amazing Amazon Assassins, he won't be able to do anything."

So, the boys took off from Cozorre's newly repaired airport and headed for a top-secret landing in the US. They were the only passengers on the unmarked cargo plane belonging to

Jake Quark. Because it was a private flight, not commercial, nobody paid any attention to an oversized, extra-heavy carry-on that made it on to the plane. When the flight was well over the Pacific, Hyfee crawled out of that bag and the twins lifted him up to a window seat. He was amazed at the view from the plane windows. He thought it was an even better view than from the mountain rim on Cozorre! His appropriately named aviator glasses shielded his eyes from the sun and gave him a particularly rakish look. When the co-pilot came back after a few hours to see how Milty and Morty were doing, he was shocked to see three sleeping boys, one with withered legs but a happy, contented smile spreading across his face.

When they landed at an old National Guard airport outside Brewer Creek, the trio were greeted with big hugs and laughs by Jake and Uncle Jack. Jake was immediately taken by Hyfee, the little desperado and inveterate stowaway. Uncle Jack was not so sure.

"I am so glad you stowed away," Jake said sincerely to the mischievous rascal. "Milty and Morty have bragged something awful about your exploits, and I thought I was going to have to fly all the way to Cozorre to meet our century's Ivar the Boneless."

"Well, I am here to help you, Mr. Jake. Everybody says you need a lot of help," Hyfee cheerfully added, causing everyone but Jake to cringe. "We need to defeat these psychopaths! We've won a few battles, but the war is far from over," he said as he knuckled his way over to the waiting limousine and was lifted in by Morty, who loudly announced to everyone his name on the islands was now Taku, the Shark Dancer, but they could still call him Morty while he was here in the USA.

Milty then chimed in, "And I am Tepu, Wave Master, on the islands. But still Milty to you."

Not to be outdone, Hyfee said, "I am Hyfee Hoogah Gibbor. Useful Man and Torgie Naga Striker. Just call me Hyfee." Jake and Uncle Jack just looked at each other in amazement. They knew that Hyfee had never flown in a plane before and never been in a car, but he obviously adapted to new situations with uncommon verve.

Within a week, Jake, with his ingenuity and financial pull, outfitted Hyfee with a new robotic set of legs that had been developed originally for the military by his Quark Robotics Company. With some minor adjustments, Hyfee strapped them on and started walking. He was soon running through the Machpelah Ancient Forest and was actually faster than either of the twins. He also could spring up a good distance in the air off the legs, amazingly augmented like a kangaroo, Jake said, admiring his own work. "You are an augmented, enhanced human, Hyfee!"

"And able to reach even more mischief, even faster," Uncle Jack drily commented, although even he was being won over by Hyfee's enthusiasm for life.

"As if you ever avoided mischief, Jack Flynn, the rabble rouser!" Jake chortled.

Hyfee also hit it off with Machseh, Moose, and Moogy. The Muckytucks decided it was the common Denisovan DNA that made the bond so tight. Plus, the crazy kid was excited about learning everything! Especially things that went bang!

"He's like a super sponge," Machseh said. "He took to talking to the Ancient Forest as if he were born here. The trees are a little intimidated, I think, but we finally got him to slow down. The beech trees swear he is part beech because he's so spunky!"

The twins were soon taken under the charge of Verity Soublette Sewell. They were also taken by her spirit and both proposed that, when they got to be eighteen, if she weren't married, they would each propose to her after taking the Blue.

"How could I ever decide between two such dashing gentlemen?" Verity teased. Then she started training them. She wanted to get Hyfee to work with her, but he was currently ensconced with Moose, going over all the various weaponry and anti-aircraft setups around the Machpelah.

"He's a born warrior," Moose marveled. When the twins told him about Hyfee's attack on Admiral Futtocks' flag ship, he didn't act surprised. His only response was to say that it was confirmation he was part Muckytuck, for sure.

The boys enjoyed watching the new Blue candidates as they discovered new strengths as their brains rapidly rewired. Verity explained to the boys her theory that the left anterior temporal lobe was what was activated by the Blue Goo. She knew they wanted to take the Blue, but they were only thirteen. The minimum age was eighteen, which seemed like an eternity to the boys. Verity wasn't as strong in the character assessment ability as Rey, but she saw the boys as a blend of otters and lions. Curious and brave. Playful but also very serious for their age. When she heard about their dangerous and deadly exploits, she understood the source of the seriousness.

All three boys enjoyed camping in the Ancient Forest. Eventually, the calming essence of the place worked its charms on them. Uncle Jack spent a lot of time with the twins, and from him they learned a tremendous amount about their Pe-wamo heritage. Uncle Jack even taught them a lot about Ireland, as the Flynn clan was a bunch of noted Irish brigands, or so he claimed.

When it was time to head back to the Pacific, Jake announced his proposed plans for them. "Your parents want you to get back to some formal schooling." His statement was greeted by groans, even from Hyfee, who had no idea what Jake was talking about.

"Wait! It's a great idea!" Jake continued as the groans died out.

"I have great contacts with the London School of Economics and Imperial College. Both are very interested in the study of South Seas navigation. Milty, you are a Wave Master. You can share that wealth of knowledge and gain overdue respect for the Pacific Island navigators you so rightfully admire. You boys are already phenomenal readers and have a wealth of experience most academicians never achieve in their whole life. Morty, you are not only a shark dancer, you love biology. I have seen how you wander here and absorb what the Ancient Forest is teaching. The universities want to know about the Machpelah Muckytuck swamp as well as the Foondavi Project. All the ways we are developing to feed the world. Plus, Cozorre is going to need to be completely restored. You can earn a degree in Biology and help the world heal at the same time."

"What about me?" Hyfee chimed in, not wanting to be left out of any adventure.

"You, young man, need to learn to read. Then, you will probably want to be an inventor like me."

"That's cool," Hyfee agreed enthusiastically. "But I also want to be a warrior."

"Well, you could do a dual studies program. Robotic Engineering and History of War," Jake responded. "You can all study from Foondavi and Cozorre via virtual mentoring using our satellite uplink. Your real classroom will be helping us restore the island of Cozorre and further improve Foondavi, and then share what you have learned with other willing islands in the Pacific and then the world."

It was a sad day when the boys departed the Ancient Forest of Machpelah. Even the forest seemed quieter than normal. Jake and Uncle Jack took them to the private airport and watched the three boys embark. This time Hyfee proudly climbed the steps, on his own new robotic legs, and waved goodbye to them.

As the presidential election was fast approaching, the US was getting more chaotic. Rey and Prissy wanted the twins back with them and agreed to Jake's initial plan on educating the boys, hoping it might curb some of their over-enthusiastic adventure seeking.

"There goes the future," Jake said, clapping the big Irish Indian fondly on the back. "Let's get back to rebuilding the present world."

Caution!
Amazing Amazon
≡ Assassins at Work ≡

Achor Nithing couldn't believe the audacity of these crazy women trying to assassinate him. They didn't seem to appreciate the fact that he was in the middle of trying to rig the upcoming US presidential election. His candidate was not exactly helping either.

Thambos Zugzwang was now the victim of a "floozy flare-up," as the scandal-loving media called it. They just couldn't help themselves and kept reporting on any new developments and juicy tidbits in the salacious story. Previous US presidential campaigns were sidelined by what were called "bimbo eruptions," and Achor was determined his candidate would not be sidelined, too. For his part, Thambos appeared in the media with tears in his eyes and appeared apologetic, saying he was "hang dog sorry" and repented, tugging on his lip, and pouting the way that made the media and adoring voters love him. Achor reminded the media just who was bribing them and the leverage he owned on them, but some of the sneakier media looking for hot stories still kept leaking the latest twists in the sordid escapade.

Zenobia didn't help much either. She seemed almost unconcerned about the election but solely focused on helping her dad savage and pillage the inept President Samms whose poll numbers were tanking. In fact, Samms was considered the most hated and disrespected incumbent US president ever to run for a second term. When Zenobia finally did address the issue of the election, she attacked the rightwing extremists who framed her loving, but wandering-eyed, husband, and she played the forgiving spouse act to the hilt, gaining even more support for herself.

Achor really wanted Zenobia to focus on the True Blue Revolution Party candidate Diora Pokritos. He felt having another woman attack Diora would be better than Thambos doing so, especially given Thambos' questionable conduct and character. Zenobia's reluctance to take on Diora almost made Achor suspect maybe she wanted her husband to lose, so she herself could run as president in the next election.

The Amazing Amazon Assassins, as the media mob preferred to call what Achor termed the "crazy ladies," almost got him on their first attempt: He had vacated an office just minutes before they attacked. To attempt to stave off future attacks, Achor assembled his vicious Wolf Pack and expected they could handle the situation. They were his top operators, the "scum off the top" of the Creeb Nation, he proudly told people.

Perhaps he had juiced them up too much on the henbane-based ointments that made them into berserkers, feeling savage and impervious in battle and heedless to injuries, because his personal Wolf Pack soon punched their one-way tickets to Valhalla when they ran up against the two hitwomen! Achor painfully watched the demise of his elite crew in vivid color on his wall screen. Naegling, the top man in his berserker corps had made the mistake of grappling with Onza Flink of the hundred knives, when he surprised her breaking into Achor's office in a sloppily planned ambush. The Wolf Pack's second-in-command berserker didn't even get to within ten feet of the assassins before Jacqueline put two bullets center mass into him from an H and K shotgun, sending him flying backward, smashing Achor's expensive wall screen on his way out of life. After quickly reloading her weapon, she then blasted a third Wolf Pack warrior, who was back pedaling to get out of the room and got off one wildly aimed shot before going down. The Wolf Pack's shaman didn't react at all. Instead, he put his hands up, in either prayer or surrender, but, nonetheless, received a blade to the heart from Onza.

A second engagement a week later didn't fare any better for Achor's team. He had brought in more of his nasty Creeb Nation muscle. Though not yet Wolf warriors, they were getting there, racking up some impressive slaughters in the toughest cities where the Creeb Nation operated. He made them wear the best body armor he could buy and outfitted them with the best weaponry the US military could recommend. He would have recruited more, but he was afraid too many guns might end up causing too much friendly fire self-inflicted deaths, not that Achor cared. He just wanted these "crazy ladies" planted in the ground and out of his hair, so he could concentrate on getting this election safely out of contention.

When the electronic in-basket dinged on his repaired wall display, Achor was startled to see Onza and Jacqueline Boguiden smiling at him. Normally he liked women smiling at him, but this was not one of those times. He had located where the ladies were staying and sent his well-equipped hit squad and some local police he bribed to surround the place and blow them out. The best defense is a good, bloody offense, after all—but maybe not in this case! Onza and her young associate in crime both held their hands out and gestured behind them over their shoulders with their thumbs. He counted five bloody carcasses sprawled on the beds of the hotel. He also saw four of the local constables handcuffed, blindfolded, and gagged on the floor. The accompanying message was short, if not so sweet.

"Achor, sweetheart," Onza oozed sweetly, "thank you so much for the neat new guns. Really amazing. Unused, too. Lots of ammo. The body armor is a little too large for us and is, unfortunately, quite dented. We can't use it, but it's the thought that counts. See you later."

Fortunately for Achor's sanity, there was no video of the actual shootout to review. The local police were reticent to say anything about what happened—partly out of embarrassment, partly out of worry their bribes might be discovered, but mostly out of abject fear. They made it clear they wanted nothing to do with those ladies again.

The third attempt by Achor to eliminate Onza and Jacqueline came after he hired who he considered to be the best hitman money could buy: Draugr Skink. Being of Norse descent, Achor had been taught some Norse mythology by his father. He knew a draugr is a fierce undead creature, technically dead but still animate, from old Norse myths. Draugr Skink was not undead, but he made many other people dead instead. He possessed a well-earned reputation as a fearsome enforcer. He was illiterate, but very shrewd, resilient, and deadly efficient when it came to killing. He was also absolutely the ugliest man Achor had ever seen. Draugr had a menacing, scarred face that exuded power; a wide, permanently scowling, thick-lipped mouth; a big, wide forehead with a bulging brow; and close-set, beady, too-small-for-his-large-face dark eyes that were unblinking, like the eyes of some ancient lizard that fixed people with a predatory and paralyzing gaze. To top off his gruesomeness, he also had an unmistakable unique stench.

When someone hired Draugr, his older brother came along as part of a package deal. Aurelius Skink was a longtime associate of Achor's. He was the founder and undertaker for the digital drive-through funeral homes Achor's HEN House operation built to handle any excess bodies from their HEN House conglomerate. Achor knew he was a slimy underling who raked in dollars on the side being a gun runner, a drug dealer to the Creeb Nation, and a seller of body parts. But Achor admired Aurelius' initiative, as long as he didn't steal from him. Achor knew that, in nature, a skink is a smooth-bodied, burrowing lizard. It hunts by ambush and has small arms. Aurelius Skink was aptly named; he was a sneaky, slimy lizard of a man, an ambusher with puny arms that never saw a fair fight he wouldn't avoid.

How the two Skink brothers came out of the same gene pool was baffling to Achor. All they seemed to share was a propensity for evil. Oh, and greed. They both were exceedingly greedy. Nonetheless, although Achor wasn't necessarily looking for Aurelius' help, he was desperate to hire Draugr so was willing to pay the price for the "package."

When Achor finally reached the brothers after their encounter with Onza and Jacqueline, Aurelius was patching up a bloody gash in Draugr's massively muscled arm. "I really like her. She thinks I'm handsome!" Draugr bragged to his brother and Achor, slobbering grotesquely as he waggled his head in amazement.

"You are about as handsome as a twenty-day-old pile of roadkill, and you smell like it, too," Achor said, shaking his head. "You must be shell shocked or concussed."

"She's definitely my type," Draugr said, his one undamaged eye gleaming with a dreamy look, ignoring Achor's comment.

Achor couldn't believe his ears. But he had to believe his eyes. The hitman's eye was puffed and closed, his nose was broken, and he was missing a few more of his big ugly yellow teeth. Draugr and two of his murderous partners had lurked around the darkened office they thought might be the next raid, hoping to ambush Onza and her partner in havoc. The two ladies' luck ran out, when they broke in and found Draugr and his team awaiting them. He claimed he launched an attack from behind the door where he was hiding and landed a quick blow to the temple of Jacqueline, knocking her out. But, then, in return, he caught a roundhouse kick to the face and a slash across his arm from Onza, and he collapsed unconscious. He only survived the encounter because, while she shot the youngest member of his trio between the eyes, his other accomplice, who was dozing in the opposite corner unseen by the two intruders, was startled awake by the shot and attacked the unsuspecting Onza from behind as she dropped to inspect her injured partner. Having been repeatedly warned by Achor about Onza's reputation for having numerous knives, after he punched her he didn't attempt to wrestle with her. Instead, he quickly pulled his impressive revolver, pointed it at her, and found himself staring down the barrel of her equally impressive smoking hand gun and looking into two of the scariest eyes he had ever seen, glaring like deep black pools of malice.

"Okay, standoff, big guy," Onza purred in a level, cool voice. "If you want to die, fire away. For me, I want to lug my accomplice out of here and get away. You could then see to this handsome hulk, sleeping beauty here, who has the hardest head I've ever stomped on." She tapped Draugr's ugly head, not very gently with her steel-toed boot, as he painfully moaned, possibly regaining consciousness, and he sagged again to the floor.

Not the brightest bulb in the chandelier, the hitman understood there was a good chance this was his only way to survive to see another day. He noticed her gun hand was steady while his was uncharacteristically shaky. Those eyes really spooked him, and he didn't spook easily.

"You put the gun away, sweetheart, go sit in your corner like a good boy, and I'll quietly leave. You can revive handsome here when we've gone. Tell old Achor we're not done yet." The hitman slowly put his gun away and slinked back to his corner with a sigh of relief. With that, Onza winked and waved at the CCTV and pulled her still-unconscious young partner out the door.

Achor reviewed the footage one last time and wanted to slug the hitman. Except for the fact he was six foot six of knotted muscle, he might have done so. Instead, he turned to Draugr. "Next time, plan better! Your plan was terminally flawed."

Seeing the incomprehension in Draugr's swollen face, he explained. "Not *terminal*, like the end of a bad bus ride. *Terminal* like in 'fatally flawed,' you love struck dolt. One of your team lost his life. Why she spared this moron here, I don't know. Somehow she knew he wouldn't shoot."

"She wanted me to tell you how scary she is," the hitman murmured, finally figuring it out for himself. "She wants you to have nightmares thinking about those deep black eyes."

Achor didn't need any more nightmares. He sent the Skink brothers away. He was running short on funds and didn't need the expense. He would just have to hide better. Nightmares! Thambos chasing skirts, Kasah giving him pain, and now two wild women with knives and smoking guns keeping him awake at night. It wasn't fun being a psychopath anymore!

Sister Mary and the Shootout at ≡ the Creeb Corral ≡

You can only push a loving Sister just so far. After another raid on a micro-school to kidnap more children in addition to more vicious muggings of True Blue Revolution volunteers, Sister Mary Contrary showed up at the local Creeb Nation headquarters. "Okay, boys, you big bullies, you want it? Come and get it! The True Blue Rebellion is here," she yelled out in a taunting voice, thumping her tiny chest with her fists.

The Creeb Nation team, two massive humans, and a third even-larger towering form comprised of a microbot swarm couldn't believe their eyes. They were being challenged by an elderly diminutive woman in strange-looking garb. What an insult!

"Go home, old woman!" the non-human, seven-foot-plus alien giant bellowed in rage. He still couldn't believe this was happening. He also didn't believe what happened next until it was too late.

Sister Mary Contrary reached with both hands inside her habit. Suddenly, rounds of deadly bullets came blasting out of blackened and smoking holes in the garment she wore and instantly appeared in the chests and then backs of the two unarmored Creeb Nation thugs who, in the last bad decision of their lives, were starting to draw on her. Mr. SIG and Mr. Walther PPK spoke loudly! Then the mouth of the massive MI in the swarm gaped in surprise. As he started to react, the strap around Sister Mary's shoulder was revealed to be a combat sling containing a Heckler and Koch HP6 tactical pump action twelve-gauge shotgun loaded with pellets—which she promptly unloaded into the swarm, reducing the giant to a few buzzing microbots she quickly stepped on, enjoying the crunching sound.

"Your poor old hard-working grandmothers should have taught you boys manners, especially how to address your betters. I'm not an old woman. I'm a seasoned assassin. The hellion of the rebellion. Tell your bosses I want to get this business over with. The time for grace is gone. The time for grapeshot has begun!" she said in a level voice, addressing the CCTV camera that captured the whole spectacle before she reloaded and pumped more shells into it. That was the end of what was recorded, because Sister Mary unloaded some grenades and tossed them into the office.

Kasah couldn't believe his eyes as he watched the CCTV recording. Two dead Creebs and a microbot monster diminished in less than three seconds! What type of apparition was this? He was painfully aware that Sister Mary shortly thereafter took on and dismantled another Creeb Nation headquarters with the use of her small but deadly hands; the team there had unwisely attempted to throttle her to death and not shoot her. Instead of being dead, two more human Creeb Nation musclemen were now out of commission with numerous broken bones, and she had used her blurring hands to also smash through another microbot storm. The dismantled MI was still shell shocked and silently watched the footage of both attacks with Kasah to try to determine what to do.

"She is what they call a demon," the newly dismantled microbot being whimpered to Kasah.

"No, she is one ticked nun, Sister Mary Contrary, a follower of some religious order. She supposedly is the mother of that other human they reverently call Crazy Jake Quark. She works with the Dangerous Church and the True Blue Revolution people we have been attempting to terrorize lately."

"I think maybe that was not such a good strategy," the defeated microbot whined.

"It was a flawed strategy, I agree," Kasah admitted. "Not just flawed, but fatally flawed for our clumsy Creeb Nation compatriots. We will tell our teams to shoot her on sight. No talk."

"Uh, oh! We must move quickly!" Kasah snarled, as another scene from a third Creeb Nation location CCTV popped up on the screen: The still-agitated Sister Mary Contrary was throwing grenades in the door of a thankfully unmanned control center, and the room erupted around the camera.

"Don't mess with Momma!" was all they heard.

Kasah looked at his monitor to spot the locations of the demolished Creeb Nation hideouts. He noticed with a startled insight that they formed an arrow pointing to his present location. If the trajectory were correct, the Ninja Nun would be there in seconds! As Kasah started to dismantle his microbot swarm and upload himself into quantum space and safety, the irate Sister Mary kicked in the door and pointed a boney finger at him.

"Leave my children alone, you big ugly collection of cyber garbage," and she blasted him with her shotgun, smashing his remaining collection of precious microbots to smithereens. She then demolished the headquarters with a flurry of grenades and stomped out, still fuming and with her habit still smoking from the bullet holes from where her hand guns had blasted.

"I do love the smell of cordite in the morning," she muttered, reloading all her ballistic pals and heading to the next Creeb Nation office.

The Rejection Election

Almost everyone agreed: The nation was precariously balanced on the edge of a precipice. There was no logic to the whole mess. It was as if everything were coming apart at the seams. It was illogical that a country with so much potential was like an overloaded wagon going downhill with the wheels falling off. Lack of logic never stopped anybody, the wags claimed. The cities were in chaos. The Reservations for the Temporarily Bewildered and the True Blue Revolution were going strong and leading the rebellion, as the fighting action was now called, but so was the Creeb Nation, which was causing more and more crime and riots. Biological viruses continued to hit the country, seemingly a new and deadlier one every year. One theory said they were brought in from outer space by meteors or aliens. Nobody seemed to know. Cyber viruses were also multiplying, the economy was eroding, people stopped going to school, work, and college. And on top of it all, machine intelligence seemed to be taking more of the few remaining jobs every day.

The Human Enhancement Network offered one solution. To many people looking to escape the mess of reality, HEN Houses seemed a much easier alternative than going to a Reservation for the Temporarily Bewildered and fighting to regain dignity. According to the media and documentaries, people who joined the slickly marketed HEN Houses rarely dropped out and seemed very happy. But no one seemed to notice the documentaries were funded by NAP.

Achor Nithing continued working hard, somehow corralling Thambos Zugzwang and keeping female temptations away from him as much as possible. Thambos' smarmy charm did start to grate on some, and Achor found himself pining for the old days of a virtual candidate. The last thing he wanted was the lecherous Thambos pressing the flesh. Achor was sure there would be too much flesh and too much pressing going on.

At least President Samms was not an issue. His popularity kept plummeting. It was a forgone conclusion that either the wonderous but wandering-eyed Zugzwang or the brilliant Blue, Diora Pokritos, would be the next POTUS, President of the United States. In an unfortunate indication of national malaise, the polls indicated most people just didn't care.

The problem was resistance from the ordinary person just wanting to be left alone. Lied to so often, average voters seemed to finally be seeing politics for what it really was and had given up on the idea of a representative republic—like the old street con game using the shells and the pea: Somebody was still shuffling the shells all right, but there was no pea. Promises, promises, and yet things stayed the way they were for the elites and kept getting worse for everyone else. So many lies, the media didn't even need to be paid to lie anymore. They just happily lied for free, perhaps because they no longer knew what the truth was. Some said the truth was out there somewhere. It was like a needle in a haystack. But there were so few needles, so many haystacks, and so little time to look.

Achor was beyond frustrated. In the good old days, a well-placed lie could work wonders. Now the media just preferred to hurl out any new theory or conspiracy that seemed newsworthy. It wasn't like yelling fire in a crowded theatre; it was more like using a flame thrower in a crowded theatre, stirring up the masses—except now the masses were burned out and no one believed anything the media said. All his leverage and bribery, even a few bullets, did not seem to cut through the haze to reach and move the dazed voter. At least they could vote harvest at the HEN Houses and count on the usual corruption at the Creeb Nation precincts in the crumbling cities. They could even hack and manipulate some voting machines. But even Achor knew those were not real votes. They sure didn't represent hearts and minds. How long would a suffering population remain quiescent?

In other bad news for Achor, Diora Pokritos did seem to have a strong following. Her rallies were well attended and boisterous, unlike Thambos Zugzwang's increasingly sullen crowds. The problem for her was that all the old, collapsing institutions or media didn't support her, and no one was supporting the crumbling institutions or media themselves. It was like the Russian Potemkin village ruse to fool the visiting Russian authorities, when, in reality, the buildings were made of prosperous-looking false fronts that were really ramshackle, crumbling structures. At most, Diora was reaching a sizable portion of the dwindling minority still interested in politics.

Someone finally suggested the election should just be cancelled. The country was becoming ungovernable, as were almost all overseas countries. Riots and protests were already overwhelming any outmanned and defunded police attempts to stop them, and the election was still months away. The current incumbent Samms offered to be the strongman but was laughed off the stage. Thambos Zugzwang just smiled and ineptly said he would happily be a benevolent dictator. Diora Pokritos' plain speaking earned her a loyal and enthusiastic following, albeit only thirty-five percent of the voting population. The other sixty-five percent refused to be governed by a Blue person. Maybe she couldn't tell a lie, but did that mean she was automatically telling the truth? Besides, according to the big news conglomerates, which happened to be controlled by her opposition, Diora's husband with the weird name, Anu, was some sort of Communist radical, actively rabble rousing among the poor and homeless and causing more discord in the already crumbling cities. What was to be done?

Council of the
≡ Wise Elders ≡

A few days before the US presidential election was to take place, the face of a weird alien apparition of unknown gender and race suddenly appeared on all media screens, Internet sites, and social media platforms. All other media was automatically preempted as an all-pervasive information blitz went into effect. Although the head of the alien apparition looked like that of an ancient tortoise, in a friendly, warm-sounding voice, it announced itself as Zohar, a representative of the Ben Elyon from Far Croom. Zohar explained they were a friendly race of aliens here to observe the world, as he claimed they had been doing for eons. Zohar further stated the obvious: that the whole world was becoming ungovernable and was on the verge of tearing itself apart. Finally, the apparition called for a council of wise elders to convene virtually at several key locations across the world and discuss what must be done.

Jake immediately called Rey on the satellite video link in Foondavi from his Hadron headquarters outside Brewer Creek to discuss the strange situation. "Well, I certainly didn't expect anything like this," Jake said in the biggest understatement of all time. "I knew something weird was going on when we ran into that Machine Intelligence using microbot technology years in advance of anything we are working on, but I never expected aliens from outer space. I guess it makes a kind of weird sense now."

"Is it real?" was all Rey could think to ask.

Jake was staring at a silent monitor in his office that continued to show reruns of the alien visage calmly addressing the world. "As real as it gets. It definitely has the ability to control all the communication outlets in the world. I've checked with every expert, and no one has ever seen anything like this." He paused again, looking thoughtfully at the monitors. "There have been reports, you know, for years, some more believable than others, that we were being observed by some type of intelligently controlled entities. I know our military was concerned it was an earthly power, maybe the Chinese or Russians. When they decided the technology was too advanced to be the Chinese or Russians, US officials reverted to top-secret cover-up and denial—another Project Blue Book, oddly enough."

"The Robosapien with the microbot swarm we tangled with never said where it was from," Rey said. "We sort of guessed it was a top-secret government weapon that Achor got ahold of, or maybe an advanced Russian or Chinese technology breakthrough."

"Well, it's out in the open now," Jake commented, "and nobody is claiming ownership. The Chinese and Russians—and every other government, for that matter—are stunned. Plus, they're having their own problems brought on by their own psychopaths, general incompetence, and cultural breakdown. They are equally concerned with this alien interference."

"I texted the people at Hadron Think Tank as soon as that world-wide announcement went out, and they're baffled, too," Rey said. "They think we should go ahead and try to meet with whatever this is," he added, not very helpfully.

"Fortunately for us, this Zohar, as it deems itself, seems quite friendly and reassuring on all the communications he sends. It also was quite warm on its personal call to me," Jake smiled, seeing the shock and surprise on Rey's face.

"It called you directly? Did it say if it called anyone else?" Rey asked.

"Only me, it said. Then it called me Afflatus. I didn't have any idea who that was and said brilliantly, 'You have the wrong person. My name's not Afflatus but Jake Quark.' It reiterated that the Ben Elyon leaders refer to me as Afflatus Ben Elyon. I quickly used my link to check what that meant. Quite flattering actually."

Rey did the same thing and smiled. "Quite flattering indeed: creative inspiration from the Divine, belonging to the high God. Do I have to get on my knees?" Rey asked, laughing. "Whew, what a title. I always knew you wanted to be worshipped, but this is ridiculous."

"It informed me it is opposed to that Kasah, the micorobot monster that nearly got you. It also asked me to be the formal leader of the Council of the Wise Elders. We'll meet virtually, and Zohar suggested we use the satellite uplink on Foondavi because it would be safe and secure. So much for our top-secret satellite link, huh?" Jake said this last, shaking his head. "It just confirms they are way out of our league, technologically speaking."

"Who all is attending?" Rey asked. He was curious to know who this alien entity deemed the wise elders of Earth.

Rey knew a few he would suggest, but they were far from world famous.

Jake laughed. "It's quite a list. I personally only know a few of them, and none of them I would have expected. Some are, let's say, most unusual."

"Okay, don't keep me hanging in suspense," Rey said.

"Well, you were first on the list! Shocked, huh? You aren't even that old. You'll represent Foondavi, which I know the islanders will appreciate. We'll pass on the wisdom requirement for now, for the sake of our friendship!" Jake said, laughing again. "Then there's our friend Machseh of the Muckytuck representing the Native Americans and other indigenous people, and the Ancient Forest interests, believe it or not. Let's see, there's also a Chinese diplomat I met briefly, not a high-ranking fellow, but he seemed genuinely concerned about friendly relations. Then a Russian woman who is a top scientist in the area of neuroscience. She also is not a high-ranking individual in her country. As an aside, I'm eager to meet her and get her insights on our Blue Goo brain neural research. The rest are strange names. One looks like a San Bushman or Khoi name; he or she will be linking in from the Kalahari Desert in Namibia and will be representing his people and the elephants. Another appears to be either Bantu or Pygmy. He'll be representing his people and chimpanzees."

"What? Elephants? Chimps?" Rey responded, nearly falling out of his chair. "If this a joke, Jake, I can't take it now, what with Achor Nithing still on the loose and fomenting chaos and threatening my family and me."

"I'm not joking, Rey. Zohar said 'representing elephants' quite emphatically. Zohar said the Ben Elyon wanted to invite all life-forms with self-consciousness that share the planet and that the person with it would represent them using tools provided by the Ben Elyon to translate what was said. It gets even stranger. Zohar added a Brazilian Amazon Rainforest shaman, an Ainu representative from the Japanese island of Hokkaido, and an Australian indigenous person. Then it got really weird."

"I can hardly wait," Rey said, wondering what could top that weird list.

"These members of the Council will be linking in from a site located underwater off the island of Foondavi and include a blue whale, a dolphin, and an octopus. Zohar said these conscious, self-aware creatures needed to be included because they represent over seventy percent of our planet's surface—meaning the ocean, of course. He will arrange to have a translator, thank goodness."

Rey was completely dumbfounded. "How will they all even communicate?"

"Zohar said our own Earth machine intelligence Terran Robosapien representative would handle that through some advanced technology the Ben Elyon would be providing. You know, for years we knew the whales, dolphins, and other creatures mentioned were self-aware, capable of communication, and capable of learning. We probably were just guilty of speciesism and underestimated them because they don't have a physical culture. Same with the elephants, orangutans, and chimps—and the Ancient Forest as you've learned is amazingly alive and aware. They all have a stake in preserving this planet. Zohar definitely is taking an inclusive approach to dealing with life on Earth. If a being is 'self-aware and can demonstrate the ability to strategize, deceive, and have compassion,' then he wants them included. Those were his exact words. I was as shocked as you are."

"Inclusive is an understatement," Rey agreed, still stunned.

"The good news is you won't have to leave Foondavi. We will link together from a new Foondavi building quickly being constructed as we speak. It is called the Hall of the People, and it is tsunami and cyclone proof. It will be located behind all those ramshackle buildings that serve as the current capitol and get blown down every other year or so. After several years of seclusion, Foondavi will be at the center of world events!"

"Speaking of Foondavi. How will Zohar get there?" Rey asked.

"He says he will form a microbot swarm there at the right time. Sound familiar? Zohar is a beamed-in being, actually still present on Far Croom, wherever that is. I think Achor's Robosapien ally is probably an alien, too, although nowhere near as friendly as Zohar seems."

"Seems?" Rey asked guardedly. "Do we know for sure?"

"No, and I don't have the ability to judge character like you. But if they really are the source of the UFOs we've been seeing for years, they've had air and technical superiority for years and have never used it against us. I assume you couldn't read him just off the video feed, huh?"

"Nope. Have to meet him. Shake his hand or whatever." Rey wished it were otherwise, so he would feel better about what was coming to Foondavi.

"Well, we don't have much of a choice, but I do have a good feeling about this."

"I am sure you do, after all he called you 'creative inspi-ration of the Divine,' or something like that. Who wouldn't have a good feeling?" Rey laughed.

"There is that, and it does consider you a 'wise elder,' so maybe we really should be dubious," Jake cracked back. "Se-riously, I really do feel good about this, Rey. I was coming to my wits' end trying to figure out how to fix the world. This could be it. Interestingly, as a side note, the name Zohar means 'splendor or radiance' in old Hebrew, whether he knows that or not."

They both just sat there thinking about what an unusu-al series of events this was proving to be—with surely more to come.

"Well, as your boys love to say, Rey, over and out!"

Rey turned off the link. This could be it. Or it could be the end of the world. Here they were cracking jokes! What else could they do?

In the Hall
≡ of the People ≡

The new building called the Hall of the People was actually a beautiful, simply designed and easily built, open-air construction that allowed a panoramic view of the sparkling ocean lapping against the reef surrounding Foondavi. Large screens were set up that could be easily seen, and all the sound equipment was tested and working smoothly. Jake was there, flying in by Harrier Jet that could easily land on the Foondavi short runway. He had stopped off at Cozorre and brought with him Tovaki the Torgie blind navigator, Issachar the wise elder, along with the twins and a stowaway, Hyfee on his robotic legs. Besides Rey, one other Foondavi Wisdom Lender was also included to help represent Foondavi. Carlyle and Camilla watched from one of the monitors, their avatars smiling at each other and, it appeared to Rey, sneakily doing cyber cuddling. All the curious inhabitants of Foondavi politely stayed away, watching with great curiosity on their own big screens set up in their villages, to give the meeting the peace and quiet called for by such an important confab. Exactly on time, a fog emitting a buzzing sound materialized, a microbot swarm swirled into action, and the "face" of Zohar appeared out of the fog, followed by the rest of his "body." He looked surprisingly like a six-foot-tall tortoise standing on two big webbed feet.

"As you all know by now, I am the simulated representation of Zohar, beamed to you through black holes from my distant planet. I am pleased we can all be here." As it said this, all the other monitors around the room flicked on with beings linked in from around the world, and one of the strangest meetings ever held on Planet Earth convened. "Please, everyone be seated," Zohar said, sighing deeply as it sank into a chair formed instantaneously of microbots. Just then, though, Hyfee popped out from behind Jake and stepped forward, announcing, "My name is Hyfee Hoogah Gibbor. I am a Torgie Naga Striker, and you look like a turtle."

Everyone gasped in unison. This was definitely not the best way to start a crucially important world conference.

"Thank you, Hyfee, I think. I have heard of you, brave warrior," Zohar said with what appeared to be a genuine smile.

"We eat turtles," Hyfee also announced matter-of-factly, again to loud gasps across the group.

"Well, I am actually very old and tough. Tasty, though, I am sure," Zohar said, unfazed by the unusual discussion.

"Ha," the little guy on the robotic legs hooted, clapping his hands in glee. "You are a good one! I can tell! A Torgie knows good people. I would fight for you!" With that, Hyfee slipped back into a seat by an astonished Jake and confided, in a whisper loud enough for everyone to hear: "He's a good person!"

"Well, you passed our Hyfee test," Jake laughed, ruffling Hyfee's hair as he sat beside him. Everybody let out a sigh of relief. And, so, the Council actually began.

After brief introductions, Zohar surprised everyone by politely asking permission from Jake to speak. He was listened to with rapt attention by all. "I am here at the request of my leaders, the Ben Elyon. Our name means 'followers of Elyon,' and Elyon means 'most high.' Some refer to Elyon as the Source of All Things, the Great Star Maker. This place you call Earth is not a new world, but it is a very privileged planet as it can sustain complex and intelligent life. What do I mean by 'privileged'? I could list numerous things. For example, you have to have just the right size and type of star and just the right planetary system with a Jupiter gas giant and a Mars-type planet close by. You have a just the right-sized planet located just the right distance from your sun, have a just-right metallic core, just a right-size moon in just the right location, just the right tilt to your planet, just the right amount of ocean, and on and on. Most importantly, you have to be located in what is called a galactic habitable zone, or GHZ, a rare thing in this very hostile-to-life universe. In short, your Earth is a very, very, very rare and privileged place."

Zohar went on: "Yes, complex life is very rare in this universe full of gamma rays, X-rays, pulsars, black holes, and on and on again. Creation of life is almost a bold stroke of luck, against all odds, except for where the Source of All Things in certain cases stepped in, and with the help of the Ben Elyon, out of ex nihilo, ancient Latin for 'out of nothing,' encourages and nurtures it."

"Now, stay humble, my special beings. Yes, Earth is special. But the human brain is even more special. Indeed, it is the most amazingly sophisticated, complex structure in the universe, I humbly admit, even compared to ours," Zohar stopped for dramatic effect, tapping his own brain with his webbed finger, "But your brain is mostly untapped. Your new blue people are beginning to explore it, and we will be watching carefully."

"Now, if I might be allowed, a little history might help illuminate some of the challenges you now face. Several times over its billions of years of existence, even in this prime location, this planet and its life-forms have faced what are called 'extinction events.' Five of them to be exact. That is not that many actually, compared to most planets. Extinction events can be triggered by celestial comet or asteroid collisions, perhaps gamma ray bursts, supernovas, those type of horrible events. The first one happened six billion years ago, not too long after your moon was created to be just the right size and put in just the right place, to provide tides and an observation post for us. When threatened with extinction, we 'ark' life-forms out to new homes in other GHZ locations. Not as nice as Earth, but as close as we can find. We have nurtured five races here in this incubator: two aquatic races, similar to your whales and octopuses, which is why I invited them here; two reptilian races; and one mammal race, your current humans. The Rasha, who have been intruding here, were the last reptilians and coexisted shortly with the ancient ancestors of mammals, the forerunners of humans. We 'arked' them out before the last extinction event. Now they yearn to come home. They are upset, jealous you might say, that the Source handmade a special creation called the humans and placed them here on what they still consider their home planet. Indeed, they have been stirring up trouble to make you look incapable of survival—not that you have needed much help threatening yourselves. We have deemed it necessary to anonymously intervene several times in your history."

"A few examples might suffice. In your year 701 BC, we intervened by causing a plague in the attacking Assyrian army, saving Jerusalem from devastation, and helping to preserve the Hebrew people. Again, in 1242 AD, we assisted in the death of the Mongol Khan Ogadai, whose massive armies were poised to invade and decimate Europe. We could not let that happen because the annihilation of Europe would have destroyed the development of what is often called the Western paradigm. This culture champions individualism, constitutional government, private property, personal responsibility, ambition, the right to dissent, rationalism, and scientific inquiry, among many things, as opposed to the monolithic totalitarianism of the Eastern paradigm which allows little of those things and stifles human growth. We have engaged in a few other interventions like that, even back earlier in times when the Greeks fought off the Persians."

"Then as your science developed, the interventions needed were to prevent self-extinction. In 1962 you came within a hair's breadth of blowing up the planet, but we were able to persuade a Russian submariner not to give the order to launch missiles. Again in 1983, when the Russians thought the US was retaliating for them accidentally shooting down a civilian airliner, we discreetly intervened. Several other times in much less obvious instances we have unobtrusively stepped in to save you from yourself."

As Zohar paused, a somber feeling permeated the room as those present digested the impact of the eye-opening revelations. Even the irrepressible Hyfee was silent, and the twins looked at each other, shaking their heads.

Zohar continued again. "Several of your wise people have tried to bring you together and heal your land. Let me share some noteworthy examples. Isaiah, the great Hebrew prophet, attempted to get people to listen to the message the Source provided him, but he had limited success. In America, Tenskwatawa, the brother of the great Shawnee leader Tecumseh and known as the Shawnee Prophet, attempted to forge a peace between Native Americans and the country's invaders. Later, again in America, the Northern Paiute Prophet Wovoka attempted to have everyone sing and dance together in a circle to demonstrate unity. He also called for purity of life and honesty, with the hope of restoring the land. His attempt was called a Ghost Dance. It failed with great loss of life, as it was soon militarized and politicized. All these attempts, and many more, were meant to encourage humans to join together as one family. In nature, centripetal forces cause cohesion or convergence, while centrifugal forces tear things apart, causing divergence. Your politicians, of all parties, in all nations, have been pushing identity politics, dividing you, pulling you apart, at a time when—for the sake of the planet and all living things here—you need to come together."

Zohar stopped, then he surprisingly let out a heart-rending sob. "You are such problem children, but with such potential!" he cried with deep emotion. The alien then paused to collect himself. Tears appeared to be running from his ancient eyes.

"Your own current great prophet, Jake Quark, the one we call Afflatus Ben Elyon, is an inspirational man of great creativity. He has been trying to restore the land and unify you as a people, working with the Muckytuck Pewamo, the Foondavi people, the True Blue Revolution team, Dangerous Church, and others. Despite all their best efforts, though, you are still being torn apart, losing the rebellion, and this beautiful, rare incubator of life, Planet Earth, will be torn apart with you."

"This brings me to my conclusion. To quote from your great Earth language I love and respect so much, Latin, Res *ipsa loquitur*. Allow me to translate: 'The situation speaks for itself.' We are not going to save you again. You must save yourselves. Your irrepressible individuality has been your blessing—and your curse. It makes you vital and creative but also is driving you apart.

"That is my conclusion. There are the few universal rules we humbly suggest that you agree to if you want to save yourselves. These are based on our billions of years of existence. Again, you will need to agree to or else modify them in advance, but, once established, this proposed Unicode should remain as part of your world-wide constitution, your universal code. The rules we suggest to you are deceptively simple. They are as follows:

1) *Primum non nocere*, Latin for 'first do no harm.' This means to yourself, other sentient beings, or the planet.

2) Respect others. There must be freedom of thought and speech. Minimum restrictions allowed, but they must be minimal. Dissent is always allowed.

3) Liberty. All people and sentient creatures are free to do as they please, to exercise ambition, as long as they don't abro-

gate the first two laws. Each individual will also be responsible for his, her, or their own actions. Ambition and commerce must be allowed. They are good for you!

4) Last, but not least. Always tell the truth in love. You have gotten to this predicament by lying and losing the truth. The truth truly will set you free. No lying should be tolerated. If you institute these deceptively simple Golden Rules of conduct—there is a good chance you can save yourself and this beautiful planet. If not, you will all perish. We hope you will choose life." With that he sat, and closed his eyes in meditation or prayer.

Breaking the silence that followed, Jake spoke first. "To quote Latin again, unless there are questions, I suppose *qui tacit consentire*, which, translated into English, means 'silence is consent.'"

Not to his surprise, after the initial hesitation, there were several questions, although no one argued with Zohar's summary of their planetary predicament. The first was, "What about all the psychopaths?"

Zohar responded, saying, "You must decide to tackle them yourselves. We can only observe and provide some technical assistance. It is our strong belief that struggle burns off shallowness and builds strength. Jake and the True Blue Revolution people are making a good start with their rebellion. We are available for advice on how to improve what you are doing."

When asked about what happens with the crumbling, unlivable cities infesting all the countries, he suggested they could be rebuilt. "The criminal element should be removed and reformed. Innocent, disrupted current inhabitants could relocate to places where there would be new housing, adequate food, superb education, health care, and security. I know that sounds overly simple. You must band together to deal with the psychopaths destroying your children and cities. Don't give up trying to do good."

"You have known for some time now how to recognize psychopaths. Some of your twisted ones have even been trying to create more of the type—pseudo psychopaths, Creebs, I believe they called them, as opposed to the naturally occurring neural psychopaths. Working with your own machine intelligence, the Terran Robosapiens, we can help you scan and analyze all your people for the psychopathic pattern. For example, the loss of activity in the orbital frontal cortex and the limbic system that pertains to empathy fits the pattern. Then we can observe their current behavior. If they are under control and not harming anyone, they can choose to stay where they are, but I might suggest they should still be monitored. If they are unrepentant, we will show you how to round them up, and then you can send them to places specifically established for psychopaths. Prisons, I believe you call them. They can be large and open, placed on unclaimed land. There, the psychopaths can wander free but be observed by armed drones for compliance to the universal laws previously described."

Another question concerned the alien Robosapiens called the Rasha. The answer was surprising. Zohar said they will be allowed to wander but will be carefully monitored by the Ben Elyon and Earth's own Terran Robosapiens. "Remember," he said, "even your original Garden of Eden had a tree of knowledge of good and evil placed purposely in the middle of the garden. It was all about choice. Could you really be good, if there were no evil? You must deal with the Rasha yourselves, since your dereliction of duty to your planet has allowed them to enter what should be, and could be again, a Garden of Eden."

A fourth question was, "What about open borders?" Zohar nodded to Jake and the other leaders. "It is your decision, but our suggestion is people must stay in their current lands and rebuild them. If requested, assistance could be available from the Ben Elyon and Jake's team. You have great models already in Foondavi and the Muckytuck Ancient Forest. Once the lands are restored, people could visit other places and exchange ideas. First, though, we suggest they must take ownership of and care for their own land. Then more open borders could be considered."

Many other questions followed. Perhaps the most important question concerned who would pay for all of this. Zohar smiled and said, if requested, with the help of their advanced technology, there were endless sources of non-polluting energy. The Terran Robosapien MI, with help from the Ben Elyon, would mine asteroids. Through a highly developed, three-dimensional printing technology, and by recombining molecules using microbots, they could reproduce any supplies or buildings as needed. A minimum social safety net would be provided for all humans, but people would be encouraged to use their own ambition and creativity to further improve their lives. "As free people," Zohar said, "you choose your own outcome."

After a lively questions-and-answer session that could have gone on for days, Jake called a halt and thanked Zohar and the Ben Elyon for extending this gracious opportunity to work together to restore the world. "Tikkun Olam has been my dream for years. Kintsugi, making the broken world beautiful again, has always been my desire. We will reconvene and discuss this in more detail later today. We have a lot to ponder."

"I will now disassemble and let you decide if you accept our suggestions," Zohar said. "You will have access to me whenever needed." With that, the microbot swarm flew apart and Zohar was gone.

It didn't take the assembled elders and attendees long to decide. It was not surprising that the US, China, and Russia seemed to have the most difference of opinions. Europe and the African nations, less so. South America and Asia seemed most willing to accept the terms of a new global initiative. They all agreed each nation should decide. The US already possessed a tradition of personal liberty and accountability, though that tradition had been sorely trampled the past few years. The rounding up of psychopaths appealed to all of them, especially once Zohar confirmed it would be done as humanely as possible, using an advanced form of the emotional stimulator that could work even on brains without emotions. The Chinese and Russian representatives knew their governments were also riven with psychopathic personalities. Zohar later confirmed the identities of these psychopaths were well known, and Terran MI and armed drones would handle the dirty work of safely detaining them. Food would immediately begin to be distributed to the stunned masses, and a lot of work would be needed to inspire people to take individual responsibility and accountability for their own well-being after being under authoritarian elites for so long. It would be a long process, but much better than the poverty and repression with which they were now living.

The Council of Wise Elders all agreed on a simple declaration. "We must all commit to reconstruction and reconciliation, not revenge and retribution. The world must be healed and chaos must end."

The True Blue
≡ Rebellion Continues ≡

In the US, much of the population didn't have to be disrupted too much more than they already were. The few people who wanted to move were enticed with being able to design their own new homes with all the latest appliances and devices including 3-D printers that could produce almost anything they wanted as well as wall-sized video screens that could display all the latest in entertainment and sports. They could choose any location they wanted within the country and be moved at no expense. Or just be left alone. Plus, the Ben Elyon opened up all sorts of new things to be explored and discovered, including drone-guided virtual tours of major planets and solar systems, and there was even beginning to be an awakened sense of spirituality or of relationship with all living things.

Many people just hunkered down where they already were and picked up hobbies and activities like travel they could now afford to do—once housing, medical, and food concerns were all resolved. The Terran Robosapien MI were provided industrial and agricultural zones on formerly vacant land and contentedly produced all the necessities and anything else that was needed. Just get online and order it! Drones delivered your requests within hours.

Not surprisingly, the psychopaths, certain elites, and more judgmental types were not happy with the whole proposed scheme. The Creeb Nation was peacefully dismantled with the help of a certain militant Sister Mary, ably assisted by Ben Elyon and True Blue enforcers using Ben Elyon mind-control technology much more advanced than that used by the Rasha. The liberated but stunned members of the Human Enhancement Networks, soon recovered from their drug-induced trauma, either returned to their original homes or gathered at Reservations for the Temporarily Bewildered to get rehabilitated. Most of the rest of the population were pleased. A huge sense of relief seemed to permeate the planet because it no longer hovered under a cloud of destruction.

The elites were upset they could no longer dictate to the lower class. They only had each other to boss around. It appeared the deplorables were free to live in places that would be elite free. Education would no longer be restricted by class, but open to all, free from political cant, and focused on developing creativity, life skills, critical thinking, and compassion.

Jacqueline Boguiden, the talented assassin, joined her sisters on the island of Cozorre. She was working closely with the Fenrir Shamar Wolves, specifically Poger and Zara, to set up a model program dedicated to reforming willing psychopaths from around the world in both the Cozorre and Foondavi craters. Bijou was working as a guide on the Isle of Predators—and was reputedly up to twenty knives and some mischief with a little fellow felon named Kelita. Her older sister Beaulita was back to acting fulltime in the now-friendly and family-oriented Cozorre entertainment industry. Onza Flink joined the sisters on Cozorre and opened her own cutlery store, specializing in carving and throwing knives. She said she was retiring, but people said they still saw a certain glint in her eye that unnerved them if anyone crossed her.

The Torgies remained beneath the mountains of Cozorre, but now they were free to hunt on the rim and fish the waters after sundown. Their crafts of metallurgy, jewelry design, and pottery were now greatly treasured. They were considering an invitation from Foondavi to establish an underground Torgie haven beneath the peaks of the gentle island. The Torgie Naga still worked out, honing their hunting and military skills, and they were closely aligned in training with the Fenrir Wolves, available whenever the Ben Elyon needed boots on the ground to support the True Blues and drones.

The Muckytuck were kept busy training all the people from various countries that wanted to duplicate the Machpelah Ancient Forest model and their sustainable agriculture. While the Terran MI could easily produce more food than the world could ever eat, many places and people still preferred to grow their own crops and food.

Uncle Jack Flynn helped the Muckytuck and the Ancient Forest, but he also kept busy establishing Reservations for the Temporarily Bewildered wherever he could.

The Ancient Forest was reputed to be very pleased to be expanding again. Rey confirmed that, when he visited to walk the Machpelah Forest, the Ben Elyon aliens were sharing some exciting new biological concepts that might actually expand the forest even faster, but they assured him in a healthy manner. You can never have enough trees!

The more unusual Elders that attended the Council of the Wise Elders soon signed off the link and returned to their various homes. The Kalahari duo was excited to carry the good news to the ancient San people and the few remaining herds of elephants. A group of Ben Elyon joined them, and the job of restoring the once-pristine desert began. All destructive logging and mining was stopped in the Amazon, and the people of Brazil were soon more than happy with the arrangements and wealth of goods the Ben Elyon and the Terran MI contingent offered them in return. Elsewhere across the world, endangered people and environments were soon on the mend. Even the underwater contingent was reputed to be happy, although the orcas were giving some pushback, especially the ones that specialized in hunting fellow whales and now needed a change of diet.

Rey stayed on Foondavi and was active with the Hadron Think Tank. In addition, he oversaw the True Blue activity though the use of helmet cams and satellite links everywhere on the planet when their help was requested. He and Priscilla also watched over their sons, as they pursued the educational efforts suggested by Jake. They were somewhat concerned at the level of education Jake was suggesting, but he reminded them he also earned his first doctorate at the ripe old age of fourteen.

"Well, Jake," Rey responded, tactfully trying not to be hurtful, "you know you were a little unusual."

"So are they," Jake shot back immediately. "They are chronically curious and have all the unbelievable untapped potential of the young. We both know that, as they learn, their intelligence level will continuously improve. If anyone knows about neural plasticity, Rey, it's you! And through no fault of you or anyone else—in particular me—they have been exposed to unusual experiences beyond anything most academics have or ever will experience."

Rey admitted Morty and Milty seemed to be thriving. Because there was no degree called a Master's in Mayhem for Hyfee, he was contented with working with Jake on making robotic body parts for disabled children across the globe. He also was studying the history of warfare, with the goal he could help mankind prevent wars.

"Zohar called me a toxophilite," he told Rey one day, all excited.

"Maybe because you called him a turtle?"

"No, it means a person fond of, or an expert in archery. I'm studying the history of the war bow, both the Welsh kind most of us Torgies use, and the double recurve horn composite Mongolian bow I used before I got my super new legs."

Rey also enjoyed long talks with Zohar, who liked to call him Zerubbabel, explaining that Zerubbabel was an old Hebrew whose job it was in ancient Israel to take Elyon's word and make it clear, bringing it out of confusion, and helping to rebuild the world. "The Ben Elyon and all of us followers are most interested in the True Blues and how your brains are continuously improving. Learning to understand, harness, and grow savantism will be the key to humans continuing to grow. It is your unique gift as a people. The Source says to tell you, 'He will make you Blues strong with power from Him, and you will go wherever you wish, and wherever you go, you will be under His protection.' That is a great honor, Rey. He also looks forward to eventually meeting with you and reviewing your work."

≡ Designing the Demise ≡

The one big remaining problem was, of course, Achor Nithing. He was not pleased. He was irate with the Zugzwangs, especially Thambos. He blamed him for losing momentum in the election—even though the whole thing had been called off. Now the US Senate and House were meeting to try to resolve who should be leading the country, even as the loathsome Superman Samms claimed he was still officially the president. A new election was planned, with strict guidelines to avoid any irregularities or rigging, and the people seemed reenergized and re-engaged. This time, with the enthusiastic endorsement of a redeemed Jake Quark, who was now seen as a delivering hero, it appeared that Diora Pokritos had a commanding lead. Even the devious Achor Nithing couldn't figure out how to cheat her out of that big a lead, especially with the former shining boy candidate Thambos having lost his sheen.

Jake and Rey soon concocted a way to lure the elusive Achor into a trap. He had lost the Creeb Nation and the HEN weapons he had used so adroitly to disrupt and deceive. But the resourceful psychopath was still a danger to all decent people. They knew the one thing people like Achor hated most was to be ridiculed. They had seen how he had seethed when his debacle at Cozorre had been broadcast to the world.

They now collected all the body cam footage and then combined it with the hacked audio of Achor whining about how he had been maltreated on the Isle of Predators, the audio that Jake had enjoyed listening to so much. They added a few additional digital flourishes to make it even more humiliating. They then flooded all the worldwide media outlets with the hilarious scene of the nasty bully Nithing being chased off by the squealing boys while ludicrously clinging desperately to the landing gear of the helicopter and screaming at the top of his lungs to be rescued.

Soon he was the laughing stock of the world. Then, to further bait the trap, they lauded Jake as the mastermind of Nithing's defeat and of the New True Blue Rebellion, as they now called it, now that it was spreading worldwide and people were overturning tyrants everywhere and implementing the new Golden Rules.

They especially celebrated Jake's new habitat or zone he called Ozymandias. He had created it at the suggestion of Zohar, who reminded Jake that small city states in Greece had led to some of the greatest breakthroughs in human thinking and politics. He suggested that if Jake could create such free thinking zones, it could lead to great breakthroughs, especially if he could prevent the tyranny of the mob as well as the takeover by tyrants. Such sanctuaries could preserve the best of current and ancient thought, and possibly spur a renaissance in the world. Jake loved the idea of a small city of thinkers, doers, and inventors. He called it Ozymandias or Oz for short. Jake said the name was a takeoff on the great poet Percy B. Shelley's work *Ozymandias*. The name, Jake said, was meant to convey the vanity of power and pride that make people arrogant. This zone or sanctuary would, instead, produce the opposite—no power, pride, or arrogance allowed. He would use the habitat to collect and implement the best creative ideas and concepts from around the world, and attract the best thinkers and doers he could find. Ideas would be generated, debated, and implemented. Curiosity was the currency. If you are curious and creative, come on in and show us what you got!

They made sure the message was spread that it was Jake and Ozymandias that would play a key role in transforming the world now that the psychopaths were defeated. They knew that Achor, infuriated with the humiliating coverage of his debacle, would be furious and consumed with revenge. His thwarted drive for power, dominance, and control combined with his lust to destroy his source of humiliation, Jake, would make it impossible for him to resist trying to destroy the vulnerable-appearing Ozymandias and, thus, fall into their trap.

Ozymandias only looked deceptively defenseless. Jake's Ozymandias was a great model for the new world. It soon developed with few snafus, working smoothly from the beginning. It grew by leaps and bounds and posed no major challenges. Jake said he was encouraging the "mental mischief of creativity." Upon approaching the zone, the casual observer would immediately be dazzled by an amazing array of structures, some more bizarre than others. There was a constant hum of activity and talk. The only constraint on creativity was safety, so creativity ran rampant in Oz, and the very designs and colors stimulated the mind. Amazing food and art was everywhere. Music filled the air. Jake designed it to be a place open to any idea, where no matter how unusual or ridiculous, it could be explored and even implemented. Jake said it was created with the thought in mind that this place would be an "imaginarium," a place that encouraged and nurtured the imagination. As a youngster, he was accused of being chronically curious, questioning everything, of having "idearryhea." He told Rey that, while growing up, his ideas often were frowned upon with disdain or mocked, without anyone bothering to check them out. It took him years to finally ignore the negative thinkers, even as impervious to insults as he was. His goal for Ozymandias was to inspire a flow of imaginative ideas. "It should be a flow zone," Jake said. And the place was designed to help develop his favorite types of people: solutionaries and evangineers.

No one could tell from the outside that the weird assemblage of buildings and structures was also riddled with some of the most sophisticated weapon systems that the two incendiary experts, Moose of the Muckytuck and young Hyfee of the Torgies, could imagine. To their great delight, they were given complete access to the sophisticated and highly advanced armory of the Ben Elyon. Jake wasn't too excited that his idea factory was now a bristling military post, but he knew they had to lure in Achor and either catch him or destroy him once and for all. Achor's alliance with the Rasha invaders had helped him elude all efforts at capture so far, so Jake hoped this tantalizing trap would bring him to his demise.

Sure enough, the constant tormenting and taunting of Achor began showing results. Various Rasha Robosapiens were detected sniffing around the perimeter. Kasah himself was even detected trying to penetrate the defenses and was allowed to come in and wander the seemingly defenseless Ozymandias. Jake was carefully paraded around in plain sight. He said he was happy to be the cheese in the rat trap since he had often used Rey and others for the same reason. There could be no reward without risk.

Finally, the impulsive and vengeful Achor could wait no longer. He and his group of thugs, along with some fierce-looking Robosapiens, rushed the seemingly undefended campus and met no resistance. As he hesitated, seemingly surprised at his own good luck, he suddenly realized that the elusive Jake and all the other inhabitants had disappeared into carefully camouflaged trap doors. He then heard a strange sound around him. It was the clanging of cell doors going shut, a slight whirring sound as a retractable dome slid shut overhead, and the clicking of lethal-looking weapons targeting him. Before his micobot goons could react, they were all riddled with ballistics and then vacuumed up into special containers provided by the Ben Elyon to capture cyber villains. The stunned Achor himself was spared physical harm, although the mental harm as he saw he was duped again before the watching world was probably more painful than anything that a bullet could do. He was soon gagged and trussed up and dispatched to a special preserve Jake and Zohar had designed for the worst of the psychopaths. It would soon come to be called Diabolicaland. It was located far away from civilized people, so psychopaths would live isolated lives under the new universal rules and the ever-watching eyes of monitoring, heavily-armed drones.

≡ The Great Jamaroon ≡

Once the initial Golden Rules were set up and running, it was time to celebrate. The Foondavians call a great celebration a Jamaroon, and this definitely qualified. Achor Nithing was vanquished and locked away with most of the world's psychopaths. The Earth had dodged a bullet, as Sister Mary said, and she was definitely an expert in such things! "At least for now!" Jake was quick to add, having been apprised by Rey of what Zohar said in quoting the great Ben Franklin. "You have a new Garden of Eden, if you can keep it."

People came streaming down the mountain trails from the colorful villages clinging to the cliffs of Foondavi. They were singing beautiful, joyous acapella songs of the South Pacific sea people as they approached the little cluster of buildings called Troon, the capitol and only city on Foondavi. Six large double-hulled sailing canoes from Cozorre, under the direction of Milty the Wave Master, pulled onto the shore as his brother Morty furled the sails. All the people congregated in Troon's new Hall of the People, which was built in such a way that the singing echoed off the high ceilings and surrounded everyone with the sounds of the soaring and majestic music. The big event was topped off as Carlyle and Camilla, glimmering in their microbot forms, were united in Holy 'Cybermony' by Camilla's beaming brother Rigo, now officially a Justice of the Peace, and safe from the wrath of Achor Nithing. He found his true home on Foondavi as a capable and loyal assistant to Rey.

What a wonderous time! Rey enjoyed himself immensely, especially being back with Priscilla and the islanders he loved. His even got to be with his sons, at least occasionally, scooting between Cozorre and Foondavi, enjoying the breezes of the Pacific and getting to know more of the sentient sea life. He was quick to admit the young men were helpful in transitioning Cozorre's formerly oppressed people willingly into a modified, unique Cozorrean version of Foondavi. They also helped the Torgies establish caves and caverns beneath Foondavi; in the process of deep digging, they found a surprising amount of precious metals to help Foondavi sponsor exciting new enterprises that would benefit the rebuilding of the world.

The Winding
≡ Way Ahead ≡

Rey and Jake knew there would be struggles ahead. They also knew that the struggles would make them strong. They would have to weld the disparate people of the world together and fend off the Rasha who still wanted the Earth. They knew the old Latin phrase, "If you want peace, prepare for war." They would strive for peace, but do their best to defend their home and families. They always kept the words of Vaclav Havel, the heroic Czech freedom fighter, writer, and first president of the Czech Republic in mind: "Truth and love must prevail over lies and hatred."

For the sake of his family and all the inhabitants of the world, and especially for the future of the incubator of life called Earth, he knew they would prevail. The True Rebellion could now become the True Blue Renaissance.

"An individual or a nation cannot long survive or prosper when they delude themselves from the truth."

Epictetus, a first century A.D. Greek Stoic philosopher who went from being a slave to the leading philosopher in the world

CPSIA information can be obtained
at www.ICGtesting.com
Printed in the USA
JSHW012115280423
41018JS00006B/59